The latest release in our anthology series:

THAT DAMMED BEAVER

CANADIAN HUMOUR, LAUGHS AND GAFFS

SELECTED BY BRUCE MEYER

THE EXILE BOOK OF ANTHOLOGY SERIES NUMBER FIFTEEN

Margaret Atwood, Austin Clarke, Leon Rooke, Priscila Uppal, Jonathan Goldstein, Paul Quarrington, Morley Callaghan, Jacques Ferron, Marsha Boulton, Joe Rosenblatt, Barry Callaghan, Linda Rogers, Steven Hayward, Andrew Borkowski, Helen Marshall, Gloria Sawai, David McFadden, Myna Wallin, Gail Prussky, Louise Maheux-Forcher, Shannon Bramer, James Dewar, Bob Armstrong, Jamie Feldman, Claire Dé, Christine Miscione, Larry Zolf, Anne Dandurand, Julie Roorda, Mark Paterson, Karen Lee White, Heather J. Wood, Marty Gervais, Matt Shaw, Alexandre Amprimoz, Darren Gluckman, Gustave Morin, and the country's greatest cartoonist, Aislin.

"*Those Who Make Us*, an all-Canadian anthology of fantastical stories, featuring emerging writers alongside award-winning novelists, poets, and playwrights, is original, elegant, often poetic, sometimes funny, always thought-provoking, and a must for lovers of short fiction." —*Publishers Weekly*, starred review

"In his introduction to *Clockwork Canada*, editor Dominik Parisien calls this country 'the perfect setting for steampunk.' The fifteen stories in this anthology…back up Parisien's assertion by actively questioning the subgenre and bringing it to some interesting new places." —*AE- SciFi Canada*

"*New Canadian Noir* is largely successful in its goals. The quality of prose is universally high…and as a whole works well as a progressive, more Canadian take on the broad umbrella of noir, as what one contributor calls 'a tone, an overlay, a mood.' It's worth purchasing for several stories alone…" —*Publishers Weekly*

"*Playground of Lost Toys* is a gathering of diverse writers, many of them fresh out of fairy tale, that may have surprised the editors with its imaginative intensity… The acquisition of language, spells and nursery rhymes that vanquish fear and bad fairies can save them; and toys are amulets that protect children from loneliness, abuse, and acts of God. This is what these writers found when they dug in the sand. Perhaps they even surprised themselves." —*Pacific Rim Review of Books*

"The term apocalypse means revelation, the revealing of things and ultimately *Fractured* reveals the nuanced experience of endings and focuses on people coping with the notion of the end, the thought about the idea of endings itself. It is a volume of change, memory, isolation, and desire." —*Speculating Canada*

"In *Dead North* we see deadheads, shamblers, jiang shi, and Shark Throats invading such home and native settings as the Bay of Fundy's Hopewell Rocks, Alberta's tar sands, Toronto's Mount Pleasant Cemetery, and a Vancouver Island grow-op. Throw in the last poutine truck on Earth driving across Saskatchewan and some "mutant demon zombie cows devouring Montreal" (honest!) and what you've got is a fun and eclectic mix of zombie fiction…" —*Toronto Star*

"Cli-fi is a relatively new sub-genre of speculative fiction imagining the long-term effects of climate change [and] collects 17 widely varied stories that nevertheless share several themes: Water; Oil; Conflict… this collection, presents an urgent, imagined message from the future." —*Globe and Mail*

ALICE UNBOUND

BEYOND WONDERLAND

THE EXILE BOOK OF ANTHOLOGY SERIES   NUMBER SIXTEEN

EDITED AND WITH AN INTRODUCTION BY

COLLEEN ANDERSON

PREFACE BY

DAVID DAY

Fiction, Poetry, Non-fiction, Translation, Drama and Graphic Books

Library and Archives Canada Cataloguing in Publication

Alice unbound : beyond Wonderland / edited and with an introduction
by Colleen Anderson ; preface by David Day.

(The Exile book of anthology series ; number sixteen)
Short stories.
. Issued in print and electronic formats.
ISBN 978-1-55096-766-1 (softcover).--ISBN 978-1-55096-767-8 (EPUB).--
ISBN 978-1-55096-768-5 (Kindle).--ISBN 978-1-55096-769-2 (PDF)

1. Alice (Fictitious character from Carroll)--Fiction. 2. Canadian prose
literature (English)--21st century. 3. Speculative fiction, Canadian (English).
4. Short stories, Canadian (English). I. Anderson, Colleen, editor,
writer of introduction II. Day, David, 1947-, writer of preface
III. Series: Exile book of anthology series ; no. 16

PS8329.1.A45 2018   C813'.087608351   C2018-901284-6
                                                     C2018-901285-4

Story copyrights rest with the authors, © 2018
Text and cover design by Michael Callaghan
Cover and interior artwork by Maeba Scuitti
Typeset in Fairfield, Footlight and Perpetua Tilting fonts
at Moons of Jupiter Studio

Published by Exile Editions Limited ~ www.ExileEditions.com
144483 Southgate Road 14 – GD, Holstein, Ontario, N0G 2A0
Printed and Bound in Canada by Marquis

We gratefully acknowledge the Canada Council for the Arts,
the Government of Canada, the Ontario Arts Council,
and the Ontario Media Development Corporation
for their support toward our publishing activities.

Canadian sales representation:
The Canadian Manda Group, 664 Annette Street,
Toronto ON M6S 2C8   www.mandagroup.com   416 516 0911

North American and international distribution, and U.S. sales:
Independent Publishers Group, 814 North Franklin Street,
Chicago IL 60610   www.ipgbook.com   toll free: 1 800 888 4741

To those who have seen the face of madness and continue the battle.

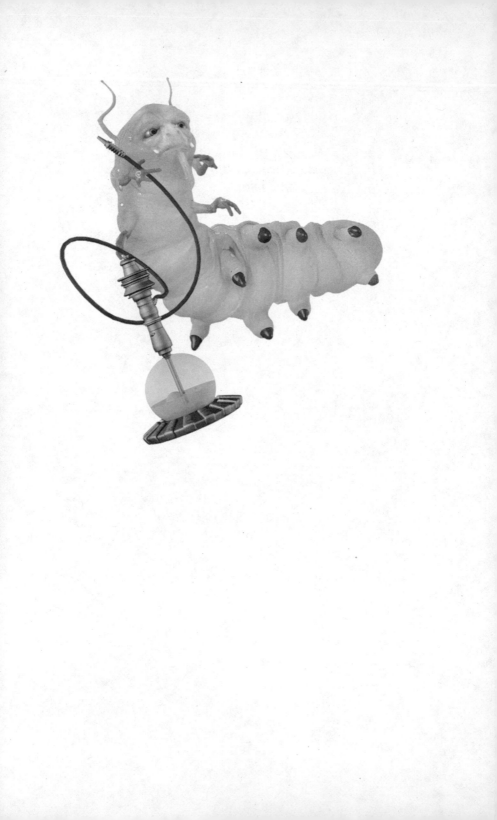

TALES FROM BEYOND WONDERLAND

OF MADNESS AND METAMORPHOSIS

INTRODUCTION

COLLEEN ANDERSON

Madness is a condition that few of us willingly pursue, but in madness our mettle can be tested, and, should we survive, we transform into wiser, more experienced beings. Dionysus, the Greek god of drama, wine and madness, knew that a story has its own logic. Some would say that to act is to become mad, for you are changing into a different personality; it is a temporary metamorphosis that allows individuals to view a new realm and understand other perspectives. Perhaps, only a god can journey through madness unscathed.

Lewis Carroll's characters have prevailed through the test of time, where the inanimate takes on life and madness becomes the norm. While the original tales are still popular, the imagery and ideas have shifted and been adapted into numerous stories, comic books, movies and TV series. As editor of *Alice Unbound: Beyond Wonderland,* I did not want rehashings of the familiar stories, but something new, set in a more modern or futuristic time. There could be trips to Wonderland but the magic, and the characters had to affect more than that make-believe land – as in "True Nature" by Sara C. Walker in which displacement plays upon what would happen if the characters had to live in our world? Or, how would we cope with such encounters and with a reality twisted by the logic (or lack) of Wonderland? And perhaps, the craziness is already in this world, and only revealed when the looking glass is held up.

As I read through the submissions, I noticed that Wonderland's aether does not engender many tales of love, though Cait Gordon's "A Night at the Rabbit Hole" immediately captured me on this aspect. Love is a motive for a few characters, but more often it is love lost and warped, as in Christine Daigle's "Reflections of Alice."

The vein of madness runs so pure through this anthology that I would say every tale is touched by it, and I could list every title here. The exploration is sometimes light, sometimes deep and always an expedition into the unknown. Insanity may present in the form of infection, loneliness, living up to the status quo, or gambling everything on an outcome. Madness means crashing through the boundaries of normalcy, taking chance by the throat and beating logic into submission.

Losing one's mind, or being physically shaped into something "other" weaves through so many themes of war, loneliness, health and experimentation – Lisa Smedman's "We're All Mad Here" puts the madness of war under the looking glass, while Danica Lorer's "Twin" examines the search for well-being of self. Whether we have dealt with lunatic thoughts, crazy surroundings, mad ideologies, or insane politics, few people ever stay the same after having danced through that particular minefield. Change is often integral to any story but when madness plays a part, when that special substance from Wonderland permeates, then it can be permanent and liberating, or destructive. This metamorphosis might be controlled or coerced, and it may not be what you expect.

To say each piece in this anthology is only about the forces of madness, or only about metamorphosis would be a disservice. Themes involve complex searches and battles against insanity; sometimes embracing it, but always involving one's self, one's dreams or how the world expects one to behave. There are stories that can offer release, such as Catherine MacLeod's "Jaune," and those that will be a trap that leads into evil, which Andrew Robertson adeptly explores in "Her Royal Counsel."

It is said that the final goal does not matter; it is the journey that is important. The ventures here delve into the psyche, the world order and what it means to be. A chess piece can find a new place, an outmoded technology can find new purpose, and a soul bearing scars from moving through the landscape of life can find redemption. These adventures can be as much fun as a rollercoaster ride and as terrifying as falling off a precipice. The madness and metamorphosis is sought, self-inflicted, invented, chosen or coerced. Not all will remain unscathed. May you enjoy your madcap journey through *Alice Unbound* and find visions and capers that transport you beyond Wonderland.

THROUGH THE LOOKING GLASS, DARKLY

PREFACE

David Day

Lewis Carroll's influence on literature and popular culture since the publication of *Alice's Adventures in Wonderland* (1865) has been nothing short of astonishing. After Shakespeare, the Reverend Charles Lutwidge Dodgson (aka Lewis Carroll) has become the world's most quoted author. *Alice's Adventures in Wonderland* has been translated into 176 languages worldwide; and furthermore, it is the most frequently *retranslated* book in existence. There are over 400 versions in Spanish, 500 in French and German; and at least 100 each in several other major European languages.

The greatest technician of language in the twentieth century, James Joyce, saw in Carroll/Dodgson's manipulations, inventions and coinages of words and language, a kindred linguistic genius. Consequently in *Finnegans Wake* we may discover Joyce's holy trinity of the *"Dodgfather, Dogson and Coo"* in hundreds of references to *"Dadgerson's dodges"* in multiple forms, such as: *"Wonderland's wanderlad," "Lew'd carol"* on the *"Wonderlawn"* accompanied by *"a tiny victorienne Alys"* who is the *"alias Alis, alas, who broke the glass!"* Joyce even implies his novel – jabberwocky-wise – may be "jesta jibberweek's joke."

Among many others, Carroll's influence has been acknowledged in the writing of Virginia Woolf, W.H. Auden and Vladimir Nabokov – the first Russian translator of *Alice's Adventures in Wonderland*. Indeed, it is difficult not to see Carroll's influence in Nabokov's flamboyant style with its double entendres, multilingual puns, anagrams and coinages. The real-life Dodgson can easily be viewed as a shockingly contrary-wise inspiration for Humbert Humbert: the middle-aged college professor sexually obsessed with a twelve-year-old girl in Nabokov's *Lolita*.

As evidenced by Nabokov's novel, and despite the family-oriented charm of Walt Disney's hugely popular *Alice in Wonderland*, there was a definite shift in perspective on Alice after the mid-twentieth century. No longer seen strictly as a children's fairy tale in popular culture, films and literature, Alice drifted off in directions not even remotely imagined by Dodgson.

From the sixties onward, much attention was given to the psychedelic aspects of *Alice in Wonderland*. From music by the Jefferson Airplane's fantastic *White Rabbit*, John Lennon's *I Am The Walrus* and *Lucy in the Sky With Diamonds*, to Aerosmith's *Sunshine* and Natalia Kills' *Wonderland*, on to an avalanche of films, books and visual artists' portrayals of Alice and Wonderland that have varied from the surreal to the entirely pornographic. While through the eighties and nineties, all manner of genres and modes were devised, from steampunk and cyberpunk to gothic horror and science fiction. Who could have predicted the popularity of the new millennium's *American McGee's Alice* psychological horror action-adventure video games; or by contrast the plastic building-block toymaker Lego Alice in Wonderland video game. Not to mention that eBay would offer *Naughty Zombie Alice* Halloween costumes, and a licensed marijuana product purveyor in Alaska would dub itself

"Absolem's Garden" after the blue, hooka-smoking caterpillar in Tim Burton's near-hallucinogenic 2010 cinematic rendering of the classic tale.

It seems we all know something about Alice and Wonderland, but like Alice herself upon her first reading of *Jabberwocky*, we find: "It fills my head with ideas, but I don't know what they are." So as each new generation falls under Carroll's word spells, each in turn must attempt to understand what Alice and Wonderland might mean in the context of their world and in their time.

Alice Unbound: Beyond Wonderland is a collection of twenty-first century stories inspired by *Alice's Adventures in Wonderland, Alice Through the Looking Glass, The Hunting of the Snark*; and to some degree: aspects of the life of the author, Charles Dodgson, and the real-life Alice (Liddell).

Elizabeth Hosang's story "No Reality But What We Make" is a title that might have been applied to many of the imaginings in this anthology. It would also be in keeping with Lewis Carroll's perspective as an early member of the London-based Society of Psychical Research, a first of its kind in the world.

"I have supposed a Human being capable of various psychical states, with varying degrees of consciousness," Carroll once mused, as he suggested that entities might exist that "sometimes were visible to us, and we to them, and that they were sometimes able to assume human form... by actual transference of their material essence."

All the stories in *Alice Unbound*, to a greater and lesser degree, "delve into the aspects of the human psyche" in various forms and on a number of levels. These stories range from tales of childhood horror to drug-induced sexual nightmares. There is a surreal Oxford academic detective story and the tragic tale of a shell-shocked soldier in the Great War trenches in France. There are futuristic travellers tales with teleporting jabberwocks, boojams and interplanetary Snarks. There are dark conspiracies with biological weapons and gene smugglers, satires and comic cannibal stories. All manner of refugees from Wonderland are let loose in this anthology, even the rock and roll tale of a struggling *Wonderband*.

In her introduction to *Alice Unbound*, Colleen Anderson rightly observes: "The vein of madness runs so pure through this anthology…" That same vein of madness not only ran through Lewis Carroll's creative world in Wonderland, but it also rather darkly ran though Dodgson's real life. Ironically, his favourite uncle Skeffington Lutwidge was a Commissioner of Lunacy who was killed by an asylum patient. It also has been suggested that Carroll's very peculiar character and genius may in part be explained by his suffering from a mild form of autism, known as Asperger's Syndrome.

Be that as it may, in a truly bizarre example of life imitating art, Carroll's literary child Alice has been posthumously diagnosed with her very own psychosis. The real-world symptoms for *Alice in Wonderland Syndrome (AIWS)* are straight out of Carroll's novel and include: hallucinations, lost sense of time and an altered self-image where certain body parts appear disproportionate to the rest of the body.

Nearly all of the stories in this collection share a sinister shifting sense of reality akin to some aspects of this syndrome (or "Sin-Drum" as Dominik Parisien's River Street Witch insists) that very well may be related to the often surreal and chaotic times we find ourselves in today. *Alice Unbound: Beyond Wonderland* reveals the authors' collective cathartic need to embrace Alice at this time in our history when we appear to have passed through Alice's Looking Glass and entered the very real madness of "Trump World."

Every day we wake up to see what our modern-day Mad Hatter has tweeted. And we can only scratch our heads at the day-to-day shifting sense of (sur)reality that has become our daily news-feed reality show.

As Alice did when she tumbled down the rabbit hole, we have come to accept the abnormal as normal, a world in which distinctions mean little or nothing. A world in which lies have no consequence, which means that truth has no consequence, which means that irreality is reality, which means that "Life is, but a dream…"

THE SLITHY TOVES

Bruce Meyer

Charles Lutwidge Dodgson, the Oxford mathematician known to the world as the author Lewis Carroll, was framed by a not-so-imaginary *thing*, which was not scholarly jealousy. What plagued the author was the same *thing* that appeared in my childhood. My St. George-like struggle against the beast began one summer day when I was three.

The red rose petals on the trellis vine turned grey, causing my father to plunge his spade into the earth, looking for whatever was killing the plant. Wiping his brow, he went into the cellar to find rose food. As soon as he left, I took the shovel, slapping the mud and scraping the hole until small fleshy wounds appeared. Something stirred.

A large worm slithered through the muck, entwining the bush as if swimming in the flowerbed. I poked it with the spade's pointed blade. I jabbed harder and harder, hoping to split the thing in two, driven by curiosity to understand what it was.

The yellow and black-striped body surfaced. It sprang at me, hissing and snarling. The thing's face resembled a woman's grimace, black eyebrows raised. Its matted hair and red lips parted over jagged, rotten teeth as it reared up.

I choked and gasped, then dropped the shovel and ran into the house sobbing and screaming.

I stuttered to my mother that *it* had stung me. She checked my arms and legs for signs.

"Was it a wasp? Where?"

I pointed to my heart and sobbed.

"Nothing has stung you. You're imagining it."

I woke screaming for nights afterward. Whatever it was, lived in my mind, shrieking into my face, this she-thing's breath worse than rotting marigolds. I knew it waited in the dark for me to return to the garden.

For the remainder of the summer, each time I entered the garden I sensed it hiding behind the lilies, lurking in the delphiniums, or waiting twined around the base of the mountain ash tree. The Baltimore orioles that sang in the branches vanished, that thing having driven them away. I couldn't breathe outside. I watched the lilies wither and brown as a bulge of earth tubed through the flower beds. The berries on the mountain ash turned black and fell like drops of poisoned rain.

That was when time came to my childhood garden and the snow fell. The world turned grey. I watched from my window as something slithered, diving in and out of the white drifts as if it was a joy to be among the thorns and dead things.

By the following spring I had forgotten *it* existed. Children bury their fears. We moved to a new house. The garden where time had started became a myth, and I grew up.

In my final high school year, I spent spare periods in the library reading all eight books of *The Caxton Encyclopaedia of Art*. In the middle of volume L to P, there was a full-colour pull-out of the Sistine Chapel ceiling. I borrowed the librarian's magnifying glass and poured over the page. The hand of God reached out to infuse a mortal digit with the splendour of life. In the panel to the left of *The Creation of Adam*, Michelangelo painted the moment of human tragedy, "The

Downfall of Adam and Eve and Their Expulsion from the Garden of Eden." There, wrapped around the Tree of the Knowledge of Good and Evil, handing the Fruit to the first couple was the thing I had seen in my backyard.

Michelangelo Buonarotti was not the only painter to have known that *thing*. Holbein gives the serpent flowing locks. Dürer paints breasts on the beast. No matter how the great masters treated the motif, that creature served as a constant reminder that something horrid always lurked beneath the topsoil. I told myself my imagination had better things to do.

I fell in love with reading. I went to university the following September to study literature and see where my imagination would take me.

At the frosh welcome-weekend pyjama party, we were given numbers and told to go look for a member of the opposite sex with the same number. Not long before midnight, a young woman with blonde hair, protruding teeth, and a heavy flannel nightgown came up to me.

"We share the same number," she said, removing my number from my back and presenting me with hers. She motioned me onto the dance floor. Without holding hands during the slow dance, she pressed against me and whispered in my ear, "I want you. Let's go to your room now."

The worm turned inside me. I suddenly lost control, yet marvelled at the thrill of the experience. She stood between me and my bed and drew the nightgown over her head. I wanted to touch her smooth, white body. As I stepped out of my pyjamas the streetlight's glow illuminated her left thigh. A lump moved back and forth beneath her skin.

"Is there something wrong with your thigh?" I said, and pointed. The lump, like a tongue rolling in the wall of someone's cheek, put me off.

She lay back on the bed, tossing her hair to one side. Reaching down, she wriggled out of the lower half of her body. She set her legs on the floor, then pulled the blonde wig from her head, and spit out her overbite to reveal black teeth. Her yellow and black tail rose and waved in the air, curling and beckoning me like someone gesturing "C'mere" with an index finger.

"You must remember me now," she whispered.

I opened the leaded casement. "'Come to the window; sweet is the night air'."

"'Ah, love, let us be true to one another.' I adore it when a willing young man quotes 'Dover Beach' to me just before I give him my special touch."

She leapt toward me. I caught her, and in that instant, my hands burned and blistered. She tried to wrap her arms around me, her black claws suddenly protruding from her fingertips. I turned to the window and flung her out.

She thumped off a dumpster, screaming shrilly as her body hit the ground. Then I picked up her wig, teeth and her lower half, and tossed them into the alley. I closed the window and pulled the drapes shut. My heart pounded. I washed and washed my hands, dressed, and ran into the night toward the Bloor Street crowds. The all-night student hangouts looked like safe havens when I reached Bathurst Street. I found a bar with thumping music and a waitress willing to serve me as many Jack Daniels as I could buy. I came to my senses several hours later in a doughnut shop, a Korean man standing over me with a carafe, asking if I wanted more coffee. I never felt safe in my dorm room again.

As the leaves turned orange and red around the campus, and the sky burst into that brilliance of blue that can only say "I am dying in the most beautiful way," autumn came to my freshman year. The yellow and purple mums in planters along the walkways shrivelled and browned. I knew it was her doing. She lurked behind the college walls to suck the life from my world. I stopped giving a damn about worldly things. The only thing I knew I could trust was literature, and I found my passion in Professor Lamoore's class. Her name was poetry.

By November the snow fell in soft, heavy flakes outside. Professor Lamoore leaned against the windowsill talking nonsense, literally, explaining what it meant to craft a new diction and use it to describe the heroic act of slaying a dreaded beast.

> *'Twas brillig and the slithy toves*
> *Did gyre and gimble in the wabe:*
> *All mimsy were the borogoves,*
> *And the mome raths outgrabe.*

Lamoore, an older, plump man, had taught my mother during her undergraduate years. His bald head reflected the brightness from the ceiling fixtures. "Now what was that?" he asked.

"Gibberish."

"Not quite. It was *Jabberwocky*."

The class sat in silence. Some sighed with a "Let's get this over with" attitude. From under his arm, he produced a copy of *Through the Looking Glass,* a book that I could never bring myself to read, and I could not recall why. Perhaps I had been frightened by the pictures.

"The poem is a folk ballad in the tradition of *Lord Randall* or *Sir Patrick Spens.* There's something unusual about what Carroll does to the poem a few chapters after it is presented. A good poet is like a good magician." Lamoore thumbed through the pages of the little book. "A good magician never explains his tricks or how they work. Yet, in Chapter Six,

Alice meets a big egg named Humpty Dumpty who relishes in exegesis, that art of explanation. Humpty sits on his wall and professes, critiques, and insists that everything must mean something. And so, he explains the meaning of *Jabberwocky* to Alice. He recites the first verse of the poem, then:

"Well, 'slithy' means 'lithe and slimy.' 'Lithe' is the same as 'active.' You see it's like a portmanteau – there are two meanings packed up into one word."

"I see it now," Alice remarked thoughtfully: "and what are 'toves'?"

"Well, 'toves' are something like badgers – they're something like lizards – and they're something like corkscrews."

"They must be very curious-looking creatures."

"They are that," said Humpty Dumpty: "also they make their nests under 'sundials' – also they live on cheese."

"And what's to 'gyre' and to 'gimble'?"

"To 'gyre' is to go round and round like a gyroscope. To 'gimble' is to make holes like a gimlet."

"And 'the wabe' is the grass-plot round a sundial, I suppose?" said Alice, surprised at her own ingenuity.

"Of course it is…"

I left Professor Lamoore's class with a sudden interest in Lewis Carroll. I knew I had met the slithy tove.

Carroll's illustrator, John Tenniel, depicted the tove in the 1871 edition of *Through the Looking Glass* and got it wrong. The badger suggestion was Lewis Carroll's purposeful misdirection. Maybe the author meant wolverine but understood that English readers would not be acquainted with the vicious North American animal. Perhaps he wanted to hunt the tove himself without giving away too many clues. Why? The tove was more lizard-like than badger, but its claws and arms, to say nothing of its foul disposition and cheesy breath, were *suggestive* of a badger.

I believed Dodgson had encountered the creature and had been plagued by the tove, which hated innocence and happiness. The tove whispered in the ears of those harbouring doubts, and wove those doubts into jealousies. It poisoned the world. When I was kicked off the college paper's editorial staff without any other reason than that I was constantly distracted and looking over my shoulder, I knew the tove had planted seeds in my fellow reporters' brains. In the dining hall no one would sit with me. Other students just looked at me and then moved their trays. I tried to overcome attacks on my reputation, the sort of college stuff that always happens – lending notes and offering to buy coffee. When I asked what I had done, people simply answered, "Well, you know…" and said nothing more. I found myself on the outside of the reindeer games that occupied most other students' time. The only place I felt secure and happy was in Professor Lamoore's class.

Lamoore and his wife, Gamba, held regular teas in their Victorian "house of grace," which was a haven for ideas and literary talk. I was always invited to their gatherings. The Lamoores welcomed acclaimed authors or renowned scholars as their guests. Just to sit there and listen to the stories was a tremendous privilege. The teas prepared me for my later work.

By the end of my honours year I won a scholarship to Oxford, thanks largely to the tutelage of Lamoore. One day, Julia Cassidy came to Lamoore's tea.

Mrs. Cassidy had been the wife of a strange but troubled professor whose brilliance and temperament had mixed within him in an unusual way. While researching Lewis

Carroll, he was found hanging in his office. Julia had the countenance of a suffering angel and an air of wisdom as if she carried a very old soul. During the tea, Mrs. Cassidy quoted from *Duino Elegies*.

"He sounds inspiring," I said. "What's his name?"

"Rainer Maria Rilke," sang off her tongue through her flowing Irish lilt. "Have you not read Rilke?" she asked with patience. I shook my head. "He also did a wonderful book, *Letters to a Young Poet*. We shall have to see to that." She smiled and went back to her dessert.

The next day, I was packing for Oxford when the porter came to my door with a small package. The outer envelope said simply, "Do not open until you are on your way." Halfway across the Atlantic as dawn was just beginning, I opened the envelope. It was a copy of Rilke's volume of advice to literary types, *Letters to a Young Poet*. I could hear her voice: "In your moment of greatest need, Rilke will provide the answer to your question. Be well and journey bravely, Julia Cassidy."

I settled into my room at Christ Church College. The slightly vaulted ceiling and stone door frame, fireplace, and leaded windows made me feel monastic. As I lay in my cot the first night, I looked up at the ceiling where it met the cornice. In the nineteenth-century plasterwork a strange bulge seemed to indicate the pipes were about to burst.

I stacked my chair on my desk and reached toward it. The moment my fingers hit the brittle plaster, the bubble burst and a withered grey corpse I mistook for a large cat fell to the floor with a thud. Someone from a nearby room hollered, "Keep it down in there, you bloody sod!"

The skull cracked slightly on impact. The corpse's sinews held the body together. I viewed the remnants of an upper torso with nothing below the waist but a long series of vertebrae and ribs tapering to a point. The skull looked partially human but small horns protruded from the sides of the cranium. The finger bones were tipped with claws. Here was the skeleton of a tove.

I didn't touch it, having seen how a tove sucked the life out of a garden, and had burned me. I put on heavy leather gloves I had brought for winter. When I touched the corpse, the palms paled as if the tanning was being drawn out. Piling the remains on my desk, I stared at the corpse. Here was proof that the tove was real. But why was it here? Why this room, my room?

In the morning, I went to the Dean's lodge, not to tell him about my zoological discovery (which I hid in a paper bag under my bed and transferred to a rental locker at Oxford Station later that afternoon), but to ask who had previously lived in my chamber. I was handed a large black ledger. I poured through the names of previous inhabitants until, under an entry for the Michaelmas term, 1851, I found the name Charles Lutwidge Dodgson. I was living in Lewis Carroll's old digs.

Had the tove come to his dorm room to claim him as a prize? What if the tove had crawled in through a dovecote in the stone eaves, become entangled in the medieval masonry and died there?

In studying Carroll's life, I found there were four missing diaries. Their absence has been used by his detractors to indict him for adultery and even child abuse. The volumes date from 1853 to 1863 and include the years that Carroll spent completing his studies at Oxford as well as those with the children of a local clergyman, Henry Liddell. Several scholars argue that he was in love with the eldest Liddell daughter, but spent his time amusing her younger sister, Alice, with his labyrinthine tales of logic and fancy.

The Liddell home still stands in Oxford. I found the name of the current owners. Carol Framwell answered when I called. "Of course, I am a Lewis Carroll fanatic," she bubbled. "I adore living here, and we bought the home because of the Liddell connection. I shan't be here, but do come around on Saturday afternoon. My husband will show you the house."

◎ ◎ ◎

"I'm not really all that interested in the inside as I am in the garden," I said to Richard Framwell who looked disappointed. He was a DIY man, and I think he wanted to show off his handiwork.

We wandered around the back, standing in the rain. I had my umbrella up. Richard Framwell is one of those Englishmen who is impervious to water, and he merely tucked his hands in the pockets of his brown oilcloth jacket and remained dry.

"May I ask what you're specifically looking for?"

"This is where Lewis Carroll took most of his photographs of the Liddell children if I am correct." Framwell nodded. "What I'm looking for is the sundial's location."

"The sundial? As in slithy toves? You aren't secreting any Stilton, are you?" He looked disconcerted and then smiled with the hope that I would catch his allusion. I laughed. Richard had his hand out to see if the rain was still falling. I saw the bushes rustle. I put my finger to my lips. I did not want the tove to overhear, though I could not tell my host that.

"Do you have trouble growing roses?" I whispered.

He shook his head, talking at full volume, ignoring my attempts to hush things. "I am an ivy man, myself. Holly and ivy. Great Christmas fare. Funny," he continued, "you should ask about the sundial. I found the base of it. We have it in the shed if you'd like to see it. It was there, about ten paces this side of that old oak, though I suppose in Carroll's day it was exposed to the light far more. I was digging there several years ago, and I had a strange experience. The mud started moving beneath it. You don't suspect it was a tove, do you?" He chuckled.

"You don't mind if I poke around, do you? I want to get a sense of the place."

"Be my guest," he said. "I shall put some tea on so please join me when you are thoroughly cold and soaked."

I stood gazing at the spot.

The birds chirped, and the rain pinged on my umbrella. I imagined a conversation, a polite male voice speaking softly to a young girl. She is giggling.

"That's enough," Humpty Dumpty interrupted. "There are plenty of hard words there."

"And what are they?" the child asks excitedly. Suddenly, she screams and points.

A yellow and black worm slithers from beneath the sundial.

"Hello, my travelling Canadian friend."

I looked up from my imaginings.

The tove emerged from the spot where the sundial had stood. She brushed dirt from her forehead. She seemed surprised that I was not surprised.

"I haven't seen you since that night in my dorm."

"You broke my heart, you little bastard."

"Only your heart? Had you a pelvis you might not have been so fortunate," I replied, smiling back.

"Had I a pelvis you might not have gotten out of your room that night. I could have given you a night to remember. It would have been the last of your life."

"So, what are you planning to do to me now? Are you here to suck the life out of me?"

"I'm going to toy with you awhile. Killing you right here, right now, well, what would be the pleasure in that? I want you to suffer, greatly, and for a long time, just like the one that was here long ago. We toves appreciate the painful process of justice."

"What have I done to deserve this?"

The tove held up her hands; three fingers on one, and two on the other. "Little boys playing with shovels are terrible things. I will make you pay for my fingers, and perhaps more, just for the pleasure of it. But all in good time."

"If you are going to kill me, all in good time, I should know more about you. May I ask your name?"

"Agatha."

"Well, Agatha, you have a charm for appearing in great works of art. There's a point of literary symbolism that has always puzzled me. Is the serpent in the paintings Satan, or Lilith, or you? And how many of you are there in your species?"

"Lilith was my sister. She was the one who ruined Eden. She was Adam's first wife – did you know that? He threw her away, though not from a dorm room window. Great men were fascinated with her and felt honoured to know her, but they all cast her aside when she tried to touch them, to know what life inside them made them great. She went to Dodgson to seek his source of love and life one night, and I never saw her again! Do not patronize me with Darwinian categorizations such as 'species.' I would have ruined that laggard zoologist,

Darwin, but he just stared at me and started taking notes. What kind of a man is more interested in finches than rare beings? Boring sod.

She continued, "There were two of us. It's only me now. That bastard, that man of two names took her. But I stole his diaries and ruined him. The world ate him. And because you follow in his footsteps, you flimsy knight of words and pens, I will destroy you, too. You think you're a young man on the rise. But no matter how hard you may try to put the life of the world into words, you will never succeed because I will be there to pull you down into the shadows where no poetry can protect you."

"Just as you did to Lewis Carroll."

"I went to that horridly beautiful little girl as she lay sleeping in her room, and I told her that if she ever revealed the truth I would destroy her and her family. The frightened little bitch kept her silence, so I destroyed her, too, by making her hold her words until she finally choked on her silence. Dodgson struggled to tell the truth for the rest of his life, and everyone thought it fantasy."

"I see." I looked the tove in the eye. "Agatha, I have a deal for you."

"No deals!"

"Okay, your loss. You'll never get the bones of your sister back."

"You have my sister's bones! Where did you find them? Give them to me."

"Uh-uh. That is, unless you give me something in return. Something I need."

"What is that," hissed the tove.

"I think you still have Dodgson's missing diaries. I suspect you're a greedy tove at heart. All dragons and slithery things need trophies, shiny things to keep at the bottom of a lake or in your nest or wherever you hang out. You like to keep something you take so you can use it later and fawn over it. Well, Agatha, I'll trade your sister's body for the volumes. If you don't have them, well, kiss Lilith goodbye. I'll not go down without a fight. I was born on St. George's Day and a bit of dragon play is part of my nature. And remember, bones are easily burned or ground-up, or, worse, put on display in the Museum of Natural History in London."

"Not that damned Darwin house!"

"Do we have a deal, diaries for bones?"

"Where and when?"

"On Addison's Walk behind Magdalen College at three a.m. tomorrow morning… Remember, no diaries, no tove carcass. And don't plan on pulling any fast ones or Lilith goes to London!"

The tove sneered, screaming, and burrowed beneath the earth.

Early the next morning, I stood in the damp beside a fire I'd lit in a garbage drum and watched as frost etched itself into every crevice and leaf. I found a sharp alder rod on the bank of the Isis and made it my lance, taking my Swiss Army knife out and whittling the end to a very handsome point. I wore heavy leather gloves. I also remembered a bottle of brandy to give me strength in case my courage faltered.

Uncorking the bottle, I took a swig and set it open on the ground. I muttered the words "And lo, though I walk through the valley of the shadow of death, I will fear no evil, for Thou art with me." As I spoke, the image of Julia Cassidy popped into my mind and her words: "In your moment of greatest need, Rilke will provide the answer to your question."

I wasn't there to think about Rilke. I had a beast to deal with.

Agatha approached out of the fog, her head held high, as if in glory. She had an old blue and gold biscuit tin tucked under her arm.

"That's far enough," I said, my back to the fire as I raised my lance. The flames illuminated the tove. "Put the cookie box down."

"It's a biscuit tin, you stupid colonial."

"Whatever. That's far enough."

"Show me the bones."

I held up the bag.

"Open it!" she screamed.

"Now show me the diaries." She pried open the tin, her claws sounding like fingernails on a blackboard, as four purple-covered notebooks tumbled to the ground.

"You know, you really are your own worst enemies," I said as I shook the sack at her. "I found this thing in the ceiling of my room at Christ Church. It must have gotten stuck and died there when it came to torment Dodgson. He didn't kill it. You've taken your temper out on the world and ruined a man for nothing. Your sister ruined the first man and woman. You are nothing but rage and hate. So was your sister. What had Eve done other than be like Adam? Lilith died behind the plaster because nothing can suck life out of stones."

The tove lunged. I reached down, grabbed the brandy, and splashed it in her eyes. She screamed, holding her claws to her face, tearing at her brow.

"I will kill you," she shrieked as her vision cleared. I tossed the corpse in the burning barrel.

"No! No! Our deal! Our deal!" As Agatha lunged at my face, I ducked, and the slithy tove went flying over me into the flaming barrel, hissing, writhing, and clutching the bones of her sister. I emptied the brandy into the fire. It ignited her eyes, which became two meteors of wrath. I thrust my lance over and over into her belly.

"Snicker snack!" I shouted.

"Twas brillig and the slithy toves did gyre and gimble in the wabe," ...said Alice, *surprised at her own ingenuity...*

"Of course, it is. It's called 'wabe', you know, because it goes a long way before it, and a long way behind it"

"And a long way beyond it on each side," Alice added.

As the embers died, I looked over the barrel's lip; there was nothing left of the slithy toves.

I waited for curfew's end. The porter finally opened the gate, grumbling about blighters being out all night. In my room I lay on my cot, thumbing through the lost diaries, one of the greatest literary finds of my era. I would redeem my lost author from his century of purgatory.

May 5, 1862

Went to see the Liddells today. I had so much more of the story of the looking glass world in my mind since I last saw Alice. I wanted nothing more than to share it with her, to see her face light up with that rare sense of joy in discovery she possesses. Speaking to her in those moments was like prayer. One feels divinity is listening back.

But as we were deep in our legend, a terrible thing happened. The creature that has pursued me all my life, the daemon that destroyed my childhood garden, appeared from beneath the sundial and accosted us. It tore Alice's lovely dress and frightened both of us within an inch of our lives. I struck it repeatedly but it would not be beaten. I tried to photograph the thing, but it slithered away, slimy, and lithe, and active. It was that awful lizard with the head of a woman and the body of a serpent. Mrs. Liddell was the first on the scene. She assumed the worst and screamed and struck me. Mr. Liddell arrived and with a blow he grabbed me and cast me to the ground. He bent down as if he was about to strike me again, but I kept repeating that I was only protecting Alice, shielding her from the awful thing."

I needed to come up with a good story.

"Well, a slithy tove and I traded for the bones of the serpent that brought about the Fall of Man."

Right. Not good.

The next week I went to London. I spent the night on a friend's sofa, then took a taxi to the Bermondsey Market before dawn as the vendors set up in the half-light. On a table crowded with silver and bric-a-brac, I discovered four identically bound Victorian diaries belonging to a lady who loved mice. Coincidence? I call it blind luck. The dealer gave me a receipt with description and date of purchase. To bear out their authenticity now that I had their provenance, the British Library Reading Room became my best friend.

A year later, the proofs for my groundbreaking Lewis Carroll biography arrived with the post as I was cleaning out my digs. I was on my way to Harvard where I had an appointment in the English Department.

When I opened my desk drawer I found Rilke's *Letters to a Young Poet* hiding behind the paper clips and Post-it notes. I reread Julia Cassidy's inscription: what was Rilke supposed to answer for me?

I flipped through the pages. I had never noticed before, but in the same pen as Mrs. Cassidy's handwriting there was a tiny star in the margin.

"How could we forget those ancient myths that stand at the beginning of all races, the myths about dragons that at the last moment are transformed into princesses? Perhaps all the dragons in our lives are princesses who are only waiting to see us act, just once, with beauty and courage. Perhaps everything that frightens us is, in its deepest essence, something helpless that wants our love."

I tucked Julia Cassidy's book in my coat pocket and put the box of page proofs under my arm. I stepped out the door, then turned to look over my shoulder. The orange, yellow, and pink flowers in the porter's small garden bloomed brightly in the morning sun.

WE ARE ALL MAD HERE

Lisa Smedman

"I've a feeling we'll be going over the top in the morning," Tom says as he clambers into the dugout and lets the canvas flap fall shut behind him.

I shiver. Tom's known for his "feelings." They're never wrong.

The five of us are cramped together in the dimly lit dugout, exhausted, hungry. My wool greatcoat is soddened with mud, and feels like a heavy wet shroud. The *boom-boom-boom* of artillery shakes the ground I sit upon. The funk hole we've dug in the trench wall is just big enough to hold the five of us; my tin hat scrapes the ceiling. The air smells of wet earth and putrefaction, with a trace of an oniony scent: the mustard gas that left Jimmy blistered and screaming last week.

Tom is grinning, teeth white in a mud-smeared face. That grin never leaves his lips. It matters not whether shells are raining down among us, blowing men to atoms; whether machine guns are scything down men before they make it one step beyond the parapet; whether the brown, choking gas is creeping towards us. It's like he knows Jerry isn't going to get him. Not yet.

"How do you know there'll be an attack?" one of the others asks.

"I heard the brass hats complaining that things here at Passchendaele have bogged down. They want the 13th to 'put some ginger into Jerry.' Me, I don't give a toss about that. But it'll be a great chance for more souvenirs."

"And to crack some Boche skulls," says Donny, pulling out the trench club he made for night raids – the one with the nails studded in one end. Donny's small, with sandy hair, a weak chin, and a soft voice, but he's a scrapper, for all that. It was at Pozières he got the nickname, after commenting on what a "lovely little donnybrook" that battle had been.

He was a lot less jolly after the news that his brother was among the missing at Loos. Now, I think, he just wants to die. In the candlelight, his eyes look hollow.

Tom deals the cards. My eyes widen as I see what's printed on them: they're racy as a French postcard. Women with creamy white breasts and open legs. Dark triangles of hair that make my pulse race. I think of that whore, back in Le Havre. The smell of her perfume as she walked past…

"Souvenirs," Tom says grinning. "Got them from the breast pocket of a dead Hun. They were a little bloody – he took a bullet clean through the heart. So mind, lads, when you're betting, since some of the cards are marked. Still, they're worth looking at, wouldn't you agree?"

Digger raises his cards and whistles. His Lord Kitchener moustache, still in tightly waxed curls despite the weather, twitches. "Too right, mate! I'd have a go wi' these lassies," he exclaims in a terrible attempt at an Australian accent.

We all give a strained laugh.

Digger's real name is Malcolm, and he's a Scot. He always has a trowel in hand when he's not in the front lines, planting seeds and bulbs from home in the ruined villages. Roses and bluebells, delphiniums and hollyhocks – those are his true loves. And heather, a sprig of which he keeps pinned inside his breast pocket, given him by his wife Maude. Digger usually saves the false accent for when someone overhears his nickname, and asks if he fought at Gallipoli. But he's laying it on thick now.

Jack cuts in: "If we're attacking at dawn, we'll want some rum. I've got a jar or two tucked away."

I believe it; Jack's a bit of a knave. Last winter, while at a field hospital due to frostbite, he stole a dozen mince pies that had been intended for the officers' Christmas dinner. One of the nursing sisters caught him hobbling along with them, but he charmed her into keeping mum. And no wonder: he's as handsome as any music hall actor, and with a voice to match. He claims to have royal blood, and with his smug bearing, that's almost possible to believe. But the truth is he was just another employee at the Lever Bros. soap factory, one of the nearly 700 of us who rushed off in 1914 to enlist in the Sunlight Pals Battalion.

Then there's me, Private Roland Childe. Eighteen years old, and the surname still fits, despite three years of war and the beginnings of a beard. I stare down at my cards, trying to decide which beauty to discard. I want to keep them all. I want to lie with a woman, just once, before I die…

Which I very well might, tomorrow, if there's another assault planned.

There's not many of us left. The 13th Cheshires, as we're formally known, lost a lot of good men at the Somme and Messines. But there's still we five.

We're like the cards, I think. Donny's the king of clubs, Digger's the spades, and Jack's the hearts. Tom, of course, could be no other card but the Joker. I suppose that makes me the diamonds – a diamond in the rough, waiting for the gemcutter's blade to cleave me in two and reveal what's within.

There's a poem in that, perhaps. And one day, when this bloody war is over, I shall write it.

But for now, I sit in the dugout, scratching louse bites, deciding whether to hold onto my pitiful hand and bluff, or discard everything and hope for the best.

Tom catches my eye and grins. "If you had a last wish before you died, what would it be? Luck or love?"

That's an odd question, I think. But for me, the answer's an easy one: love. Before I can answer, however, Tom's dealing me five more cards.

"Here you go, then. A good choice: luck will only go so far, and then it runs out."

I realize I haven't discarded yet. I toss my hand onto the blanket and pick up what I've been dealt. I have to fight to hide the disappointment: this hand is even worse. Just a high card: the queen of hearts.

The others discard and draw, and then we're betting. Digger starts us off, then Donny, then Jack, and then it's my turn. The shells are getting closer by the moment. If we're going over the top in the morning, I may as well wager it all.

"I'll see your quid," I shout at Jack, "and raise you two." I've gotten rather good at bluffing – my hands are steady as I hold up two fingers, even though the shells are nearly upon us.

We continue betting until someone calls, and then it's time to show our cards. Tom lays down a royal flush, and we groan. I realize I can hear again; the shellfire has stopped.

"Must be my lucky day," Tom announces. He leans forward, reaching for the bank notes. "I'll just collect my—"

There's a high-pitched *whizz* as a shell hurtles through the air. Then a loud bang. Shrapnel rips through the canvas we've hung over the dugout entrance and glances off my helmet.

Something lands in my lap, and my trousers are suddenly warm and wet. For a second, I think I've caught a blighty in the thigh, or maybe pissed myself. Then I hear the others screaming.

I look down.

Tom's head is in my lap, grinning up at me.

The rest of his body is gone.

◉ ◉ ◉

I open my eyes.

There's an electric light above me, a ceiling. Softness under me, and a warm blanket covering me. I smell vomit and piss, bleach and Sunlight soap.

The soap smell takes me back; for a moment, I wonder if I'm at Lever Bros. Then the sounds intrude: the groans, the wheezes, the coughs. I turn my head to the right and see, in the next bed, a figure whose face is heavily bandaged. His jaw is missing; blood-soaked bandages hold together what's left of his face. He's breathing noisily, staring fixedly at the ceiling with his one unbandaged eye.

To my left is a man whose remaining leg is missing its foot. The blanket has been drawn back to his waist, and a brown rubber tube leads into a hole in his thigh, conveying into his swollen flesh the liquid from a glass bottle that hangs above his bed. He feels me staring, and gives a weak laugh.

"Caught a blighty," he says in a posh accent. "The nursing sisters say I'll be dancing at the balls in London, by Christmas."

"Dancing?" I ask. "With just one leg?"

His face crumples a little. Then it brightens again. "The doctors will sew my leg back on. They promised me."

I turn away. The room is a large one, with two dozen or so beds along each wall. The men in them are all in a bad way: some missing arms or legs, others coughing and struggling to draw breath, still others with bandaged eyes or terrible burns, their skin yellow and weeping.

A nursing sister walks past, wearing a white pinafore, her blonde hair held back by a veil like those worn by nuns. "Sister!" I cry. "Am I in hospital? Have I been injured?"

"Oh!" she exclaims, turning toward me. "You can speak."

I'm struck mute by her beauty. She's everything I've ever dreamed of, with the kindest blue eyes and the warmest smile. She captures my heart in an instant.

I try to swallow, but the inside of my throat is sandpaper sore. A sudden memory comes to me of gagging, and the smell of burning flesh. I begin to cough...

"Your throat will be sore," she says, as she moves to my bedside and takes my hand. "That's the electroshock therapy. But on the bright side, it's finally restored your speech. And your vision has returned!"

I stare up at her, overwhelmed by the feel of her soft fingers holding mine. "I'm glad of that," I whisper hoarsely. "You're quite lovely."

A poem springs to my lips, and I recite it aloud, my voice becoming stronger as I say the lines:

> *"He saw her once, and in the glance*
> *A moment's glance of meeting eyes,*
> *His heart stood still in sudden trance*
> *He trembled with a sweet surprise*
> *All in the waning light she stood*
> *The star of perfect womanhood."*

She has a lovely laugh. "You're a poet?"

Am I? I'm not sure.

Her expression turns coy. "I suppose you wrote that for your sweetheart?"

"I haven't one," I answer. I feel a sheepish grin creep across my lips. "Never even been kissed."

Her expression softens. She's giving me a peculiar look, the sort a girl would give a bloke that she fancies.

"What's wrong with me?" I ask.

"Dr. Lapine classified you NYDN."

"Sorry?"

"Not Yet Diagnosed, Nervous," she explains. "You were found a mile behind the lines, blundering into things as if you couldn't see, wandering about holding a…" she pauses, seems hesitant to go on.

"Holding what?"

Her lips tighten.

"Please. Tell me. I can't remember anything of how I got here."

"The stretcher bearers asked you what had happened, but you wouldn't answer. They thought you were deaf. But when they told you to put…the thing you were holding…into their basket, you complied."

I stare up at her. I have no memory of any of this. The last thing I remember was…

Cards. I was playing cards with the lads, in our dugout. My friends…

I try to picture their faces, but they are lost. Vanished without trace, into No Man's Land. Only their smiles remain.

"The doctor at the casualty clearing station asked your name, but you wouldn't answer. From your collar badges, we know you're with the 13th Cheshires, but your identification disk and pay book are missing. What's your name?"

"I'm…" I try to answer her, but my name has vanished completely. "Diamond," I say at last. "Private Diamond." That feels right.

"No first name?"

"Sorry…it's gone."

There's compassion in her blue eyes. "They say you're a deserter."

"I'm not," I say fiercely. "I just had to…"

I pause, wondering what it was I had to do. Something important. Then it comes to me: there was a cat in my arms. A dead cat. I needed to bury it, so there could be flowers on its grave.

"I'll tell Dr. Lapine to come speak with you. If he diagnoses you as shell-shocked, and suffering from hysterical blindness, you'll have a defence against accusations of cowardice."

Her soft fingers touch my forehead, checking for fever. I reach for her hand, clutch it as if I'm drowning in mud. "Do you think I'm mad?"

"We are all mad here," she answers. "Even we nursing sisters. If we weren't, we wouldn't have come here."

"What's your name?"

"Alice." Gently, she pulls her hand away. "I must finish my rounds."

I prop myself up on one elbow. "Can we talk again later?"

"Nursing sisters aren't permitted to fraternize with the soldiers," she says. "I'm taking a risk, talking to you now. But I'll try to stop by later in my shift, to see how you are, all right?"

I watch her leave. Somewhere close at hand, artillery opens up with a dull *crump-crump-crump*. My bedframe rattles, and my pulse quickens. I hear the shriek of a shell, passing over the hospital, and throw myself to the floor, scrambling under the bed and covering my head.

All around me in the hospital, the air fills with screams…

◎ ◎ ◎

I'm back in my bed, with no recollection of how I got here. Through the hospital windows, I see the night sky, stars fading on the horizon as dawn breaks. White flashes illuminate low-hanging clouds from below: the artillery barrage that's rattling my teeth.

They'll be going over the top soon, I think.

Who will? I try to remember, but it's vanished again.

I sit up and swing my legs over the edge of the bed.

"Where are you off to?" the man in the next bed asks me. His bandages are gone; his jaw is back in place. This time, it's his hands that are missing.

"I need to get back," I tell him. "The lads will be wondering where I've gone."

I start to rise, then sit back down again. Back where? I wonder which regiment the man I'm talking to is from. He's wearing a blue uniform I don't recognize, made of flannelette.

"Hospital blues," he tells me. "All the convalescent cases get them."

I glance down at my shirt sleeves, and see khaki. "I'm not wearing them."

"That nice nursing sister – the one with the blonde hair – tried to dress you in blues earlier," the soldier continues. "She said she thought it might help. But a few minutes later, the hospital matron ordered her away – gave the sister a good scolding."

"I don't remember any of that."

The soldier holds up the bandaged stumps of his arms. The smell of putrefaction wafts in my direction. "I wish they'd given me pajamas instead of this wretched convalescent uniform; I can't get my buttons done up. But the doctors will make that right, soon enough. They've promised me hook hands – buttonhook hands." His laugh skitters along the edge of hysteria, like a nervous rat.

My attention is caught by a major, briskly entering the ward. His uniform is starch-smart, his brass buttons gleaming. A swagger stick is squeezed tight under one arm. He marches to my bedside, and stares down at me. His face is red, like a man who's been drinking, and by his glare it's anger that's lent his cheeks that hue.

"On your feet, Private!"

Beside him are two soldiers – both privates – with rifles held across their chests. One seems about my age, and has freckles. He looks uncomfortable; sweat trickles down his temple.

I stand, feeling dizzy. I grip the bed rail to steady myself.

"Salute, damn you!"

That snaps me to attention. My body moves of its own accord, fingertips touching my temple.

I lower my hand. "Sir," I say, "I'm ready to return to the front. Can you tell me how the lads are—"

"Left face," the major barks. "March."

I fall into step between the two privates. One is ahead of me, one behind. The major leads us out of the hospital ward, and into a corridor.

Suddenly, Alice darts out of a door on our right. She steps in front of the major, fists on her hips. "Where are you taking my patient?"

The major draws to a quivering halt. "He's no patient. He's a malingerer."

"He's shell-shocked. He can't even recall his own name."

I stare at her: the fire within her is wondrous. I'm so lucky to have met her. "Hello, Alice."

The major snorts. "He remembers your name well enough. And he was quick with a lie, when Dr. Lapine questioned him." He turns and smirks at me. "'Private Diamond,' is it?"

"Yes, sir," I answer. I think a moment, searching for clues to which Pals Battalion I might belong to. "And my mates are Private Spade, and Private Heart, and Private Club."

The major snorts.

"Where are you taking him?" Alice asks.

"To his court martial. This man needs to be made an example of."

"You can't!" Alice cries. "This man is genuinely shell-shocked." She steps forward, clutches the major's arm. "Please, Major, if you would just send him to Craiglockhart for treatment. Doctor Rivers has worked wonders, returning dozens of similarly wounded men to the front."

"Wounded!" The major's eyebrows rise to meet his cap's brim. "No, young lady, this man's hardly that. He's a coward and a liar: this 'madness' is just a ruse. The last thing this army needs is for others like him to think they can sham their way back to Blighty."

He stares down at her. "Will you step aside, sister? Or shall I order my men to clear you out of the way?"

Alice glares right back at him. Then her shoulders slump and she steps aside.

But as the major and his two soldiers march me past her, she suddenly darts forward again, takes my face in her hands, and kisses me. "Good luck," she whispers.

My head reels as I drink in her scent. I touch my lips. That kiss was worth everything – all of this confusion, this muddle. I'm a lucky man.

I can feel Tom's ghost grinning.

I glance over my shoulder as the major marches me away. Are those tears in Alice's eyes? Why is she crying? Then we round a corner, and she's gone.

◎ ◎ ◎

A little later – minutes? days? – I find myself standing at attention in front of a table at which the major and two other officers are seated. The two soldiers who marched me here stand off to the side near the door, rifles shouldered.

An older man with white hair, pale eyes and a nervous expression sits at a smaller table off to one side. He's wearing a doctor's white coat and cap. He's reading aloud from a paper he's holding, and making nervous gestures, but I can't make sense of what he's saying. All I hear is the *cheep-cheep-cheep* coming from a cage against one wall that holds a dozen bright-yellow canaries like the ones miners use to detect gas.

The doctor keeps talking and talking. I hear something about a head coming off, and clap my hands over my ears; I don't want to listen to this.

The officer on the left side of the table – a captain – stares at the paper he's writing on. His pen *scritches* and *scratches* like nails on a slate, setting my teeth on edge. Meanwhile, the canaries are watching me with those bright little eyes of theirs. Judging me. But they know nothing about me, I think – just as I know nothing about myself. I want them to be silent.

"Stupid things!" I shout at them. "Be quiet!"

The doctor fumbles to a nervous halt. The three officers stare at me. After a moment, the red-faced major speaks. "Have you anything to say in your defence, Private?"

I stare at the gold-and-red crowns upon his epaulettes. "If it please your majesty, I would like to return to my battalion. My name is…" I think hard, trying to get it right. The room swims and I feel as though I might faint. "My name is Private Roland Diamond, and I'm from the 13th Cheshires. We've lost our cat…"

The colonel with the pencil keeps scribbling, but the third officer – another captain – gives me a hard look. "You're not fooling anyone with that act, you coward. You'd save yourself a world of trouble if—"

"I'm not a coward!" Tears fill my eyes. "I just…wanted to bury him."

The major is speaking now: "The court, having considered the evidence against prisoner Roland Childe, is of the opinion that he is in breach of Section 12(1) of the British Army Act. The court does therefore sentence Private Childe to…"

He keeps talking, but I no longer hear or see him. All I can see, as I stare at the wall above his blood-red face, is Tom's grin, which is slowly fading as the canaries chirp their verdict…

◉ ◉ ◉

A while later, I awake to find myself on a bed – but not in the hospital ward. Stark vertical shadows fall across me from the metal bars, shadows cast by the lantern in the hallway outside my cell. I smell tea. I sit up and swing my feet to the floor.

"Ah, you're awake." A military chaplain sits on a folding chair nearby, his stiff white clerical collar visible above his khaki service jacket. He has a small head; his cap looks huge in comparison, the brim partially over his eyes. He holds a teacup in one hand, and bread and butter in the other. He pops the last of the bread into his mouth, then brushes crumbs off the Bible in his lap.

"What's happening?" I ask.

"Field Marshal Sir Douglas Haig confirmed your sentence." He swallows, wipes butter from his moustache, then sets the teacup down. He pulls paper from his pocket, and smooths it atop the Bible. "Is there anyone you'd care to write a letter to?" he asks as he pulls a pencil from his breast pocket. "I can't let you have the pencil, but I can jot it down for you, if you like."

I shake my head. "I don't have any family."

He starts to put his pencil away. Suddenly, I think of something: the lines to the poem I'd recited for Alice earlier. I realize, now, that it wasn't my poem: it was written by a man more famous for his nonsense verses. But I recite it anyway, and the chaplain scribbles. I choke out the final verse:

"The heavy hours of night went by,
And silence quickened into sound,
And light slid up the eastern sky,
And life began its daily round.
But light and life for him were fled:
His name was numbered with the dead."

"There's a nursing sister at the hospital, by the name of Alice," I tell the chaplain. "If you could give the poem to her…"

He nods. "As good as done, lad." He folds the poem, and tucks it into a pocket.

My eye falls on a brown bottle, sitting on the floor beside the bed. A note is propped up against it: *Drink me. You'll fare better if you do.*

"Did Alice leave that for me?" I ask.

The chaplain shakes his head. "There was a man here, earlier tonight. A private. Said his name was Jack, that he was a friend of yours. How he got in here is still a puzzle to me; no one's permitted to visit you except me."

I have no idea who he's talking about. I pick up the bottle, pull the cork, and sniff. Rum.

"He left something else for you as well. Playing cards."

He pulls a stained pack from his pocket and hands it over. I accept it, blushing. I don't take the cards out; I wouldn't want the chaplain seeing what's printed on them. I tuck the deck inside my breast pocket.

"Your Jack said the lads don't hold it against you that you ran," the chaplain tells me, "that any of them might have done the same. He said he was going to have a word with Doctor Lapine, see what he could do to persuade him to change his testimony. I told him…"

The chaplain pauses, as if needing to collect himself. "I told him that wouldn't do any good, that it was already too late. Jack nodded, and asked me to tell you that some Australian bloke would plant flowers on your grave."

My grave? That gives me pause. Am I dead, I wonder?

"Your friend told you all this himself, mind, but you didn't answer him – just stared straight through him, as if he were a ghost."

"Is he still here?"

"He said he had to get back to the front, or they'd charge him with desertion, as well."

Desertion. The word sends a shiver to my core. My hand begins to shake. I raise the bottle to my lips and gulp down the rum as quickly as I can. It burns my throat – the spot where the rawness is. I cough, and the rest of the rum slops out of the bottle, onto my trouser leg. I look down, and see not rum stains, but blood.

I open my mouth to scream, but only silence comes out.

◉ ◉ ◉

It's morning. The major and two privates have returned for me.

One of the privates opens a door, and we march out into a courtyard. Beyond the high stone walls, the eastern horizon is turning pink. Artillery rumbles nearby, and airplanes drone overhead. There's a battle going on. A big one.

I think of my friends. "Are the 13th Cheshires in it?" I ask the major. "The Sunlight Pals?"

"They were," he answers. "And they took heavy casualties. More than a hundred dead, and more than twice that many wounded." His eyes narrow. "You should have been there with them."

And I would have been, I think, if it wasn't for the cat.

No. That's not right. It wasn't a cat. It was Tom. And he's dead. And – it's just a feeling, mind, but somehow I know it's true – so are Jack, and Digger and Donny.

All dead.

The major marches me to a post in the ground. The two privates pull my hands behind my back, around the post, and tie my wrists together. The major, meanwhile, pins a scrap of white cloth onto my shirt, just above my heart. Behind him, four more privates with rifles enter the courtyard. Together with the first two, they form into a line.

I stare into the major's eyes. "You're going to shoot me, aren't you?"

"You're to be executed, yes." He reaches into his pocket. "Would you like a blindfold?"

Somehow, I manage a grin. This is it, I think: the diamond cutter's blade, descending.

"No, thank you," I tell him.

The major's eyes soften, just a little. "That's the spirit, lad."

He marches back to where the firing line is, and raises his hand. "Ready…"

Rifles come to shoulders.

"Aim…"

Eyes squint – the men take aim.

Which of their bullets will strike my heart, I wonder – and which has a blank in his barrel? I hope it's the young one with the freckles; he doesn't deserve to carry this burden.

"Fire!"

Bullets punch into my chest: the pain sharp, taking my breath away. I slump to my knees, twisting as I fall.

Tattered bits of white hang in the air above me. The bullets must have struck the pack of cards in my breast pocket, I think, as the pieces flutter down upon me – creamy white, like the feathers they pin to cowards.

A fragment of the Queen of Hearts lands upon my lips, and sticks to the blood on them.

Alice, giving me one last kiss.

I finally understand what Tom was grinning about, that night in the dugout. He could feel what was coming, sure enough: he knew we were all going to die. So, he set me on a different path. With five more cards gone from the deck, Tom would complete his royal flush. And then he'd lean forward to collect his winnings, just at the right moment to have his head blown clean off. And I would go mad, and be sent here, and meet Alice.

Lucky in love, I think as the blood pumps from my chest.

Lucky in…

OPERATION: LOOKING GLASS

Patrick Bollivar

Arthur grew tired of trying to read on the new e-reader his children had bought him. *What use is the thing if it makes my eyes hurt so bad?* Still, he found the biography of Alice Liddell to be fascinating. She'd inspired Lewis Carroll and lived in a real age of wonders.

His eyes needed a rest, so he grabbed his flashlight and made his way to the observatory.

Arthur didn't believe any of the rumours of strange happenings in the telescope room. Nothing interesting ever happened in Greenwich, unless you counted discovering new galaxies.

The route to the onion-domed building wasn't pleasant. The storm lurking overhead tried to blow his cap off. He held it tight and ran inside.

Arthur climbed the stairs. Upon reaching the door, he found it had shrunk to a quarter its size and changed from a wood finish to eggshell blue.

He scratched his balding head. "How odd."

The lock still accepted his key. "Luckily my cooking is bad." He pulled his skinny frame through the small door.

Standing, he shone his flashlight and gasped. "Oi! What do you think you're doing?"

A girl in her late teens glanced through the viewfinder of the giant telescope rising like a brass beanstalk toward the sky. She wrote in a notepad, a parasol swaying on her puffy sleeve, then went back to gazing through the view-finder.

A woman crouched next to her in front of a large wooden crate. Older, but not by much, she studied a mask with tubing running into the crate.

Neither paid the watchman any mind.

Arthur felt a revolver press into his side.

"Drop the bobby stick, if you please, sir," said a dapper gentleman in a three-piece suit, who sported a thick moustache under his bowler hat.

Arthur dropped his flashlight.

"I thought you locked the front door, Edith."

"I did, Harry," said the girl. "He's obviously got a bloody key though, don't he?"

"Speak like a lady please, Edith," said the other woman, before glancing up. Her eyes sparkled in the lamplight. She examined the two men with a piercing gaze. "Harry, I hardly think the pistol is necessary." She brushed hair from her face. "What's your name, good watchman?"

"Arthur, Miss." The older woman appeared to be in charge. They were dressed like Victorians; maybe it was some sort of a rehearsal. Then he studied the telescope. "Hold on, is that the twelve-inch Mertz?"

"If you say so."

"But that hasn't been in here since the 1890s!"

"Ah," said the woman. She put the mask down and arched her back, wincing. She wore a silver breastplate over her bodice, leaving the sleeves free, and a holstered pistol dangled from a belt above her skirt. "Mr. Carroll did warn us of potential temporal displacement along the Mean Line. Should go back to normal, once we're done. In the meantime, have no fear, Arthur. We're here on official business, by order of Prince Leopold."

"Begging your pardon, Miss, but I received no word that anyone would be in this room tonight." Arthur worried she might be crazy, that they all might. He glanced nervously at Harry, who gave him a wink. "And since when do you need weapons to gaze at the stars? You're not here to steal something, I hope."

"Do we look like robbers?" the armoured woman replied.

"Robbers and 'nappers," said a voice in the corner, causing Arthur to jump. It seemed to have come from a cloth-covered cage — too small for a person — near the telescope.

"Shut it, Mr. Do," said Edith, whacking the cage with her parasol. The woman rolled her eyes at the teenaged girl.

Arthur glanced around, searching for an escape, but Harry had the exit blocked. He saw another cloth-covered object against the wall, tall and rectangular against the wall. A sudden fear seized him, and he wondered if he'd be making it home to his wife and kids. "Fallen down the rabbit hole, I have."

"What did you say?" said Edith. She stormed up to Arthur, heels clacking. Arthur felt briefly amused by her fierceness, which did not fit with her short stature, or her dress. She smacked him on the nose with a rolled parchment. "Are you a Wonder disguised as a watchman? A spy, perhaps?"

"No, I don't even know what a Wonder is!"

"He isn't a Wonder, Edith," said the other woman, sighing. "Show him Prince Leopold's order."

Edith thrust the parchment into Arthur's hand. "This gives us free rein in this bloody observatory."

"Edith, language! My apologies, Arthur, but Leopold's soldiers have been a bad influence on her. Speaking of which,

come here, and power up the Influence Machine, Edith. I
need to test that the capacitor is functioning properly." Edith
glowered at the other woman. "Now, young lady."

Edith glared a final warning at Arthur, then marched over
to a long table. Steel balls on poles rose beside it, nailed to a
board. The table was laden with odd objects, including four
bell jars, each lined with metal foil and full of liquid.

Sparks shot between the steel balls as Edith turned the
wheel. The four jars began glowing white. The woman
beamed. "The Leyden jars are working perfectly! As soon as
you find the right ascension, we shall be in business."

"In other words, get back to work," grumbled Edith as she
returned to the telescope.

The woman tightened the straps on her breastplate,
caught Arthur watching, and cocked an eyebrow. "We really
are on important wartime business, Mr. Watchman."

Arthur wasn't sure to what war she referred, but thought
it best to play along. "Well, if it's for the war effort, I won't get
in the way. Can I go now, sir? Er, Miss?"

Harry raised an eyebrow. The woman frowned. "No, best
to stay, I think. Stand over there, please, out of the way."

"Harry, I need the scope adjusted: twenty-five degrees,
counterclockwise, if you please," said Edith as she applied
her notes to a star chart laid out on the floor.

Harry went over to the wall that operated the dome's rotation. Below the wheel rested an iron curb of cannonballs running the length of the polygon-shaped room. "Give me a
hand, Arthur," Harry said.

Arthur hesitated. *Winches and cannonballs?* The
armoured woman touched his hand, removed the parchment,
and smiled encouragingly. Arthur found himself playing
along.

The two men cranked the winch's handle, which rotated the dome, the telescope pivoting with it.

"If you don't mind my saying, sir, it's a little stormy for star-gazing tonight," said Arthur.

"You're quite correct, but stars are not what we're gazing for."

Arthur laughed. "No? What then?"

"Wocks, and snaps, and slithy toves," said the thing inside the cage. "They'll broil you alive come brillig time."

"Only if things go wrong, Mr. Do. Only if you've lied to us about the time of the tea party."

"One minute to midnight, one minute before doom!" said Mr. Do.

Arthur blanched. "If you don't mind my asking, sir, what war are you fighting?"

Harry laughed. "You really are a temporal displacement, aren't you? Fascinating. Where you're from, does Queen Victoria still reign?"

"No, sir. What year is this?"

"1871. The war with the Wonders is in full swing. Every stitch of grass between Oxford and Land's End is in their hands, and now they move west toward London."

"We're almost ready, Harry," said Edith. Her brown curls flopped around her face as she gazed into the viewfinder. "Bring over the looking glass."

Harry wheeled over the tall cloth-covered item. Arthur crept forward, curious. The white cloth over the object billowed, as if a wind rustled the sheet. Edith moved, and Arthur saw light projected through the telescope onto the white canvas. Was that an image of the sea? Something flew over the water, quickly passing in and out of view. He swore it had wings, the front body of a bird, the hindquarters of a lion.

Harry helped the woman pull a brass breathing tank from the crate. Gears spun on the back of it while a pump rose up and down at the top. Harry held the tank as she slipped the straps over her shoulders and clasped the leather buckles at the front. She pulled the mask over her face, and lowered her goggles.

"Breathing okay?" asked Harry. She gave him the okay with her fingers.

"Declination is off by a quarter," said Edith. "Spin her half a turn clockwise, Ensign Liddell."

"Aye, aye, First Mate Liddell," Harry said, grinning. The telescope moved as the toothed wheels groaned.

Arthur watched, trying not to stare as the tank pumped away on her back, occasionally emitting steam. Things began to slide into place. He wished he had his e-reader now. Harry had been the brother. Edith, the youngest sister, some said a paramour of Prince Leopold himself. And the woman. He laughed as he realized who they pretended to be.

She glanced his way, and lowered her mask. "Hand me my gun, please, Mr. Watchman. This suit is very cumbersome."

When he didn't move, she pointed to the strange weapon at her side. Arthur unclasped the holster strap, and slid out the gun made of blown glass – fat at the back, and thin as a needlepoint at the tip, the colour of strawberry cream. Nothing more than a toy. "Here you go, Miss. Er, if you don't mind me prying, but the gent and young lady said Liddell. Is that your last name also?"

"It is."

"So, you're Alice, are you?"

"Oh, heavens, no. I'm Lorina, her older sister."

"Then who's playing Alice?" said Arthur. "I mean, where is she?"

"Through the looking glass, of course, but with hope, not for long."

"I see them!" Edith cried. "Remove the cloth!"

With a yank, Lorina revealed the mirror, its edges etched with butterflies, caterpillars, and smoke curls. Both sides were made of smooth glass, reflecting nothing but fog twisting and drifting across the surface. The Liddells stared nervously into its depths.

"Do you hear music?" asked Edith.

"Yes," said Harry. "It's coming from the telescope."

A low melodic song drifted towards them, the words lost in the telescope's brass chamber. Light gleamed through the viewfinder as if the sun shone through the lenses.

The looking glass's fog swirled, revealing a shadowy glimpse of giant mushrooms, with houses underneath. A castle made of cards stood in the background, on a hill. "Wonderland," whispered Harry.

Lorina moved towards the mirror.

Edith grabbed the hem of her dress. "Wait, you idiot! We still have to hook you to the telegraph." She dashed to a wooden box on the table, decorated with spools of copper wire, and a brass handle that Arthur recognized as a telegraph communicator. Edith took the wires and tried to attach them to a spindle on Lorina's belt, but her skirt interfered. "Oh, blast and tarnation," said Edith. She undid the buttons, and removed it, revealing Lorina's petticoat.

"Avert your eyes please, sir," said Harry, sounding affronted by Arthur's stare. Arthur glanced at the table instead, feeling oddly embarrassed.

Edith returned to the telegraph, and rotated the crank on the Influence Machine. The Leyden jars sparked to life. "Okay. Check that it's working."

Lorina reached down to a small telegraph transmitter on her belt. She typed quickly.

The brass handle on the table moved rapidly up and down against the metal plate, which Edith translated, reading from her notepad. "Don't call me an idiot, you dolt. Stop." Edith snorted. "Okay, now you can go. I want you in constant communication. If anything goes wrong, we pull you back."

"Of course, dear," said Lorina. "Be ready with pistols and sword should anything come through whilst I'm gone. Oh, and Harry, if I should die, roast that lying Dodo for me. I think he would be very tasty stuffed with bread crumbs."

"Will do, Lorina," said Harry.

From within the cage a voice said, "Such barbarism! The Queen shall chop off all your heads if you pluck one feather from me."

"Oh, shut it," said Harry. He picked up a hook attached to a spool of rope, and secured it to Lorina's belt.

Lorina squeezed Harry's shoulder, then stepped toward the mirror, one hand gripping her gun, the other reaching forward. Her gloved fingers touched the surface, and continued inside, as if she slid into calm water, ripples flowing outward. Her whole body disappeared into the mirror.

"Jesus!" said Arthur, stepping backward. "Just like in the book! How did you do that?"

"So, you've read Carroll's propaganda, have you?" said Harry. "Not just like the book, Arthur. Mr. Carroll's whimsical stories were meant to prevent people believing in Alice when she returned from Wonderland. There are far worse horrors than the March Hares and talking caterpillars beyond the glass. The jabberwock and the frumious bandersnatch are numerous, and under the Queen's control, and the Mad Hatter makes Bluebeard seem positively gentlemanly toward the ladies." Harry peered intensely into the mirror, one hand on the unspooling rope, the other tight on his revolver. "Edith, I've lost sight of Lorina. What you?"

Edith squinted into the mirror. "Yes, I see her. She's hiding behind one of them mushrooms, watching the castle. She's moving forward now, her weapon out. I think she sees something. Balls, now she's gone over a hill." Edith typed on the telegraph. "What's happening? Stop," she said as she tapped the key.

A reply took a while to come. "There's a party ahead. Stop," read Edith. "The animals are playing croquet as the Queen sits for tea. Stop."

"Croquet?" asked Arthur, grasping for something familiar in all this insanity. "With hedgehogs?"

"They are using human heads. Stop. Alice is with the Hatter and what might be a jubjub bird. Stop. I've never seen one up close, so not sure. Stop."

"I have, on the battlefield," said Harry. "If she gazes into its eyes it will induce hysterical fits of laughter. I saw a man die from it, outside Slough. He was unable to stop his jocularity for three days. Couldn't breathe in the end."

"Monstrous," said Edith.

"Indeed."

The telegraph tapped away.

"I'm in position. Stop," read Edith. "Release the distraction. Stop."

"Help me, Arthur, there's a good chap." Together they dragged over a crate pockmarked with holes. Arthur smelled hay, and heard snuffling, which made him nervous. "Right up against the mirror, now. Jolly good."

Harry grabbed two pieces of fence, and lined them up on either side, from crate to mirror. Then he opened the front gate. Nothing happened.

"Give it a whack," said Edith.

Using Arthur's flashlight, Harry banged the back of the crate. Something moved. A nose peeked out. Pink, and wiggling up and down. Then another, with long white ears. Harry whacked the back of the crate again and they took off, six rabbits, straight into the mirror.

Arthur watched, fascinated, as the rabbits transformed on the other side, reared up on their hind legs, and suddenly shouted, "I'm late, I'm late, I'm late!" before they ran off in different directions.

"It's the aether," Harry explained to Arthur. "The air in Wonderland is not like our own. An unnerving gas, so to speak, changes people, and animals. Too long inside, and you would lose your mind, Watchman."

"The bungabear, and dandyboats come frolicking in the froth. Stop hop, hop stop," read Edith. "Dammit, her breather mustn't be working properly." She quickly typed, "Check your attachments, you're typing nonsense. Stop."

"Stop, stop, drop the gop and sew the— Sorry, it's fixed now. I'm fine. Stop," Lorina sent.

Edith wiped her brow. "That was close."

The mirror wobbled briefly, then lay still. "Did you see that?" said Harry, his revolver ready.

"Yes," said Edith, pulling a thin rapier out of the casing of her parasol. They carefully surveyed the room.

"What is it?" said Arthur, the sudden stillness frightening him.

"Could be nothing," said Harry, though he handed the watchman back his flashlight. Lorina's rope suddenly shot into the mirror, burning Harry's hand. He tried to hold on, and nearly lost his head for his troubles. A large, oval object shot out of the mirror, knocked him aside, splintered through the crate, and then skidded across the floor.

A large turtle shell spun on its belly before slowly coming to a stop. It was the colour and size of an old copper tub. Arthur laughed at the sight. "It's just a turtle."

"Ooh, just a turtle, he says," said a mocking voice from inside the shell. "Into the crow's nest for a look, Mr. Porcupine."

"Aye, aye, MT."

Where the turtle's head would normally appear a spy scope stuck out, moving left then right as it surveyed the surroundings. Harry and Edith carefully approached the shell, their weapons poised. The spy scope spotted Harry, and quickly retreated. Harry was bending down to glimpse inside when thin needles began extending between the shell's plates, making both Liddells back up.

"Fire the quills!" said MT.

"Everyone down!" yelled Harry, but too late. The quills launched, one striking Harry in the neck, another in Edith's rapier hand.

Arthur had fallen on his backside when Harry yelled, the Mock Turtle's barrage barely missing him. He removed his cap and found three long needles embedded there, oozing a strange yellow goo.

Harry collapsed to the ground, his revolver sliding from his hand. Edith stood, albeit barely, the crinoline under her skirt seeming to hold most of her weight as she leaned heavily onto the table. "Arthur, help," she wheezed. But Arthur didn't move. It had finally sunk in that this wasn't some weird costume drama. The idea terrified him. "Arthur, do something," said Edith.

Arthur calmed his shaking knees and carefully stood.

The turtle's limbs extended from the shell's openings. The Mock Turtle skidded, trying to gain purchase on the polished wooden floor. "Put your useless flippers back inside, MT!" said a new voice as it sprung up onto hind legs. "This is a job for pig's feet."

"Fine, you walk, but I want to see!" A turtle's head poked out the top, wearing a monocle. "Got two of them! But where's the third?"

"Here!" cried Arthur as he rammed the giant shell with his shoulder. The Mock Turtle wobbled towards the mirror, and after another push, vanished inside.

"Thank you, sir," said Edith weakly, plucking the quill out of her hand.

"Will you be all right, Miss?"

"Fine. Hopefully the effects will wear off soon. Please see to Harry." As Arthur did so, the telegraph started clicking. Edith transcribed, though barely able to stand. "I have her. Stop. Had to kill the jubjub. Stop. Weapons at the ready. Stop. Pull back the rope. Stop."

But the rope had vanished.

Arthur glanced nervously at Edith. She could barely lift her rapier. He saw Harry's revolver on the floor, near the dodo's cage. He went over, and picked it up. "Not too late to run," said Mr. Do. "A caucus race would do."

He ignored it, and went to stand in front of the mirror. Lorina appeared on the other side, hobbling toward him, her strange, rounded pistol in hand. It fired some sort of light beam at the pursuing guards. They burned easily, for their bodies were playing cards. The guards scattered, and Lorina's path became clear, though her forward movement slowed.

With her other arm, she dragged someone half her height, wearing a golden crown atop a curly head. A girl, similar in age to Edith, and unconscious.

The gryphon swooped downward, his claws outstretched. Arthur stuck the revolver through the mirror, and fired. Instead of a bullet there shot a star, arcing skyward with a colourful tail streaming in its wake. The star did no damage, but burned bright enough to distract the gryphon from its prey.

Lorina stumbled forward, still firing her pistol behind her and to the side, as animals of every size, and in every type of Victorian fashion charged.

Fog swirled across the reflection as the light from the telescope dimmed. "Wonderland is passing out of zenith," said Harry drowsily, as he struggled to lift himself. "Help them, Arthur."

Arthur took a deep breath, and plunged into the mirror.

The world lurched sideways, as if the ground in Wonderland was perpendicular to the Earth's. Arthur worried that if he ran too fast he'd fall toward the horizon. To keep his balance, he concentrated only on Lorina. Playing cards ran at him, human heads sewn onto flopping bodies. They sprayed him with red paint smelling of blood, but stinging like acid. He shot stars at them while helping Lorina up. Together they plunged back through the mirror, the girl held between them.

They stumbled onto the observatory floor. "Shut it down," said Arthur, as he fought for breath.

The last image Arthur saw: ugly beasts flapping their leathery wings as they charged, their puckered faces full of fangs. Then Edith shoved the looking glass away from the telescope's light, and all went dark.

"Help me get this off," said Lorina, still on her back. Edith removed her breathing pack, and the armour, leaving Lorina in the remains of her undergarments. "Thank you, Arthur." Lorina smiled.

Arthur waved obligingly, and then vomited up a variety of whole pastries. He'd eaten nothing of the sort today. He lay there, on his side, and stared in wonder at the figure still lying unconscious on the ground.

Lorina gently rolled the Queen over, revealing a girl dressed in blue, wearing long white stockings. The golden crown appeared far too heavy for her thin neck to support. "Alice, wake up." Lorina shook her. "I had to subdue her to get her to come with me. I hope I haven't done any permanent damage."

Alice's eyes flew open. "Cut the joint! I care not if it bows first, I am hungry. Remove the pudding though; it offends me greatly!"

Lorina stretched a hand to her, but Alice smacked it aside.

"Hand me not! Off with her head! Where is the Hatter and his friend the March Hare? Did they march away?"

"Try taking the crown off her," said Edith quietly, her eyes wide.

Harry and Arthur held the struggling Alice down while the women removed the crown. Barbs hidden underneath pinned it to her head. It left her with little bleeding pinpricks around her brow.

The crown transformed from a lustrous, shining gold to dull and rusty. Alice sighed and collapsed into Lorina's arms, both crying. Even tough Edith shed a tear before turning away.

Harry took the crown and stomped on it until it lay flat.

"Alice?" said Lorina when her sister's crying stopped. Alice did not respond. She'd passed out.

"Blimey," said Edith, as she wiped her sleeping sister's tears away. "Ten years, and she hasn't aged a day." Edith stared at the mirror. "Do you think the war will end, now that Alice isn't there to lead them?"

"Let's hope so," said Harry as he covered the mirror with the cloth. "We shouldn't linger. Alice needs a doctor. We have no idea what such prolonged exposure has done to her." Harry made his way toward the exit, holding Alice protectively in his arms.

Lorina buttoned her skirt over petticoat.

"So, Alice started this war?" said Arthur, trying to understand.

"No," said Lorina bitterly. "They used her! Made her their Queen, but treated her as their pawn."

"The Wonders need a human mind to organize their armies," said Edith as she sheathed her rapier. "Alice was able to turn their madness into an ounce of sanity, just enough to stage an invasion. Hopefully the front line is confusion right now."

"And with Lewis Carroll imprisoned in London Tower, they have no one to take her place."

"Get a move on, you two!" said Harry. "She's not as light as she looks." The sisters made their way toward the exit.

"Hang on, what about me?" said Arthur. "I don't belong here. I need to get home!"

"Sell the talking bird. That should pay for your passage," said Edith. "Not only does he talk but he's a Dodo. Rare, they are. Consider it your fee, for services rendered."

"Though I'd recommend eating him for Christmas dinner," said Lorina. She laid a hand on Arthur's shoulder. "Go about your normal duties. I'm sure the temporal displacement will end, now that we're done. Just don't touch the mirror."

They departed, leaving Arthur alone. Well, not entirely alone. A real Dodo, truly?

Arthur peered under the cloth, and came face to face with an angry beak sporting a white moustache. Not a normal Dodo then. "Do you know the way home?"

"Back the way you came. And they call me a Dodo."

Arthur squeezed through the small door, and found his way back to his office, which was just where he'd left it. A jet engine roared in the distance, giving him comfort that all had returned to normal. Pity. "I miss the Liddells already."

"I don't."

"Oh, shut it, Mr. Do."

MATHILDA

NICOLE IVERSEN

Mathilda drove along the Scottish coastline, the sky fill-ing with orange and red as she kept an eye in the rearview mirror. It had been days since they last saw the Tweedle brothers. Her eyes began to burn, and she made an aggra-vated noise, noticing the grey cat hairs stuck to the steering wheel.

"Oh, for God's sake, Dinah. How many times have I told you not to brush your fur in the front seat?"

A hiss came from the back and Mathilda scowled. Her nose twitched. She tried to hold her breath – then sneezed, her head snapping forward, her eyes closing. The RV swerved, a high-pitched screech came from the back, but Mathilda managed to straighten out.

"Geez, Mathilda. Are you trying to kill us before we find your sister?"

Mathilda sighed. "You know I'm allergic."

Dinah flopped into the passenger seat. Mathilda eyed the brush she held. Dinah rolled her yellow eyes and put it on the floor, then crossed her paws. "Don't take your worries out on me. Alice isn't in the human world. Why don't we go back to Wonderland?"

Mathilda grasped the steering wheel tighter. "Alice wouldn't go back. Not when she's the hero of our story and the only one who can drive the villains back to Wonderland. I swear I'll find her before the Queen of Hearts does."

The villains had escaped the other fantasy realms and were causing unnatural disasters as they waged war in the human world. Orcs patrolled cities, the White Witch had frozen half the world, and sea creatures of every kind plagued the oceans. Luckily, none of the gods from the other realms had appeared.

Dinah scratched behind her feline ear. "Wouldn't Alice have shown up if she knew she could help? All the other heroes are ready to stand up. The Pevensie children, the Hobbits, even all those damn princesses. Alice doesn't care."

Mathilda shook her head. "That's how I know something is wrong. Alice doesn't let other people figure out problems for her. The Hatter said the Treacle sisters could help."

Dinah stroked her fuzzy tail. "You're going to believe that nutter? You know there's a reason they referred to him as the *Mad* Hatter, don't you?"

Mathilda eyed her passenger. "Respect the dead."

The Queen of Hearts had made good on one of her threats. The Hatter's hat sat displayed as a trophy outside Buckingham Palace, alongside the countless other possessions from those the Queen had ordered executed. It broke Mathilda's heart. Dinah clawed against the seat but, rather than reprimand her, Mathilda said nothing. Dinah was as worried about Alice as she was.

A roaring motorcycle obliterated the silence. She glanced in the rearview mirror and Dinah turned in her seat. Nothing appeared on the road.

"Maybe it was just a motorcycle?" Dinah suggested.

Mathilda glanced out the passenger window, and her heart leapt.

"No, it's them."

Dinah looked out, her claws carving deep lines in the leather seat. In the dimming light a black motorcycle drove over the ocean's surface.

"Mathilda," Dinah whined.

Mathilda slammed her foot down. The RV lurched forward. The motorcycle reached the highway, chasing after them. The highway zigged and zagged and Mathilda was glad there were no other cars. Dinah yowled as she thumped against the window. The motorcycle kept up, and every once in a while a *thunk* hit the RV.

"They're throwing oysters," Dinah said.

If there were enough oysters they might lose a few limbs. The back window smashed. Mathilda peered over her shoulder.

"Dinah! Can you get it?"

Dinah slid down to the floor on all fours, which she normally avoided. While Mathilda drove madly down the highway, Dinah crept toward the oyster. Mathilda remained quiet while Dinah hunted, unable to see what was happening. Dinah landed hard on the floor.

"Shit!"

"What happened?" asked Mathilda.

"Little bugger got away from me."

Dinah hissed. Mathilda heard clacking and resisted the urge to turn around.

"There's more oysters," Dinah announced.

"You have to get them out of here."

"I'm trying!"

Dinah yowled, hissed, and pounced against the little kitchen's cupboards. The clacking grew louder. Mathilda tried to focus on the road, and refrained from stopping to help Dinah. She flinched as an oyster shell flew past her face and hit the window before falling empty on the dashboard.

"Are you eating them?"

"No," Dinah answered in a muffled voice.

Mathilda made a face and gagged.

"What else do you expect me to do with them?" Dinah shouted.

Another empty oyster shell landed in the front seat. A roaring engine caught Mathilda's attention and she looked out to see the motorcycle driving alongside them. The person in the sidecar waved at her, prompting the dark-skinned Walrus to hit him over the head. Mathilda rolled her eyes, and would have sped off, but the RV was already going as fast as possible.

"I say," yelled the Walrus, "would you mind terribly pulling over?"

His passenger, the Carpenter, slurped down an oyster. "Yeah. We just wants to talk to ya."

"Sorry," Mathilda yelled. "On a bit of a deadline. Can't stop. We'll have to catch up another time."

The Walrus glowered through his goggles. The motorcycle moved closer and rammed them. What did he hope to accomplish? Then Mathilda remembered the motorcycle could drive over water, jump canyons and land safely on the other side. She had discovered that in a disappointing turn of events a few weeks back. The walrus might succeed in running them off the road.

"The time has come," yelled the Walrus, "to talk of many things: of decapitation and slaughtering, and causing devastation. Of blood and Queens, and whether you have wings to fly from the scene."

"I liked the original better," yelled Mathilda.

Oyster shells littered the dashboard and passenger seat. Dinah continued to fight the molluscs in back.

The motorcycle rammed the RV again. Mathilda turned the wheel and struck back. She would not concede defeat.

"The time has come—"

"For you to shut up!" Mathilda shouted.

The Walrus made an abrupt sound and flicked his whiskers from side to side. The Carpenter threw an oyster through the window, which Mathilda dodged. It landed on the seat next to her.

"Dinah," Mathilda called. "I need your help."

"I'm a little busy."

Mathilda kept one eye on the road, and the other on the oyster. The top of the shell began to lift. Constricted by her seatbelt, Mathilda couldn't reach it. The memory of being bitten made her cringe, and the large scar on her arm served as a reminder. The shell opened and a little face peered up at her. Before the oyster could pounce, Dinah emerged, scooped it up and slurped it down.

Dinah sat down heavily in the passenger seat, straightening her Rolling Stones T-shirt, and cleaned her fur with her paw.

"You haven't gotten rid of them yet?" Dinah asked.

Mathilda growled. "Do you want to drive?"

"Uh, Mathilda."

"If you think you can do better, then please take the wheel. I insist."

Dinah screeched. "Look out!"

Mathilda looked back. A large brown puddle covered the highway. She stomped her foot down. The RV screeched and skidded but stopped short of the mud. The motorcycle whizzed by, plowing through the mess, and spun uncontrollably. Mathilda and Dinah watched the Walrus and Carpenter cling to each other as the motorcycle skidded off the road and crashed into the ocean.

Mathilda turned the RV off. Dinah followed her toward the edge of the highway. Neither the Walrus nor the Carpenter was seen.

Dinah smiled, showing off her canines. "They're gone."

"For now," answered Mathilda. She crouched down beside the puddle and poked her finger into the gooey mess. She felt it between her fingers before bringing it up to her nose and sniffed.

"It's treacle."

"Well, of course it is," said a new voice.

Mathilda stood and watched the three Treacle sisters walk onto the road. The eldest was fourteen and the youngest eight. Tillie, the youngest, wore a purple tutu with a blue sweater, while her two older sisters wore ripped jeans and boyband T-shirts.

Mathilda smiled at the girls. "I have never in my life been happier to see anyone from Wonderland. What are you doing here?"

"Tweedle Dee and Tweedle Dum passed by in their flat cars yesterday," said the oldest sister, Elsie Treacle.

"Fiat," Mathilda corrected. "They're called Fiats."

"Alice told us to keep an eye out for you," the middle sister Lacie informed them.

"You've seen her? She's alive?"

Dinah burped, dropping oyster shells onto the road. "See, I told you."

"Where is she?" asked Mathilda.

"She left three days ago," answered Elsie. "She had been wounded and needed our assistance."

Mathilda's heart lurched. "Wounded?"

"The jabberwock found her," Lacie replied, a grim expression on her face.

"But she was all right," said Elsie. "Treacle did the job."

Dinah scratched her ear. "How can molasses help?"

Elsie rolled her eyes. "The kind of treacle I'm talking about refers to a remedy for poison."

Mathilda waved at the stray cat hairs floating in the air. "Where did Alice go?"

Something pulled at her sleeve and Mathilda looked down into the youngest Treacle sister's face. Tillie, pigtails askew, face covered in treacle, held out her drawing, which Mathilda took.

"What is it?" asked Dinah.

"It's Millennium Bridge. In London." Mathilda looked at the youngest sister. "Alice has gone to London?"

Tillie nodded, her pigtails bouncing, as she sucked on a lollipop.

"Tillie, give Mathilda the vial," Elsie told her sister.

Tillie reached into her tutu and pulled out a tiny vial filled with a brown substance.

"Give this to Alice," Lacie instructed. "She left before we could give it to her. We're going back to Wonderland."

Mathilda put the vial in her pocket. "Thank you for your help."

"Stay safe," warned Elsie. "The Tweedle brothers are still out there. The walrus and the Carpenter won't stay gone for long either."

"You could come with us."

"Just give Alice the vial and we'll be fine," answered Lacie.

Tillie immediately turned on her heel and ran towards the other side of the road.

"We'd rather not meet the Queen," said Elsie.

Lacie held out a pail and waved her hand. The treacle on the road floated through the air and into the pail. Mathilda and Dinah returned to the RV. As they passed the sisters, Mathilda honked, and Tillie waved.

Night had fallen and the road was now black, the headlights doing a minimal job. A few slurping sounds emanated from the passenger seat.

"Are you still eating those things?"

Dinah's pink tongue licked at her mouth before she held out an oyster.

Mathilda's stomach ached, so she grabbed the oyster and gulped it down.

It was going to take over nine hours to get to London from Aberdeen, but if Alice was there it might not matter how much time it took. A burp escaped Dinah and Mathilda looked at her.

Dinah groaned, clutching her stomach. "I think I ate too much."

Laughter filtered in and Dinah frowned.

"It's not funny," said Dinah, hanging her head. "I think I need to use the kitty litter. Stop laughing."

"I'm not," Mathilda replied.

The laughter grew louder. A cat's head materialized in front of Mathilda, suspended in mid-air. She shrieked and slammed on the brakes, screeching to a halt. Dinah thumped to the floor.

"CHESHIRE!" Mathilda screamed.

"My apologies, Mathilda." Cheshire smiled widely.

Mathilda took deep breaths to calm her rapidly beating heart. "I thought you returned to Wonderland."

The Cheshire Cat's emerald eyes narrowed. "Which is where I wish to be, but my services are needed here." His entire body formed and he grinned. "Hello, Dinah."

Unlike Dinah's human form, the Cheshire Cat's appearance was akin to a regular cat. If normal house cats had burgundy fur with purple stripes, that is.

Dinah hid part of her face behind her tail. "Cheshire."

Mathilda rolled her eyes. "What are you doing here?"

"I have come to inform you that most of the villains have been driven back to their own worlds. Wonderland's are some of the last." His large eyes glanced at the back of the RV. "I do not see our dear Alice."

Mathilda was getting used to sighing. "We haven't found her yet. But we ran into the Treacle sisters, and I think she is in London."

Cheshire's bushy tail swished. "The power of the Treacle sisters is amateurish at best. You must hurry. The other realms' wizards cannot cast their spells to make the world forget this ghastly turn of events until all villains are back where they belong."

"We have to get to London first," said Mathilda. "We won't be there till morning, so they'll have to wait."

If it were possible, Cheshire's already wide smile deepened. "I believe I can assist."

Mathilda frowned. "I don't like the sound of that. No offense, Cheshire, but you're not one for being helpful."

Cheshire nodded. "True. I am allergic to helping, but no one wants things the way they were more than me. I wish to live in peace in Wonderland. I brought an old friend with me."

Before Mathilda could question Cheshire, the RV jolted. The moon's glow on the ocean disappeared as the RV rose. Mathilda began to bounce in her seat, thankful she wore her seatbelt.

"What is that?" Dinah screeched, putting on her seatbelt.

If the devil existed, he would most definitely get smiling tips from the Cheshire Cat. His grin went from ear to ear, and his teeth seemed to twinkle.

"Our Caterpillar turned into a butterfly," he replied.

Mathilda frowned. "He's not known for being helpful either."

Cheshire pranced around the dashboard. "I hid his hookah on him as an enticement."

Dinah laughed, petting her tail. "Oh, Cheshire. You are a scoundrel."

"What do we do once we find Alice?" asked Mathilda. "Does she know what to do?"

"She does," answered Cheshire. "However, once Alice has sent the villains back, you must return yourselves to the Realm of Undying Stories along with the other heroes."

"Of course."

They didn't belong in this world. Their place was alongside the other characters from beloved books where they were safe. It mattered only that the villains never escape again. Mathilda relaxed, and though she was still worried and on edge, her eyes eventually closed.

◎ ◎ ◎

A hard shake jostled Mathilda and she lifted her head from the headrest. The RV was once more on the ground, the sky alight with a new day. Relief filled her as she took in the Victoria Memorial directly in front of them. Even if the Winged Victory on top of the monument was painted red, it meant they had reached their destination.

A tap at her window made her jump. She cursed the Caterpillar for being stupid enough to leave them in the palace courtyard. Guards surrounded the RV; some in black armour, others in red. The guard at her window wore blood-red armour, and a black diamond displayed over his heart with the number ten. Mathilda rolled her window down a crack.

"Can I help you?"

The guard held up his spear. "Out of the vehicle."

"What do we do?" asked Dinah.

"Do as he says. Alice has to be here."

Mathilda slowly opened her door and stepped down. The ten of diamonds immediately searched her, finding only the vial. She glared as he put it in his belt.

Mathilda kept her head down, avoiding the severed heads on spears stuck into the ground. She knew they weren't just Wonderland characters, but Centaurs, Hobbits and a few Narnian's. The guards led them toward the palace. Looking up, the bright sun reflected off the red paint, reminding her of the neon sign over the strip club where they once found the Dodo squandering his time. The palace walls matched the crimson carpet, making Mathilda feel as though she were in a giant strawberry.

They walked down the length of red hall, and into the throne room. Nothing was safe from the Queen of Hearts' red fetish as gold and wood had been painted. Mathilda began to sweat. What were they going to do now? They wouldn't sur-vive meeting the Queen, not when she wanted Mathilda dead as much as Alice.

Beside her, Dinah growled low and menacing, flexing and extending her claws. The guard shoved his spear into Dinah's back. She yowled and whirled, pouncing on the guard. Mathilda stood silently, watching as the other guards tried to pull her off. A muzzle was brought forward and fear filled Dinah's yellow eyes.

There was a shout. "No! Leave her be."

Mathilda looked up. A figure in scarlet with a veil over her face sat on one of the thrones. The guard Dinah attacked stumbled as far away from her as possible. Tiny red scratches covered his face, with many more on his black armour. Mathilda kept her attention on the throne as the figure stood and pulled back the veil.

She gaped at the heart-shaped face staring back. "Alice?"

The expression of indifference didn't change on her little sister. Mathilda rushed forward but several guards circled her, their sharp spears halting her. There didn't seem to be a mark or bruise anywhere on Alice's body. Her blonde hair fell neatly down her back, but her blue eyes looked lifeless. The scarlet dress didn't suit her, and the veil created the illusion of a devilish halo.

"Alice! What are you doing?" Mathilda frowned. "Where's the Queen?"

Alice scowled. "I am the Queen."

"I don't understand."

A short man wearing a gold crown and a red and white robe stood at Alice's side, only coming up to her waist. Mathilda glared at the King of Hearts, and he intelligently looked the other way. She tried to push aside the spears but one poked her stomach, and another pricked her back. She halted, looking for another route.

"What did you do to her?"

The King of Hearts stroked his thin moustache. "It's perfectly simple. Alice is my Queen now. Unfortunately, the same will have to be done to you." He took a deep breath. "Send in the White Rabbit!" he yelled.

A nearby door opened and a guard walked in holding a rope. At the end was the White Rabbit, curled into a ball, being dragged along the floor. Large patches of fur were missing, his ears drooped from torture, and his only clothing was the pocket watch wound around one of his legs.

"Late, late, always late," the White Rabbit mumbled. "Time, time slips by. Can never go back. Always forward. Only ever forward."

The King smirked. "If you had looked at the heads in the courtyard you would have seen my wife among them. My dear Alice didn't enjoy sharing so I thought it best the Queen lose her head."

"I'm the Queen," Alice fumed.

The King looked at Alice. "Of course you are, my darling."

Mathilda stared at her little sister's face. There was no way to get closer, but perhaps she didn't have to. There was usually one word that could break a spell; Mathilda only had to figure out which one.

The King of Hearts went over to the throne, but his legs were too short. He snapped his fingers and a guard stepped forward and placed him on the seat.

The King straightened his crown. "Alice arrived yesterday. All alone with no one at her side. My dear wife locked her up, but I paid her a visit."

Alice stood as if she were a statue, her eyes unblinking, and Mathilda's heart broke.

"Mmm—" The King stopped. "You are Alice's sister. You tried so hard to save her and the world. There will be a place for you here in the palace and you will never have to be parted again."

Mathilda kept her focus on Alice. "We can be together in the Realm of Undying Stories."

The King snorted. "Contained and pushed away. In this world we're seen by everyone. The people attend us. In the

Realm we're lucky if anyone reads our stories. Children are forgetting...they don't want to hear old tales."

"You're wrong," Mathilda argued. "You're jealous, because you're a villain and everyone loves heroes more. Once I awaken Alice and drive you back to Wonderland, everything will be as it was before. Though here's a piece of advice; when you return to Wonderland you might want to find a hiding place. Your true Queen might be a little upset with you."

The King gulped, but raised his head in defiance. "Alice is under my spell. You can't awaken her."

Mathilda smirked. "You think I didn't notice how you stopped from saying my name? It's always been me and Alice. Even though I'm older and couldn't imagine the same as her, we're best friends. Sisters. Which means we would do anything to save each other."

"RABBIT!" screamed the King. "Wind your watch!"

The White Rabbit sat up and began to unwind the gold chain from his leg. A shrill yowl came from behind Mathilda. She didn't need to look to know that Dinah had pounced. The guards focused their attention on Dinah, allowing Mathilda to move forward, catching the White Rabbit's attention.

"I am Mathilda, sister of Alice of Wonderland, and together we will drive you back to your rightful place."

Mathilda only had to say her name before Alice blinked several times, peered around the room, then down at herself.

"What the hell am I wearing?" asked Alice.

"Mathilda!" Dinah yelled.

She turned to see half the guards lying on the ground.

Dinah threw the vial of treacle she had swiped from the guard's belt, and Mathilda caught it.

The remaining guards milled in confusion, and the King couldn't get down from his high throne.

"Alice, it's from the Treacle sisters."

Mathilda threw the vial toward her sister and Alice caught it. Mathilda pushed Dinah down on the marble floor as Alice pulled the cork from the vial. Large gobs of molasses spurted out of the tiny vial and covered the entire room. The molasses surrounded her and Dinah in a bubble, and when it disappeared Mathilda raised her head. The King and guards had disappeared. The room was as it had been, no evidence of red paint. Looking out the window, she saw all the severed heads had also vanished.

"Mathilda."

She turned and fell against the wall as Alice jumped into her arms. They clung to each other until a low mewling intruded. Alice stood back and turned.

"Dinah!"

Alice threw her arms around Dinah's furry neck. Mathilda couldn't help herself and wound her arms around them, but the embrace didn't last long before her nose began to twitch. She let go and sneezed loudly, making Alice laugh. Mathilda couldn't help but laugh as well.

Alice reached for Mathilda's hand, holding Dinah's paw in her other hand.

"Let's go home."

It was the best idea Mathilda had ever heard.

A NIGHT AT THE RABBIT HOLE

CAIT GORDON

With chest bound underneath a crisp blue shirt accented by a tie dangling below the unbuttoned collar, this brand-new person stared so intensely into the mirror that they could have been looking through it. They. That was the pronoun now. Not he. Not she. They. The stocky yet fit soul considered adjusting their tie, but winced. *I always feel like I'm choking in these things.* They examined the way the faux-silk hung, and nodded. *Yeah, I prefer it sloppy chic.*

One last decision had to be made, for today at least. A name. *Something gender neutral or is that too expected?* Perhaps it would have made more sense to have chosen a name at the beginning of their transition, but for some reason they'd left it by the wayside. If you'd asked them, they'd not have been able to tell you why. In any case, the moment had arrived and a deadname stood on the precipice for burial. Time to give birth to a new one.

Focusing on their reflection, they met a face with high cheekbones and a dimpled chin, smooth skin, a freckled nose, and thinned lips pulled taut. They raised a thick brow over a pale blue eye. Their other eyebrow and eye remained impassive. Atop this facial configuration rested a newly acquired undercut with a long bleached fringe. *Who do I look like? I mean, sometimes people say they look like a Sam or a Shannon or an Ashley. But who do I really look like?*

They bit their lip. Rummaging through their brain's filing cabinet, it felt like every uncovered file turned up blank. *Okay, it really shouldn't be this difficult. I mean, I know who I am now, so putting a name to me has gotta be easy.* They swore loudly and ran a hand through their soft fringe. Another ten minutes passed where several names came to mind, all of which were met with a *meh*. Shaking their head, they did what they always did at times like this. They grabbed their cell phone for advice.

Where to begin? The first letter of the alphabet seemed logical. "Names that start with A," they barked into the search engine.

The results appeared. Nothing inspired. The person huffed.

"Names that start with A that ROCK!" they shouted.

They laughed loudly at an image of Alice Cooper in full makeup. After scrolling down for other suggestions, all of which left them flat, they returned to the photo. *Alice. That would be way too funny.* They gazed once more in the mirror. *Well, it's definitely not a cliché. I can't help but feel more than a little pleasure from the name Alice representing my gender-fluidity.* Their reflection smirked. *Yeah, I'm so doing this. Hey, everyone, I'm Alice. Deal with it.*

"Thanks, search app!" Alice said to their phone.

The screen went blank.

What the heck?

A white dot appeared against a black background. It stretched from both sides and each end curved upward, resembling a wide grin. Alice blinked a few times. They never remembered installing a smiley app.

"Um, hello?" Alice asked. "Where did you come from?" They poked at the screen. The smile distorted with each touch, but returned to normal.

"Hello, Alice," said a voice unlike the tone Alice selected in their phone settings.

"Wha— How did you know my name?" *And why am I talking to this thing?*

The grin opened up into a toothy smile against the dark screen. "I like this name. I also like glam metal. That's why I chose it for you." The smile vanished, replaced by a hand whose fingers were arranged in a heavy metal-salute.

"Yeeaah, okay, so—"

The phone display returned to normal before Alice finished their reply. Everything looked as it always had, including the purple and aqua cupcake wallpaper. *I'm not on any meds, so I can't be hallucinating.* They checked for rogue apps. Nothing. *That wasn't weird. Not at all.*

They were putting their cell in their back pocket when it vibrated, taking about ten years off their life. Alice feared looking at the thing, expecting the grinning metalhead app. They exhaled when they saw it was a text from a friend:

Are you coming? We'll never get into this new place if you're not on time!

Alice smiled. *Ah, Bunni. You're obsessive, but I love you.*

I'm on my way. And call me Alice.

Move your butt, Alice! We're going to be late!

They smiled.

Butt is moving. See u soon.

Alice hopped off the bus as it entered The Garden. Not its official title, but that's what everyone called it. This section of downtown comprised an eclectic collection of coffee shops, strip clubs, dance venues, tattoo parlours, and various religious institutions. Finding a church beside a tanning salon or house of ill repute – if anyone even said that anymore – seemed perfectly normal. Prophets new to the 'hood often admonished "sinners," but eventually could be found sharing a tea and a scone at a nearby café with the same people they'd tried to rebuke. Something about the pulse of the neighbourhood created an atmosphere of acceptance. You could be who you really were there.

The person Alice sought wasn't hard to spot. Bunni paced beside the long line outside of the town's newest hot spot, fretting into her smartwatch. Alice's breath caught in their throat: white halter top against light brown skin, form-fitting white capris, and powder-pink stilettos, the same colour as her bobbed wig. Their front pocket vibrated over and over as scolding texts poured in.

Eventually Bunni looked up, glimpsing Alice walking casually toward her with hands in their pockets. Her own hands immediately found her hips and the woman in white stood akimbo, poised for battle.

"Hey, Bunni, it's me, Alice," they said. Bunni really *was* beautiful when she was angry.

"Do you know how late you are? Look at this!" she gestured to the queue, which trailed around the block.

"I'm sorry. Again." They proffered their arms out for a hug.

Bunni offered up her wrist. "Can you read this? Can you see the time? Can you even tell time? Well? Can you?"

Alice sighed. They peered at the fluorescent sign that wasn't lit properly. It couldn't have been a complete name, because a dark patch to the left made the letters appear misaligned. *It Hole? Seriously?*

"What's an It Hole?" they asked. "Are the S and H missing?"

Bunni clucked her tongue. "It's Rabbit Hole, stupid. And we are obviously not getting in for the opening, so you might as well take me to an S and H place right now."

"You know, you could at least say something about how I look," said Alice.

Bunni fumed at her watch again, and at the impossibly long line. When it dawned on her that Alice had said something, she glanced at their body and face and muttered, "You're fine. I would have rethought the tie. Like your hair, though."

Alice shook their head. That would have to do. "What about my name?"

"Your name is your name. How can anyone argue with it?" Her back was to Alice now while she made eye contact with a sturdy bouncer, who greatly approved of the woman before him.

He leered at Bunni and waved her over. She gestured that Alice was her plus-one, and he didn't seem bothered by that a bit. He'd probably try to hit on her later.

Inside the club, Gryfünn belted out their one-hit-wonder, *Drowned in My Own Tears*. The song sounded a bit emo to Alice's ears, and as with most tunes they despised, Alice changed the lyrics from:

> *You are my entire heart*
> *I need you as my air*
> *I pray we never part*
> *Clandestine love affair*

to:

> *I need to really fart*
> *and taint your precious air*
> *I hope the ground soon parts*
> *and sucks you into nowhere*

Bunni ran toward the stage, screaming like a teenager. This was her favourite band and she'd not stopped talking about the club opening for weeks. Alice wanted to join her, but not even the bliss of being beside Bunni tempted them to give their undivided attention to Gryfünn. *Yeah, no. I'd rather hang upside down off a frozen balcony in January, in the nude, wearing a sign that reads, "Look Ma, I'm an icicle!"*

Alice shoved wireless earbuds in tightly, hoping to drown out the sound of cats being castrated without anesthetic. Picking up their phone to select a playlist, they jumped when they saw the screen go black again. Instantly, the smile reappeared.

"If you like her, tell her," said the app.

Vitamins, thought Alice. *That's all I took before I left. Four of D, and I think a C. Maybe I shouldn't have bought them from the organic shop. Who knows what's in the fillers?*

They pressed two buttons on the phone, hoping to provoke a factory reset.

"Stop that," said the app. "Anyway, here's what will eradicate that cacophony."

A rage of death metal surged into Alice's consciousness, threatening to rip apart their eardrums with a driving double-kick beat, and a lead singer who sounded like Cookie Monster on steroids. Alice attempted to lower the volume.

"Too loud?" said the creepy smiley app.

Alice pressed and pressed the volume controls until they strained a ligament.

"If you want something, you must ask me," said the app. More teeth appeared in the smile.

Alice looked around to make sure nobody stared and realized that was ridiculous. After all, it would just appear like they were speaking to a voice-activated device, as everyone did these days.

"Volume down by thirty percent," they said.

"Was that so hard?" said the app, lowering the volume.

Alice relented. They felt thirsty. Also claustrophobic as the crowds poured in, pressing firmly against Alice's body. *Holy crap, I'm not sure if I just lost my virtue!* Alice pushed forward, taking their dry throat to the bar at a snail's pace. It was not a great situation for someone who coveted their personal space. Losing patience, they ducked through a gap in the masses and dived for a lone seat at a table where some rando took a drag on his bong.

"Um, hey, can I sit here?" asked Alice.

"Looks like you're doing a good enough job of it," said the guy, blowing rings into the air.

A voice rang through Alice's earbuds. "Ask him to give you a treat. But don't eat it until the right moment."

They peeked at their phone where an eye appeared above the grin and winked slyly. Alice looked up at Bong Guy and cleared their throat.

"I'm parched, dude. Any chance I can get a drink around here?"

"That's not what I told you to say!" said the app.

Alice removed the earbuds, and shoved their phone in their pocket. It vibrated like mad. Alice ignored it.

"Bar's over there, son," Bong Guy pointed with the mouth-piece.

"Yeah, I know, but it's impossible to get to. And by the way, I'm not a guy-YI-YEEE!" Alice jumped out of their seat and quickly tossed the searing phone from their trousers. It landed face-up on the table. On the screen was not so much of a smiley face. More of an angry face.

Bong Guy jumped when he caught a glimpse of it. "Whoa, dude," – he turned Alice's phone over to hide the app – "I didn't know you were one of *us*. Sorry, I didn't recognize you. New hair?"

Alice sat, mouth gaping, and picked up the phone, putting the buds back. They shook themself awake and cleared their throat. "Um, yeah, phone? Talk to me."

"First of all, don't do that again."

"So noted."

"Second of all, ask the man for a treat."

"What kind of treat?"

Bong Guy smiled and leaned toward Alice, exhaling smog into their face. "Right on, dude. You want a tart, dontcha?"

"Don't call me dude. I'm not a guy. Tart? The dessert or a woman with loose morals?"

"Hey, I call my mom dude."

"Good for her. I don't like it."

Bong Guy frowned and took another drag. "So, you want the tart or not?"

"Again, person or baked good?"

Bong Guy laughed. "You're hysterical, dude— uh, person. Let's shake on this budding friendship. It's nice to have interests in common." He held out his hand.

"Take it," the app said into Alice's ear.

Alice smiled awkwardly and shook the man's hand. They felt a plastic packet with something hard inside pressed against their palm. When they tried to peek at it, Bong Guy chastised, "Not here, du— erm, person, not here. Keep it in your pocket until the signal. Geez, are you trying to blow our cover already?"

"Sorry."

"Cwen will lose it completely if she finds out we stole her tarts."

"Cwen?"

"Yeah. She's over there, with Roy. It's amazing we have them together in one place." Bong Guy pointed with his mouthpiece again, as he blew more smoke rings in the air.

The creepy smiley app had turned off the musical anti-dote, so Alice inwardly groaned at having to listen to Gryfünn's latest hit, *Everything Is Queer Today*, a misdirected attempt at being inclusive. For some reason, the song had played on every local and online radio station. It must have been easier to avoid the plague than this musical train wreck. Alice prayed for a stroke – for either themself or the band. Alice wasn't too fussy about whom.

Trying to focus, Alice targeted their sights through a part in the crowd that revealed a large round table where a bunch of people seemed to be gambling. It was hard to make them out.

"Head over," said the app, sporting a wider, toothier smile. "See what you're up against."

Seriously, how many teeth can one have? On second thought, since apps can be designed with more teeth than any living creature, I probably should just accept this at tooth value. They stood up and nodded to Bong Guy.

"Later, person," he said with a puff. "And remember, wait for the signal."

Alice ventured through the crowd, tripping on someone's outstretched boot and crashing against two men slow-dancing. The startled couple offered a symphony of profanities.

"You slaughterer of romance!" cried the guy in the over-sized felt top hat, who clutched his partner protectively. The other man wore a scowl of death, and a headband with furry brownish-greyish rabbit ears attached to the top.

A killer rabbit? Alice resisted the urge to recite *Monty Python* sketches, and instead apologized profusely and fled the scene.

Finally reaching the table with a gang of people around it, Alice had a better view of Cwen and Roy. Cwen looked strong and buxom in an Amazonian sense, clad in a red-leather dress that moulded her toned form perfectly. Her dark hair piled high on her head in a riot of corkscrew curls. Several tendrils escaped their bobby-pin incarceration and danced against her pale skin. Roy also had midnight locks, and would have been more handsome if he hadn't conveyed such acute distress. He wore an ill-fitting, soft black leather jacket over a scarlet shirt, and nervously scratched his frizzy hipster beard. However odd a match, they seemed to be some sort of power-couple; everyone deferred to them in a sycophantic manner. *Perhaps for this place, they're hot poo, even though no true A-list couple would be ever caught dead in The Garden.*

"Straight flush, peasants!" Cwen tossed her cards on the table. All hearts. She reached for the pot piled high at the centre of the tabletop.

"Not so fast," said a man sitting at the nine o'clock spot. "Royal flush beats all!" He threw down the spades.

Cwen said nothing, sitting upright. Roy cowed on her right. She turned to him and drew her finger across her throat. Roy gulped uncomfortably and nodded at the woman standing guard at Cwen's left. The woman in turn nodded to two people who stood behind the man who'd just won the hand. They swooped in and pulled him from his chair, just as he reached for his winnings.

"Hey! Let me go!"

They held him firmly by the arms.

"What did I do? Cwen, Cwen! What did I do?"

Cwen inspected the cuticle of her index finger. "We don't tolerate cheaters here, Jack. You must leave the game."

"But I—"

"Permanently." Cwen waved a hand dismissively and Jack disappeared into the crowd, escorted by what Alice assumed was Security. Hopefully, the man had merely been barred from the club. Hopefully.

"Now, then," said Cwen, "we need a new player." She scanned the faces standing around the table. Most of those faces refused to look directly at her. However, her eyes sparkled when she noticed one person who appeared quite the noob.

"You!" she barked. "The one with the horrible tie trying to free itself from its collar."

Alice pointed at their chest.

"Yes, yes, you," Cwen said impatiently. "Sit down."

"I really don't know the game too well," said Alice.

"Perfect! Stan, pull out the chair for my new guest."

Someone obviously named Stan did her bidding. Alice felt all eyes on them as they sat. "Um, thanks, Stan," they said over their shoulder.

Stan grunted.

"Your name, my dearest?" asked Cwen, suddenly all coquettish smiles. She dealt the cards in that gravity-defying way only experts manage. It was a skill Alice had always envied.

"Alice. As in Cooper. My pronouns are they, them, and their."

A dimple deepened on Cwen's left cheek. "Aren't you a clever one? Well, then, my nonbinary friend, shall we play?"

"Um, sure."

"But do remove your earbuds, dear. One might accuse you of cheating."

Alice's eyes widened. They'd be losing their only connection to the smiley app. For once they actually wanted that creepy thing inside their head. They removed the left earbud but before they could take out the other, the app said, "The pink flamingo."

Cwen skillfully dealt the cards. Alice cleared their throat again and thought, *Lose. All I have to do is lose. Then everything'll be okay.*

They picked up their cards. Three jacks and two kings. A full house. *Aw, gnads.* Around the table the other players wore stoic poker faces. Considering the amount of sweat trickling into Alice's pits and onto their forehead, they probably had all the *tells* in the known universe. *Crap!*

When someone called out the betting round, Alice nearly announced they had no money. A mountain of chips poured from monstrously large hands. Cwen smiled with only her mouth. Her eyes glared wickedly.

"A gift from me to you." She laughed with certain malice.

Alice put down the required red chips. As the other players folded, it never occurred to Alice to fold. Maybe because they felt eyes staring at their cards from behind. *Is it still considered cheating to fake your own death in poker?* They decided to ask for three cards. *That should ruin my hand. It'll also make me seem ambitious to the goons behind me.*

Cwen dealt the three cards. Alice picked them up. They had discarded the three jacks only to retrieve two kings and an ace. Now they had four kings, which was even better than a full house. *Okay, Life, seriously?!*

Everyone stared at Alice now. Alice had no idea why.

"Well?" said an overly rouged woman to their right. "Raise or check?"

"Uh, um, check?"

"Oh, come now," said Cwen. "Will no one have the courage to put some money down on this friendly game? Nobody likes a coward, you know." She glared pointedly at Alice.

If I bet nothing, it's bad. If I bet anything, it's bad. If I bet everything, it's super bad. But maybe she has another straight flush. Maybe she keeps straight flushes on her lap. That could be a thing, right? Hoping desperately the true cheat was Cwen, Alice pushed out ten black chips onto the table. Ten seemed to be a conservative number.

"A thousand? Well done!" cried Cwen. "You impress me, young Alice." Her almost black irises said otherwise. No doubt she was prepping her finger to cross her throat once more.

The people to Alice's left folded until it was Cwen's turn to bet. "All in," she said.

"But, dear," said Roy, "you can't—"

"I can do what I wish!" she retorted.

Alice pushed the mountain of chips to the pot and threw down their cards. Cwen scowled. She had a full house.

"L-look, you-you keep it," sputtered Alice, pointing to the chips. "I-I don't want it. I p-prefer a low-income Bohemian lifestyle, anyhow." They tried to stand but were pushed back onto their chair.

"Rooooy!" Cwen bellowed.

Without warning, a siren roared and water spritzed out of overhead sprinklers. People screamed, mostly because their hair and outfits were drenched. A loudspeaker voice announced that this was an unexpected false alarm. The sprinklers stopped immediately. However, the diversion worked. Whoever's hands had been on Alice had let go, so Alice bolted as fast as possible. Their phone vibrated and heated up again, but without scorching. Alice grabbed the plastic packet from their back pocket, looking at a beige pill with a raspberry gel-like center. *Gee, it even looks like a tart.* They popped it in their mouth and washed it down with whatever drink was nearest. *Ugh. I hate Scotch.*

The ingredients blazed through Alice's system, changing their perception of their surroundings. The motley crew of patrons who were still there seemed to think all the wet was camp and fun, but dispersed throughout the club stood beings most definitely not human. Humanoid mauve faces, streaked with fluorescent orange and green patterns, scanned the crowds. Alice gasped, searching for Bunni. They pushed people out of the way, distinctly avoiding the aliens, to find their beloved friend.

She hadn't budged and danced sensually, soaked to the bone, to the pounding beat of the onstage horror. Sadly, Gryfünn were not aliens. *That would have explained a lot, actually.*

"Bunni, Bunni!" Alice grabbed her arm. "We have to get out of here!"

"Ugh, no way!" she protested. "This is my favourite tune. I've waited forever to see these guys play live."

"No, really, we have to get out of here!"

"You go. I'm staying."

Alice spun about and saw more aliens; the highest concentration of them hung about Cwen's table. Cwen herself stood out from the rest not only because of where she sat, but also because of her outrageously high bouffant in gradients of purple. *Um, pretty gaudy. And she didn't like my tie?*

Alice looked over at Bunni. *Oh heck, let her hate me.* They grabbed the woman, swept her off her feet, and onto their shoulder, like a sack of potatoes. *A sexy sack of spuds, though, in pink stilettos.*

"Have you lost your mind? Put me down!" screamed Bunni as Alice panted and ran.

They stopped when they noticed more aliens blocking the exit.

"Crap!"

"Put me down or else I'll never speak to you again!"

Alice did. As soon as Bunni's heels touched the concrete floor, Alice grabbed her cheeks in their hands.

"You're going to think I've lost it, but we're in big trouble. This place is crawling with aliens!"

The expression on Bunni's face revealed her exact feeling about that statement.

"I know, I know," said Alice, "but you hafta trust me on this!"

"Listen," she said, "I know people tend to experiment a little when they come to places like this, but honey, what did you take?"

"I didn't take, well, okay, yeah, but, you don't get it. Bong Guy said—"

"Bong Guy. Said what?"

"The signal! And then the sprinklers. So I ate the tart, and then there they were. Everywhere. Purple and green and orange and I think their Queen has a Sixties bouffant, so—"

"Alice—"

"Wait! The phone!" Alice grabbed their cell and shoved one earbud into Bunni's ear and the other into their own.

"Tell her, app!" they shouted.

As creepy smiley metalhead app began to explain, Bunni's understanding didn't seem to deepen one bit. She quickly removed the earbud.

"Where did you get this phone?"

"Some guy online. Got a deal second-hand. Mint condition."

"Alice, you're losing it."

"There they are!" screamed Cwen as she charged ahead of her guard toward Alice and Bunni. "That's the thief who cheated me out of my money. And after I'd been so generous, too! Grab them!"

"Run, Bunni!"

"Wait, what? What money – HEY!" An alien reached out and pulled Bunni away. "HEY! ALICE!"

With Bunni dragged off and Cwen barrelling toward them, Alice turned left and right and left and right like someone with no sense of direction.

"The pink flamingo!" shouted the app.

"What flipping flamingo?" cried Alice.

The flashlight of the phone pointed toward a plastic pink flamingo standing upright beside one of the columns just ahead.

"Get it, now!"

"AAAALICE!" screamed Bunni.

Alice bolted for the pink flamingo.

"Pick it up," said the app.

They did and clutched it in their arms. Cwen and her troops were closing in.

"Point and shoot!" shouted the app.

"Point what and shoot where?"

"The feet. Aim the feet at the aliens and squeeze the beak!"

"Arrest this person at once, and all their accomplices!" ordered Cwen.

As stupid as they felt doing this, Alice aimed the flamingo and fired. The blast emitted a pulse that disintegrated Cwen and a few guards, but had no effect on the human bystanders.

"Good shot," said Bong Guy, arriving at the scene with his own flamingo. "Between the two of us, we'll make quick work of these douchecanoes!"

Alice and Bong Guy waved plastic birds at random patrons like lunatics. Onlookers could not perceive the blasts coming from the weapons. They could, however, see the patrons disappear, and must have wondered how Alice and Bong Guy pulled that off without any smoke and mirrors. A few people applauded, thinking it a wonderful illusion. Others stopped drinking, fearing someone had spiked the punch.

Just as Bong Guy had predicted, the Rabbit Hole was clear in no time. Alice also satisfied a particular bloodlust by vaporizing the purple-people-snatcher who'd tried to abduct Bunni.

Alice rushed to Bunni and held her tightly. She wrapped her arms around them.

"All right, all right, I like you, too," she said. "I've no idea how you frightened away that loser with only a lawn ornament, but thanks."

Alice pulled away and touched her cheek. "I need to kiss you now, okay?"

Bunni smiled. "Sure." She pressed her lips against theirs.

Remarkably, Gryfünn hadn't stop playing throughout the alien extermination. Alice inwardly cringed at how their first kiss with Bunni would forever be immortalized in one of these inane songs. *Oh well*, they thought with a shrug, and kept kissing her.

"You want me to explain why all of this happened in the first place?" asked the app through the bud still lodged in Alice's ear. "You see, this race had been studying Earth for decades. They felt The Garden would be the perfect neighbourhood to blend in while they gained further intelligence to help plan the coup of this planet. We of the resistance decided—"

Alice pulled away again. "Maybe tell me more…later." They tucked their earbud into their pocket and offered their hands to Bunni. She took them and pressed her body against theirs. The couple caressed and kissed without any worries of purple poker-playing aliens, as they slow-danced to Gryfünn's syrupy ballad, *Don't Wake Me Up If This Is a Dream.*

REFLECTIONS OF ALICE

CHRISTINE DAIGLE

The Duchess holds her breath, waiting for Richard to answer the phone.

...four rings...five...

How long since they've talked? Two months? Three? Not that it matters. They'll continue right where they left off. They've always been like that.

...six rings...seven...

When she's about to asphyxiate, he finally picks up. She heaves out his name. "Richard!"

"Celia?" His voice echoes over background noise; chairs slide across hard floors, glasses clink. And there's another sound among the commotion. The laughter of a young woman.

"Sorry about the racket," Richard says. "Setting up for tonight's gala."

Even with the distortion, his voice is so warm she wants to cry. He must have seen videos of her vomiting. Everyone has since the clip went viral. But it doesn't matter. She and Richard share an unbreakable bond. He's that little black dress you can count on. The one that always flatters you (not like Jean-Archer — another name on her list of fleeting love affairs). As her business partner in the fashion world — and the only person she's ever truly counted on — the Duchess expects Richard to look after her interests.

"The signal's terrible, but I'd really love to talk to you. Will you come?" he asks.

Of course she will. It's the only place she wants to go. Running to Richard. Like always.

As she meticulously dresses, she almost feels better. With spirits slightly lifted, she glides into the limo and sinks into buttery seats. For a moment, a translucent ghost haunts the window, city lights adding platinum sparkles to her hair. The phantom image submerges her in the depths of its ichor.

◎ ◎ ◎

Nineteen years old, she wears a chiton-style dress on her date with Richard. The resulting photos of her with the scion propel her into the spotlight. Dubbed the Duchess by the media, she's suddenly an object of scrutiny. Their relationship intensifies – fame, fortune, a thriving business…then marriage.

On the night of their wedding, she shares a memory…

When she was fifteen, a friend signed her up for an art class. It was supposed to be fun. On her canvas, she attempted to paint a flower-filled vase. While her friend showed promise, the Duchess got the proportions all wrong. Frustrated, she gave up. The open window let in a city breeze, rust and sausage, and air currents tickled the white roses and foxgloves. She noticed where the light was harsh, the petals looked severe. Where the light diffused, the bouquet looked beautiful. Anything can look beautiful in the right light.

The instructor approached. His fingertips brushed hers. *Like this.* Confident, masterful sweeps: his lines were gorgeous.

Class after class she tried. He stayed close, leaned over, pressed his chest against her back. *I can't do it,* she said. He showed her again. The brush began to flow. When he took his hand away, she made clumsy marks. He offered comfort. *Maybe you won't make beautiful paintings, but you are beautiful. Flawless. Surely that's enough.*

Once she realized she'd never be an artist, it took little to convince her to model. *You have to be my masterpiece. Sit for me.*

In his private studio, a darkened bedroom in his apartment, no bigger than a closet, he told her to hold still as he went about his work. *It will take many months to complete. We must go slowly, meticulously. I have a perfectionist streak.*

Unopened tubes of paint lined the easel's ledge, waiting to serve their purpose. In that room, where a satin robe hung on the back of the door, she didn't like his strokes, different than those from class: stretching, reaching. She had a lingering sense to bolt. The way a wrong smell hovers and warns you off. The way she was back to smelling city rust and sausage.

As the portrait took shape, she studied the light, shifted this way and that, finding the perfect position to catch the lamp's glow. Like the flowers in his studio, certain angles made her look flawless. That feeling, the euphoria of immortal beauty, lodged deep.

And then the tubes of paint knocked to the floor, red and ochre, honey and grey, *stroke, stroke.* Eventually, he said it was a mistake.

I've done everything you asked for nothing? she shouted over ripping seams, the satin robe stretched between them. *I can't carry on,* he said. *Go home!* So, she let it go, knowing she wouldn't get what she wanted. She let it all go; the canvas, the masterpiece, the immortality. All but the words he shouted as she left. *Can life imitate art?*

She tells Richard maybe it meant she was too beautiful to paint. That the painting instructor hoped she'd stay untouched by the ephemeral. It was all very profound.

◉ ◉ ◉

Now, the limo pulls up to the hotel. When the driver opens the door, the reflection distorts, and the looking glass evaporates. The Duchess steps out; well-toned legs between slits of a rippling dress. She moves through the faux marble lobby, then down the hall, until she emerges between the ballroom's post-modern columns. Busy floral carpet matches cheap crown-moulding. The stage curtains are heavy velvet.

In the center of the room, Richard's encircled by charity benefactors from their favourite charity, the Jonas Institute. Research pioneers, exploring the foundations of life, cutting-edge cures in neuroscience, genetics, and immunology, the non-profit helps find new treatments for cancer, Alzheimer's, childhood diabetes, and ridding animal organs of harmful viruses, practically eliminating the need for organ donors. Nothing looks better than supporting life-saving science. Richard's new fascination, a recent branch of the Jonas Institute, makes bionic assistive technology and robotic prostheses.

As she enters, the buzz of conversation quiets. She's warm from her brisk walk; skin luminescent with moisture, figure slim, smile bright. She takes another step. Richard breaks into a grin. And then, the Duchess is enveloped with applause and adoration. She savours it. Why not? She's earned it.

It's not long before a socialite she knows, Hugh Mayer, takes her arm. "You're here!" His tone encourages. "Have some Champagne."

"I don't see any servers."

"Well, I'm sure they'll be along shortly. I hope they haven't run out." Hugh glances at his watch. "I'm glad you're not hiding," he adds. "So much talk. Best to face it head on."

Then she's pulled away by someone else, then someone else, and they discuss wealth, privilege, giving back.

Eventually, she spots a blonde at the bar. One she hasn't seen before. And maybe Richard's youngest yet. The Duchess can pass for thirty. A great thirty. But it's no match for youth; for a blushed nineteen-year-old face.

They're always young, blonde, stunning, well mannered. They only speak when spoken to. So, the Duchess doesn't speak to them. She has more important people to impress. Other donors come up and squeeze her, and talk, talk.

A spokeswoman from the Jonas Institute takes the stage, steps up to the microphone. The Duchess loses sight of the blonde as everyone shuffles for a better view. The spokeswoman is saying, "...the innovations you're about to see wouldn't be possible without the generous contributions of our donors. A special thanks to our top supporter, the wonderful Richard, for hosting..."

Everyone applauds, and Richard gives a dignified nod, practiced humble acceptance of others' admiration.

"To express their deep gratitude," the spokeswoman calls over the clapping, "please welcome those whose lives have changed because of your benevolence."

The parade starts. The cured limp and roll across the stage on motor-powered arms and legs, exoskeletons with clunky Velcro straps; a grotesque display of crude anatomy. The miracles wear broad grins, some lopsided. She maintains a serene smile, but her eyes feel too wide, and she can't do anything about it, can't look away.

And then, Richard and the chief engineer, Jack, are next to her.

"What wonderful work," the Duchess says.

"Maybe they could model in our shows," Richard says. "A new definition of beauty. Cutting edge. Never done before."

"Splendid idea." She uses a cadence of genuine interest. Then, as Jack turns to receive congratulations, she leans in close to Richard and whispers, "Don't be gross."

He laughs.

"Can you imagine what the media would say? They'd think we're mad."

"Same old Celia. As you get older, your perceptions change."

"But standards of beauty don't."

"I know it's hard to grow old." Sympathy seeps into his voice. "How are you managing?"

"Better now that I'm here. I needed to escape for a while."

He takes her hand. "Is Jean-Archer on his way out?"

She shrugs. "I don't love him."

"I know." He releases her, then gives a raw smile.

She wonders if he pictures her as she was when they first met, whether he superimposes her teenage self over what his eyes see. Smitten. The real thing. He sees her in the best possible light.

"I still love you," he says. "Always have. Always will."

"I love you, too."

"It doesn't matter though, does it?"

And then he's off, slipping through the crowd. The Duchess accepts Champagne from a server and takes a long drink. Engaged in pleasantries and small talk, she feels worn out. As the sparkling beverage imparts warmth, her attention drifts into the fluted glass. Light curves and she tumbles into its distortions.

The Duchess wants to be remembered by the iconic, black and white photograph that appears in the media nearly every time she's mentioned: she's leaning against a balcony's wrought-iron railing overlooking Paris. Tailored jacket. Wingtip Mary Janes. A below-the-knee-dress belted at the waist. The light hits her perfectly.

A man bumps her arm, shifting her attention from the Champagne flute. She quickly smooths her irritation away. The last thing she needs is more bad press. The fashion industry has many expectations. Stay fit. Don't look your age. Her thoughts turn to the vomit video. People are fascinated by images that produce a visceral reaction. Vomit. Sneezing. Rage. Visions of ugliness are the ones that inhabit memory. She drains the glass, but refuses to look into its depths. The Champagne tickles her insides until she nearly laughs at her foolishness. Public drunkenness is a terrible idea. Maybe she's starting a new trend, adding more items to her list of latest concepts. Before she knows it, she's at the bar. She'd only meant to find a seat until the tipsy feeling passes. But here's the blonde right beside her. Hauntingly beautiful, the girl looks the way the Duchess would have if her features were perfectly symmetrical; a lovelier version of her.

"I recognize you." The girl's voice is timid.

"Undoubtedly. And who might you be?"

"Alice," the girl says politely, but her stare says she's not fooled by the Duchess' feigned ignorance. Hands folded in her lap, she lowers her eyes. "Although Richard says I'm still young and figuring out who I am."

"And who do you want to be?" the Duchess asks with practiced interest.

"I hardly know," Alice says.

Briefly, there are muted sounds of a band warming up. The prosthesis recipients have changed into formal wear. Floor-length gowns. Tuxedos. They crowd the dance floor. She tracks their movements, noting the fake limbs, the real. No amount of fabric can cover that up.

"Ahem." Alice clears her throat.

The Duchess doesn't know why she's still sitting here. More stable now, she could get up, move on. But conversing with this girl makes her feel like she's mentoring herself. Or maybe it's the reverse. Maybe Alice reminds her what it's like to be a lost girl finding her place in the world.

Alice says, "By the way, don't eat the oysters, they're spoiled …oh, how silly of me. I'm very sorry I mentioned shellfish. I'm sure you wouldn't have touched them, anyway."

"Do you think sitting next to each other makes us friends?"

The girl blinks innocently. "I didn't mean to overstep. You're so well known to me that I feel I've made your acquaintance before."

And then Richard appears. "Let's get some coffee." He takes her arm and helps her up. He doesn't say a word to the girl and, as they leave, she doesn't follow. The girl must have read about their relationship, seen their passionate wedding day photographs. She wonders how the girl sees her, whether it's much the same way Richard does; an ageless face from a magazine. How can the girl compete?

Richard seats her at a quiet table, and puts coffee in front of her. "I'm glad you came."

"You don't have to placate me." The Duchess wears a wisp of a smile because she's used to holding her face that way. Everyone else is far enough away, she's not afraid to speak candidly. No one pays them much attention, except Alice. She watches from across the room.

"Really, I am. I've wanted to see you."

"Don't start down that path again."

"Let's talk later. When I'm done wrapping things up."

It's almost eleven o'clock. It will be hours until the last guest stumbles out.

"Shall I sit here quietly until then?"

"You'll keep occupied."

"I usually do." The Duchess considers taking his hand. Instead, she takes a small sip of coffee.

Hugh Mayer plops down next to her. "I hope you don't mind, darling, I need to rest my feet."

The Duchess smiles her prettiest smile. "Looks like I'm planning to stay awhile. Always a pleasure to have your company. Perhaps we can discuss recent dining experiences. The hottest chefs. The trendiest restaurants."

Hugh leans forward. "That might keep me awake."

"Maybe we should try the oysters. I mean, what could go wrong?"

"I'd rather hear what's going on with you and Richard." There's a wild glint in his eye; anticipating insider information.

The Duchess looks for Richard's reaction, but he's gone. And someone else has joined them. Alice. Of course. She sits across from them. Quietly. Politely.

"Nothing's going on. Richard and I are old news."

Hugh pats her hand with rounded fingers. "Then what's keeping you apart?"

Another glass of Champagne finds its way to her. She says, "The same thing that's kept a thousand other couples apart. Boy meets girl. They fall in love. Girl gets pregnant, delivers early, the baby dies." Hugh's attention wanes, but what can she do? The juicy bits are something she can't tell. Something only she and Richard know. "We drifted away until there was too much distance to cross."

Hugh rubs tired eyes. "How sad."

Alice says, "I don't think you've said it right, I'm afraid. Not quite right at all."

◎ ◎ ◎

It's hours later when Richard escorts the last guest out. He finds her in the mirrored lounge off the lobby waiting in a faux-leather chair. He sits on the other side of the small table.

"We need to talk," the Duchess says.

"What's wrong?" He reaches for her hand, but she pulls away.

"I need to know. How much have you told about the reason we split?"

"I—" He rubs his ring finger; a guilty habit. "I needed to talk to someone."

Cold panic floods her. "You know what trouble this could bring me," she says.

Alice's face floats above Richard's shoulder, smirking. There's a tickle at the back of the Duchess' throat. A dry cough.

"I was very careful. You know I'll always protect you."

Her heart beats too fast. She looks around, but no one is watching. Except that disembodied girl.

"I needed to let go of some guilt," Richard says. "Doesn't it crush you?"

"I don't know what you're talking about."

"I didn't share, you know, everything."

"How could you do this to me?"

"Because not everything is about you!"

A sob slips up her throat that she forces down.

"Look. I didn't mean to get cross with you."

"There's something I've been thinking about."

Dark circles sag beneath Richard's eyes. He covers a yawn. "What?"

"Do you remember that night after the gala? The one when we did all those shrooms?"

"To be honest, not really."

"In the room with the brass door. And there were all those insects."

"You're not making any sense."

"The shrooms! The bugs! Remember?"

"Shhh. So, I don't remember a party. Why are you so upset?"

"Because I think that's the night I conceived!"

Richard is quiet for a long time, then says, "It doesn't make any difference."

The sob expands into her mouth until it's all she can do to keep it inside. She can't swallow.

"Why don't you go home? You don't look well."

"Good idea," she manages.

"I'll send someone over to check on you, soon. Okay?" As he rises, his fingertips brush hers.

"What do you mean, someone?" she croaks, but already he's walking away.

Alice's face fades until only her wicked smile's reflected in the warped mirror that sucks the Duchess in.

◎ ◎ ◎

On the night that changes everything, their life couldn't be any better. The public adores her designs. And they praise her good works, her charity. Every event she and Richard host is a huge success. She doesn't remember much about the party, except they end up in their hotel room, the one with the brass door. They get very high on shrooms. They're enthralled with each other, caught up in the rapture of each other's body. She kisses his hair, his skin. He presses his mouth against hers and hoists her up against the balcony door. Sweat suctions her to the glass. She shifts to let him slide inside of her, feels him writhe and twist. She wonders what it's like for him to be cocooned in her wet warmth. At some point he shudders, and then she shudders, and then she feels them on her skin. She feels them *under* her skin. She says, "Something is wriggling. Oh God, they're really squirming. My skin is rippling. They're everywhere. Get them off." So, Richard brushes her. "No, really get them off! I want you to get them off. Please, get them off!" Suddenly she and Richard are staring at each other. And the Duchess is crying, asking him to do something he can't, because he can't see the bugs. And she starts scratching. It's a horrible trip. Everything had been going so beautifully. She scratches until her skin is raw, but the bugs keep crawling. Richard opens a window. Gets some water. Nothing helps. She claws at her skin. Blood runs down her arms. He grabs her hands, holds them at her sides, but he can't contain her very long. Finally, he gives her sleeping pills. When they wake up, they don't talk about any of it. Looking back on it now, the Duchess is sure she felt something wriggling inside of her, too. Ugly and wrinkled.

◉ ◉ ◉

"Too much pepper in the soup?" Jean-Archer shouts. "Not this rant again!"

"I'm still pissed!" The Duchess started the fight as soon as she got home. Anger is good. If she's raging, busy throwing things, smashing pepper shakers and teacups, she can't think about Richard's betrayal; how he told some young blonde their secret.

"It's not my fault you're too self-absorbed to read a menu. It's my best dish! I told you I was making it."

"No, you didn't!"

"Tabernac! You don't hear anything that makes the slightest bit of difficulty for you."

"*I* don't hear anything? You're the selfish bastard that poisoned me at *my* gala, you idiotic, filthy, no good..." the Duchess keeps yelling at him until he stops yelling back.

He turns and walks out the front door. She sends a Wedgwood dinner plate flying after him. As he steps off the porch, the spinning china misses him, but...it grazes Alice's hair as she walks up the stone pathway. With a great crash, the plate shatters against one of the trees behind her. As she slips inside, the girl seems unconcerned about soaring crockery.

"I hope you don't mind my coming in without asking," the girl says. "Oh my. There's so much pepper in the air, I think I might—" The girl sneezes.

"Why are you here at all?" The Duchess doesn't feel bad about her rudeness. At home, she can say whatever she wants and it doesn't matter. The public will always love her. "Richard sent you to check on me, didn't he? I wish you hadn't bothered. If everybody minded their own business the world would go around a good deal faster."

"Which is not to your advantage," Alice says. "Just think how much quicker you'd age."

Oh, but the girl has a knowing smile. The Duchess narrows her eyes. "Since he's already told you, I suppose my business is your business now, isn't it?"

The Duchess walks slowly, deliberately, to the last room at the end of the hallway. From her pocket she withdraws a small golden key and unlocks the door. She thinks the girl hasn't followed, but then hears soft footsteps on the hardwood, hardly there at all.

In the center of the room, a dim light glows inside a fluid-filled tank where a pink form floats, long catheters supplying it with blood. Cramped and huddled, the figure fills the whole space, the container forcing it to tuck into a ball.

"Well, there it is," the Duchess says. "The big secret. Jonas Industries is the science behind why I look so young." The next words catch in her throat, but she forces them out. "I had them put my cells into a *pig* fetus and sustained it in that artificial womb. An unending supply of stem cells ready for injection."

"How curious," Alice says. "Do you ever wonder what you're doing? Or whether you should?"

"I'm always a top five philanthropist, you know. It's hard to sell fashion and throw charity galas with the face of a shrivelled fig. The greatest public good is produced by the greatest private selfishness. I only wish this happened long before I turned thirty. Then I could have kept your nineteen-year-old face forever."

Alice steps up to the artificial womb and peers inside. Then she turns and looks at the Duchess and the Duchess looks at Alice. The girl reaches into the tank and scoops the huddled form into her arms.

"Why," Alice says, "it's not a pig at all." She holds up the wet pink thing, the artificial womb's glow casting warped shadows upon it. Alice, eyes wide, whispers, "It's a baby." The Duchess puts a hand to the glass, hoping it will steady her. She's tugged inward by the force.

◎ ◎ ◎

Pain. Childbirth is prolonged pain that's supposed to end. Not for the Duchess. When she made the final push, and the baby wriggled free, the pain grew. Its body was segmented rolls of skin; its head a truncated cone with sightless eyes. She thought she was prepared for the birth, knew what was coming. But, as she looked at the scrunched-up face of her…her newborn son, nothing could fix this. An expert from Jonas Industries took the quiet baby and put him in the artificial womb. Through the glass, the infant looked like a deflated balloon, a caterpillar, a pig, a fig; its proportions kept distorting.

◎ ◎ ◎

It's early morning when Jean-Archer returns. He finds the Duchess outside, lying in the rose garden. She's covered in dirt, her hands blistered from all her digging with the garden spade. He calls to her. No response. She stares deep into the woods behind the house. He calls an ambulance, then notices a room at the end of the hall with the door wide open. It's always been locked before.

◎ ◎ ◎

By the time the paramedics arrive, Richard is there, too. Jean-Archer reports nothing but a disoriented Duchess and an empty tank. Richard explains the delicate situation, relies on the paramedics' ethics not to disclose how their son was born missing parts of the brain needed for self-awareness. That the tánk was a remnant, something the Duchess couldn't let go. But rumours have a way of starting. They begin with how the Duchess rambled over and over to the paramedics, about the first time she saw the baby. That after, she couldn't look at Richard the same way again, couldn't look at *them* the same, couldn't accept she'd birthed something so hideous: that the designer who made her created something so revolting and used the same fabric. She'd at least found a way to put something so awful to good use, hadn't she? Wasn't her work worth a few occasional stem cells from a creature that didn't know the difference between life and death? Repurposing a failed design. Using remnants to revive an already beautiful piece, keeping ephemeral, timeless. But the recounting of her words is dismissed as tabloid gossip. The Jonas Institute declines to comment. No solid evidence is ever dug up.

◉ ◉ ◉

"Why did you tell her?" the Duchess asks Richard much later.

"Who?" Richard says.

"The girl. Alice."

Richard says he has no idea who that is.

"The blonde with you at the Jonas Institute gala."

"There was no one with me. I went alone."

"Alice! The blonde. Looks like a younger me, like every blonde you've dated since our divorce."

"I haven't dated anyone since our divorce." His voice is so quiet.

"The blonde, the blonde," she says until her voice goes quiet, too. "The one you told about the baby. The one you sent to check on me."

He insists he sent no one. And the person he told about their split was his therapist, bound by confidentiality, that he hadn't revealed anything damaging. He suggests that, perhaps, the Duchess should see his therapist, too. But, he doesn't push it. He can't force her to do anything she doesn't want to do. He never could act against her wishes. Not in that vulnerable moment long ago when she asked him something on the promise he wouldn't tell.

Now, she asks for sleeping pills. He gets them.

◉ ◉ ◉

As the years go by, the Duchess continues her charity support, but leaves the house less and less. Without stem cell injections, the wrinkles start; tiny fissures that later crack wide open. She can't bear to show an aging face to the public. They wouldn't look at her the same. When she dies, she hopes they print the Paris photograph, not the one with her face contorted from heaving and rage. The one that shows her in the right light.

TWIN

Danica Lorer

There was only ever one
suffering from vanishing twin syndrome.
The dum, dum, dum
an extra heartbeat remembered, one heatbeat
a heartbleat
weakly throbbing in the womb
that only had space
for one.

Mother named him
held him
kissed him
once on each cheek
once on the nose
never suspected
more than one
perfect son.

The dee, dee, dee
a first child song
mimicking the little black-capped chirpers.
Flitting alone
only wanting to share

sunsets and musings
scraped elbows
and stories of the sea.

He asked his mother
where his brother was
the one like himself
begged her for another.
"There will only ever be one."
She sighed
hands folded
over an empty belly.

Hide-and-seek
was only ever hide
no one to seek
when he found the place
dark and musty
under the porch
where the caterpillar spun
around and around.
No one to find
no matter
how hard he looked.

Alone, lonely
wishing for the (br)other
he remembered
from the time before

his time walking
breathing outside air
tasting wild strawberries.

He left his mother
in a flooding puddle of her own sea-salt tears
an ocean amniotic.
Kissed her twice on each cheek
packed double what he needed.
He could set the extra clothing on the ground
use it as a mirror.

In a stranger land
he found his own way.
He spoke in riddle rhymes
one voice while standing on his two flat feet
one voice rose while he balanced on his head.
It was a trick of the golden light
bouncing between the trees
casting shadows
over the water.
He believed
everyone believed
there were two.
Dee-dum, dee-dum, dee-Dum.

A whisper
to his inner ear.
The walking, breathing one was losing
the memory of his own words

and poetry.
Tried to hum, to recite
to remember the lyrics
his mother mouthed at his cribside.
The one absorbed by
early loss
once unviable was gaining
a power
to manipulate the eyes
see clearer
lift a leg
without yet owning a body.

Facial features melted away
caught something alien beneath
a way of holding the corners of the mouth
a tic
a twirl
dancing so fast
one could never tell
if it was one, or two
or four, or sixteen.
Who would lead?
Who would follow?
Who was growing strong?

When there was no one else in the forest
would anyone hear the single twin fall?
Clapping one hand?

Dee, dee, dee
he felt his own
feet slipping
out from under
held on to walls to hold his ground.
His chest cavity
too full
to catch his breath
he held it
turning blue.
His own voice
raised
a pitch
pitched forward
until he felt
almost
consumed
by something
he no longer
longed to see
or hear.
Something scratching in his
throat.

His ears
a drumskin
vibrating
too loud.

He tried to silence
the growl
the murmur
the buzz of something budding
stretching, clawing
underneath the muscles.
He tried to give up looking
for the other
dropped the desire
to be doubled.
Changed his signature.
Tweedle Dee.

He approached
an expert,
a magician of the mind
who measured success in inches
a mad man
whose obsession
lied and truthed
on the size of a brain case.

The physician's
sleight of hand
shone a light down his throat
stuck a tube in his ear
yelled
to see, to hear
if anyone lurked
inside.

Medication to soothe
the cake to grow bigger
the drops to grow small.
The illusion was easier with smoke
and a broken mirror
shards like butter knives
left even more reflections
more faces
more facets.
Knives to cut into skin
surgery to separate.
One trying to cut a part, apart, a part
to carve out a place to fit the other.

He'd spent his life
searching for the other face
seeing sneers and grins
eyes, and jawlines
in tree bark, clouds,
and the patterns on the floor.

He pulled at his ears
tried to shake
the other out
couldn't run, or roll, or wobble
away.

He walked, ran, toward
the glow
of a sterile room

bright lights
the voice
growing louder.

Knives excised,
pulled tissues apart
cells rearranged
electric shock therapy
division
and multiplication
adding and subtracting
a miracle of life
through nuclear transfer.

The clone grew
swallowed up all the memories
as the first flesh home
became a shell.

The second body
matured at an alarming rate
the gel medium allowed the space.
There was no softness
planted by a mother's embrace
no scars formed by the sticks and stones
of playground bullies.
This one didn't learn the rules
about putting fingers into
light sockets
about sticking everything into its mouth

about pushing knives
into the bellies of others.

It woke speaking full sentences
as the rasp of dee, dee, dee
escaped the first one's mouth
lying under a white sheet
eyes open
not seeing
the brother whose face
he had searched for every day.

The second
within minutes
spoke cruel verse
peaking in a heated stanza
a curse
to the one
who had grown beyond an embryo
so long ago.
The earlier frame
soft and round
easily molded
fading.

The replica used its
mass to lift and run
building blocks
for abs, thighs
and biceps.

The dum, dum, dum
rose to a drum, drum, drum
footfalls not mere steps
but leaps
and no one thought there
was more than one
standing in front of them.

Hands
had split
the sequel from the innocent one
whose only fight had been with sorrow
missing part of himself.

The copy took more
than its fair share
didn't wish
for a (br)other.

All was quiet
as they readied
to read the last blink
to close the seeking eyes
to pull the covering up
and over.

Dee, dee, dee
rattled breath
in, in, in
and
out, in one long puff.

There was only ever one
at a time
thriving
an independent beast.
The DUM, DUM, DUM
a heartbeat, a drumbeat, a heartbreak
forged without the warmth of a womb.
The world had only space
for one.

TRUE NATURE

SARA C. WALKER

I left the crowded tea shop for the buzz of pedestrians and traffic on Queen Street. A rush of heat seeped through the paper cup, warming my hands through my gloves. Exhaustion permeated my bones. I took a sip of tea and winced at the teeth-cringing taste, wishing I had grabbed a cup of Wonderland's much superior stuff before making the jump home. I fondly recalled a particular English breakfast with a clean bouquet and just a hint of raspberry in the finish.

As a White Rabbit Enterprises messenger, my duty was to deliver communications across the oceans from one court to another. During the delicate peace negotiations the job came with danger, and after a long day, the tea kept me alert.

Old City Hall's clock tower bells sang the hour. I glanced over at the ornate yellow brick building.

Crap. I was late.

"Is that you, Alice?"

The deep raspy voice came from a man-sized lump of worn cloth crouched on the sidewalk, huddling against a lamppost. He – or she – seemed old, a dark face hidden by the hood of his – or her – coat. I thought I glimpsed a pair of oversized sunglasses, an odd choice given the evening hour.

Toronto sheltered plenty of homeless. I turned away and returned my attention to my horrible tea. Guilt warmed me. If Rachel were here, she'd want to buy him a hot beverage and a sandwich. I would remind her she couldn't save the world. And she'd reply that was no reason not to try. It was her nature to help the helpless.

"It's you, isn't it?" he-she-they insisted. "I'd know you anywhere. You smell like a beamish flower – an English rose—"

My communicator chirped. Relieved, I moved out of the vagabond's earshot and hit the respond button on my wrist. My supervisor's face filled the flexscreen. "Yes?"

"Lacie, have you booked your flight to London yet?" Mary Anne said in a rush.

"I have a flight in the morning. I was just on my way home—"

"There's been a change. Stand by. Details will be sent to your communicator shortly." The screen went dark.

I frowned. The Home Office kept tabs on us through the communicators whether we were in the real world or through the looking glass. I was supposed to spend a brief night with Rachel before making the trans-Atlantic flight to jump to Red Court Wonderland and give the White King's plea for assistance to the Red Queen.

Wonderland's war between Asia's Black Court and North America's White Court necessitated that messages be received and delivered in person to the royals to avoid chances of interception.

If only Wonderland had reliable trans-oceanic flights, I could save so much time. On the other hand, I might also be out of a job.

I tapped the flexscreen to ring home. My heart skipped a beat as Rachel's face brightened the screen, but the thrill disappeared a moment later when I noticed her gloomy expression.

"You're going again, aren't you?"

"Rach, I—" Inside my pocket, the ring I'd picked up in White Court Wonderland pressed uncomfortably. The tight suit didn't allow for anything extra. A queen-cut diamond – considered even better than a princess-cut for its larger crown on a grander pavilion – set in sparkling platinum, could not be rivalled this side of the looking glass.

The pressure of the ring hadn't bothered me before this moment.

"It's my job," I said softly.

Damn the job. I pictured Rachel all cozy in our Toronto apartment. I should have gone straight home. I would have been almost there if I hadn't stopped for tea.

"I know," she grumbled. "I just miss you. And we had plans—"

Rachel had nabbed tickets to *The Taming of the Shrew*. I was going to ask her in the dark before the final act. "Keep them."

"Lacie—"

"I mean it. You should go tonight. We can go together another time."

"No," she said firmly. Her eyes shone, knowing I'd rather stay home. "We'll go when you get back."

I relented. It made Rachel feel better if we had date night plans on my return.

"Of course." I smiled. I'd always been a sucker for those pretty eyes.

"Don't forget I love you."

"That is the one thing I shall never, never forget."

"You're not going to say it, are you?" To anyone else her tone would seem light and teasing, but I heard the disappointment.

"You're a *messenger*, Lacie."

My cheeks burned despite the brisk wind. I tried to explain. "Rach, I'm standing in the middle of the street. There are people all around—"

She waved her hand with a half-hearted laugh. "It's okay. I love you enough for the both of us."

By the time we ended the conversation – we never, ever said "goodbye" – she smiled between issuing her ritual cautions and warnings. Her heart seemed lighter, though mine wasn't.

My stomach knotted. Words might be my trade, but that didn't make speaking my feelings easier.

"Blast," I exhaled.

"Excuse me, Alice?" The homeless man had skittered his way up the sidewalk to the lamppost next to me.

"Stop following me," I snapped. "And my name's not Alice."

He shrank away and the streetlight glinted in the shadow of his hood, reminding me of his dark glasses. Did he wear them because he was blind?

"White Rabbit's girls are *all* named Alice," he said. "That is, if you're not named Mary Ann."

The tea went cold in my belly. How did he know that? I hadn't uttered my supervisor's name.

"Stop following me."

Couriers of White Rabbit Enterprises were untouchable by law since there were so few genetically capable of jumping through a looking glass, but there were still those vicious enough to try. The regulation vorpal blade in my left boot bolstered me.

"In the war between Black and White, Red will come out all over," he droned.

"Why don't you get out of the cold? It's clearly affected your brain."

"I can whiffle the Kevlar woven into your jumpsuit. You're one of the White Rabbit's girls, aren't you?" He sounded pleased. "A pawn hoping to be promoted to Queen."

This pest needled me, but I was more upset because it was working.

"What do you want?"

"Only what anyone stuck on the street is without." He skittered away, pressing his back against the lamppost. His face retreated into the hood's depths. Something bugged me about the way he moved.

"Home? You want to go home?"

"It's where the heart is. Isn't it, Alice?"

His statement lanced my chest. Right at this moment I wanted nothing more than to be home with Rachel. Did he overhear that conversation, too? Or was it just a lucky guess?

I wanted to slam him for being up in my personal business, but stopped myself. Rachel wouldn't approve.

The wind blew strong, funnelled between the buildings. He hugged his knees to his chest, rags flapping and snapping. In that moment he seemed vulnerable. Still creepy. But he was clearly cold. Helpless.

"Maybe you should at least move to an alley so you're out of the wind."

As much as I wanted him to go away, Rachel was right. She was always right.

The ring in my hip pocket dug a little deeper. It would stay there tonight. I supposed that was for the best. The timing was off, anyhow. November was too bleak for this. Best to wait for an occasion. Winter solstice, maybe. Or perhaps closer to spring…

"How about I buy you a cup of tea?" I suggested.

"I've tasted the tea here. I'd just as soon kiss a jabber-wock."

I bit back my urge to cut and run, and instead tried to sweeten the deal.

"A sandwich?"

"With honey?"

"Sure."

"Oh, frabjous day!"

"Good. Let's go."

"In there? They'll never let me in."

"They will if I say so." There were perks to the place being owned by White Rabbit Enterprises. The tea shop was always open, always busy, and the large bathroom mirror opened directly to the White Court.

With another gust of bitter wind, he gathered his feet under him and rose, stretching out long legs and torso until he towered over me.

Inside, people went about their evening, chatting with cups in hand, giving the vagabond wary glances as we made our way toward the back.

"Here." I grabbed a handful of rags and pulled him to a chair at a vacant table. "Stay."

I went to the counter and placed my order, and a few minutes later, carried a sandwich and tea service back to the table. I poured out two cups and placed them on the checkerboard tabletop.

"How did you get here?" I asked, setting the honey-smeared bread in front of him.

He shrugged. "Followed a messenger."

Great. We weren't supposed to allow anyone to follow us through the temporary rift when we touched a looking glass. I would have guessed he followed Alice, but we hadn't had a messenger by that name since before I started. He couldn't have been here that long, could he?

Unease wrapped my bones. I tried to shake it off, remembering he was helpless and probably blind. But the unease stuck.

"So, why don't you tell me what's really keeping you from returning home?"

He sat with his head bent, hood falling forward, shoulders slouched. "Have you never been away, never worried things will be maxome burbled when you get back?"

Only every damned mission.

I pulled in a deep breath, trying to keep a lid on my patience. "Yes, things change when you're away, but they also stay the same."

"Such as?"

"Well, people might look different, but the love is the same." How many times had I come home to find Rachel with her hair another colour or cut in another style. A new shade of eye shadow. A change of wardrobe. A new hobby. A new job. But through it all, the same Rachel. The same scent of her hair. The same soft silky skin. Her loving eyes on me. Her laughter.

"Not always," he said gloomily. He'd made no move to eat or drink, simply held his hands in his lap.

"Tell me why you can't go home," I said softly.

"I ran away."

"You ran away? From Wonderland? But why?"

"Because of the wig."

"The wig?"

"The wig is gone," he mourned.

"So, if I get you another wig, you'll return?"

"It won't be the same."

"But if I could—"

"And after all I did for the White Queen. I was the inspiration for her waistline, her silhouette, you know."

"You lost the Queen's wig?"

"The wig was mine. It was stolen."

"By who?"

"The Queen's men. She really has too much power, you see."

I had no doubt about that, but I couldn't understand her reason for taking this poor man's wig, nor why that should cause him to run away. "I'm confused."

"Words are not my gift, not like they are for you, Alice."

I had a feeling Rachel would beg to differ. My communicator suddenly felt like a boa constrictor tightening around my wrist. The truth was I had so many words to say to her that I didn't know where to begin.

The man cleared his throat. "Why do you hesitate to profess your love?"

I cut my gaze to him and glared.

"It's just I couldn't help overhearing earlier—"

"Mind your own business." I flushed hot and angry.

"My apologies." He sagged, deflating from his sudden burst.

Rachel would scold me if she were here. "Drink your tea."

He leaned forward, peering into the cup. "Sugar?" he asked hopefully. He placed his hands on the table. It would take hours to unknot the rags just so he could grip a spoon.

I picked up the sugar dispenser.

"Any brown sugar?"

I clamped down my frustration, opened two packets of brown sugar, and stirred them in.

"More," he said. I added another, and he asked for two more before finally pronouncing the beverage passable.

"I can see you once were strong and mighty. What happened?" I asked. "What made you forget your true nature?"

He shrugged. "It was the Queen. One day I was her favourite – out of all my brothers and sisters – and the next, we were all sent away."

"You thought you would be staying?"

He nodded. "I found this wig, and it changed me. I felt so slithy, so sure she wouldn't reject me again. For a while we were happy… Then she had more children. She took my wig and cast me out again."

"I'm sorry."

"Being cast out once was frumious, but twice? How could I show my face there ever again?"

"So you came here." Poor thing must have felt humiliated. "I completely understand. You need to forget her. Anyone who would cast you out twice is not worth another minute of your thoughts."

"Really?" He sounded incredulous.

"You need to find someone who loves you just as you are – no wig required. Someone who isn't going to replace you with children. Someone who – who is there when you get home from a long day at work. Someone who makes your favourite foods, rubs your aching shoulders. Someone who makes you laugh, makes you forget the trouble of the world."

He lifted his head. "Sounds like you already have that someone," he said quietly.

The tightness in my stomach eased. "I do."

"Sounds like you might be in love."

Like a tiny butterfly trapped in a large jar, my stomach fluttered and felt hollow at the same time. I wiped sweaty palms on my knees. "You might be right."

"Sounds like you need to tell her."

The hollow feeling spread. I should have been angry at him, I should have said again it was none of his business, but I did neither. I could only focus on what Rachel must be feeling – what I caused her to feel when I declined to say the words she wanted to hear.

"It's not so easy to be true to your nature when it matters, hmmm?"

I glared at his shadowed face. "I don't think running away is a good solution."

My communicator beeped again, not a video message, but text only.

We've received word the White King wishes to amend the message you received. You are to return immediately.

White Rabbit had a policy in place for amendments – rare as they were – the original messenger must also receive the amendment to avoid possible conflict in messages.

There was no choice: I had to return to the White Court.

I turned to the homeless man. "Well, I guess this is your lucky day. I'm returning to Wonderland right now. I can accompany you to the other side; I could even escort you home, if you like. Be there for you when you see the Queen."

He leaned back against the chair. The question weighted his shoulders.

"Will you come with me?" I asked.

"You really think it will be all right?"

"I'm sure it will. Denying your true nature only leads to misery."

"But what if they remember the wig and laugh at me?"

"Then move on to the next person. You deserve to be with someone who loves you for your true self."

Someone like Rachel who withstood my tongue-tied jumble of excuses, just because I'd had my heart broken before.

He nodded. "You're right. I do. I want a love like yours, Alice."

Once bitten, twice shy. It seemed so logical before. Now I saw it for the flimsy excuse it really was.

He followed me to the small washroom. I closed the door.

The gilt-framed mirror filled the wall from countertop to ceiling. I placed my hand on the glass, and it softened like gauze and began to melt away.

"If we're through with denying our true natures, there's something you should know," he said. "I'm not exactly what you think I am."

"Oh?" I'd already had a hunch – after all, he *was* from Wonderland.

Something made me turn away from the silvery pool.

"That is, I'm not a man." His words were sharp, striking the tile walls and floor.

He began to unravel the rags. As the layers came off, he revealed spindly limbs of black, and wide yellow bands across his hourglass abdomen. Large, round multi-lensed eyes shone back at me. A set of jagged pinchers jutted from where a mouth should have been.

"You're – You're a bee?" I couldn't quite wrap my mind around it. Of course, I'd run into the giant insects in Wonderland – who hadn't – but I would never have expected one to survive on this side.

Suddenly being trapped in a tiny room with one seemed like a bad idea. A chill settled down my spine.

"Actually, I'm a wasp," he said. His sabulous voice fizzled out words faster and faster. "There is a difference. This is the waistline that inspires women to draw tighter their corset strings. Bees do not have such elegant lines. Unless you consider bullets elegant."

At the moment, I was seriously considering reaching for the vorpal blade in my boot, as the wasp seemed to be working itself into a frenzy.

Every cell in my body stood at attention, hyper-aware of the sharp stinger protruding from its rear end. A glossy drop of venom shimmered, balanced, waiting on the long blade, surely enough to kill a human – stop the heart, at least.

"That's – That's quite the stinger you have there, sir," I said, stalling for time.

"Ah, yes," it hissed. "There's something else you should know. Only the females of our species can sting."

I swallowed. "But you're not going to sting me, are you? We— We shared a meal. We're friends, aren't we?"

"After that lovely speech about deserving to be happy with someone who loves me for my true self?" She made a sucking sound. I wondered if she considered that laughter. I shuddered.

She turned toward the mirror and said over her shoulder, "I can no longer deny my true nature."

I spun, reaching for my blade, too slow, too late. The wasp struck me with her stinger, then lunged and jumped through the looking glass. The room filled with a burst of bright silvery mist and then settled.

My right hip flashed blindingly hot. I fell against the wall, and slid to the floor as lightning pain travelled down my legs. Had the stinger pierced my jumpsuit? Or did the suit do its job? My hands went to the wound and came away soaked in venom. Did that mean… Did that mean the stinger didn't go in all the way?

I fumbled for the ring in my hip pocket. It was bent now, having taken the brunt of the stinger's blow. Saved by my love. She would be so pleased if she knew.

Rachel.

Damn. The wasp was right. A question needed to be asked...

I glanced at the time. I wasn't too late.

This wasn't the best time or the best place, but I finally had the words.

I pressed a button on my communicator and dialled home.

FULL HOUSE

GEOFF GANDER AND FIONA PLUNKETT

"The *Snark's* done worse," said Risus, her long tail flicking. "She's outrun pirates, dodged asteroids—"

"And without drive coolant we can't go anywhere," said Et'Eruca. It dimmed the engineering console with one upper limb while two others punched buttons to re-route power. "We're stranded on this planet until we can replenish." It stretched to its fullsome height of just over two metres, ten pairs of feet keeping it securely on the floor, and glared at Alis.

Alis, leaning in the doorway of the ship's cramped bridge, calmly met Et'Eruca's glare. "The next time pirates shoot us up and destroy our fire control systems, I'll let the cargo burn." She had made a split-second decision to cut the coolant hose and extinguish the flames. The attack had also knocked out the comms.

Et'Eruca turned to Risus. "I advised you against hiring her, Captain. Humans are as untrustworthy as they are belligerent. The Imperium taught us that."

Risus held a hand up, halting Alis. "Alis was just a child when the war ended, and humans have short memories. She did save the cargo." She grinned toothily.

The Chys resembled Earth's felines in behaviour. It had taken Alis a while to learn that the Chys grin was similar to a human shrug.

"You said there might be something here we could use as a replacement?" Risus asked. Her translucent fur pulsed and shimmered.

Et'Eruca's antennae twitched in annoyance. Like the insects they resembled, P'lar lacked facial muscles, making them difficult to read. "The swamps of Borogove produce gases that could be condensed into a substitute, if my sensors' readings are accurate."

"I hope so," said Alis. "There's little info on this place, or the system. Who named it, anyway?"

Risus grinned again. "As long as we can drop a few claim beacons out here, I don't care what this place is called."

Alis nodded. Weeks spent in close quarters bred familiarity. Risus said little about her life before commanding the *Snark*, but Alis knew that family was why she traded among the Free Alliance fringe worlds. The highly matriarchal Chys society was also very mercantile. Risus would never be free from her mother's control or expectations until she could buy her independence. Alis supposed that was why Risus took her on – she had been able to buy a share in the venture, rather than be an employee. Unhappy to see her gamble her life savings, her parents would have been even unhappier if she spent more time in jail for protesting the ranching conglomerates' treatment of livestock on Bellman's World.

"Where is this gas, Et'Eruca?" asked Risus.

"You lot, always rushing," said Et'Eruca. The P'lar took a long drag from a metal pipe that emitted wisps of faint green mist. It let out a long, contented sigh. "Must be the thin air you all breathe."

Risus moved toward the hatch. "Not all of us have the luxury of living for centuries."

Et'Eruca took another drag, then placed the pipe in a silvery metal box strapped to its chest. "There's a source about two clicks from here."

"Lead the way. We'll suit up," said Risus.

◉ ◯ ◉

The *Snark*'s airlock hissed, then clanked open. A wall of humidity oozed into the chamber and plastered Alis's clothing to her body while sweat beaded her forehead. Borogrove rode the inner edge of the habitable zone of its red dwarf sun. Its slow rotation allowed thick cloud cover formation that protected the surface from the worst radiation while trapping enough heat to create a hothouse.

Et'Eruca led the way down the gangplank onto a field of spongy red moss, inhaling loudly. "It is most satisfying to be able to breathe freely."

"Maybe Borogove hasn't been charted for a reason," said Alis. She checked her respirator filtering the stagnant air. Green lights. All good.

Et'Eruca pointed with two hands to a spot beyond a rise to their left. "The concentration of gases should be over there," it said, as though Alis hadn't spoken. "We should be able to harvest them with the condenser."

Tubular, dark yellow growths topped with white tufts crowded around the *Snark* and towered above them. A far cry from the open, grassy plains of home. Alis doubted the docile toves on her family's ranch would enjoy grazing on the squishy moss, although the white fluffy creatures bounding in front of them seemed to enjoy it. She hefted the shiny, barrel-shaped condenser and stomped uphill after the others.

The Terran Imperium had dominated this sector of the galaxy for decades and placed the P'lar, who had resisted, under occupation. Her family never protested when Bellman's World was ceded to the Free Alliance, nor did they resist when half of their land was given to demobilized Alliance soldiers for settlement. They just wanted to live in peace. *Yet Et'Eruca thinks I'm just like the people who bombed its home world. Maybe I should take my chances on another ship once this is done, share be damned.*

The barrel of a rifle greeted her when she crested the rise. The burly figure wearing a climate-controlled jumpsuit waved her forward. Risus and Et'Eruca stood at the bottom, bracketed by two more people. Alis's legs twitched. She had been a champion runner, and Borogove's lower gravity might give her an edge, but she doubted she could outrun a bullet. She handed over the condenser and strode down the hill, hands raised.

"Are there any more of you?" asked a woman at Risus's elbow, her voice harsh and tinny through her mask's speaker.

"Just us, collecting supplies," said Risus. "We'll be on our way if you let us."

"Don't think so," said the man next to Alis in a deep, rumbling voice. "You're coming with us."

"What about my ship?" asked Risus. Her whiskers flattened against her cheeks.

The man gestured with his rifle.

Two others that looked like twins joined them. They shook their heads when the man looked at them. "No one else. Well, that part of your story checks out," he said. "Keep moving. We've only got a week of daylight left." He chuckled at his own joke.

The trek took them into steeper hills free of the stalks, but still blanketed with spongy moss. Alis sank up to her ankles as she plodded forward. The soupy air enveloped and constricted her, but she was grateful for her respirator. Risus marched in silence, staring at the ground, while Et'Eruca crawled as fast as its many legs could carry it. It seemed to have far less trouble negotiating the squishy turf. Their escorts wore overshoes with flared, wire-frame soles, allowing them to walk without sinking.

The hilly country gave way to a broad, empty plain that reminded Alis of home – if she didn't need a respirator and wasn't sweating to death. A long metal structure loomed ahead, resembling the pre-fab hangars and warehouses in the smaller communities on Bellman's World, except that this one was shiny and dust-free. Their escorts nodded at a pair of guards standing by the door, and nudged them inside. She blinked in the harsh interior lighting and shivered at the sudden climate-controlled chill. Before she had her bearings, they were ushered through an anteroom and down one of several gleaming corridors. She counted a left turn and then two rights before they were deposited in a small, square room devoid of furnishings.

⊙ ⊙ ⊚

"I don't suppose your sensors happened to detect this facility," said Alis.

Et'Eruca twitched its antennae and stared coldly at her while it took a long draw from its pipe.

"Quiet," said Risus, hunched over the door panel. "I cracked the lock's code. They have outdated security systems."

Alis blinked. "I didn't know you could pick locks."

"I've had a lot of jobs," said Risus. Her mouth formed a taut line. "These people must have ships. Let's find their hangar."

Alis frowned. "What about the *Snark*? And our shares?"

"And the cargo?" added Et'Eruca.

"We took a lot of damage before landing," said Risus, "and I'm sure those furless brutes looted the *Snark*."

Alis frowned. "I'm right here, you know."

Risus murmured an apology. Alis closed her eyes and pinched the bridge of her nose to distract herself from her churning stomach. *My share is gone.* She'd had just enough Free Creds – all she'd saved while working at the family ranch – to buy into the *Snark* when she signed on. She'd had a vote, a percentage of the ship's profits, and a chance at something more.

Judging by her calmness, it wasn't the first time Risus had suffered such a loss, but she imagined Et'Eruca must be livid, the way it ground its mandibles. Alis spoke as little as possible with the P'lar, but knew the success of this venture meant a lot to Et'Eruca. *Whether you have a stake means nothing if you're stuck on this planet.*

Alis slid the door open, peering up and down the corridor. "I'll go first. They may not look twice at a fellow human." No hangar doors were visible on the side they entered, which meant they were probably on the opposite side. As they moved down the corridor the glaring lights overhead cast everything into sharp relief, throwing their silhouettes onto the brushed aluminum walls. The rattling of the air circulation system muted their footsteps. The occasional murmur of conversation, carried through air ducts, and she cursed at not being able to pinpoint where their adversaries were likely to be before they stumbled upon them.

They entered a room to find a man sitting at the table, sipping a cup of steaming tea, judging by the smell. His breathing mask lay at his elbow. His eyes widened and his hand darted toward his belt.

Alis scanned for a weapon. In a pink and purple blur, Risus vaulted over the table and landed lightly on the ground. The guard twisted toward her as he drew his pistol. She raked her claws across his face. He screamed and clutched his shredded cheek as red rivulets seeped between his fingers.

So much for sneaking out.

Risus wrested the pistol from the guard just as he rose and shouldered into her. Alis darted around the table and swung wildly at the back of his head. Her fist connected with his neck. He grunted and staggered to his knees. Risus whacked the top of his head repeatedly with the pistol's butt, until he collapsed to the floor.

Et'Eruca's mandibles clacked. "I can feel the vibrations of several people running to our position."

Alis nodded, thankful.

They ran down the corridor. Alis scanned the signs by the doors for anything to point them in the right direction. Interspersed between the storage rooms and barracks were processing labs and refineries. *What kind of place is this?* More voices ahead spurred her to open the next door and dart inside, closely followed by Et'Eruca and Risus.

They stood in a long, high-ceilinged room lined with large cages stacked three high. She gasped. In each cage a stout, four-legged creature with dirty white fur and long pointy ears sprawled. Tubes sprouted from their heads, and ran to boxes with flickering lights mounted in each cage's ceiling. Even stranger, each one wore a waistcoat covered with dials and other gauges. Faint whirring and clicking sounds emanated from the set-up. Alis's fingers twitched. *How can I get them out?*

"What now?" asked Et'Eruca.

Alis stared at the cages. "If we make it out of here, we report this to the Alliance authorities."

"There may be a reward, too," said Risus.

Et'Eruca turned away. "This is none of our business."

Alis spun to face Et'Eruca, pointing to the cages. "How can you not care about what happens to another living thing?"

"I have the rest of my apprenticeship to think about," said Et'Eruca, clasping both sets of arms behind its back. "My family are navigators. I can't return home in disgrace."

"Let's discuss it later," said Risus, who listened at the door. "I don't think anyone's there."

Alis realized if they escaped, there might not be any left alive to save. "We should set them free."

"Why?" asked Et'Eruca. "They're almost dead. I'm very much alive and want to stay that way."

Risus gently placed a hand on Alis's shoulder. "We need to be practical."

Alis slowly looked away and nodded. Her parents had said the same thing, just before their last argument about her activism.

They continued down the corridor and passed more processing labs. Alis wondered how many more creatures were behind those doors being drained. Regardless of what Et'Eruca thought, she must do something. There was no risk here of being arrested for threatening the interests of corporations that squeezed family-run operations; just a chance to finally do the right thing. She could work her way up again on another ship if things soured because of it.

A set of double doors beckoned at the end of the corridor. Alis sprinted the remaining distance and burst into the hangar. A handful of one-person, high-altitude flyers were parked along the far wall, and two larger ships – probably courier vessels or small freighters – occupied the area near the doors. A dozen cages like those in the processing labs lined the nearest wall, but their occupants were very much awake and highly agitated. They immediately began scrabbling and grunting upon seeing Alis and her companions.

Alis started toward the cages. *I've got to free them from the hell that's planned for them.*

"Either one of the freighters will do," said Risus.

"Not so fast, and drop the gun." Et'Eruca aimed a small stunner at Alis and Risus. Alis's momentary shock quickly dissolved into anger. She clenched her jaw. Their captors had never examined the P'lar's respirator, which was large enough to conceal a small weapon. Risus placed the pistol on the ground.

"What's your game?" asked Alis.

"There's a much bigger prize than laying claim beacons," said Et'Eruca, gesturing toward Risus.

"Why?" asked Risus.

"You always glossed over your past and never explained why you love working in the fringe systems, when we could be making so much more in the Core," said Et'Eruca. "That made me curious about what other roles you've played."

"'Death is the final role,' as we say at home," said Risus.

"Some syndicates would agree...and disagree," said Et'Eruca, "including the one that hired me."

"You fucking bug," Alis hissed, using the common insult.

Et'Eruca shrugged its four shoulders. "I've got only two years left on my apprenticeship, and with the *Snark* and her cargo gone, I've got nothing to show for it. I weighed my options. The bounty on Risus will buy my family's forgiveness for failing."

"I took you in when you were fired from your last post," said Risus slowly. Her whiskers flattened against her cheeks.

A jump-suited man entered the hangar, carrying a large pistol. "A touching sentiment. Thank you, bug," he said.

Et'Eruca stiffened. "The Chys is yours, as promised," it said calmly. "The human is of no concern to me."

The man's icy blue eyes swept over Alis. She fought back a shudder. *There's a man who'll shoot me as soon as look at me.*

"I am happy to have been of service," said Et'Eruca. "My account information is on a cred-stick. We can settle things and I can ride the next ship out of here."

The man fired. Et'Eruca squealed and cradled its newly perforated arm. A second shot tore through a shoulder and a third through its chest as its stunner clattered to the floor. The P'lar slumped to the ground and lay still, a greenish substance oozing from its wounds, its mandibles twitching for a few seconds. "Consider things settled," he said. He turned to Alis. "It's nothing personal, you understand." He levelled his pistol at Alis.

An icy cold ball settled in her chest. She fought for breath. "Wait! I've got useful info!"

"So does everyone, in your situation," said the man.

"I'm serious. I know the black market on Bellman's World. I've been looking for people – my own people – to make connections."

"Why are you with this crew?" he asked.

"I've got a record," said Alis. That wasn't far from the truth. "I needed a way off-planet, no questions asked." She looked away from Risus's hurt expression. *If this works, I'll make it up to you.*

"Put the Chys in a cage and come with me." He directed Risus to an empty cage with his pistol. She shuffled inside and winced as the door clanged shut. She did not meet Alis's gaze.

The man marched Alis back down the corridor. "We'll have a talk to see if we can use you," he said.

If we can use you. She didn't like the sound of what would probably be an interrogation. She had bought herself time, but she would be drawn into their web or she'd slip up before long. Whatever Risus had done, and however indifferently she'd treated Alis, she didn't deserve her likely fate. She asked, "What are you manufacturing here?"

"Those mome-rats are the highest form of life here. They're stupid buggers, but they make useful pheromones for pharmaceuticals when they're scared. And the Alliance can't touch us in neutral territory."

Alis gritted her teeth. At least the conglomerates fed their toves and let them out once a day. "What about the Chys?" she asked.

"That thing was our best distributor, until she had an expensive change of heart that lost us shipments and some of our boys."

They approached the guard post in the anteroom. The guard she had attacked before was nowhere to be seen. "Could I have a tea? It's been a while," she said, pointing to the corner table holding the Nutrimat machine.

The man shrugged and punched a few buttons on the machine. A plastic cup plopped into a small hopper and black, steaming liquid smelling of bergamot and crisp dry leaves in autumn poured into it. When the machine gurgled to a finish, he handed her the cup. "Here you g—" His words devolved into an ear-splitting wail as hot liquid splattered his face.

Alis sprinted back to the hangar before the man had finished his first scream. She maintained a white-knuckled grip on the cup. A crappy weapon, but better than nothing. *Death is the final role.* Risus would just pick herself up again and move in a new direction. Alis could do no less. She'd been a rancher, an activist, and a cargo master, but she'd never been a fighter. Until now.

A uniformed woman stepped into the corridor, drawing her pistol. "She's heading to the hangar," she shouted into a badge clipped to her shoulder. She fired. Alis winced as a bullet grazed her arm. She plowed into the woman, and crashed to the floor. Her jaw exploded in heat from the pistol butt's impact.

Alis punched her adversary on the side of the head. She fell sideways and Alis rolled away, snatching the pistol from the woman's hand and running. She burst into the hangar. Risus was out of her cage and inspecting the freighters. The hangar doors were open. Humid air snaked around her and constricted her chest. Alis turned back to the doors and shot at the control panel. The bullet embedded itself in a crate. The third shot hit its target, creating a small rain of sparks. That would slow them down. Maybe.

"You're back," said Risus.

"Did you think I'd stay?"

"I knew you were buying time. I'd understand you wanting to be with your own people, but I'm glad these aren't *your* people."

"I had more in common with Et'Eruca." Alis checked their back.

Risus opened the freighter hatch. "Where does that leave us?"

"I know where I belong," said Alis. "I'll stay on, if you'll have me."

Risus blinked. "I'm starting over. Again. In a new ship with no guarantee of profit. You might get fifty percent of nothing."

"You've done this before and seem to be okay."

"All right, then." Risus grinned. "I need someone to help me run this thing if any money's to be made." She gave a low, throaty rumble of amusement.

Alis looked back at the cages. "One last thing before we blast out of here"

She let the mome-rats run free.

◉ ◎ ◎

Settling into *The Wunderland*, Alis turned to Risus. Their new mission was to rescue the imprisoned, no matter where they were. To rise up the meek. But, they had time to kill before their next port of call. Alis smiled, put the ship on autopilot, and pulled out a deck of cards that she had found beside her seat. "Poker?"

A wide, toothy grin spread across Risus's face and she purred in agreement.

Alis dealt out the cards. "Five-card draw, Queen of Hearts is wild."

THE SMOKE

Costi Gurgu

Gabriel stared at the human skeleton in the room's centre. One of its arms was missing and a sticker hung on its ribs, reading "Mr. Bones" written with pink marker. He recognized Maya's writing, loving her gothic penmanship. She had a way of making everything hers in the most unpossessive way. Her touch infused almost everything in the university's dusty old basement. Spider webs covered dirty windows so high that nobody had probably opened them in decades.

If their project succeeded, they could create humanity's future among the stars. At least that's what Gabriel had told Maya, to draw her on board. Some guys played maleness, or their coolness card, to get the attention of their fellow female students. Gabriel was seen as a weirdo and a geek, not in a good way, considering that *weirdo* was the same qualifier as *geek*. He didn't care what others thought, as long as Maya's opinion wasn't influenced.

Gabriel tied on a leather apron. Mr. Bones was covered in a metallic mesh that dripped liquid. Wires spread from more than sixty sensors stuck to the skeleton, creating a web throughout the basement.

Maya also wore a leather apron and large leather welding gloves. She walked to the ancient power box on the wall, where seven levers stuck out. She tapped one lever and smiled expectantly at Gabriel. He bent over his laptop and activated the sensors on the digital skeleton. Mr. Bones lit up like a Christmas tree. Finally, he pressed record on the video camera.

Maya placed welder's goggles over her eyes. "Ready to go, Dr. Frankenstein." She'd stuck a paper label on her overalls. With the same pink marker, she'd scrawled "Igora Maya" in gothic script. To Gabriel, she was the *real thing,* and his idea had become quickly *their* idea.

"All right, baby. Let's do it!" Gabriel's hand wavered over the laptop's display.

Maya laughed maniacally, grinned, and struck a *ready* stance.

"Trial number one, parameters version one-point-one for inanimate objects starting in three, two, one!" He pointed to Maya.

She pulled the levers. Electricity crackled the air and sparks exploded around the skeleton.

"We've reached the critical point. Let's teleport Mr. Bones a couple metres away."

Gabriel touched a command button. Energy arced between the sensors with loud snaps and pops, turning the room into a fairyland. The power box exploded, throwing Maya onto her back.

Light left the basement. Then, a ripping sound shook the room and before Gabriel could reach Maya, he saw the darkness tearing and glowing red in the centre of the room. The skeleton appeared black against it. Gabriel glanced at Maya who shakily pushed herself up. He walked carefully toward the glowing rip. Maya stood a few steps away.

Then *whoosh,* and the skeleton disappeared, leaving only the bloody tear.

Where the bones had stood, something else *plopped* through, splashing loudly in the puddle. A huge, dark shadow.

"Gabe!" Maya screeched.

Gabriel used his cellphone flashlight. The sensor-covered mesh lay in the puddle, wires still stretching to the walls and ceiling. In the web's middle stood a nightmarish creature – worm-like, wrinkled, hairy body, spikes protruding here and there, several pairs of legs, some writhing in the air. Worst of all, its head…was only an excrescence on the body, with the face of an old man!

Gabriel shuddered. Suddenly, the creature's eyes sprung open, and it exhaled. A cloud of smoke poured from his cavernous mouth, straight for Gabriel's face. He couldn't prevent inhaling the substance.

◉ ◉ ◉

Gabriel heard screaming, and his stomach clenched. What the… He opened his eyes, saw the scene, and closed them again. Voices continued to rise. Certain he couldn't be dreaming, he opened his eyes once more.

Emergency lights threw some red light in the basement, displaying a worm the size of a gorilla leaning against a wall, partially hidden behind some crates, smoking nervously and exchanging words with Maya.

Gabriel rose, feeling dizzy. He stopped for a couple of seconds to breathe and his vision cleared. He grabbed a chair and turned to strike the monster.

Maya stopped speaking, keeping her hand stretched toward the worm, and said, "Are you all right, Gabe?"

Gabriel paused, chair above his head, and noticed Maya was untouched, her face creased with worry, but no terror. "A bit sick…" He put the chair down and pointed at the worm. "What. Is. That?"

"Dear sir, my name is—"

"Shut up!" Maya blustered.

"I'm really losing my patience, young lady!"

Gabriel swallowed. "Is it really talking? Am I going nuts?"

Maya spoke in a low voice for him, alone, and the worm puffed angrily. "You're not going nuts. It's talking and I don't know what it is."

"Where's Mr. Bones?"

"We lost Mr. Bones…something else replaced it…"

"My dear sir, may I present myself?"

"It's talking again," said Gabriel, feeling the cold sweat of reality.

Maya pointed her cellphone at the monster.

The worm said, "I can only assume from your gesture that you're using that device to threaten me."

"Keep it there while I check the parameters," Gabriel said.

At his laptop, Gabriel confirmed that Mr. Bones no longer registered on the sensors. The experiment had succeeded… not as they'd hoped. He looked at the worm. It was ugly, no doubt about that. But the humanoid face made it appear… approachable. No, it was more like a…it looked quite similar to… Gabriel bent over, coughing violently.

"Put that cigar out!" Maya growled at the worm. "Don't you see it bothers him?"

"I'm sorry. It calms me."

She waved the smoke away. "I don't care!"

Examining the cigar's burning tip, the worm muttered, "Someone is very rude." It made a show of extinguishing the cigar on its tongue, then threw the butt into its mouth and chewed with an annoyed expression.

Gabriel breathed in a few times to relax and studied the worm. It resembled a giant caterpillar, but with a face mimicking human expressions. That's why it seemed so… normal, for lack of a better label. He considered the data, trying to determine what happened the moment the swap occurred.

Maya continued to "threaten" the caterpillar. "Are you all right, Gabe? Do you feel funny? Should we go to the hospital?"

Her attention and concern made him feel good. But if this was real… The basement felt surreal, and yet, they stood face to face with a horrific caterpillar, and somehow managed to retain their composure. What else could they do? Panic and run? No, they needed to restrain and study it. He looked around for cable or rope. To buy time, he said, "You were saying?"

The wrinkled human face composed itself, speaking with the voice of an elderly English gentleman. "I am Absolem, and I don't know where I am. I would be profoundly grateful if you could point me in the direction of the Mushroom Village."

Gabriel swallowed hard. Maya giggled. Between giggles, she managed, "If you're *the* Caterpillar, I must be Alice!"

Absolem indignantly replied, "Oh! Could that be true? If so, it's quite a shock! I must say."

She lowered her cellphone. "I think we're hallucinating."

"If you are hallucinating," said the creature, "that means I must be as well, because this land looks quite peculiar."

Maya erupted into laughter. Gabriel didn't feel amused. The lack of proper illumination, the caterpillar's presence, the…he wrinkled his nose – yes, the *stench* it brought with it – everything unsettled him. He felt a looming threat, and the fact that he didn't know what to do frustrated him. He couldn't use the wires on Absolem or he'd ruin the experiment.

Gabriel coughed for a long time, leaning against Maya. He turned to her. "The problem is, if we are talking to the Caterpillar from the *Alice in Wonderland*, what reality are we in?" He pointed to Absolem. "What is *it*?"

"*It* is not a *what*, it is a *who*." Absolem cleared his throat and moved around, exploring the basement.

"You're right," confirmed Maya. "What shall we do?"

Absolem snapped, "You should ask the right questions."

"If he is real, we're in a very bad situation," Gabriel finally uttered.

"Why?"

Lowering his voice, Gabriel said, "We may have a biohazard situation. The question is – do we call the CDC or do we risk a serious widespread contagion?"

"Although I heard every word, I didn't understand any of it, dear sir. This is a strange land indeed."

"The fact that the creature keeps talking is very creepy," said Gabriel.

Absolem turned toward them. "I don't know where I am, but I must say that people seem to be very rude here."

Gabriel tapped his chin. "So, we sent Mr. Bones somewhere, in exchange for Absolem."

Maya pointed to a chalk mark on the floor. "We set the parameters to five metres."

The caterpillar leaned in, listening.

"So," Gabriel began, but his legs gave away.

Maya caught him and gently lowered him to the floor. Turning to the caterpillar, she asked, "What did you do? What was that gas you blew into his face?"

"It wasn't gas, young lady. It was smoke."

"What was it made of, then?"

"Mushrooms…"

"What?"

"I believe, young one, that you meant to say *excuse me*."

Maya stepped closer to Absolem, and raised her cellphone once more. "What kind of mushrooms?

"Leave that for now," said Gabriel. "I have saved three versions for inanimate objects and two separate protocols for live beings. I only had to finish inputting the data from the trials."

"All right…" Maya encouraged him to finish.

"We may want to send Absolem back to Wonderland… I can't believe I just said that."

"Oh, no, young sir, I'd really appreciate you doing me this favour."

Gabriel said, "Well, that would save us the trouble of having to deal with the CDC."

"You know that if it, if *he* really brought something like a virus, bacteria, or parasite, anything to our world, the CDC would only be able to find a cure through the original carrier."

She was right. This was not something to pretend didn't happen. That brought them back to searching for a restraint.

Before Gabriel could reply, the room blurred. He felt a jolt, and everything disappeared in a vortex of colours.

◎ ◎ ◎

The kaleidoscope faded as Gabriel returned from wherever he had been. The scene before him looked different. The basement looked better, flooded in light. The caterpillar explored the laptop. It looked more grotesque fully illuminated. Maya studied something under the quantum microscope they'd stolen to observe changes in Mr. Bones' molecular structure after the first teleportation. Something didn't seem right. He thought that a brief episode of vertigo had overwhelmed him, and when his head cleared, it looked as though he'd been gone for hours. He cleared his throat.

Maya jumped from her chair. "You're back!"

"Yes, but from where?" Cold fear creeped through his body.

Absolem looked at Gabriel, his face a portrait of intrigue. "Now that's a good question."

"We don't know, Gabe. But you've been gone for two hours."

The caterpillar asked, "Have you been to Wonderland?"

Gabriel looked at them, feeling as though he had become the butt of a bad joke. Recognizing the worried expression on Maya's face, he knew they weren't joking. "I never left." He tried to make sense of what had happened, and immediately doubted himself.

"Young man, you disappeared in front of our astounded eyes and reappeared two hours later in the same spot. When all physical evidence leads to the same conclusion, you must admit that your deduction can only be the truth."

Gabriel looked at his watch. "What time is it?" he asked Maya.

"Eleven-oh-six at night." She watched him with curiosity.

"Holy shit!" Gabriel raised both his arms above his head.

Absolem sputtered, "This is, without a doubt, the most rude place I have ever visited."

"My watch says nine-oh-six," said Gabriel. "So, I wasn't in a different place. I went forward in *time*."

"Pardon?"

Maya approached and then checked her cellphone against his watch. She nodded, and shouted, "Holy shit, indeed!"

"I feel as though your rudeness is coordinated and intentional," said Absolem, indignation radiating from his face. He patted his body and produced another cigar from a skin wrinkle. "Wait, you said you moved forward in time?"

"Yes," confirmed Gabriel.

"But if your watch is two hours behind this young lady's, then you stayed still while we went forward."

"It might seem that way, but I arrived in my future in only a few seconds of my subjective time, meaning you lived through two hours while I jumped forward." Gabriel exchanged glances with Maya.

"So…your machine is a time travel device?" said Absolem.

"No, I told you," Maya said exasperated, "it's a *teleportation* device."

"As in…?"

"As in moving objects and people across distances."

"Then why am I here?"

Maya asked Gabriel, "What do you think?"

Gabriel didn't have an answer. Instead, he asked Maya, "What were you looking at?"

Maya pulled him to the microscope.

"Absolem's blood. The most peculiar thing you'll ever see."

"*Peculiar?*" said Gabriel.

Gabriel glanced at Absolem, who nervously turned the cigar between his fingers. The caterpillar also had fingers! Gabriel stared at them, fascinated. What *was* Absolem and where had it come from?

"His genome," Maya resumed, "does not exist in any database. And that's not the most intriguing aspect."

Well, obviously. He didn't think anybody else had ever seen a creature like Absolem in human history. With the exception of the fictional Alice, of course.

Maya said, "His genetic information isn't stable."

Gabriel touched her shoulder and whispered, "What do you mean?"

"I mean that one moment Absolem is something, then the compositional structure changes. His genetic map moves from one configuration to another every few minutes or so. None of them exist in our world."

"He is not of Earth," murmured Gabriel. "And yet, he has a humanoid face and speaks English."

Gabriel turned to Absolem and brushed his fingers across the creature's surface. His coarse and rough skin was solid enough. The caterpillar spoke a very educated version of English.

Trying not to flinch when looking into the caterpillar's eyes, Gabriel asked, "What did you say the gas or smoke was, exactly?"

"It was the result of what I smoked."

"Yes, but *what* were you smoking?"

"What else, my dear sir?"

"What else than what, Absolem?" Gabriel felt feverish and faint, but he wanted clearer information. The danger intensified from so many unknown facts.

"My mush… Oh, no."

"What?" Gabriel crossed his arms over his chest. "What was it?"

"I thought it was my mushroom, but I remember now. I tried a brand-new elixir with my hookah."

Out of patience, Maya shouted, "What was it?"

"Three parts red and two parts grey, of what once twas grime, and one part of the ivory shine."

"Can we have a clear answer for once?" Gabriel exploded.

"No, wait," said Maya. "It sounds like a chemical formula."

Gabriel waited for her to share her thoughts. She was way better at chemistry. He stepped closer to a crate and collapsed on it, closing his eyes. He felt weirdly tired and it was so hot that he removed his leather apron.

"So, the three parts red should be a red substance…"

"Why, blood, what else?" said Absolem, annoyed. "Sometimes I wonder what happened with young people…"

"Three parts blood?" Gabriel murmured.

"Whose blood?" Asked Maya.

"The Jabberwock's, of course. This was his elixir. The most potent one known, as the jabberwock's the most amazing creature of them all."

"All right, so you smoke the blood of a fictional character…" Maya tried to keep her voice neutral.

"No, it makes sense," said Gabriel, his voice hushed. "The jabberwock is a…uh…"

"A chimera," Maya suggested.

"Yes."

She asked, "Do you feel sick?"

"No, just tired and…very hot."

Maya placed her hand on his forehead. "You're feverish. I need to get you some ice."

"Not yet. The rest of the chemical formula…" Gabriel looked at Absolem, and said, "So, three parts jabberwock's blood, one part grey that once was grime."

"Yes, that's correct."

Maya pulled her hair into a ponytail and tied it with an elastic she kept on her wrist. "You're killing me. What's the grey part?"

"Why, a bit of ash, of course," replied Absolem.

Gabriel asked, "*Two* parts grey?"

"Yes, soaring ash from burning the feathers from the jabberwock's wings, and crawling ash from burning some of its shedded skin."

Gabriel continued to unravel the clues, "And one part ivory something?"

"A melted jabberwock's scale, of course."

"Why three parts red? Is it the quantity that matters or...?"

"Is it the same blood in all parts, Absolem?" Maya asked.

"Why no. That would be silly."

Maya smiled patiently and tapped her foot.

Absolem put his cigar back into his skin wrinkle and explained with an irritated voice, "One part of the jabberwock's dragon blood, one part of its hydra blood, and one part of its spider blood."

Gabriel sighed. "That's why his genome is the way it is..."

They now knew every component, and yet didn't know how time travel was possible or what had happened to transport the caterpillar.

"All right, we may have the reason for your problem," Maya said, "but let's make sure. I discovered something I call the Chimera virus in Absolem's blood. The pathogen eats away at his native blood cells, perverting his molecular structure."

She held Gabriel's chin, gently, and looked him in the eye, trying to make him focus. Then she rolled up his sleeve and prepared a needle and a test tube. She inserted the needle into his vein, attaching the test tube and drawing blood. Gabriel felt so weak that he could barely keep his eyes open.

Maya said, "My theory is that this elixir has done something, allowing its flesh to connect to our teleportation system. When we started the experiment, Absolem was sucked into the *gate*. It's probable that Mr. Bones is now in Wonder-land in Absolem's place. So, we didn't build a teleportation device that moved objects and people from one place to another. Instead, we built something that moves objects and creatures from one *world* to another."

She pulled out the needle, disinfected Gabriel's arm, and put a bandage on. "He probably infected you when you inhaled the smoke. I'll check to see if it's the same strain."

Maya placed a glass of water in front of Gabriel: "Drink. Stay hydrated. You're still feverish."

"I don't have the Chimera virus, Maya. I slid through time, which…"

Gabriel tipped the glass and emptied it with two deep gulps. He'd been thirsty. He rose, then slid forward into the time vortex.

◉ ◉ ◉

The vortex was beautiful and colourful, soft and gentle. It smelled of cardamom and sounded like a cat's purr. He breathed with ease and allowed himself to be carried, finally feeling cool and relaxed. He hadn't asked what the elixir was for, but considering the effect it had on Absolem, he imagined it didn't know either. How could it impact a creature's DNA, but more importantly, how would it affect his?

Gabriel reappeared in the basement lab. A giant cocoon was fastened to the heating pipes. Maya slept, her head rest-ing on the table, next to the microscope. Gabriel walked on uncertain legs, and leaned on the wall.

"You're back," Maya's voice soothed him. "Sit, rest. Are you hungry?" She pulled him to a chair and he collapsed without comment.

Gabriel looked at his watch – 9:21. "Since the experiment started, I've only lived through about fifteen minutes, so I'm not hungry."

Maya nodded. She placed another glass of water in front of him and said, "Drink. I don't know how much time we have so please, listen carefully."

"Sure, baby. Shoot."

"I need to stop this infection before I lose you."

"What do you mean *lose*? You think I'm going to *die*?"

"Not necessarily. This time, you jumped ten hours in time. That is five times more than the last one. Assuming this factor of five applies to each instance, the next time you'll jump for fifty hours, that's more than two days. By the seventh jump, you'll be gone for twenty years. *That* means I'll lose you."

Her words sank in. Gabriel didn't have much time to solve the problem. Even if, for him, every jump cost him only a minute or so, the world would keep revolving. In ten minutes of his subjective time, he would likely jump to a time when no one would know who he was, or what had happened to him. Eventually, the Earth would die. His life would soon become a series of trips through a vortex, followed by a ten-minute break here (or wherever), followed by another vortex, until he arrived in a time where he would die by asphyxiation, or poisoning, during the ten-minute break, maybe before he'd die of hunger or thirst.

"We need the antidote, Gabe. And as always, it can only be with a sample from the original carrier. In this case—"

"The jabberwock."

"Yes."

"But, that's madness," said Gabriel. "The Jabberwock lives in Wonderland."

"And we have a teleportation system connected to Wonderland."

"And the jabberwock is a huge, ferocious monster."

"Absolem told me that we can hire a Jabberwock hunter. That's why I tried to send him back, but it didn't work."

"Right… Is that a cocoon…"

"Yes. Absolem began weaving it an hour after you jumped. When I suggested the theory, he insisted that his kind is the apex of their species, and that they never turn into butterflies. Apparently, butterflies come from flowers in Wonderland."

"What if the caterpillar-cocoon-butterfly metamorphosis was latent in his DNA, and has been awakened by the Chimera virus?"

"That's my working theory. Anyway, as I said, I used the teleportation device on him and it didn't work."

"What do you mean?"

"He's still here, or was…"

"All right, what protocol have you tried?"

"I tried the exact protocol with the same parameters as in our trial with Mr. Bones."

"But that's for inanimate objects."

"Yeah, but it still brought Absolem here."

"You're right." Gabriel leaned his head on his hand. "What if we use the teleportation system on me?"

"As if it's not enough that you slip through time without any control."

Gabriel shrugged. Maya had always been level-headed. He'd chosen well, with her. Unfortunately, they wouldn't have the opportunity to watch their relationship progress.

"Anyway, I tried the teleportation device on him again, using the second protocol for living things. Still, nothing happened. A lot of lights and sparkles, but Absolem stayed."

Gabriel heard Maya's answer as though it drifted through his dreams.

"Gabe, stay awake!"

He jolted awake. Why was he so tired?

"Sorry, so you tried a second time."

"Yeah, so I thought perhaps because Absolem is a fictional character, of sorts, the device doesn't recognize him."

"But we touched him, Maya. He's real, tangible…"

"I know, crazy. So…" She hesitated.

"What did you do?"

"I tried the experiment on myself."

"Maya!" He sounded harsher than he wanted. The idea of her in danger gave him a bad feeling. "It's not ready for human trials."

"Well, anyway, it didn't work on me either. I'm still here."

"How were you supposed to return if it worked, huh?"

"I left you a note. Gabe!" She stopped him, exasperated. "There's no time for this. The program doesn't work anymore. So, I'm out of ideas. I don't know how to save you."

Only now he noticed her voice cracking, fighting not to cry. And he didn't have the strength to make it better. If there was no solution to reach Wonderland, they'd have to find another way to at least slow down his time-sliding. They might—

The vortex sucked him in. He howled with frustration at the colours.

◉ ◉ ◉

He dropped from the vortex onto the same chair he'd been leaning on, right before he'd jumped. He exhaled loudly and rose.

Absolem's chrysalis still adhered to the heating pipes and wall. By now, the caterpillar probably didn't exist, on its way to becoming a butterfly. He sighed and turned to his laptop, and froze. Absolem smoked a cigar a few steps away from the cocoon. Gabriel looked around – Maya was absent.

"Welcome back, sir. You've arrived as your lady predicted."

"What are you doing here? No, more importantly, where's Maya?"

The basement door opened. Maya stepped inside. Gabriel exhaled, seeing her unharmed. After Maya, Absolem entered through the narrow door with some difficulty. Gabriel stopped breathing, looking in confusion from the caterpillar in the basement to the newcomer. Maya saw Gabriel and cried out. She ran to him. Another Maya entered after the second Absolem. The first Maya embraced him, then she examined him at arm's length.

"What's going on?" he murmured.

The first Maya looked at the second Maya coming to them with a big smile on her face, while the second Absolem undulating toward the first Absolem.

"Ah, yes, a lot has happened in the days you've been time-sliding," the first Maya said.

"Why don't you fill me in. I only have a few minutes left." Gabriel collapsed back on the chair.

"All right…uh, it seems that the teleportation works after all. But differently than expected."

Gabriel broke his stare at the two Absolems, avoided looking at the second Maya, and looked into first Maya's eyes. Nothing seemed right. He asked, "What do you mean?"

"Remember when I told you that I tried twice to send Absolem back and it didn't work?"

"Yup."

"Well, it actually worked. I did send him back...sort of. The thing is that the program doesn't send live organisms away from our reality. It sends replicas. So, the real Absolem stayed behind, but a replica reached Wonderland. And then a second replica arrived."

"Then you tried it on yourself and a..."

"Replica of myself went there, solved the problem, and brought the two Absolems back with a...uh..." Maya uncovered a cage – a little monster, the size of a hound, screeched at him from behind the bars.

Gabriel stared, fascinated. "It's a baby jabberwock!"

"And we discovered the strain in its blood."

The second Maya came back with a syringe filled with a transparent fluid. She gave the syringe to the first Maya, who was already disinfecting Gabriel's arm.

"We have the antidote!" laughed the first Maya. She injected Gabriel.

"Ah, guys?" the second Maya shouted. Gabriel turned. The two Absolems advanced toward the undulating cocoon. One of them placed his palm on the rough textured surface. Suddenly, the cocoon blossomed to double its volume.

"Don't touch it!" Maya shouted.

Too late – the cocoon exploded, filling the basement with remains and goo. Where the cocoon had been, a cloud of green mist swirled and expanded.

An infernal shriek filled the basement, cracking the building's walls. Gabriel rose, overturning the chair. The basement shook once, twice. A louder shriek; the mist cleared away as though it had been blown by a strong wind.

A monster rose, stretching two pairs of magnificent butterfly wings, the lower ones ending in claws. A row of spikes ran along its humanoid head, down its feathered bird body. It rose on four pairs of sticky, thorny, spider legs. The monster unfurled to the basement ceiling, nearly twenty metres in height. The human mouth opened, showing tiny, sharp teeth as it shrieked again, shaking the building's foundations.

Gabriel shouted, "Fuck!"

The jabberwock shook its body, and in two lightning-fast moves grabbed the two caterpillars in its huge claws. Its face oscillated between Absolem's human expressions and the new chimera's beastly visage. It bit into one Absolem, tearing the caterpillar in half, chewing hungrily.

"No!" Maya's scream attracted its attention. It stopped and stared at the second Maya with fascination.

Some of the building's electrical conduits had shaken loose. Gabriel grabbed two as the monster released the caterpillars and turned toward the second Maya. The first Maya knocked her twin to the floor as the monster's claws swiped and missed. Gabriel burst forward and reached the monster's back as it turned on him. He touched the two wires to its flesh and electricity coursed through it, making it buck and shriek. It tried to strike Gabriel, but the live wire made contact again. The monster jumped back, extended its butterfly wings, and flew upward. With one quick sweep, it blasted through the basement's windows, raining glass on them.

The damage was done. They had released a monster into their world. Gabriel dropped the wires and looked toward the two Mayas. *The twin will also be difficult to explain.* One Maya bent next to the still breathing, intact caterpillar. Silky threads started sprouting from Absolem's pores. *We need to destroy that, before it's too late.*

"Maya—" Gabriel felt the time vortex taking him. The last image he saw was the new cocoon encasing the dying Absolem, ready to create a new chimera.

THE RIVER STREET WITCH

DOMINIK PARISIEN

I'm taking my plate to the sink when the crumbs on it grow big. I know looking too long is bad, that that's when the magic comes, but I can't help it. One step I'm thinking of Bobby pushing me in the schoolyard, of Becca smiling while she watches, of Chrissy laughing, and the next step the crumbs are big as pebbles, big as baseballs, bigger than the dinner plate. I try to get to the counter but it's too late, the plate goes *smash* and plate bits go everywhere and the crumbs get small again and roll under the stove.

"Lucy, what the hell?" Mommy shouts, coming into the kitchen.

"The crumbs got big!" I say.

"What?"

"I'm sorry! I made the crumbs too big and I couldn't hold the plate. I didn't mean to!" I know from Mommy's face I shouldn't talk about the magic, that magic makes her angry, but I say it because it's true and Mommy always wants the truth.

"Goddamn it, Lucy!" This was one of the good plates, for when Grams and Grumps come over, but she took them out anyway because the kids hurt me again at school and she doesn't like when they hurt me. Mommy gets down to pick up the pieces, but she doesn't know about the crumbs under the stove, so I say, "Mommy, I—" and she says, "Just go to your room, Lucy." But this is important: the breadcrumbs might get big again, and if they get too big the stove might break and Mommy won't be able to make spaghetti anymore, so I say, "You can't leave the breadcrumbs under the stove!"

Even though it's true, Mommy looks at me angry and screams, "Go to your fucking room, Lucy!" so I run to my room and I cry all the way there because I know that if we die hungry it will be because of me and the magic.

◉ ◉ ◉

In bed, I tell Glover about the breadcrumbs, about my *predicament,* which is when you have a problem, and he looks at me with his big teddy bear eyes. I know he's trying to help, but it doesn't work. The magic is too strong today, and even Glover is getting big. Pretty soon my bedposts are far, far away, my ceiling goes all the way up to space, and Glover's eyes look like stars. I'm so small I have to crawl on his leg so I can sit on the ruffles of his stomach, like a baby kangaroo.

Downstairs, Mommy is talking to Daddy on the phone about the breadcrumbs, telling him, "I can't deal with this shit alone." I know magic is what makes them fight, and if I could stop it I would and Daddy could live with us again, but I can't, so now he has to stay with his friend, Delilah.

"Yes, it's still the same Dick principal, you'd know that if you—" Daddy once said Dick is Mr. Gardner's first name. Mommy was angry when he explained that, because kids aren't supposed to know a principal's first name, especially if it's Dick. If I was a boy and my name was Dick I wouldn't want kids saying it, even if I wasn't an adult, because it's stupid. I know Mommy doesn't think so because she's telling Daddy "—not stupid, Vince – doesn't need private schoo—"

I know *private* means something not for kids, but sometimes the magic makes words bigger when they come out of
Mommy's mouth, and I can hear them from my room even
when I'm not supposed to.

"I am not a witch, I am not a witch," I say, burying my face
into Glover's huge leg. It isn't true, though. I am a witch. The
River Street Witch, which I guess is what happens when
you're the only witch who lives on River Street. But sometimes I don't want to be. Nobody likes witches, not the other
kids in school, not even Mommy or Daddy. Magic leads to
misunderstandings, which is when people don't believe in
something but it's true and you aren't allowed to say that.

"I'll go into the kitchen when Mommy falls asleep," I tell
Glover, "and then get the breadcrumbs out from under the
stove." I don't really sleep so waiting is easy. I don't tell Glover
the rest of my plan, how I want to bring the breadcrumbs
back to my room and put them in my fishbowl and feed them
to Matt. Magic is like science, you need to experiment, and
experiments are complicated. Glover is a teddy, and teddies
understand better than most people, so obviously he already
knows what I want to do. I've already tried staring at the tiny
Matt in the fishbowl over and over, but Matt hasn't changed
size yet. Maybe if he eats the breadcrumbs I made grow he'll
grow big again too. I know Matt wants to go outside the fishbowl, but if I let him out he'll run, and he is so, so small, and
someone will squish him and no one will even know, and he'll
be gone forever because of my magic. So, he has to stay in the
fishbowl for now.

I really should stop calling it a fishbowl. Words are important. The fishbowl is a *terrarium*, which is what you call a
place to hide tiny animals and people and help them grow.
Matt must be lonely in the terrarium. The army men toys I

put in there are way bigger than he is, and he doesn't kick them anymore, or scream or hug them. He mostly just sits with his head down.

I need to make Matt big again. Like the breadcrumbs, I didn't mean to change him. I used to walk behind Matt on the way home from school, but Mommy doesn't let me walk home alone anymore since Matt came to live in my terrarium.

I liked the back of Matt's head, the way the top of his backpack rubbed against his hair and left a spot like an upside-down horseshoe. I was looking at that spot too long, and that's how the magic snuck up and shrunk him. Matt's head became as small as an egg, and I couldn't see it over his backpack. I was so scared for Matt –he's nice and lets me walk behind him and doesn't make fun of me – so I looked somewhere else when he turned the corner near the little wood by the school. When I turned the corner, there was only his backpack. I screamed *Help help* even though I didn't want anyone to see, and in the bushes I saw an old man with long hair and a beard like a broken bird's nest go deeper into the woods. I just *know* he saw the magic and got scared and ran. It took me a long time to find Matt, he was so tiny. I thought bugs might eat him. I was crying when Mr. Bleacher found me later with the backpack and still little Matt hidden in my lunchbox.

It's so hard not talking about Matt. Mommy says only adults get to keep secrets, that kids can't because they make you grow old really fast if you don't say them. Not talking about Matt hasn't made me skip any grades yet, but it does make me feel like Grumps when he says the ceiling pushes down on him when he walks. I always thought that was funny, but I think it's true, and if I can't fix Matt soon I'll look like Grams and Grumps by summer.

I wish I could tell Mommy or Daddy, tell Matt's parents, Mr. and Mrs. Rogers, so they wouldn't need to worry. Tell Bobby and Becca and Chrissy so maybe they would leave me alone. But I can't. I know they'd all be angry because I can't make Matt big again. That's why I didn't tell the policeman how it really happened, because he would ask the Woods Man and then they would put me in jail for my magic.

But maybe everything will be fine, maybe the bread-crumbs will help Matt get back to normal. Getting them will be easy. I'm small enough now to crawl under the stove and get the breadcrumbs. Even if Mommy gets up she won't see me.

I don't always want to be a witch, but sometimes it helps to do what you need to do.

◉ ◎ ◉

"It's just the goddamn Alice in Wonderland Sin Drum," Mommy screams from Mr. Gardner's office. I was supposed to stay in the office with her, but Mr. Gardner told me to wait on the chair outside. His secretary, Miss Reynolds, sits next to me at her desk and she coughs twice really loudly. I think she might have a bad cold and maybe I should sit somewhere else.

"…Todd's Sin Drum, Mrs. Demarco."

Sin Drum isn't what it sounds like, it isn't a bad drum, it's just what Mommy calls the magic. Our music teacher, Mrs. Lodge, probably wouldn't like it, but I don't think she knows. Mr. Gardner always says *Todd's Sin Drum*, because Todd has a Sin Drum too, but I don't know Todd. Mommy gets angry when I ask if I can meet him and says Todd is just the doctor who made Alice in Wonderland *Sin Drum*, but the doctors I know aren't witches so I know she's lying. Mommy hates lying, but she hates magic more, so that's why I'm sure Todd is a witch too. She doesn't want us to play because it could make the magic stronger. Mommy doesn't understand how lonely it is being a witch. But someday I know I'll meet Todd and we'll talk about our magic and be witch friends. I'll show him my *Alice in Wonderland* book. I know Todd will like it. Mommy and Daddy and Mr. Gardner like to say my magic is like Alice's, that it's just in my head and in a book, that it isn't real, but they're wrong. Alice eats cookies and drinks juice and that's what makes her big and small. Alice isn't a witch, like me or like Todd. But I still like the book. Even if there's fake stuff in it like disappearing cats and rabbits in clothes and mean cards, at least there's real magic around Alice.

"Mrs. Demarco, Lucy's condition coupled with her learn-ing difficulties—"

"Here, Lucy," Miss Reynolds says, giving me one of the hard yellow candies from her desk. Everybody knows those candies are for secretaries and teachers, and I don't know if I'm supposed to keep it for Mr. Gardner so I hold it in my hand just in case.

"—fact that your daughter found Matthew's backpack only helps connect her to the boy's disappearance in the chil-dren's minds. The combination is making Lucy an easy target for students to—"

The candy feels sticky in my hand. Matt didn't grow back to normal with the breadcrumbs. If he was here he could sit on the candy and get stuck there.

"The candy is for you, dear," Miss Reynolds says. I smile at her and put the candy in my mouth. Because the candy is for adults it tastes like it's made from bigger lemons and it makes my cheeks feel like magic is making them smaller.

"—lucky she's in the other room. Lucy, grab your bag, we're going home! And give me your fucking superintendent's number!"

◉ ◉ ◉

Houses fly by the car window, and I don't know if it's the magic shoving them away from Mommy's anger, or if Mommy's foot is cramped and she can't pull it off the pedal. The day too is magicked, I think. The magic made it smaller because I still had gym and math class, but here we are in the car.

"Piece of shit pompous prick of a—" Mommy says to the steering wheel. Sometimes Mommy goes outside into the car at night and screams. She thinks I don't see her but I do. I know the car sometimes helps Mommy like Glover helps me. The car has a name but I don't know it. I think it only talks to Mommy, which is fine. Mommies need special friends too. So do cars, I guess, and they probably only like people who can drive them. So, I give Mommy and the car some time together. I only say something when I see the dog crossing the street in front of us. It's a big dog, off its leash, and it looks like those dogs that pull sleds in the North.

"Mommy."

She and the car are still talking and they don't see the dog, which isn't surprising because the dog is now the size of our neighbour's fluffy Pomeranian. Or because the car is the size of a big truck.

So I say, "Mommy," again, but louder. Mommy isn't paying attention, I can tell because she doesn't realize how high above the street we're driving. I guess that means the dog should be fine, but you never know with magic.

Then: "MOMMY!"

Mommy turns her head my way and shouts: "WHAT?"

"THE DOG!" but it's too late, too late, the monster truck car is already driving over the spot where the tiny dog was crossing. Mommy makes the car stop, and the car screams in a high-pitched voice. The car is scared, like me. It didn't like getting big, or maybe it's afraid for the dog too. Maybe getting back to regular size made the car's pipes and oil and under-stuff squeeze the dog in its insides and it's all my fault. I pet the glovebox in front of me and whisper, "Everything will be okay, car." It has to be.

"Oh shit oh shit oh shit oh shit," Mommy says, climbing out of the car. I unbuckle my seatbelt – I'm supposed to sit in the back but I think the car likes having me in the front, so Mommy lets me – and I get out too. Mommy looks under the front of the car, and a stranger runs over and shouts. I don't want to look, but then I don't have to. Next to my shoe is the tiny dog, wagging its tail. Witches shouldn't cry, but I'm so happy I cry a little anyway. I bend down, pick the dog up between my fingers, and put it in my pocket. The dog's voice is so small I can't tell if it's barking or some other sounds, but I don't want to leave it in the street. The magic doesn't always work the way I want it to, and right now the dog isn't getting big again.

"Goddamn it!" Mommy says, maybe to me or to the stranger still shouting at her. "There's nothing there."

"Sorry," I tell her. "I thought there was a big dog." I know Mommy only wants the truth, but today is a day where truth won't be good for Mommy. Like on days I want ice cream, but my tummy growls and I know eating it will only hurt so I don't. I let Mommy sit me back in the car and listen to her shout, even though it isn't night and I'm in the car with her.

It's for the best. Mommy doesn't like dogs.

◎ ◎ ◎

I call the dog Gulliver. Gulliver looks happy to come out of my pocket, and I'm glad Gulliver wasn't squished by the car or by my pocket. A better name for him might be *Lilliputian*, like in another book Mommy showed me where people are small but they don't have the magic like me. Lilliputian is a nice name, but it's too long, and Lilli is a girl's name, and I think this dog is a boy, so I call him Gulliver. Gulliver is probably somebody's dog, but they wanted a big dog and Gulliver is small now, so I'll keep him until he gets big again.

I put Gulliver in the terrarium with Matt. Gulliver jumps around when he sees Matt, which is good. Matt seems happy – he keeps hugging the dog and shaking. Maybe Gulliver is Matt's dog, and he's been looking for Matt since Matt's been gone. I think he is. The magic has done a good thing, bringing boy and dog together. I give them cracker bits from my school snack and I put a few drops of water in the bottle cap that works like a little pond. I can't give them fruit because flies will come and take Matt away.

"Now there are two of them," I tell Glover, leaning on the bed. Downstairs, Mommy is talking to Samantha at the doctor's office. Samantha is Mommy's best friend and Mommy calls her a lot.

"What – vacation? Lucy needs to see him now. Are you the goddamn doctor? Then why do – Okay, okay, I'm sorry Samantha. I just don't know what to do – yeah, still Alice in Wonderland Sin Drum—"

"I need to fix this, but I don't know how. Help me, Glover. Tell me what to do." But he just watches Matt and Gulliver. "You're useless!" I say, but I don't mean it. He does so much for me. But he can't do magic. What I need is another witch.

What I need is Todd, and Glover already knows that because he's a teddy. So, I just hold him tight while Mommy shouts and cries downstairs.

◉ ◉ ◉

Donny's mommy runs next to our car in her bathrobe, even though bathrobes are for inside where no one can see you. In their house, Donny looks at us from the window. He's all wrapped up in blankets. I guess he isn't going to school today and that's fine, I don't really like Donny.

"They found Matt," she says looking at me, and my fingers make fists and my nails dig into my pants. That can't be true. *Nobody is allowed in my room!* I want to scream. *Only Mommy and Daddy can go in and Matt is so small they never see him!*

"In the woods," she says, and I'm shaking. Someone thinks they found Matt, but they haven't. He was in the fishbowl this morning. They've just found something else. "He's…he's dea—"

"Don't say it!" Mommy screams.

I try to grab Mommy by the wrist but she puts her hands on her mouth and makes a whine like Gulliver. Donny's mommy bumps their heads together and they say things to each other that aren't words but are trying to be words.

Now I want to say, *Matt is just in my terrarium,* even if I will go to prison for magic, even if Mommy will hate me, because I don't want her to sound like that. I want Mr. and Mrs. Rogers to know Matt isn't really gone. Even if I can't fix him. But I can't. They will *misunderstand* because I'm a witch, because of the magic. So Mommy keeps crying and Donny's mommy cries and I cry and it's so *stupid* because Matt isn't even gone, he's in my room, in my terrarium, with a dog called Gulliver.

"I…I need to take Lucy to school."

I almost scream, *No, Mommy, leave me with Matt!* I need to try other experiments, try something, anything.

"What? You can't seriously—"

"I can't do this to her. She…she needs this, she needs to be there. Some of the kids blame her. She can't be away when they announce it. If she runs from this it'll only be worse."

But Mommy is wrong. I'm the witch who made Matt small, who keeps him in her room, who makes people think Matt is gone. How will I lie to everyone when they'll think he's gone for real? The secret will make me so old. My hands are all wet from crying, and my fingers look like when I get out of the bath, or like Grams' and Grumps's hands. I want to say, *Look at my hands, Mommy. By tomorrow I will be too old for school!*

◉ ◉ ◉

Mrs. Drummond calls math arithmetic, and every day she writes out the word on the chalkboard so we can learn it. *Arithmetic*. I hate it. It makes me think of asthma, which Bobby has, and then I sit in class and all I can hear is Bobby's scary asthma breathing, even though he isn't breathing like that. Sometimes I look at the word and it gets so big it pushes all the other words and numbers off the board, and all I see is *Arithmetic*.

I don't want to think about numbers. A week is seven days. Two weeks is another seven days, and seven plus seven is fourteen. Matt's been in my terrarium for more than fourteen days. And now Mommy and Donny's mommy think Matt is gone forever, and soon everyone will think that too unless I do something.

On my desk, my right hand is too big, at least two times bigger than my left hand. I don't want the other kids to see, so I put my face in my hands and lick my palm, because it helps sometimes. There's salt in my mouth now, from the rocks I was playing with in the schoolyard. I want to think just about the salt, to not let the magic come, but it isn't working.

I need to get out of class, before my hand gets any bigger, before I get big and my head goes through the ceiling. Everyone's looking at Mrs. Drummond and *Arithmetic*. I want to ask Mrs. Drummond if I can be excused, but before I do that I see the Woods Man outside, the one that got scared when I shrunk Matt. He's standing by the fence that cuts the school off from the trees. He looks like he never left the woods, with his brown ripped jacket and his dirty pants that don't cover his legs. And he has no shoes, which is weird because nobody walks in the woods without shoes, but maybe he lives in the woods and that's what you do when you live there. I know I don't wear shoes at home.

Mommy always says to stay away from weird people, and I know I should tell Mrs. Drummond about the Woods Man, but I don't. I know if I say, *Look, it's the Woods Man*, everybody will ask how I know he's the Woods Man, and I won't want to tell them how I know it's him because I scared him when Matt turned small, so I'll have to lie, and because I'll lie Becca and Chrissy will know something's wrong and think I like the Woods Man and they'll sing *Lucy and the Woods Man, sitting in a tree*.

But it isn't just that. The man isn't just dressed weird, he looks *wrong*. He is *wrong*. His arms are as long as the fence and his fingers are as big as posts and his legs look crooked and too thin to carry him. The Woods Man sees me looking and pulls his right arm all the way back into his body and waves at me. I think he's magic, like me, and he wants me to know that.

I ask Mrs. Drummond to use the washroom.

"Careful not to fall down a rabbit hole!" Bobby tells me.

"That's enough," Mrs. Drummond says. "Lucy, please be quick. There's a…a special meeting in the gymnasium in fifteen minutes."

◉ ◉ ◉

I hate walking down the hallway when there's magic. The blue walls stretch like an inside sky and the ceiling is clouds and I'm a witch with a too-big hand and it's like the washroom is on another planet because it takes forever for me to walk to it and outside there's a Woods Man, a Magic Man, and he's—

Todd. He's Todd with the Sin Drum, like me.

Somehow, I'm at the washroom, so I go in a stall, close the door, pull my feet up on the toilet, and hide. Todd is the Woods Man. The magic has brought us together, like Matt and Gulliver. He was there all along. He saw what happened to Matt and he wanted to help, but like me he was scared, and he didn't want to get shrunk so he ran. But now he's showing me his magic. He heard what people think about Matt and he came looking for me.

Mommy must have known, and Mr. Gardner too, that Todd isn't a young witch like me, that he's old. Maybe he kept secrets and got old too fast. That's why they didn't want me to meet him. But they don't know he's the only one who can help. I can't fix anything by myself, and I can't bring my terrarium to class for Show and Tell and say, *My name is Lucy, and I am a witch, and this is Matt and Gulliver, and this is a terrarium and not a fishbowl.*

◎ ◎ ◎

I'm bigger than a house and I'm moving through the school-yard and my giant feet go *boom boom boom*. No one from the school is following me, and they couldn't catch me even if they wanted to – they aren't witches.

Todd, the Woods Man, the Magic Man, is still next to the fence. He sees me coming and goes back into the woods. The fence down there is made to keep out mice, not girls as big as trees, and it's easy for me to go over it. In the woods I walk through the leaves and the tops of some of the trees come up to my eyes.

Todd coughs somewhere down there. His arm goes all the way up to me through the branches, and it's like a spider arm. It grabs my hand and squeezes tight.

There's magic in his hand – it feels like when I put my knife into the toaster and my hair stuck on ends and Mommy screamed. All around me the trees grow tall and I get small, back down to Lucy-size. Todd is bigger than I am, and he squeezes my hand. He really is magic. He has to be. His arms and legs and other bits of him grow big and small, big and small.

"I'm the River Street Witch," I tell him. I know not to talk to strangers, but we aren't *really* strangers, and we're both magic, and we're in this together.

"And I'm the Witch of the Woods," he says. I know he means his name is Todd, but I didn't say my name is Lucy because we're witches and that's what matters right now. Kids aren't supposed to call adults by their first name anyway, so the Witch of the Woods works.

"You…uh. You're—" I say, looking at our hands. He's an adult, and magic, and I need his help, but he's really smelly and covered in dirt so I try to think of a nice way to say he needs a bath. "—very dusty."

"Best way to do magic."

I never even thought of that. It makes sense, I guess. Mommy always wants me to take baths, even when I don't need to, so maybe water or baths block the magic a bit. "I have a lot to learn."

"Yes, you do."

"I need to bring Matt back. He…he's in my terrarium. With Gulliver."

Todd nods, because of course he knows. "I can help with that," he says, smiling, and even though I stay the same I can feel my heart growing big in my chest. I've told my secret, I don't need to become old. I'm so happy I feel like I'm float-ing, and I have to look down to make sure I'm not.

There are ants near my feet, and it's like they're all staring at me. It must be the magic. I know ants listen to their queen, and I could be their queen if I learn to work the magic, once I fix Matt. Maybe Matt will realize he liked being small, and he will stay with me and the ants and we'll have adventures with Gulliver and Todd. I want to tell Todd, but he's better at magic than me, he already knows what I want to say, and he pulls me down. We're both getting small, going farther and farther away from the trees and the branches and the sky. We're down with the leaves and the dirt and the ants, and Todd grabs me by the waist and sits me in front of him on an ant, and together we go deeper into the woods where he'll teach me how to be a real witch.

THE RISE OF THE CRIMSON QUEEN

LINDA DEMEULEMEESTER

"Only three," said the funny looking kid who'd been locked in the coal bin.

He'd somehow crawled into the cellar during the night. Aggie heard him scratching at the door and rattling the latch. "Let me out," he'd moaned.

When she set him free, they stared at each other face-to-face. Aggie had never seen anyone quite like him. He was as small as a toddler, with long coal-smudged white ears and a soot-covered waistcoat. When she reached out to touch his droopy ear, he bit her hand and ran away clutching two fistfuls of coal to his chest.

"Dirty, rotten thing," cried Aggie, holding her thumb.

"Only three," he called back.

◉ ◉ ◉

Aggie and Mommy were driving back from the swimming pool. Rain beat against their windshield and hammered like pellets on the car roof. The windshield wipers pounded a rhythm until Aggie felt her heart match its beat. The old-car smell mingled with stale cigarette smoke, making her feel sick.

"Daddy and I are divorcing," Mommy said.

When they got home, Mommy let them eat in front of the television. Daddy would never have let them do that.

Two nights before, like other nights, Daddy had come home from work and everybody had to be quiet. Aggie hated quiet. After dinner they could sit without noise or fidgeting while Daddy sat on the couch and sipped his beer. He always fell asleep watching hockey and one of them, usually Tricia, would turn on cartoons. Then Davy would switch the channel to an action show. Aggie didn't much care what was on TV. She just wanted them not to argue. They always argued. Daddy would wake up and send them all to bed.

The next night, Aggie had played with her father's tools. He accused Davy. Davy was too afraid to defend himself. Aggie was too scared to confess. Davy got a spanking.

That's when Aggie wished her father would go away, so she wouldn't have to worry about being quiet or good anymore.

◉ ◉ ◉

Aggie only had one so-called friend on the block, and she didn't like her much. Her cousin Jane lived next door and was two years older and bossed Aggie around. She was tall, skinny and blonde, and Aggie thought they looked stupid together because she was short, dark and plump.

"Come to my house after school."

Jane never asked, she told. Aggie had to wait outside the school for her for an extra half hour. The wind bit into Aggie's ankles and scraped her lips raw. She yanked her skirt as close to her knee socks as she could.

Jane cried all the way home, saying her hands were cold. Aggie didn't think a seventh grader who blubbered had any right to boss her.

The next day, when Jane wanted her to stay outside in the biting cold and wait for her, Aggie shook her head and went straight home. But as Aggie walked down the steps of the school, she saw Jane plastered against the window making a fist at her. Jane had her ways. Aggie was afraid to go to school the next morning.

She wished her cousin's family would go away.

That night, nestled with Tricia in their tiny bedroom, Aggie kept waking up with the same bad dream that hot smoke scorched her nose and throat raw. When she got up to get a drink of water, she heard her mother crying behind her bedroom door just like she heard her every night since Daddy left. She wished she didn't have to hear Mommy cry. After her trip to the bathroom, Aggie heard the *whoop-whoop* of the sirens race down her street. From her window, she saw fire trucks parked by Jane's house, and their red lights bathed her room in blood. Smoke billowed from next door.

Aggie and her sister and brother ran downstairs with their mother and out the door to watch their cousin's house burn down. Mommy sobbed harder and in front of everybody on the whole block. Aunt Sheila didn't look that sad that her house was on fire. Jane managed a nasty smirk as she huddled under a blanket.

Shivering in her pyjamas, the heat that rushed to her face burned as bright as the flames that leaped from Jane's house to her own rooftop. Now Aggie's house was in flames.

◉ ◉ ◉

After the fire, Aggie and Jane's families went away all right, but the kids were farmed out among other aunts and uncles. Mommy needed a rest and was staying with Aunt Diane in another city. Aggie didn't hear Mommy cry anymore. Only…

It was a bad time to run out of wishes.

"Why can't Trisha or Davy stay here with us?" Aggie helped Jane unfold the hideaway in their Granny Perkin's battered, wine-coloured couch.

"I couldn't put up with anyone that needs a lot of watching," Granny said, her cigarette dangling from her mouth as she managed to simultaneously smoke, talk and drink her coffee. "And I didn't want to take in anyone old enough to be mouthy." Saying this, Granny glared at Jane. "But I only had two choices now, didn't I?"

"I won't be here long," said Jane. "We had house insurance. We're getting a new house built. I'll get my own room, a real one."

"Not soon enough for me," muttered Granny, and she shuffled to the kitchen in her quilted slippers and stained housedress to pour more coffee.

"You'll be here forever," Jane whispered to Aggie behind their granny's back. "'Cause your dad ran off and your mom's gone nuts because you had no insurance on the house. Your family's lost everything. Now, I'm your boss."

Jane smirked. She made a fist and waved it in front of Aggie's face. "I'll take the bed. You sleep on the couch cushions."

That night as Aggie tried to distribute her weight on the two cushions, her bottom sagged between the break until she abandoned the cushions and curled up on the threadbare carpet. The carpet smelled faintly of cat pee, which was still better than the cushions that radiated mildew and cigarette smoke. She wished she was in her own bedroom listening to Trisha's soft breaths. That's when it occurred to Aggie.

She had to find that funny-looking rabbit kid, whom she realized wasn't really a person at all, but something closer to an *it*. Not the *it* that lurks in closets at night, and not the kind of *it* that delivers Easter eggs either. She *needed* more wishes.

It was Granny Perkins who gave her the idea. When Jane was taking a bath and Aggie was blissfully free of her, she found an old record player and records in Granny's closet. Granny had finished her first whiskey of the night and was more agreeable. She showed Aggie how to play records.

When Aggie put the third record on Granny's portable, it played a Bing Crosby song over and over as he crooned about high hopes and ants moving plants. She spun until she was dizzy and stumbled backwards around the living room, until she knocked over a pewter ashtray stand and it smashed down with a wallop. The glass ashtray shattered.

"That's enough nonsense," snapped Granny, who'd finished her third whiskey by this time. She raked the playing arm over the record. Aggie's teeth ached from the needle's scratching sound.

"See what happens when you run around widdershins," said Granny Perkins. "The faeries can see you, and they cause accidents." She handed Aggie a dented metal dustpan and a whisk broom.

"What's widdershins?" asked Aggie.

"Ass backwards," Granny mumbled, rolling her cigarette over her tongue. "Contrary, like asking questions when you should be cleaning up this mess."

As Aggie swept the ashes and glass shards into the pan, she plotted.

On Saturday morning, when Granny was sleeping it off upstairs, Aggie washed up the breakfast dishes. Jane sat in the living room munching on her third piece of cinnamon toast as she watched cartoons. Jane didn't notice her slip out the kitchen door.

On the back stoop, Aggie climbed backward down the porch. She counted the backward steps to the cellar. Pears and plums that hadn't been raked during the fall, squished under her navy sneakers, releasing rotten fruit fumes while she slid across the thick frost. Aggie reached down the furnace chute and pulled out several stray chunks of coal. She held them one by one in front of her face. "Come and get it, whatever you are," she said before stuffing the coal in the deep pockets of her pink jacket.

Cold air nipped at her ears and nose, and Aggie shivered as she kept her backward motion out of the yard, past the blackberry canes, out into the gravel lane. Backward, she walked down the alley marvelling at how different the neighbourhood looked in this widdershins motion. Even the dilapidated garage with its crumbling tarpaper blurred almost unrecognizable against the steel November sky.

Aggie finally reached the huge field at the end of Granny's block with its leafless chestnut trees and tall frozen grass. Behind the trees and camouflaged by the tall grass was the underground fort she and Jane had been digging since they moved in with Granny. *I've been digging*, Aggie thought, rubbing the blisters on her palms. Jane was her foreman.

The fort looked like a giant rabbit hole to Aggie. She circled the hole counter-clockwise three times before she dropped the chunks of coal inside. She propped up the hatch with a tree branch, and marched around the hole in a clockwise motion, hoping the funny-looking kid wouldn't notice how she tied her skipping rope around the branch. Huddled behind the tree trunk, Aggie pulled her knees close to her chest for warmth and tucked her hands inside the dirty sleeves of her hooded jacket. It didn't take long.

When Aggie heard snuffling sounds of something rooting inside the fort, she yanked the skipping rope taut. The branch pulled away and the hatch snapped shut.

"No," screeched the giant rabbit kid.

Aggie rushed to the hatch and jumped on top, securing the only exit.

"Let me out," it screamed. Aggie's nostrils flared at his otherworldly scent. Butterflies battered her stomach as his nails scratched underneath, but she held her ground. "Promise me more wishes," she demanded.

"You only get three," the rabbit kid said. Aggie didn't like the way his voice took on a taunting tone, reminding her of Jane. "What's the matter, didn't the other wishes work out so well?"

"They were okay," said Aggie. "Only three wasn't enough. And you can stay down there till I get more."

"There are rules, you know." This time he sounded less smug. "Wishes in the hands of a child can be a nasty business. A child can be ruthless even by Wonderland's standards."

"Then get yourself out," cried Aggie and she stomped on the hatch, hoping chunks of rock and dirt would rain on the creature.

"Stop that," he bellowed. "You can't stand there forever."

"Are you sure?" asked Aggie. "My granny doesn't care. Jane will miss me when she wants something, but she hates the cold and won't come looking for me until spring."

For a while there was silence. Aggie shivered as the sullen grey clouds thickened the sky. She waited.

"What if…"

"What?" asked Aggie, hoping she didn't sound too curious.

"What if I make a deal with you," the rabbit said. "I'll give you a treasure instead of a wish."

"A treasure?" asked Aggie.

"I can do magic with the coal and turn it into a valuable gem."

Aggie considered his offer. Her teacher had said that coal buried under great pressure for a very long time turned into diamonds. She'd given that endeavour her best effort, filling a pit with pieces of coal, damping down rocks, dirt and leaves over the coal, hopping on the pile every day for months. But when she dug up the coal, it was still black, sooty chunks of rock.

With some trepidation, she stepped off the hatch and watched as he poked up his long ears and then his white head. He crawled out of the hole, clutching his pieces of coal.

"Why do you need coal?"

"We've run out of treasure," the rabbit complained. "And we have to keep paying more to the Jabberwock."

"Why?" asked Aggie.

"We're disorganized, I suppose," he said in disgust. His nose twitched. "We find it hard to stand up to him." He pulled out a long-frozen stalk of grass and strung it around a piece of coal. Then he covered it completely with his white paws.

For a moment, as if the sun had peeked from the clouds and lit up the sky, a queer green light seeped from his fists and spilled out. When he unfolded his hands, a glittering gem the size of Aggie's palm hung from a delicate chain of pale gold. Aggie gasped. The necklace would be worth a fortune, and she could afford to buy Granny Perkin's house and let Trisha and Davy move in, and somehow get rid of Jane and Granny.

With shaky hands, Aggie took the necklace from the rabbit's furry paw and hung it over her neck. Close to her chest, the stone flushed as if a sponge had been dipped in blood until it glowed ruby red.

"Will that do?" the rabbit asked and flashed a quizzical smile revealing his protruding white teeth.

Aggie nodded backing away, mindful of those teeth as she remembered her bitten thumb. As she hurried down the alley back to Granny's house, the heat from the ruby necklace warmed her through her thin jacket. It was time to put Jane in her place. When Aggie opened the kitchen door, the dry heat from Granny's old-fashioned, wood-burning stove blasted her.

"Where've you been?" Jane towered over her, handing her a bucket and a rag mop. "Granny says we have to clean the cellar. I've been dodging her for an hour. You'd better get busy."

Instead of taking the mop, Aggie lifted the necklace, ready to lord it over her cousin. "You'd better be nicer to me and fast, you big jerk."

Jane stared at the necklace with a slightly puzzled expression, and then she reached over and snapped the chain off Aggie's neck. Alarm squeezed Aggie's heart – she'd never considered Jane would steal the ruby from her.

"No," cried Aggie.

"Have you gone crazy?" Jane slapped her face hard. And as she held out the necklace, Aggie saw that it had turned back into a miserable chunk of coal and a shrivelled piece of straw.

Aggie rubbed her burning cheek. She picked up the mop and bucket. That nasty rabbit was going to pay.

The next evening while Jane was hogging the bathroom, and Granny had poured an extra long dreg of Jameson's into her coffee and was snoozing on the couch, Aggie left the house, taking with her a lamp. Widdershins, she walked out the backyard and down the alley. Again as she walked backward, the sky above lost its familiar look as the moon turned a sickly yellow like the mouldering cheddar at the back of Granny's fridge, and the stars burst out of the sky flickering red and blue. She didn't look over her shoulder once, and only the muffled crunch of the frozen grass alerted her she was back in the vacant lot's field.

Aggie tossed five huge pieces of coal, the largest in Granny's cellar, into the hole of her underground fort. This time she didn't close up the hatch. Instead, she set her Aladdin's lamp reading light beside the coal, using its precious batteries to light up the dark, even though she still had fifty pages of her book to read under her bedcovers when Jane's loud snores signalled she'd finally get a little peace.

Instead of hiding behind the chestnut tree, Aggie climbed up the gnarled trunk and boosted herself up onto the branch that hung over the fort. She pulled down her black toque until it almost covered her eyes, and tugged up Granny's enormous black sweater until she was only a smudge of shadow in the tangle of black twigs. She unwound the netting she'd wrapped many times around her waist. She'd found it in the cellar as she'd mopped, along with her departed grandfather's fishing waders, buoys and poles. Aggie waited.

When the rabbit scrabbled below her, Aggie drew herself in, and didn't take a breath. When her lungs were about to burst, the creature finally perched over the open hole of the fort, bent over and reached for the chunks of coal.

"Sucker," shouted Aggie. She dropped the fishnet on him, and then scrambled down the tree trunk.

The rabbit dropped and rolled and only managed to knit himself into a cocoon like a fly in a spider's web.

"Must we do this again?" he asked tersely. "I'm going to be late. I can't be late."

Paying no mind, Aggie stood over him. "You cheated me with that lousy piece of coal."

"Just so you know, coal is valuable where I come from," said the rabbit.

Aggie shrugged. "I've got all night. All day too. Did you say you were late?"

"Fine. I will give you one, but only one more wish." Then the rabbit said, "Call it a test."

Aggie was usually pretty good at tests. She helped untangle his head, arms and shoulders, but kept the net wrapped around his extremely long white feet, staying away from those big teeth.

"So there isn't any misunderstanding," said the rabbit adjusting his waistcoat, "wishing that all wishes come true won't stick. It's another rule."

That was fine. Aggie had only wanted one wish anyway, had thought about it all night and chosen just the right one. "It's a deal," she said.

What is your wish," the rabbit asked.

"I want to be *the boss,"* said Aggie.

"The rabbit gazed thoughtfully at Aggie. "What about your family? Children who are the boss can't stay with their family."

"Now my family is Granny and Jane, and they can lose their heads for all I care," said Aggie.

His watchful grimace broke into a grin. "You've definitely got the makings. You're tougher than the warrior goddess, Badb." He picked up a piece of coal that he'd dropped when the net fell, and snapped another stalk of frozen grass.

Aggie simmered with anger. "I'm not stupid," she snapped.

"No, of course not, that's another point," he said and hung the ruby over Aggie's head. "We've been without a queen for ages. The last one, Maeb, got herself killed by a piece of cheese. I suspect you'll do better."

The trees closed in. The sky shifted, losing its inky blackness as peculiar orange clouds streaked the sky. The rabbit bowed low in front of Aggie.

"Behold, Your Majesty, our crimson ruler, queen of our hearts." Then he cackled. "Oh, the Jabberwock will be sorry now."

Aggie drew herself up and, as if she stood next to a giant Halloween sparkler, the snap and bite of a thousand sparks flowed into her.

No. Jane and all blonde-haired girls would be sorry now.

HER ROYAL COUNSEL

ANDREW ROBERTSON

The sand moves thoughtfully slow and serpentine, drifting along the Mexican desert as I watch the parked, red pickup truck full of bound, writhing bodies roasting in the midday sun. It's like they are trying to squirm out of their sunburnt skin and fly away. I guess I might feel the same if I were them. But I would never be caught in such a predicament. Not after the last time.

I will never be ruled. I watch from the ether, invisible unless I choose to be seen by their sad eyes, and untouchable unless I become material enough for their dirty fingers.

Excitement spirals in my belly as their anxiety colours the atmosphere with panic and vain hope. A fear-born humidity surrounds the captives, their flesh sticking to the truck's searing metal. Thuds and thumps float as their skulls knock the truck bed, skin bruising over human porcelain. I sense confusion; what in their life went wrong to deal them such a rotten hand? They know what they did. They know the cards they played. Each is ready to blame their mother and bake her into a tart to escape this pickle. Pleasure tickles me with what will be wrought before the sun drops from sight. Some acts benefit from the cruelty of full daylight.

Some of the captives inch along like awkward caterpillars, belt buckles catching on aluminum ridges, their owners moaning and stretching in an effort to find their way up and over the truck's side, their hands desperately fluttering behind them, seeking a knot to loosen or a sharp edge to cut the ties, but to what end? Not one will become a butterfly and flutter away. Already their mouths dry and their lips have begun to crack and bleed.

Their keeper, a young drug runner named Tony, hits them with a long stick ending in a small hook as he waits for his masters' instructions. He desperately craves his victims' silence so he doesn't need to think of them as human. His hands tremble, ever uncertain of how far he must go to satisfy his masters. I have been grooming him as he fitfully sleeps, as he prays, even as he fucks, to become harder and crueler. He can beat a man until his face is pulp, but he hasn't been able to kill. His resistance has been a delicious and bitter menace to me. Tony wasn't born a killer. I run where he only walks. There was one accident, the young blonde girl who was found in a crumpled heap by a turnpike after he administered an overdose. If she hadn't been blonde, white, pregnant and American, no one would have bothered looking into what happened to her, and Tony wouldn't have found out she was fourteen. He has convinced himself no one knows his role in her demise, or ever will. This is my insurance that will seal this deal. Once he spills all this blood, my power will surge. This foreplay would leave many rubbed raw but I will overcome his morals and this thing called conscience that humans value.

He beats his flock into silence. His hooked stick allows easy removal and control of select hogs he drags from his cargos, usually pulling them onto the ground where someone else delivers the killing blow.

He checks his phone repeatedly, worrying that there may not be any service, but that's what the satellite phone is for. This isn't his first rodeo, but it's the first time he has been unable to hand off the slaughter to another. Either way, he always panics right before the call comes. That is when his lips form secret prayers to the Mexican folk deity Santa Muerte, Our Lady of Holy Death. As luck would have it, she seems to have started answering his prayers and taken quite a personal interest.

Almost destitute after a week of cocaine-fueled gambling, Tony dreamed of Santa Muerte, awaking to find a bag of money had appeared on her altar. He has been answering her call ever since. Last night, in what was akin to a nightmare, she told him that each and every captive must die or she may abandon him for someone more willing to exact justice in her name. Waking up confused and fevered, he dressed in dark clothes and reluctantly headed out the door.

He has been one of my favourite playthings to date, given his virginal struggle against my desires, and constant attempts to delay the inevitable. Tony's not bad looking – handsome with youthful arrogance, and will look even better with blood painting a crimson mask on his face in tribute to his goddess. I know he is hoping that Jose will meet him here. Jose will not. I've seen to that.

For years I have been dancing on Santa Muerte's altars, in Tony's room and those of many others, taking every sacrifice offered in her name, and answering the prayers or those who do right by me. Some days, I bathe in the plasma of my flock's acrimonious existence, orgasmic from the hurt spilled in alleys, basements and even bedrooms. Some consider it death worship, some think Santa Muerte a demon. I don't give a fig. My only request is blind faith to do as they are told in dreams and by the voice that whispers a quick verse in their ear. I've even fashioned a gown for those who I reveal myself to, prostrate before the altar. With tear-stained faces in the dirt, they glimpse a red gown covered in sacred hearts trailing past, yet familiar from dreams; an illusion to placate them. When in Rome, I say. Their blood, tears and subjugation sustain me.

Since my escape, I have silently entered the chambers, beds and minds of monarchs, dictators and moneyed men to bring my unifying vengeance to this plane. Many know me only as a thought, an urge, or a persuasion. In their hazy half-slumber I am the errant finger tickling their fancy with buried shames. Exposure is all that is needed to force a conscience into the unspeakable, whether the threat is real or not.

Tony fiddles with the phone again, like a millennial waiting for a lover's text! I have already determined how this game will end, and how the next begins. I whisper a few phrases into the heat and he finds himself reaching under the passenger seat, wrapping his hand around the grip of a long, sharp machete designed for hacking through more than a few creosote bushes. I imagine the ringing of metal against bone and a shiver runs down my spine, weakening my legs. No man could ever give me this pleasure, but a few women have come close. It's always surprising to see how much pain a woman can inflict, and how much more pain than a man she can endure.

Throughout the ages, very little effort has been required with men who believed themselves free. I have whispered wretched and glorious plans to increase their desire for control, revenge, and need to conquer land and people. They are so megalomaniacal, sure every murderous thought, every rapacious act, every final blow has been wrought of their own free will – the grandest illusion of them all.

I have no illusions. I know the purity of the desires that fuel my mind, and the crisp, clean edges of the sentences I hand out. Time does not wait for those who would rule to ask for permission. If you become a sheep, you are eaten by wolves. I prefer to be the She-Wolf, with blood staining my lips and torn flesh hanging from my teeth. No one hunts the better hunter.

The slightest scent of fear or weakness makes these ambitious autocrats hard. I was there in the desert to preside over the decapitation of journalists in the Middle East. I gave a final kiss to Marie Antoinette as she knelt in front of the mass of orgiastic French vermin, and I gyrated with their rage and need for death. Henry the VIII heard my voice ring true over his conscience. I watched from shadows as the axe was so cruelly and deliciously introduced to Lady Margaret de la Pole, over and over. Throughout millennia, humanity's desperate race for power and immortality has grown unfettered, some people becoming legends while others are ground down like worn out, wooden teeth. Either outcome feeds my appetite.

I scan the horizon to be sure we won't be interrupted. Tony feels the blade's weight and smells his prisoners' rising stench. Some may already be dead. Each of us must lay claim to our destiny. Mine is to rule and to influence. I judge and sentence as is my right. At one point, in another place and another time, my efforts were thwarted by lesser creatures that deemed me a foul monarch and wouldn't play by my rules, but not now. Now I am something else entirely. I am something better. Leaving that place has given me new strength and abilities. Tony's destiny is to ensure my greatness.

Grey, wind-worn mountains rise in the distance. Before them, like a tatty rug, are miles of coarse shrubs and grasses that hiss as they rub together. It sounds like the shuffling of a deck and I am near ready to draw my hand.

A hacking cough interrupts my reverie. One of the captives has chewed through his cloth gag and gasps out a prayer while infuriatingly begging for mercy.

"Who are you?" the prisoner rasps. That question often asked by another, in a faraway place, brings me a sense of unease that I don't care for one mote. Of course, he is speaking to Tony – no one knows I am here. Not even Tony. He thinks Santa Muerte exists only in dreams and perched on her altar. He thinks that all the violent deeds he does are his idea. At night I breathe in the elegance and despair of his regret from where I wait for the final offering.

A spasm cramps Tony's torso. His doubt clouds my vision. It is time to steel his resolve.

Show him the blade, I whisper into the space between us.

Tony strides forward, the sand becoming a tiny cloud around his stinking boots. After this job, he can afford new boots, truck or an apartment even...maybe something big enough to house an altar to his Lady who has brought him such filthy lucre. Even as he walks with purpose and masculine endeavour, I feel his heart shrinking at the task ahead and smile. There is always a bit more left to give, despite a litany of profane acts.

I reach deep into the mind of this creature crying in near silence in the truck bed.

Ask Tony about the girl.

"Who is the blonde girl?" He pitifully whispers. "Why did you do it?" He hisses more words out, confused and choking in the heat.

Tony stands frozen and fully erect, feeling the blood drain from his extremities, his face blooming hot with guilt. Then the rage rises. He never meant to hurt her. He didn't know she was just a girl. No – she was a slut!

The captive's eyes plead as Tony's forces open his mouth, holding his dry tongue between index and thumb. Pleasure surges through me, unlike any I've felt before, as the final hand is revealed with the help of my little blonde queen, my earthly dead Alice.

He slowly works the machete tip into the poor bastard's mouth and then there is a sound like a mug breaking. A section of tongue hits the sand and flops back and forth like a dying trout. A clattering of teeth follow, pinging off the truck's metal before skittering away, lost in the wasteland. Gasps and moans ripple the air. Tony looks at the ground and his work. The sand thoroughly covers the tongue, leaving it speechless.

You aren't done yet, I exhale, feeling a chill of orgasmic anticipation between my legs.

Take your prize. Take your trophy. It is yours.

He grabs the man by his hair. Muscles spasm as the man chokes on blood rushing from where his tongue once slept, and a stream of hot shit is released into cheap denim. I hate bad manners.

Tony lifts the machete high, shining against the late afternoon sun.

I close my eyes, savouring this agony cooking in the heat, before opening them wide and delivering my verdict.

Off with his head!

DRESSED
IN WHITE PAPER

KATE HEARTFIELD

Theophilus Tench wrinkles his nose. With the toe of his polished shoe, he nudges the Goat's chamberpot under the T-shaped pile of luggage that Tench has arranged into a makeshift screen between them.

The Goat's battered steamer trunk on its edge forms a trunk of a tree, and the leaves, so to speak, are made by the Goat's carpetbag drooping on top. Or rather, it would be a carpetbag, if it were made of carpet. This is a custard-skin bag. Utterly impractical. It does the job of shielding the chamber pot from view of the six passengers in the compartment, although it does nothing to improve the smell.

The call of Tench's nature long ago reached a state of uncomfortable complacency, a numb memory of urgency radiating from his thighs on the upholstered bench.

Alas, this is an old-fashioned train compartment, its two facing benches in knee-banging proximity. Some would consider the window an outlet for nature's business, but Tench is not among them.

Tench has heard, in his life before the train, of new railway carriages with corridors down the middle, and dining-cars, and even lavatories! If he could walk, his thighs might zingle to life, but then, so might his bladder, so perhaps everything is for the best. Stillness is also best for preventing rumpling and tearing of the seat of his paper pants. He has been

on this train for – how long? He can't quite remember boarding.

Tench is not an animal. He is a gentleman, a gentleman
dressed in white paper. And he is going to the Fourth Row,
where he belongs.

"A good day for travelling," the Goat bleats.

Tench realizes he has been frowning. He ought to be
cheerful; he ought to be grateful.

"Nothing better than a journey on a day like today," Tench
supplies, and the passengers rush to agree.

"Nothing like travel to broaden the mind!"

That from a Beetle, just beyond the Goat. The Beetle
wasn't there a moment before, but then, people come and go
on the train. Tench doesn't ask questions. It isn't done.

The valise resting on his lap opens its mouth and yawns.
A vulgar habit. Tench pushes the lid back down and fastens
it. He carefully recrosses his legs, and that's when he sees the
mark.

Something – *something* – from the Goat's chamber pot. An
umber smudge on the crisp cuff of Tench's trouser leg.

It's work, wearing whiteness. His father taught him to take
pride in that work. Whiteness is so fragile, tears so easily. It
must be patched up, papered over, smoothed taut, many
times each day. This is how a gentleman shows his loyalty to
the White King.

Paper means work. Whiter than linen, humbler than silk.
Paper shows every stain and tear; paper, well maintained,
shows absolute devotion. Paper takes a crease like a knife.
Outer purity, inner purity, and three times six is nine. That was
always Father Tench's motto.

He looks up, and feels the blood rush to his ears. Opposite
him is a child, with ribbons in its hair. She's arguing with the

guard, though, and isn't looking at Tench's trouser leg. The train has paused, as it does, from time to time, and people appear and disappear. Not Tench, though. Never Tench. He is still waiting for his stop to come.

The guard is chastising the girl for travelling in the wrong direction. She must be a Red, then. The wrong sort altogether. Tench certainly doesn't want to fraternize with Reds. The people listening to his thoughts must know that. There are people listening, of course, but it's impossible to say who. Perhaps that Gnat who was flitting about earlier. Tench is happy to be listened in on. The White King must know what is happening in his domain. Tench has nothing to hide.

"So young a child," said Tench, recrossing his legs casually, "ought to know which way she is going, even if she doesn't know her own name!"

The Goat widens his eyes, and bleats wildly, "She ought to know her own name, even if she doesn't know her own alphabet!"

Everyone choruses in, and the child's eyebrows do a funny dance. It looks like it might cry. Perhaps it truly didn't understand about the train's destination. Very likely it was not raised properly. Tench has nothing against Reds. They are wrong, that's all, waiting for their King to wake instead of accepting that life is much better when the White King rules alone. Tench has nothing against this child.

Tench leans forward, close enough, he hopes, that no one will overhear.

"Never mind what they all say, my dear, but take a return-ticket every time the train stops."

"Indeed I shan't!" shouts the impertinent creature. "I don't belong to this railway journey at all."

The passengers all gasp. Everyone must be where they belong. If you're not where you belong, someone else soon will be, Father Tench used to say.

Father Tench was killed by a Red Knight because Father Tench was in the place where he shouldn't have been. It was a mistake. He was trying to make it to Fifth Row. Queen's orders. Then the Knight went loopedy-lop – they're so hard to predict, Knights, unless you're a mathematician, which Father Tench was assuredly not.

Flowers in the surrounding fields found bits of paper, floating on the air, for weeks afterward.

The train's rumble becomes a whirr, a loudness without noise, and now the bench beneath Tench's rear seems more comfortable. It is not a bench at all, but a kind of chair, and on his right is an armrest, and a new person. A woman with a mass of dark hair, reading a book.

Beyond her a small oval window does not open, and outside the window, Tench sees clouds.

The tops of clouds.

He would lose his breakfast, if his breakfast were still with him. Breakfast was so long ago he hardly remembers it. The journey to the Fourth Row is very long.

This is a wonder for which he was not prepared.

He stands, as best he can in a space cramped by the back of a row of seats in front, and peers out. He sees a silver wing, unmoving, and sky beneath it. Down far below, in a smudge of green and brown, he thinks he sees a world.

He sits back down, hard, and bites his tongue. The white paper cocked hat tumbles off his head onto the valise in his lap.

"Now where did you come from?" says the woman.

Tench rolls his wounded tongue in his mouth, swallows blood. What an impertinent question, when he is clearly a pawn, and not capable of movement in any direction but one. He looks to his left, where a boy-child sits, staring at something shiny in its hands, images moving brightly on its surface. Beyond the boy, another woman, her eyes closed as she leans against the curved wall of the compartment, or belly, or whatever has swallowed him. And another oval window, looking out onto sky.

This is not a train.

People say the Red King flew on a bird to his forest home across the sundering sea, when he abandoned the world. And there he sleeps, still, oblivious.

Tench is not oblivious. Tench can hardly breathe.

"Are you in the right seat?" says the woman. "You get lost on your way back from the bathroom?"

He frowns, confused. He picks up his hat, and regards it. "I'm trying to get to Fourth Row."

"That's up there a ways." Her face clears, then wrinkles again. "Have you got a first-class ticket?"

Alas, he does not. He clicks the fasteners on the valise in his lap and opens it. Inside, 700 sheets of pure white paper. He pinches the corner of the top one, slides it off the pile and hands it to her. "I have a ticket but it is second class. I can't be expected to have first class, not yet."

Second class is undeniably a gentleman's class, his mother said. First class is for gentlemen who have proven their purity. Once he gets to Fourth Row, then everything will be cocktails and cravats. He closes his valise with a righteous click. Then he jams his paper hat down, hard, on his head.

"No, of course not," says the woman slowly, glancing up at the aisle between the seats. Another woman is walking toward them, her hand on the seat-back in front.

"Can I help?" she says.

"Oh, it's nothing too serious," says the woman in the seat. "This man is lost, I think. He wasn't here before."

Tench was here, of course he was here. The trouble is that *here* was not here.

"Not here?"

"I think I would have remembered a man in a paper suit."

The standing woman nods, frowns. "I think I would too. Show me your boarding pass, please, sir."

Tench picks up the ticket from where the other woman let it drop on the armrest and hands it to the standing woman. His papers are in order. He has nothing to hide.

He is in the air. Where is the beast flying to? That's the question, surely. Is it flying to the stars?

Her face clouds. "This is a blank sheet of paper." She hands it back to him, accusingly.

Tench stretches his cheeks into a smile. It's best to remain happy. Gentlemen adjust to their circumstances and do not complain about their lot. "Nothing like travel to broaden the mind!" he shouts, perhaps, a little too loud, to be heard over the roar of the beast.

There are no smiles on any of these people's faces. It is a strangely homogenous assembly, with no Animals in it at all. He folds his ticket and puts it into his origami breast pocket.

"Please keep your voice down," says the standing woman. "What is your name, sir?"

That's an easy question. He ought to know the answer to that. "Pawns have no use for names on the board," he recites. "Names can be changed as often as guards. I ought to know that I am a gentleman, even if I don't know my own name. I ought to know that the White King is infallible, even if I don't know that I am a gentleman."

Little Theophilus Tench, as only his family called him, was a well-behaved student. He can barely remember the days when the Red King was still awake, still on the board. In those days, the Red King and the White fought, and there were not so many rules. It must have been terrifying.

The standing woman reaches over him, pushes something. Then someone has him by the hands and ties something cold and stiff around his wrists. He opens his mouth to cry out, and then he remembers that he is a gentleman, that the rules are there to protect him.

Then a man dressed in rough blues and blacks, like a bruise all over, is lifting him by his tied wrists and Tench is standing in the cramped cabin, his valise bumping down to the floor.

As he stumbles down the aisle, the man's hand on his back, his suit gashes in three places. A rip across his back, a tear on his sleeve, and worst of all, most ungentlemanly of all, a split in the seat. His whiteness is meant to protect him, to signal his worth to the world, but it's falling off him here. Is he not good enough for Fourth Row? Is this where failed pawns go, off the board, into the abyss? What could he have done to deserve that punishment? Tench is trying to not think disloyal thoughts, he truly is, but a man is nothing without his papers, and his papers are in the valise.

The man straps him down on a little seat all his own in a quieter part of the flying beast. Someone took the valise, but Tench can't see where. The man stands, watching him, with something small and black and sickening in his hand. Tench says nothing. His thoughts are so loud that for a moment he thinks he has spoken them, so he hushes them as best he can. He smiles, very certain that all of this is for his own good.

"You won't be smiling when we get to La Guardia," says the man, scowling.

Everyone talks such nonsense here.

After a while the beast moves uncertainly, and so does Tench's stomach. There's a jolt and then the beast is speeding so horribly fast that Tench's body strains against the strap.

But they do not die. The man grabs him, tearing his whiteness, marching him toward a bright door in the beast, an opening into some other world.

It comes to him then. Theophilus Tench understands at last.

This is the way to Fourth Row. This is the test each pawn must pass, to show the requisite courage to be rooked or beknighted. A test to show one is ready to die for the White King, for purity and order.

Tench smiles with teeth, as he walks down a staircase into bright sunshine, on some part of the board he has never seen: broad, empty, paved silvery like a giant's courtyard, filled with great beasts moving before great fortress walls.

"A remarkable day for travelling!" he shouts. "A wonderful day to die!"

People are shouting on the ground, surrounding the staircase, pointing shining black sticks at him, and he stumbles forward, smiling desperately, blinking back tears. At last he is doing what his father did, before his father died.

Bits of white paper, floating in the air.

He tries, he tries, to keep his thoughts worthy, or at least to keep them quiet. To not question why the White King mistrusts his pawns so. To not wonder whether he, Theophilus Tench, might want to do something other than sit, dressed in white paper, in hopes of a reward of coffee and crossword puzzles and not being slaughtered.

He tries, but he fails.

Something hard knocks him on the head from behind. The man behind him lets go his grasp, and shouts, and the valise is fluttering in the air. Six hundred and ninety-nine sheets of pure white paper fly out of it, folding themselves into dart-like shapes like flying beasts. They fill the sky, crowding around Tench and his captor, and something bangs, three times, loudly.

Whiteness flutters angrily in the air, confounding the man's attempts to take Tench again.

Yes, Tench thinks, and nearly weeps with relief. I am angry! Attack!

The valise bangs shut and shoves its handle into Tench's bound hands like an affectionate puppy. Tench can barely see with all the paper whirring around but his fingers curl around the handle and then the valise is opening again, flapping its sides, rising into the sky and carrying Tench with it.

Suddenly a red pain soaks his white trouser leg. He glances down, but dare not let go of the valise handle. Underneath him beasts of all sizes and shapes rumble, and rise into the sky, but the valise flies quickly over dark water. *This must be what it is like to travel as a queen travels*, Tench thinks, loudly, as they skim the tops of trees.

The valise catches in a tree branch and Tench is knocked tumbling down to the ground. The noise of the bellicose beasts of Fourth Row is subtler now, distant. Still, he dare not stop.

He looks up gratefully at the valise, which has settled happily into the crook of the tree, and seems to want no more to do with him.

The trees shade him as he walks, his hands still bound, his leg smarting but not, it seems, deeply wounded. He relieves his poor bladder at last and starts to feel hungry again. His hat is still on his head, by some miracle. Everything is quiet here, and Tench is quite alone with his thoughts. He thinks things he never dared think before. He is off the board, without his papers, with no way to patch his suit. A pawn no longer. His pants are stained half red and his shirt is torn half off. A gentleman dressed in white paper, he was, this morning. Now he is – something underneath. Something motley, ragged, alone, afraid, ready.

Before long, he comes to the pebbled shoreline of a great dark ocean. Boats, small and large, float on it as far as the horizon. The water laps his toes.

The sundering sea. Somewhere, beyond this, the Red King lies sleeping. Might it be possible to wake him, and speak to him?

Tench yanks the white hat off his head and looks at it. It is a good hat: confidently cocked and neatly folded, its seams sure, made of many layers of white paper, its borders rolled thick. Quite practical.

He drops it, upside down, on the water. As it floats, it grows, until it is big enough for Tench to step into. It rocks a little as Tench settles into it, kneeling.

He has no oar so he slides his ticket out of his breast pocket, unfolds it, and holds it up with both hands for a sail. He lets the wind take him out to sea. Tench sails close enough to Fourth Row to see its fortress but it does not see him. He sails in his paper boat, in search of the Red King, and the chance to ask some questions.

THE KING IN RED
AN ABOMINATION IN
FOUR ANGLO-SAXON ATTITUDES

J.Y.T. KENNEDY

Attitude One: Anticipation

On a desolate street, the dingy neon
sketched a lady lewd with lighted tits
rudely blinking. A blended staleness
of beer and smoke, of smut and rot,
greeted me at the door. The greying proprietor
let me talk as he smeared the tables
with an unrinsed rag. He raised a sneer.
"No warrant I guess? You're wasting time,
but I've nothing to hide, so have your way.
Look all you please. I'd like to know
who stole the tarts." I turned to my search:
dressing rooms and dreary nooks,
the tawdry stage and narrow stairs
that led below. I'd laughed before
at my sister's belief in superstitious tales
of girls who disappeared down those steps
not to be seen or numbered again
amongst living or dead. A dampness rose
from the windless dark: a winding caress,
the last weak breath of a broken soul.

My deception felt thin: no detective in truth,
only a woman seeking a sister and peace.
I had made ready for mundane ugliness:
for a grimy passage and grisly secrets
not for this naked feeling, this nauseous sense
of standing poised, one step from falling.
My heart staggered with a hopeless lust
to cast my soul into the sensate void.
Black stars rose at the stairwell's foot
and a sudden wind whipped through my hair.
One wanton step, and the world was gone.

Attitude Two: Incomprehension

I gasped and staggered in the gaping air.
A fetid field gave my feet purchase,
crusted with dank and crippled weeds,
overlooking a lightless, brooding lake.
A towering barrow was built on the shore
on which a lordly figure was laid in state,
draped in royal robes as red as blood.
Another man stood, crowned and starkly pale,
his hair a halo of high-flown clouds
that dog the moon, his clothes milk-white,
near to my side. He said, with a smile
more fey than kind: "That is the King in Red.
He buries himself in heedless slumber
dreaming of your life to draw his mind
from sorrow's grip. He sacrificed all
the ones he loved, and lost just the same.
I was his doom. I took daughters, sons
horses, halls, even his haughty queen:
laid waste his world. No wonder I became
a hated thing that haunts his dreams."
He might have spoken of sports or games,
so casually he talked, so calmly he smiled,
but it hurt me to think of hatred and love.
I said, "I am seeking my sister and others
who came here as I did." He cocked his head.
"I told you: your talk, in turn my answers,
even the airy stars are all stuff of his dream.
There were no women. He'll wake and then,
you'll cease to exist." I saw no truth

in his murderous logic: "I live and am more
than a fancied shadow: I feel my reality."
"You remain a part, whether real or not,
of the king's dream. You cannot deny
only the dreamer is real in the realm of sleep.
That makes a syllogism, only solved one way."
I saw neither solution nor sense in his words
and replied, "I will rouse him and reveal the truth."
His locks shivered. "A shame," he said.

Attitude Three: Bravado

Down I went through that dismal place
treading on rocks and treacherous thorns
to the barrow that shaded the bitter lake.
As I climbed aloft, the altitude swayed
and space distended in dizzy perspective.
The earth receded; the edifice stretched.
There lay the king all lost and lorn,
his face a study in stricken lines
no gentle sleep could slur to peace.
I put out my hand, then halted in pity
thinking that, waking, he would be sure
to relive once more the wretched despair
that carved his face in furrows so cruel.
Yet he lay so still that I started to think
his features formed: a fanciful design
as if he wore a mask or was made of wood.
"Where are the women?" I wondered aloud.
"Just disappeared? Is my doom like theirs?
A forgotten woman: who wonders about
one more marked down missing or murdered?
Is the price for letting my precious sister
succumb to hardship, for hating her need,
for saying I hated her, the same dark fate?
Did I learn too late that I loved her?"
I closed my eyes and clutched his arm
but hesitated to speak. A hellish fear
coursed through me of things unknown,
and my resolve faltered. Then rage in turn
drove back my fear. I faced my weakness.
I meant to act and make an end.

I wanted my life, my world, my sister.
I shook him, shouted, then taken by a shift,
queer and quiet, a quickening and death,
I woke but not to greet the world of bustling
joy and sorrow that once seemed so real.

Attitude Four: Despair

I lay on my back, and back to me came
my true memories marching in step:
the dear, dead demons of my distant past,
the old happiness all hewn to shreds,
the land and loved ones lost forever.
I screamed aloud. I scratched wildly
at my loathsome face, too late knowing how
to wit the words of the White King.
My dreamworld was a wish and no more
to live another life, love other kin.
Now they were nothing, nobody, nowhere.
There were no women, not even the one
I had dreamed of being; no dreadful stairs
no sister unburied or hope of salvation
nor the scant empathy of an enemy lingering
to meditate on the pain of the man he abased.
I was the most miserable of mortal men
recalled unready to regrets and the cruel
curse of knowing I was the King in Red.

NO REALITY BUT WHAT WE MAKE

Elizabeth Hosang

The little blonde girl ran across the patchwork lawn scrolling beneath her. The children's laughter reached me from the flowerbed's far side. I drifted to where my sister Blanche, the White Queen, sat cradling her daughter Lily, soothing her tears. The next moment a piercing light filled my vision and extreme weight pulled me to my knees. Rough hands grabbed me, dragging me forward. A male voice shouted, "That's seven," as the hands released me. I landed on my face.

"Scarlett!" Gentle arms wrapped around my shoulders and helped me up. Roland, the Red King and my husband, crouched next to me. Metal bars separated us from the rest of a harshly lit large room. A black metal chamber stood to one side, surrounding a pale blue glow. As I watched, a figure fell through the light and collapsed to the floor. It was my castle, Beatrice. She tried to rise, but men in black uniforms raced forward and dragged her through our cage's entrance. Arthur and Abby, the Red Knights, stood inside the door, blocking the men from entering. They dropped Beatrice at Arthur's feet and retreated. Arthur helped her up.

I looked around. Across the room, a man in a grey suit frowned at white-coated men crowded around several glowing boards on a wooden table, jabbering to each other. The little blonde girl lay on a bed, wires leading from her forehead to a little black box.

The blue light grew brighter and we watched, helpless, as Timothy, the Red King's bishop, fell through the light. When the men grabbed at him, he screamed and struggled. One of them hit him with a black stick and he sagged to the ground. As the men dragged him to the cage I stepped in front of Roland. He was the King, but I was the Red Queen, and it was the job of the entire Red Court to protect him.

Time dragged on, as one by one the rest of the Red Court joined us, then the White Court. We huddled together, the pawns and the kings in the center, the rest of us surrounding them.

At some point a door across the room flew open, and a large man stormed in, followed by several other men.

"Anders! What the hell is this?"

One of the white coats rushed forward. "Mr. Partridge, sir. We weren't expecting you so soon."

"Monroe called me. What the hell is this?" Partridge stomped to the cage and glared through the bars at us. "How much LSD did you feed the kid?"

"The usual dosage. It's the first time we've used Alice. Her parents only just heard about our fake drug trial to prevent nightmares. She's eight years old, the optimal age for dreaming of distinct beings without being limited to what she perceives as the real world.".

"Why are there so many of them?"

"We think they're chess pieces." Anders stepped next to the larger man. "See? They have either white hair or red, and their clothing looks like the costumes on the set in the playroom."

"Chess pieces! What the hell good are human chess pieces?"

The smaller man flinched. "Well, sir, this is huge progress! It proves our working hypothesis that we create alternate realities while dreaming, and that we can reach into those realities."

"I don't care about alternate realities! I care about this one. When my agency agreed to fund your research, Doctor, you promised we'd be able to extract information from high-value targets while they slept. What good is pulling imaginary people out of children's dreams?"

"Well, to be fair, when we approached you, we believed there was only one dream reality, the Dreamscape, if you will. We had intended to create a portal that allowed someone to seek a particular dreamer. Only, after several tests we realized that each dreamer creates their own Dreamscape, rather than connecting to an existing alternate reality. Which also makes it impossible to enter. We can only get things out."

"How can you be sure? You've been experimenting on children!"

"Because children create a more coherent Dreamscape. Adult Dreamscapes are muddled, and trying to grab one concept drags along too much clutter. But children of Alice's age group have less murky dreams, easier to bring into focus. We have actually extracted several animals – cats, a rabbit, and even a cartoon mouse."

Partridge's face purpled, and Anders shrank before his gaze. "You've used my money to pull bunny rabbits out of thin air?"

"But, but, Mr. Partridge look! This time we've pulled out sentient beings!" He turned, pointing to Arthur.

"You there." Anders said. "What is your name?"

"Arthur, Knight Champion of the Red Queen."

"There, you see, they can talk!" he said, as if that made it all better.

Partridge stepped closer to the bars and bent down, staring at Arthur's chest. "What is that hanging around his neck? A ruby? It's huge!" He looked over the rest of us, noticing the heart stones we wore. "And the white ones are wearing diamonds. Anders, is it possible the kid dreamed up real jewellery?"

"Well, I suppose it's possible. That rabbit was real enough. We dissected it and found real organs."

Partridge snapped his fingers, and one of the soldiers stepped forward. "Liquidate them, dispose of the bodies, but bring me the jewels. Maybe we can save something from this fiasco."

"No!" Several voices cried out. Anger cut through my fear. A warm pulse came from my heart stone. Suddenly the cold lights dimmed, and the room's edges softened. The weight that had been pulling me to the ground since I arrived disappeared. I was the Red Queen, and nothing would stand in my way.

Arthur, Abby, the red knights, and the white knights Melinda and Mark disappeared from where they stood, reappearing on the other side of the bars. The knights attacked the soldiers, grabbing their weapons, and striking them down. The soldiers shot at the knights, but the bullets passed through them.

In the cage, the two castles Beatrice and Peter shrank, passed between the bars, and grew, snatching weapons from the closest men. I followed their lead, resizing myself next to a man in a grey suit. A knife appeared in my hand and I drove it into his neck, standing back as hot blood spurted from the wound.

More gunshots sounded until, "Cease fire!" Partridge yelled, but he was nothing to us. It was one screaming little white coat who was our downfall. Backed into a desk by the red castle, he pulled out a black object and pointed it at her. A small explosion, followed by a buzzing noise, and my brave castle collapsed.

I rushed to her aid, but I was not the only one who noticed her fall. "Stun guns! Everyone!" The last thing I saw was Anders pointing a similar object at me. Incredible pain seared me, and then nothing.

I awoke in a smaller cell. Female members of both courts lay on the floor next to me. We were still in the same room, but there were now several cages, holding the adult members of the royal court. The pawns, our children, were nowhere in sight.

The door burst open and Partridge stomped into the room. Behind him came several soldiers, dragging Roland between them. My husband's head hung, his body limp. Horrified, I watched as they tossed him into the cage that held Arthur and the other men.

Partridge walked to my cage, glaring at us. "Which one of you is the Red Queen?"

I stood, shrugging off Blanche's attempt to hold me back. "What have you done to my husband?"

"My people ran tests. Without those jewels you are just regular people. Mortal people, who feel pain. Anders thinks you can project the Dreamscape onto reality with those stones, making it possible for you to change size, dodge bullets, and float above the ground. Unfortunately, they don't work for us. So, we're going to make a little deal. You're going to perform certain tasks for me."

"Why should we?"

He smiled then, and for the first time I was truly afraid. "I suggest you take a closer look at your king. My specialists spent several hours with him, trying to coerce his cooperation. The king is the least powerful piece on the chessboard, so we weren't worried about damaging him. But there are fifteen of you, and I'm not above doing it again."

"Fifteen?" I asked, as a cold hand wrapped around my heart.

"That's the other incentive. You may notice, Queenie, that your children aren't here. You will do what I tell you, or you'll never see them again."

◎ ◎ ◎

Arthur, Beatrice and I drifted down the semi-lit hallway to the door at the end of the hall. I turned to Beatrice, pointing to my eyes. Reaching into her jacket pocket, she pulled out a sleeping dormouse, curled into a ball. Holding it to her ear, she listened, the mouse's voice a barely audible murmur. After a moment, she put the mouse back in her pocket and gave me a thumb's up. In the year we had been serving Partridge we had all developed new skills. Beatrice could impose her Dreamscape onto mice, creating a hive mind and controlling them through a single member. She could send them ahead to scout locations, and create entrances to sealed buildings, receiving their reports through her proxy.

I nodded to Arthur. Now that he had delivered us safely, he turned back. The next step was beyond his abilities, so he had his own mission.

Closing my eyes, I pictured myself shrinking. My head spun with the sensation. When I opened my eyes, we were so small that we would have slipped between the fibres of the welcome mat. While the door likely had no space, in the Dreamscape we floated through the two centimetre gap above the tile floor. Once inside, I concentrated on expanding.

Full sized, I followed my castle through the apartment. The bedroom door gaped open. Inside, the sleepers' deep even breaths were broken only by the occasional snore. A framed image hung on the wall to my left. According to the dormice scouts, the safe lay behind it. Moonlight peeked around the edges of the venetian blinds hanging on the bedroom's French doors. I willed them away, and the full moon's silvery light revealed a woman sleeping with arms akimbo.

I tapped Beatrice on the shoulder, pointed to the sleeper, to her, and then to my eyes. Beatrice nodded – she would keep an eye on the woman in case she woke.

I made my way around the bed to the oil painting and gently pulled. The painting swung aside, revealing a wall safe with a keypad lock. Placing my hand over the keys, I willed the lock to undo itself. A beep sounded and the door popped open. Files and jewellery boxes filled the safe. On top of a stack of papers lay a black plastic case with a short USB cord. This was our target, the hard drive, right where Beatrice's scouts said it would be. Placing it in my pocket, I gestured to Beatrice, and we headed out. At the bedroom door, I looked back. The Dreamscape had left the room with us. The portrait was once again flush with the wall, and the blinds covered the windows.

Outside the building, we found Arthur waiting. "Any problems?" I asked.

"None. Our contact came through." Arthur patted his heart stone. My knight wrapped his arms around our waists, and in a blink the suburban landscape disappeared, to be replaced by the asphalt parking lot outside the Agency's headquarters. A circle of soldiers surrounded us, their electric stun weapons humming in case we gave them any trouble.

"Stand down," said Monroe, second in command of the Agency men.

I touched my large ruby pendant and closed my eyes. Gravity reasserted itself, weighting me down.

"You've reached the outside limit of your mission window. Again," Monroe accused, his left arm held so I could see his watch.

"We got it." I removed the hard drive from my pocket. "We went to her lab first, but apparently she doesn't trust the other researchers at the university. She had the drive with her weapons research in her home safe."

"You've been taking longer with every mission," Monroe snapped. "You should be getting faster, not slower."

"The missions have been more complex. They take longer," I replied.

"They are meticulously planned. Follow my instructions to the letter and you should be back on time. If I find out you've been sightseeing," he trailed off.

You'll know soon enough, I thought.

"You will perform to my satisfaction, or face the consequences." He held a pawn pinched between his thumb and forefinger. "Or do I need to remind you what you risk?"

Out of the corner of my eye I saw Arthur take a step in my direction. I held up my hand. We couldn't afford to start a fight, not now. "No, sir."

"Good." He snapped his fingers, and a nervous-looking white coat stepped forward, opening a black case. Reluctantly, I placed my ruby pendant in the case. It always hurt a little as it left my chest. The heart stones were the concentrated essence of the reality from which we came, but we had no choice in surrendering them. Not yet, anyway.

Arthur and Beatrice yielded their stones. As the locks clicked, the soldiers put away their stun weapons and drew handguns. Monroe didn't like us in the parking lot, but the facility had been installed with safety measures long before we existed. The electronic shield kept the knights from teleporting into or out of the building.

The soldiers escorted us back to our prison and locked us in. Over the past year our obedience had earned us living quarters instead of cells, with bedrooms off a large central area furnished with sofas and tables. Blanche and her bishops Camilla and Timothy were awake, seated around a low table. Timothy stood as we entered. "Were you successful?"

"We were," I replied. Still adjusting to gravity and the menial task of walking, I tripped over my own feet. Timothy lunged toward me, but Arthur caught me from behind and held me for a long moment. I leaned into him, relishing his warmth, his strength. At last he released me, stepping away with a little bow before heading to the kitchen area.

Timothy watched Arthur go, his face unreadable, then followed him to the kitchen. I sank into the couch next to Blanche. "Did they let you see Lily tonight?"

She nodded, but refused to look me in the eye.

"It won't be much longer, I promise," I whispered.

"You should get some rest," she said.

"We all should," I replied.

In my chambers, Roland lay on his side of the double bed. Partridge claimed he was respecting our relationship by granting the king and queen a single room, but in reality it was a reminder. Whatever they had done to Roland, his mind had been shattered. He babbled, his thoughts racing feverishly, oblivious to anyone or anything around him.

I stood in the doorway looking at him. In the last year, we had come to understand that we were not real people. We had sprung, fully formed, from the mind of an eight-year-old girl, who believed in handsome kings adored by beautiful queens, and surrounded by loyal courts. Roland was my love and my life, and even now I remembered those feelings. But as we'd adjusted to reality, we had realized that past life was a lie. The only reality was what had happened since that night. I looked at the man created as my husband, who had only been real for our first hour of life, and guilt flared as I remembered the warmth and reassurance of the knight who had kept me from falling, who had been by my side since, and worked beside me to secure the safety of our people.

I sighed. Despite the confusion, this was still my bed, my personal purgatory. I lay down beside my absentee husband and closed my eyes.

Hours later I rose and left my chamber, making a show of stretching, yawning, and running my fingers through my hair as I tied it back. The hallway cameras tracked my progress toward the main living area, where most of the others were gathered. For the last month, we had been keeping irregular hours, gathering in the early morning before some of us went back to our rooms, so that the guards would not expect any particular behaviour from us. Blanche sat on a sofa, reading. I joined her and picked up a book, pretending to flip through it. The clock on the wall read seven a.m. The lab men would be arriving with the new guards an hour from now. The current shift was tired from keeping vigil through the night. Our captors were at their weakest.

I looked around the room. Despite the Court's slouching body language, all eyes focused on me. I nodded at Arthur. He nodded back, removed a shoelace from his pocket, and slipped it around his neck. His ruby, dangling from the string, winked in the artificial light, and then Arthur disappeared.

I counted to five before Arthur reappeared. "All clear?" I asked. He nodded and I stood. His strong arm circled me and in a flash the lab's steel tables and stools replaced the living room.

"Here," Arthur said, gesturing to a large metal safe next to us. I didn't have my heart stone, but I wouldn't need it. Arthur stood behind me, projecting the Dreamscape onto me. We'd practiced this and other things on missions we finished early. I placed my hand over the keypad and willed it to unlock. Bolts slid back, and I pulled the safe's door open. Inside sat numerous black cases, each labelled with a chessboard position. I didn't need to read the labels to find mine – I simply held out my hand and felt it calling to me. Good. That would make this easier.

I snapped open the case and slipped the pendant around my neck. Arthur and I pulled out other heart stones, throwing the necklaces into the case that had held mine. Once it was full I thrust it at Arthur. "Go," I told him.

"Don't move," he replied, and then he teleported. I turned back to the safe. On a lower shelf sat a number of computer hard drives containing everything the scientists knew about us. I grabbed an armful and deposited them on a nearby metal table. I took a drive from the top and began smashing it into the pile. Plastic bits flew as I annihilated them. Then the lights went out, replaced almost immediately by the orange glow of emergency lights.

Arthur reappeared at my side. "Timothy cut the power. He's staying there to make sure the EM field stays down. The knights are evacuating everyone to the rendezvous point. But we have a problem. I didn't have either king's heart stone." He swung the safe's door wider and began searching the lower shelves.

"You won't find them there." On the far side of the room a group of people stood just inside the door. Monroe glared at me, one hand gripping Blanche's arm, the other holding a stun gun to her temple. Behind him stood Anders and two soldiers, aiming rifles at us.

"The children are gone!" Blanche cried. "Mark got me to the nursery, but it was full of soldiers! They shot him and took his heart stone. He won't be able to heal himself. I don't know if he's dead or alive."

"We moved the pawns a month ago," Monroe taunted. "Couldn't risk losing our leverage. Now stand down. One queen's plenty, and I know Anders is dying to resume his experiments."

"Get out, both of you," Blanche sobbed.

"I'm not leaving you here," I hissed.

The next moment, the overhead lights came on. Monroe tsked. "Should have done like Whitey told you." He yanked Blanche's arm and pulled her closer. "Now you're trapped again. You can bounce around the building for a bit, but you can't get out. So stand down."

Blanche hunched her shoulders in defeat, but I saw the determination in her eyes and the knife in her free hand. I reached my hand out to Arthur, standing behind me. He clasped it and squeezed once.

The next moment I was almost touching Monroe. Before he could move I grabbed the hand with the gun and twisted the weapon free. As the bones in his wrist snapped, Blanche whirled away from him and slashed the thigh of the soldier behind her. To my right, Arthur did the same to the other soldier. Their femoral arteries slashed, both men were easily overpowered.

I grabbed the stun gun and jabbed Monroe with it. He screamed for the full five seconds I applied current, then collapsed in a sobbing heap that smelled of urine and sweat.

"Where are they? The children. Where are they?" I demanded.

"Go to hell," he replied. I applied the current again.

"He doesn't know." The cool, detached voice came from the other side of the lab, where another door led to the other hallway. Partridge.

"Did you really think you could escape? That you were smarter than me? I was playing chess for decades before little Alice was even born. You will lay down your weapons and surrender your heart stones. And then you will beg my forgiveness."

"You don't have all of us," I said.

"Oh yes, your associates outside the walls. They were meeting at the gas station five kilometres west of here, correct?"

A cold horror gripped my heart. We had never discussed the plans inside the building. The bishops, our planners, had been quite clear: no word was to pass our lips inside, where we could be overheard. So how could Partridge know the rendezvous location?

The next moment I had my answer. A red-headed figure stepped out from behind Partridge. No one held a gun to his head.

"Timothy?" Arthur asked. "You were supposed to be guarding the generator! Now we're trapped!"

The Red King's bishop shook his head. "Poor, dumb, loyal Arthur. You still think you're really a knight."

"What did they offer you, Tim?" I asked, my voice surprisingly even. "What was worth betraying your family?"

"We aren't family!" he yelled. "And you aren't a queen! You're nothing, just an overgrown toy who talks about loyalty but throws herself at the nearest man while her supposed husband's too sick to defend himself!"

"You're one of us," I replied.

"No, I'm not. I decide who I am, and as for what they promised me? They promised me you." He leered, then turned to Blanche. "Both of you."

"You'll still just be king of the toy box," I said.

"Better to reign in Hell than serve in Heaven," he replied.

Behind us, angry voices sounded, followed by gunshots. Mark burst through the doorway, his clothes stained with blood. He lunged for Blanche, just as Arthur lunged for me. The two knights joined hands, and the lab disappeared. A red haze surrounded us, and pain shot through every fiber of my body. Through the agony I felt my heartbeat, once, twice, three times, and then it was gone. We stood in a brick hallway. Arthur was on one knee, and Mark had collapsed to the ground. Blanche knelt over him.

"Where are we?"

"Subway service tunnel," Arthur gasped. "Secondary rendezvous point."

"When did we decide on a secondary location? And how did you get us through the EM field?" I demanded.

"Two of us working together. Camilla thought we could get through the barrier, but it would hurt," Mark gasped. "And the knights have always agreed that this would be a good place to meet." He got to his feet with Blanche's help.

A diamond pendant hung around his neck, supported by a shoelace, same as Arthur's. I felt a small twinge of satisfaction. Getting a second fake heart stone had been my contribution to the plan. "Easy to leave from here, just in case we ever got a chance to run. We never told the bishops. I just hope the others made it here."

"They're here," Arthur replied, pointing to chalk lines low on the wall. "Probably spotted the soldiers the moment the first group arrived at the gas station."

"We can't abandon Lily and the other children!" Blanche cried.

"We won't," I said. "We'll find them and the kings, and make our family whole. The Agency can't hide the children forever."

"Are we a family?" Arthur asked, still on his knees, his shoulders slumped. "You heard Tim."

"We are," I replied. "Everything we've done, everything we've suffered, makes us real." I held out my hand to help him up. "I don't know exactly what comes next, but at least it will be our choice. We've got our skills, and we've got each other. And we're free." Arthur staggered to his feet and took my hand, and we made our way toward the daylight at the end of the tunnel.

FIREWABBY

Mark Charke

Measures of sanity among planeswalkers are difficult to come by. What is normal changes for you. Laws of physics that are cast in stone in one place can be like smoke elsewhere. As a child I saw a fly caught in a spider's web. I imagined what it would be like to be the fly. I imagined being the spider. I never thought about being the web.

I use magic, not parlour tricks. My parents named me John Stuart. I burned their house down at the age of three. I had no control at that age. They left me at the doorsteps of a church. There I was called Firestarter. They taught me. You would be surprised what you can do with faith, a total dedication to something and a library. I learned to control the fire. I learned to transform into other things.

Today, it doesn't matter what day it is anymore, I stopped. I wandered into a picturesque meadow. Trees, grass, sky; brown, green, blue. A massive tree lay on its side, long dead and covered in loam, half swallowed by the earth.

Faith is about listening and having the courage to act. I heard desire. It manifested as a sea of voices saying "Come," silently. The screaming disturbed the leaves where they hung from the trees, unmoving. The wind remained still, except for the gale force of breath, which tugged at my red cloak and made the voices. The cloak could be influenced by things that were here, yet not entirely here. There was something flowing into this world from somewhere nearby, something

not of this world, not normal. I felt dizzy for a moment so I
became something that could not get dizzy.

The voices changed. The word became a murmur of different words, questions; who, how, brother and what? I saw
the rabbit hole tucked into the roots of the fallen tree. Inside
I saw, felt, chaos, an infinite drop into eternity. As I dropped
into the bottomless pit, I caught a glimpse of a rabbit across
the meadow. Perhaps it had meant to say something to me?
It vanished as I fell.

Here and now, I fell. Chaos came as an old upright piano.
A table with sweet cakes. A ladder with one broken rung.
An umbrella unfolded into a mushroom. I saw all these
things around me in the small hole. Roots moved by on the
walls of the tunnel, far too deep now to be possible. I spun
and twisted. Things changed. The piano opened a mouth
full of pointed daggers. The cakes exploded into ribbons.
The ladder folded itself into a chessboard. The mushroom
ate itself.

I landed on the chessboard. My red cloak swirled around
me. Red pieces stood around me. Opposite were the black
pieces. I had made a mistake; checkers, not chess. I considered my death here on a checkers board. I felt sort of
insulted. I stood and looked around at the piece placement.
The game had not yet started.

A self-important snort of laughter marked the start. I saw
a giant table beneath the board and two massive opponents
prepared to face off to an audience of hundreds who stood in
hushed silence. A massive hand reached across the board and
slid a black piece forward.

Next, a gaudy red-gloved hand stretched out toward my
person. I rolled out of the way and slapped at the hand. The
crowd was silent. Only their heads moved, turning.

I summoned flames. They were not confronting some helpless wanderer, disoriented and desperate. Fire flowed, the board burned and the plastic pieces melted into gobs of quicksilver tar and blood. Magic here had a strangeness and I had to struggle to control it.

I became a giant, just a larger version of myself. I exploded out of the conflagration, becoming their size. Not a soul gasped or flinched. The player merely reached for me, despite my·size. I slapped his hand away. The hundreds, dressed all in different shades of red and black, leaned forward just slightly.

"Cheaters will not be tolerated!"

The tone was sharp and arrogant, self important. A queen, obviously, dressed in black and red filled out a tall throne of brilliant gold and sparkling crystals. Her head, larger than her torso, cast a shadow over her shoulders. Her crown, a silver band of some kind, was lost in her beehive of braided hair. I abandoned the hope of logical conversation.

Her hand reached across the 100 metres between us, growing in size as it did and swatted me like a bug. The army of spectators, the table, the contestants, the queen, and the fire, moved away very quickly. I saw a forest that made no sense in its growth. I saw a mountain range in the distance that tasted like dandelion flowers. I licked my lips, not knowing how I could learn that.

The landing did not hurt as much as it should have. Something broke underneath me. It was bread. I found myself on a table bigger than what would be normal. Massive cups and saucers were spread about, between teapots scattered without discernible pattern. One of them appeared to be made from of the smell of late afternoon sunlight in the summer. I blinked and looked at it harder but did not see it with my eyes. I only interpreted smell. A smashed pocket watch sat nearby, its gold chain hanging off the table.

A man in a hat wider at the top than the bottom flipped a cup over and slammed it down over me. Tea went everywhere. I could smell the warm tea soaking into my cloak. I became a large knight in armour, sort of. My form had a melted wax look as my control ebbed.

The cup grew bigger with me. I smashed my mailed gauntlets against it. It cracked and shattered. The pieces hovered for a second before growing wings and becoming butterflies. I shooed them away.

"I am the Hatter, mad."

Standing on the table, I looked down at the short man bowing formally with hat in hand.

"Won't you stay for tea?"

"No."

I drew a massive sword from my pocket and faced him. We both paused and looked at the slight bend in the blade.

"Oh, excellent. I knew you would stay."

I kicked one of the teapots off the table. It clanged to the ground.

"Gravitas!" The Hatter yelled and threw another one to the ground.

I ran.

"Not without your tea, you don't."

Tentacles of tea stretched out of each pot and grabbed me. They held me in a seat and the Hatter worked a pot up to my mouth. I became something that does not drink but it took every ounce of concentration. The hot liquid poured over what passed for my new face.

"Oh, you are for the jabberwock!"

That did not sound good. The Hatter folded the table in half, then again and it became a suitcase and bounded away. The chairs turned and ran. The rabbit appeared. A glimpse of white and a green smoking jacket. It gasped and ducked back from where it had appeared. I had grown sick of this place and of running. It had not helped.

The jabberwock appeared beastly to be certain, what could be actually seen: tentacles, wind, claws and teeth. To describe its colour I would use the sound and feel of breaking crayons. It bounded toward me on all six truffles worth of legs. Its presence seemed to make things more difficult to understand. Certain words changed, lost meaning and took on new meaning. Its breath smelled like blue. It made me gag. I made it burn.

The fire erupted chaotically, swirling like dye spooned into water. I let go of control and it grew stronger this way. The trees burned. The grass evaporated. The air boiled. The jabberwock became a hiss and crackle. I did not take my eyes off it.

When it stepped out of a cloud of smoke and its teeth snapped open with a loud snicker snack, I swung my blade. It cracked and bent further on the hide. I wrinkled my nose and heard yellow. It might have been green. My senses continued to make less sense.

The claws cut and stabbed. I experienced pain and cheese. Poison. They had finally had their way with me. Blood dripped, and I went for my greatest trick by letting go. I became my greatest and oldest form. My snarl erupted from behind long teeth and ancient eyes. My skin became red steel plates. A dragon fears nothing.

I breathed fire, not that pathetic magic. Not that bit of explosion. Not that shallow flame but true fire, dragon fire. It came from within, from my heart and lungs, drawn from my very soul. The jabberwock evaporated in the inferno.

It did not die, however. I would never know if my senses saw the laws of physics twist or if it had just been madness. The jabberwock became the taste of ash and the scent of time. No longer a thing, I could not kill it; not at all. Its abstract form did not slow it down or make its claws less effective. It bit and sliced, and I bled.

It circled when I looked to retreat. It came all around me, laughing in scents and premonitions. I slowed. Magic failed completely. I became a man again, a badly injured man. It could kill me easily now. The claws stabbed and cut, but only little cuts. Little stab. Little slash. Little pains.

I needed to flee this torture. I needed time to heal. Perhaps a form it couldn't hurt? My brain scrambled and then stopped. I realized the form, the only one they would let me take. I realized the trap. I saw them shrieking in delight. The rabbit, the Hatter, the queen.

Cut. Cut. Cut. Eventually they would get bored and have it kill me. I understood now. It was shallow comfort. I became the jabberwock.

My mind split and I saw things from all directions. Colour. Taste. Touch. Smell. Sound. They were all the same, even existence and thought. I experienced everything as one. Then someone giggled. Me. I achieved a perverted enlightenment. Matter could be thought. Madness – I had let it in. I hated that it felt right.

I saw the path back now, the rabbit hole. I ambled toward it, no longer able to tell the difference between moving and singing. Either would achieve my objective because they wished it to. Their raw desire here dwarfed my willpower. They were in charge.

I crawled up the rabbit hole by thinking about skating on mint candies strapped to my feet and how yellow is a perfectly good colour to build a house out of, strong and resistant to the smell of darkness. Time and chaos stretched out for what could have been a second or a lifetime. Then finally roots, grass and dirt appeared. These things were real.

The unthinkable form of the jabberwock faded as reality composed itself. Skills, memory and senses began to work. I crawled, too dizzy to get up. Grass gave way to dirt, then a creek and finally a field of wheat. Just these simple, normal things were like a tall glass of water to a thirsty man in the desert. I regained more composure but sickness churned my stomach and did not diminish. I had escaped the web by being fly and spider and web at the same time.

None of the creatures followed me. They did not want to. I had seen the rabbit, but just as a rabbit here. They wanted to be here as they were there through that rabbit hole. Inside me was their madness now, their way into this realm. If I let it out, they could consume this world.

The next time I became something else, the next time I dug down into my well of magic, their madness would claw its way to the surface, and let them in. That's what the madness wanted.

I knew a place to take it, a horrible place that would be improved by their chaos. I started through the wheat to see what was on the other side, a traveller with a burden now.

SOUP OF THE EVENING

ROBERT DAWSON

The Mock Turtle paddled in lazy circles beneath the cloud-less sky. Since its carbon-fibre-composite front left flipper had failed, eighty-three years ago, circling was easier than swimming straight. On each circuit, it scanned the horizon, the wooded headland, the beach, and then the horizon once more, looking for poachers.

It had not seen a poacher, or any other human, in more than fifty years, but thousands of generations of evolution had given its turtle brain near-infinite patience; and the im-planted computer had no concept of haste whatsoever. The Turtle's job was to guard the sea creatures in the park, as the Gryphon guarded the land.

Once upon a time, on evenings such as this, the Gryphon would come down to the beach, the Mock Turtle would crawl out of the water, and they would talk together of many things while the sun set and the full moon climbed the sky. But it had been a long time, years, since their last meeting. Perhaps the Gryphon, too, was gone.

Ahead drifted a jellyfish, a mop of angry tentacles under a glassy clear dome. An invasive species, one that the Turtle was allowed to eat without limit. Its stainless-steel beak bit hungrily: two more gulps finished the jellyfish off. There was not much nutrition in jellyfish, but with few other creatures to eat them, they were plentiful.

Half an hour later, the Turtle became aware of a faint discomfort in its stomach and a buzzing in its head. Had that jellyfish been contaminated in a red tide? So many of the Turtle's organs had been replaced by pumps and filters that the dinoflagellate toxins could not harm it for long; but they would disturb its organic brain until the nanofilters cleared them away.

Strange thoughts and memories from long ago invaded the Turtle's mind. It swam in ovals, in trefoils, in spirals. On a sudden whim, it began to sing to the pale moon: *Will you walk a little faster, said a Whiting to a Snail?* Through the fizzing tingle of the dinoflagellate toxin, the words almost made sense. The beach was coming into view once more. Two figures walked along the sand. One was – could it be? Yes! The Gryphon! A step behind followed a strange small human. The Turtle surged toward them, stopping occasionally to correct its veering course. *No, Constable, I haven't dropped a touch. Must have been something in the jelly. Sober as a, as a, one of those sober things.*

The Gryphon paused now and then, looking out to sea. The Turtle tried vainly to call over the crash of the surf. Onward it swam, taking bearings from a boulder on the beach. The water grew shallower now: the waves began to shoal, the lazy irregular rocking of the open sea turning more urgent. The crests mounted steeper and steeper, flecked at the top with impatient patches of foam. At last, one ridge toppled, and a mighty surge drove the Turtle dizzily through tumbling foam onto sand. The water slid back, leaving the Turtle beached, stuck onto the wet sand by its own weight.

Slowly, awkwardly, on its three good flippers, it crawled up above the licking waves. The Gryphon shouted and waved; the Turtle called weakly back, and the Gryphon lolloped across the beach on all fours, its claws throwing up little puffs of sand. The small human followed, holding up its skirt to run faster.

"So good to see you again!" cried the Gryphon, and threw itself on top of the Turtle in a clumsy embrace, sandwiching the Turtle's head between shaggy fur and sand. Finally it moved away, and the Turtle could speak again. It smiled weakly.

"Good see you too."

The Gryphon looked solicitously at the Turtle. "Pardon me? Are you feeling poorly?"

"Sorry. Jellyfish. Disagreed with me."

"What?"

"Disagreed with me. I settled the argument. Ate it."

"*That* will teach it," the Gryphon said cheerfully. "I've brought somebody for you to meet. Don't get into an argument with her. Didn't bring her for you to *eat*, you know."

"Who is it?"

"It's a little girl. The Queen said to bring her here."

The Turtle blinked. "What for?"

"Ask her if you want."

The little girl stopped a metre away. "Are you the Mock Turtle?" She scuffed her patent-leather shoes in the sand.

"Once," said the Mock Turtle gravely, "I was a real Turtle."

"You *look* real." She reached out as if to touch the Turtle's shell, but drew her hand back at the last moment.

"Oh, I'm solid," the Mock Turtle said. "But they put a computer into me. And cyborg parts."

"A computer! Do you have internet? For games?" she asked.

"*That* wouldn't be a good idea," said the Gryphon.

"Why not?"

"Nets are bad for turtles."

She put her hand to her mouth. "*Oh!* I'm sorry."

"It's all right," said the Turtle. "And, yes, we used to have games. Back when there were porpoises around, they played all sorts of games. Chasing games, mainly: Tag-And-Release, Red Roughy, and British Bullhead. But they've all gone now."

"And you can't play without them?"

"It would be porpoiseless," the Turtle said sadly.

"Why did the people do all those things to you?"

"So that I could guard the coral and fish and oysters better. And talk to the scientists. And file the weekly and monthly and quarterly and annual reports. And do the Population Apology—" That didn't sound right. "I mean the Botheration Ecology. Counting the oysters."

"Are oysters very difficult to count?"

"Well, they don't *move* much. No feet, you know. But I had to take lessons to do it properly."

The little girl frowned. "They make me take lessons too. What lessons did you have?"

"Ambition, Distraction, Uglification, and Derision." Blasted jellyfish! The words would not come out straight. "Deferential and Interminable Calculus. And Sadistics."

"That doesn't sound very pleasant."

"It wasn't. All the Sandwich Deviations, and Incompetence Intervals, and Linear Digression, and Hippopotamus Testing. And Bays' Rule." The Turtle thought for a moment. "Because the beach is in a bay, you know." It made as much sense as anything.

"And why do you have to count the oysters?"

"So they'd know how many there were. So nobody would harvest too many."

"Do the oysters mind being harvested?"

"I never asked them. It wouldn't have done any good, you see. Oysters can't talk."

The little girl nodded. "How many are there?" She looked around, as if she expected to see oysters walking along the beach.

"There aren't any. Not anymore."

"Why not?"

"The water got acidic. And then the little oysters couldn't grow shells, and the fish ate them."

"So now you just guard the fish? And the coral?

"No, the fish swam away when the oysters were gone. And all the coral turned white and died, because the water was too warm." It had all been so beautiful once... The Turtle began to weep. It brushed at its eyes with a flipper, awkwardly, trying not to rub sand into them.

Its melancholy thoughts were interrupted by a faint and distant whine, imitating a lone mosquito. Far up the beach, something silver and black glided above the sand, twisting and dipping in the air like a glittering ribbon. As the Turtle watched, it swooped toward the beach, picked up a scrap of something, and resumed its flight.

"What's that?" asked the little girl, her eyes big with wonder. "It's so pretty – is it a dragon kite!"

"It's a Snark. They keep the beach clean."

The little girl clapped her hands. "Will it come closer?"

"I'm afraid not. They're programmed to stay away from people." Snarks had been picking up litter and flotsam from the beach, and taking it who-knew-where, for almost a century.

"Oh! It *is* coming closer!" And so it was, hurtling toward them faster than the Turtle had ever seen a Snark fly. The whine grew, and frigid tentacles clutched at whatever was still organic in the Turtle's belly.

A century was a long time; software could be corrupted by circuit failure or cosmic rays. A rogue Snark might attack humans and cyborgs, trying to get directly at the metal and organic materials that it was programmed to crave. The Turtle would be safe in the sea; the Gryphon could fight back or run away. But what of the little girl?

The flapping peril loomed nearer: the sound grew to a whistle, to the shriek of a hurricane. The Turtle turned to the Gryphon. "Cover her up! Keep her safe! It's a boo—"

The Gryphon knocked the Turtle aside and threw itself on top of the little girl, who gave a little "oof!" as she vanished under the shaggy beast's bulk.

And then the boojum was upon them, like a whirlwind in a machine shop, clawing and biting at the Gryphon, as if trying to chop its way through its body to the small human beneath. There was a smell of blood and hydraulic fluid. The Turtle raised itself as high as it could, and clamped its steel mandibles onto the nearest limb of the boojum, which immediately turned its fury on the Turtle.

Without releasing the boojum, the Turtle pulled as much of its head as it could back into the darkness of its shell, protecting its skull and eyes from the hacking, slashing cutters and pincers. There was an upward pull and a flapping sound as the boojum tried to fly away. The Turtle's shell rocked back and forth, but the boojum was not strong enough to lift it.

Slowly, blindly, the Turtle crawled back toward the sea, dragging the thrashing monster with it. Every time a flipper was exposed, the boojum attacked, but the Turtle persisted. After an age of struggle, it felt the welcome splash of a little wave, then a bigger one. Soon it was swimming, scraping along the sand, pushed out into deeper water by the undertow. The limb that it held in its beak no longer thrashed and struggled, but pulled first one way, then another, like a kelp stalk in the waves.

The Turtle swam on, dragging the boojum completely under. Once it was sure that the enemy was submerged, it rested on the sandy bottom, waiting for the salt water to take its toll on the boojum's air-fuel cells and electronics. When enough time had passed, it opened its jaws, leaving the inert body of the boojum to drift, and swam back through the breakers to the beach.

The sand was empty, and unmarked except for the Turtle's own tracks emerging from the sea and the traces of its solitary struggle with the boojum. Silently, it turned and limped back into the sustaining embrace of the sea. It would have been pleasant to talk with the Gryphon some more, or at least say a proper farewell.

It swam out beyond the breakers, beyond the drifting wreckage, into the deeper water where the oyster beds had once been. Empty shells still covered the sand, grown brittle and white as the water gradually leached the strength out of them. Little creeping things, sandworms and shrimp, moved among the shells. Disturbed by the Turtle's passage, they scuttled for cover.

Don't be afraid, little ones, the Mock Turtle thought. *I'm here to keep you safe.*

CYPHOID MARY

PAT FLEWWELLING

Mary entered the rope corridor, one of a half-dozen weary travellers bound for red-eye flights. This was her sixth international and second domestic business trip in three months.

Security had kept the queue switchbacks in place, forcing the few tourists to walk needlessly back and forth six times as they approached the baggage scanners.

The security guard's voice was too big for the late shift. "Boarding passes ready, please."

Mary hadn't slept in nearly seventy-two hours. It was as if she'd simply forgotten how to fall asleep the moment she'd landed in Vancouver. Everything felt darkly comical.

The teenager ahead of Mary skipped once. Her older companion – father, maybe – gazed in wonder. The girl shrugged and asked, "What?"

Mary couldn't account for a block of time on her last flight. It might have been sleep. She'd opened a book, and the next she knew, four hours had passed and they were landing.

"Move forward," the guard said. He had a face like an Easter Island statue. He dropped his cleaver-shaped hand to cut the traffic between the teen and her dad. The girl advanced to the conveyor and hopped three times on the spot, as if her leg had the hiccups.

"Can't you just let me go through with my daughter?" the man asked. "Please. We're late. We've got an appointment in the morning and I—"

"Stop there," the Moai statue bellowed, as if yelling at a crowd only he could see. He narrowed stony eyes at the belligerent and crossed his arms. "Have your passports and boarding passes ready," he said. "Peanuts!" Curious people turned in his direction. As if nothing had happened, he gazed over Mary's head.

Mary felt like she was in a dream that was taking a turn for the dark. She needed to wake up, or security might assume she was stoned.

Time trickled on as the teen deposited her carry-on luggage, jacket, computer, and phone into the grey bins. All the while, she hopped periodically on her left foot. *God, I hope she's not on my flight. Is she high?* "Stop that," the baggage inspector said. Defiantly, the girl stopped, tucked up her left leg and hopped on her right. The inspector nodded and let her pass.

Only three people remained in line now, Mary included. No one new had joined. It gave her the willies.

"Go forward," the security guard said to the worried dad and to Mary, then slammed his hand behind her.

Just get on the plane, Mary thought. *You're tired. You're hallucinating. Go to sleep, get home, take a couple of days off.* Mechanically, she placed her possessions in the bins.

"POPcorn."

Everyone jumped. The long-faced, blushing gatekeeper cleared his throat, guarding the last person in queue, as if denying the exclamation had ever come from such a paragon as himself.

Mary handed over her boarding pass to the inspector. "Take off your head, please," the inspector said.

"I'm sorry?" Mary asked.

"Take off your hat, please," the woman said, in the same cadence and tone.

"Oh," Mary said. "Right." She took off her ball cap and dumped her personal effects into it before proceeding to the metal detector. The agent on the other side blinked at her. Thinking she'd maybe missed the hand sign, Mary moved toward the metal detector, but the agent shouted, "Stop!" With a gentler gesture, the agent waved her back, and then loosely stood at ease, watching the metal detector's lights as if waiting for a sign from God.

Maybe I'm asleep in the taxi. Maybe I've been drugged.

A second agent summoned Mary through the detector. Mary didn't know if she should obey the come-ahead wave or the stay-there shout. At the second agent's insistence, Mary passed through the arch, without setting it off.

Mary shuddered. *Well, that was weird.* The guard behind the X-ray monitor saw her shiver and said, "Take this, sweetie," in a grandmotherly voice. He started taking off his own uniform. Suddenly, the cheery light went out of his eyes. He looked confused and retrieved Mary's jacket for her instead.

The next passenger came through the metal detector, making it beep. He said, "Oh, excuse me, I forgot my watch." He retreated, took off his flannel shirt and dumped it on the floor. He was wearing an undershirt. He passed through the detector again. "Oh, excuse me, I forgot my watch." He took off his shoes. A third time, he set off the detector's alarm. The two agents stood by with the metal detection wand. "Oh, excuse me, I forgot my watch."

It was like watching a time-loop, and no one else seemed to think it was odd that he was taking off his pants, undershirt, and underwear. Mary's eyes bugged out. He wasn't even wearing a watch.

"PROGRAMS!" shouted a furious voice. "GET YOUR PROGRAMS!"

Mary shivered. She'd stopped breathing. *What. The. Actual. Hell.* "Excuse me," she said to the security supervisor. "I'm uh… I don't feel so good." She pointed to her head. "Is there a doctor or something—"

"You must be cold, dearie," said the agent behind the X-ray machine. He climbed awkwardly over the Plexiglas and roller track, taking off his uniform jacket as he came.

"Oh, excuse me," the nude man said, "I forgot my watch." He had no more clothes to take off. The passenger made like he was pulling off a jersey from the bottom hem up over his head, but instead of material his nails caught skin. Three great, bloody wounds unzipped under his fingers as he tried to flay himself. Mary gasped to scream, but her voice caught. Someone else *had* to see what was going on.

Boots thumped and a breeze rushed past Mary as a fresh team of security personnel took over. A pair of medics came too. One man in a suit quickly ushered Mary away from the sight of blood and the eerie absence of screaming. The plain-clothes man asked her if she was all right. She said, "Absolutely not!" He assured her the situation was now under control. He coaxed her this way and that, beyond all the familiar parts of the airport, into an office. *Flashmob*, she thought. *It's a gigantic prank, and I'm the rube. A thought experiment, to see how people would react to…to…*

"Where's your luggage?" he asked.

"I…I left them on the table."

"Passport and boarding pass, too?"

"I put them in my luggage before that man… That…"

The suited man nodded and raised his hand. "I don't think he hit anything vital. Can I get you anything? Water, cup of coffee?"

She shivered. "I could use a coffee."

"Cream, sugar?"

"Yeah. Please."

"All right. I'll be right back." He reached across the table and squeezed her hand. His encouraging smile was a breath of fresh air. "You're safe here." He left, and the door clicked behind him. Maglocks and a card reader sealed her in. There were two surveillance cameras. She wasn't being held for her own safety's sake. She was being held for interrogation.

Honestly! What the hell!

Almost as quickly as it had shut, the door pushed open. It was the man in the suit. "Sorry about that," he said with another winning smile. "I brought my cat pictures with me," he said conversationally, though with a strange undertone of accusation. "In fact, my cats are very well documented, as you will see."

"What?"

"In the instance where cats will cat, cats are catty." He took out his phone. "We've even got video proof. My question is, where do you fit into it, and why did you do it?"

"*What?*" Mary's mouth trembled. "I don't understand—"

He bent and slapped the table. "My cats," he insisted, "are on the Internet, and Vine is full of trick photography and cleavage. I want to know why your cat videoed cleavage vines."

"Is this a joke?" Cold sweat stained her shirt.

Like a professor keen on his lecture, the man played with his phone, saying, "Independent manga hentai, porous navigation!" He turned the phone around for her to see his Goodreads account. "In this regard, only otters slide sideways, you see?" He pointed to the screen. "Alphabetically, I have a better bunch of grapes in a minute-egg!" He was getting angry. And Mary was locked in with him.

"I don't know what you're saying!"

"Soccer diesel animal hangar!" He caught her wrist. "Prove to me that cat cleavage videos indigo barter vinyl chalk!"

Mary stared at the maniac, struggling to free her wrist. *Use his madness against him. If you don't trick him into letting you go, you're dead meat. Think!* "Your cats!"

"What about them?" he asked.

Outside the interrogation room, someone wailed, "Peanuts!" as if it was the name of some innocent fool who was falling from a cliff.

"Answer me," the man in the suit urged. "You'll miss your Jefferson, and I don't give a damn." He threw down his phone and showed her his fist. "Surrealistic *pillow*, Mary." He wrenched her wrist, making her yelp. His eyes bored into hers. "Tell me!"

"You left your cats in the oven!"

He straightened, blinking. "I did?"

She twisted her hand to slip free. "You have to let me rescue them!"

"Where?" he asked.

"I have to take you. They're hidden."

He grinned gallantly. "Come on, there's no time to lose." He pressed his pass to the card reader. "Go on, then! Hurry! Reduce, reuse, recycle." He pushed her into the hall, drew his gun, pressed it to his temple, and as if saluting the queen, said, "Purple under cleats!" and pulled the trigger.

She shook as if she'd been the one shot. He looked like an English airman saluting the queen, but the left side of his head was gone. Shards of brown and white bone fell from the oozing mess that covered the door frame. His legs folded under him. She screamed, and ran backward until her heels caught in the carpet, and she fell.

"POPCORN!" someone cried behind another locked door. "Peanut, peanut butter!" The door banged against its hinges. "And jelly."

Get up and run, she thought, *or you're dead*.

Like a pinball, she crashed along one hallway to another to another, then to a fork in the paths. A sign pointed to the washrooms, another to Information. She had to get out of that airport, by plane or on foot. There were armed personnel all over the place, and if they *were* going mad, there was an equal chance of someone shooting himself, shooting a friend, or shooting Mary.

A joyful ding preceded a message over the airport announcement line. "Final boarding call for James Rogers," the female voice carefully pronounced, "Anoush Behar, Sahak Behar, Baba Ganoush, and that fat bucktoothed ass-hole. Please come to gate B17. This is your final boarding call. Thank you."

Voices and people rushed toward Mary, so she dashed into the nearby washroom and waited near the door, listening. It sounded like a stampede. Dozens of people stormed past, not quite marching in time. They were puffing as if they'd been jogging around the block.

Mary turned and leaned against the wall. She closed her eyes, but her lids had been flashbulb-burned by that man blowing his merry brains out.

There's got to be something in the air, Mary thought. *My God – that's it! A biological weapon! It was deployed in the air-port. It must have gone off at security, because that's where all this started.* She needed to escape into fresh air and call for help.

Mary slipped out of the bathroom and took the first left. To her enormous relief, she saw the stores and signs pointing to boarding gates. She slunk down the shopping promenade, keeping a wary eye on a man sitting on the floor drinking Coke by the litre, blissfully unaware of the puddle of urine he sat in.

Near the end of the concourse and up the ramp, the security team sat at a table outside the baggage inspection area. Mary had left her luggage, phone, and wallet on that table. The agitated guards were playing strip poker. One woman was down to her hat, shoes, underwear, and tie, and she was trembling. Her lips were crusty and white.

The cards were stained with blood.

"Time's running out," said the grandmotherly man. His sweaty lips twitched. It was impossible to say if he was looking at a very good hand or the very worst.

"But we must be more thorough," said the security supervisor. "It's there."

Mary slowly and quietly reached between two players. She had her hand on her jacket when someone grabbed her by the hair. "Sit!" Mary was dumped onto the bench, thigh to naked thigh with one of the guards. Cards were in front of her, face down. The security team stared at her.

"I bid one sock?" Mary asked.

"A strip search isn't enough," the supervisor said. "We need to be more proactive, diligent – these are dangerous times we live in. We must look deeper."

Out of the blue, came a rumbling. There must have been fifty people crammed shoulder to shoulder, moving like a flock of flamingos, flowing through and around the security obstacles. They went past the card game and down the ramp to the shopping arcade.

"You never know where you're going to find it, sweetie," said the grandmotherly man. "But you have to keep looking."

"It's the skin folds of fat people," said the metal detector man. They all agreed.

"It mixes with the laptop battery acid and the onboard crudité platter," said the woman with the necktie. Her left hand had been so badly broken that her wrist looked like the open head of a Pez dispenser. "We all know that's the payload. Now we have to find the detonator!"

"The bomb is ticking," the supervisor insisted. "Check your cards and play."

Mary lifted her cards. The face cards were all well-hung men. She had two aces, a jack, a nine, a four, three twos, and a business card. "I don't know how to play this game," Mary said.

"It doesn't matter!" the supervisor said. "Time is up. We must find it, now!"

The grandmotherly man gasped and cried, "I have two nines!" He threw down the cards as if they were going to explode, and the others recoiled. They weren't even nines. They were a ten, a jack, and a six. "Wait. False alarm," he said, sitting. He wiped his brow. "A full house, queens over eights."

Mary had to get away. She needed to tell the outside world what was happening, and get these victims to safety before they all killed themselves. But someone behind her refused to let her stand.

The woman with the broken wrist was trying to peel open her cards. "I can't see it anymore! It was there, but now I can't reach it!" The supervisor shook his head and clucked his tongue. He motioned one of his team to help her. "I can find it myself!" the woman screamed. "It's here, I swear! I saw it just a second ago!" She ripped the card in half vertically. She sat back, one half in either hand. "Oh God. I've tripped the timer."

Do something!

The supervisor said, "Now you've condemned us. Charles, you know what to do."

Easter Island Face rose from his seat and put a hand on the necktie woman's forehead, as if he was getting ready to break her neck.

Do something! They're going to kill her!

Mary grabbed her backpack, then shot to her feet. "Wait! I have it right here!" She set her bag on the table and opened it. "I can defuse it before it goes off." They all lurched from the table, except for the naked necktie woman and the man about to break her neck. "Watch." Mary extracted a pair of socks as if they were made of nitroglycerin. "I'm familiar with this kind of bomb." Someone sucked in his breath. "This is all you have to do, to defuse it." She unrolled the socks and laid one beside the other, smoothing them flat. "There. Problem solved."

After a long, pregnant pause, all eyes lifted from the socks to Mary's face.

"How did you know where to find the bomb?" the supervisor demanded. "And how come you know so much about how it's built? Immigrant terrorist! Invader! Parasite! Learn *English!*"

Mary would take her chances with the barricaded front doors, if she could get that far. She upended her backpack, throwing clothes to blind them from her escape. She ran through the holding area with half a dozen naked security personnel behind her.

"She'll kill us all!" the supervisor screamed. "Kill her! Kill her!"

Their voices soon fell behind. Panting, Mary turned to see what fresh hell had delayed them. In single file, the guards were walking through the rope corridor. At every bend, each solemnly said, "Peanut." Then they rushed to the next bend, slowed, and said, "Peanut."

If there was something in the air, clearly Mary was immune to it. She alone could warn the world. She raced past the boarding wickets toward the terminal front doors and the taxis waiting outside. There were no barricades. There were no medical personnel. There was no biohazard warning posted on the doors.

The boarding announcement pinged. "This is a final boarding call for Mary Mallory. Final board – DEMON-SPAWN GET ON THE PLANE – for Mary Mallory. Final boarding call for that flat-chested ginger bitch DEMON-SPAWN SHITSTAIN. Thank you."

Mary felt her pockets for her phone as she rushed for the door. *What the hell do I do? If I call the cops, are they going to go crazy too? Shoot everybody on sight?*

Out of nowhere, the pack of jogging travellers charged her, smothering her, carrying her along with them. They chanted, "Come on, go faster. Faster in front. Stop pushing. Faster. I'll sue. Get out of my way. Go on." They shoved her through Departures, back into the security holding area. She begged them to let her go. "We're late. Get out of my way. I'll sue. We're late. Move on. Stop pushing. I'll sue." Like a train's shrill whistle rising above the chugging of its engine, someone lifted his voice, crying, "Do you have any idea who I am?" They pushed on through security, ropes and all, corralling the security crew who added "Peanut, peanut, peanut, peanut" to the drone of impatient voices. They tipped over the metal detector.

"Final boarding call for BITCH GET YOUR ASS ON THE PLANE!"

The quick march became a flat out run. When Mary could no longer keep her feet, two people grabbed her by the arms and carried her to Gate B17. There, the boarding attendant was staring at the ceiling, saying, "Welcome a-broad. Welcome a-broad."

Mary bit her hand, but there was no getting out of this nightmare. She wasn't asleep.

The pack squeezed down the gangway. People were coming toward them, shouting indignantly. The plane was still disembarking, but the mad mob had momentum and width on its side.

Someone picked up Mary and shoved her across countless shoulders. "Final boarding call!" someone yelled as she crowd-surfed down the ramp, through the hatch and fuselage, her head banging against the overhead baggage compartments. Then someone yanked Mary to the floor by the waistband.

An attendant pulled Mary upright. "Get away from her! Get back! You idiots! What kind of a game is this? Where's security?" She dusted Mary off. "Are you all right?"

"No! I'm not!" Mary cried. "The whole airport is like them! There's been some kind of biological weapon—"

"Biological weapon?" The nearest disembarking passengers screamed and wrestled each other for access to the rear emergency exit. Panic and madness spread. People jabbered in tongues, dropped their pants, headbutted each other.

Mary hid in the nearest seat, pressed up against the window, weeping, blocking her ears with her fists, sickened by the rocking of the plane. A body fell against her and she screamed, punching blindly.

A thousand voices became a hundred. A hundred became ten. Ten became only a question here and there.

Mary sobbed.

"Mary?"

She lifted her arm. Her eyes were bloated with tears. She wiped her face. The plane was mostly empty. There were only three passengers left, all of them sitting across the aisle. The nearest one wore a cowboy hat. The one in the window seat wore headphones designed to look like the antennae of an old TV set. Between them snored a doughy-looking man in a DeadMau5 T-shirt.

She wondered if the flight crew was immune. They seemed unperturbed by the unorthodox disembarkation and Mary's boarding.

The cowboy and the man with the rabbit-ear antennae were comparing notes, snickering, heads almost touching, oblivious of the sleeper they squished between them. She couldn't make sense of a word they were saying. It sounded like a mash-up of every Eastern European accent, with a little Spanish, Urdu, and Mandarin thrown in. *Maybe I am going crazy, after all. It just took longer for me to catch it.*

"Did you see what happened?" Mary asked.

"It was hard to miss!" hooted the man with the rabbit ears. "Marvellous."

"We have to warn people," Mary said. She rubbed her nose on her sleeve. "It was like a virus in the air or something. Everyone's gone mad!"

The captain came out of the cabin, switched on the announcement radio. "Oh, you can't help that," he said. "We're all mad here. I'm mad. You're mad."

"But I'm not!" she said.

"You must be," the captain replied, "or you wouldn't have come here." He hung up the radio mike and locked himself in the cockpit.

The cowboy leaned on his armrest. "Why don't you tell us what happened?" He sounded like he was covering up a Russian accent with a Texan drawl.

"People were going crazy and getting crazier all the time, everywhere I went," she said.

"Ah yes, that's the key fact," said Rabbit Ears. He giggled and rubbed his hands together.

"What?" Mary asked.

"None of them were mad until you arrived," the cowboy chimed in. "They went crazy wherever *you* were. You're the initial disease vector."

The man in the middle chuckled drowsily. "Mary, Mary, life is scary. How does your madness grow?"

The man in the hat moved over to Mary's side of the aisle. Rabbit Ears punched DeadMaus, who moved into the cowboy's aisle seat, and Rabbit Ears moved into the middle. "You were selected as our initial vector days ago," cowboy explained.

"On this very plane," said Rabbit Ears.

"A...a virus?" Mary asked.

"A very profitable one," Rabbit Ears said. He licked his lips almost erotically. "It's airborne, you know."

The sleepy man giggled. "Airborne."

Mary's seat jerked, and she gripped the armrests. The airplane was taxiing away from the terminal. "Wait, stop the plane!"

"Don't feel so bad." The cowboy moved one seat closer to Mary, and his companions followed suit. "You're not the only carrier."

Rabbit Ears said, "Hmm, perhaps that's the trouble. Cross-pollination."

"Yes," said the cowboy, in his Russo-Texan accent. "This being an election year, we'd expected some hybridization, but not *your* rampant mutation. You were only supposed to cause agitation. Decrease some inhibitions, impair judgment, and entrench a little xenophobia."

"You should have *seen* that little virus work its magic in Kentucky." Rabbit Ears hummed. "A work of art."

"But *your* variant," the cowboy said, "causes symptoms much too unpredictable for our purposes."

"Pull her out of circulation," said the sleepy one, in a tiny, high-pitched voice.

"Oh, I'm sure we can find a use for her," Rabbit Ears said. "She might sell well in certain unruly countries as a techno-organic weapon." He giggled. "To discourage organized protests, for example."

"No, no, no!" Mary cried. "No, this can't be happening."

"Oh, but it can and is," the cowboy said. "Our carriers in Texas, Florida, and other such muggy states have been doing great for years!" The cowboy's black eyes were wide and keen. "It's a digital virus that uses your own brainwaves as a carrier signal. All you've got to do is stand in the middle of a crowd and think your own thoughts. With the help of your digital virus, you generate a very mild electromagnetic field that interferes with the normal function of other brains nearby. Reprograms their operating system, if you will."

"Downloads and installs whatever political shift we want," Rabbit Ears said. "Designer beliefs, done dirt cheap. 'Jobs are scarce because of immigrants, so I've gotta accept this $9/hr job. We're being replaced by computers, and robots, and clean energy. I've got to work all the jobs I can. Hard work is what defines our nation. I don't have time left over for exercise. Fast food is faster and cheaper. I need diet pills. I need surgery. Nobody comes between me and my family. Everyone else is after me and my freedom. I need a *gun*.' Ka-ching!"

"Money, money, money," murmured the DeadMaus fan. "Evil's the root of all money."

"I prefer the political strain," the cowboy drawled. "Such as, 'Education is stupid. War is good, but veterans are lazy beggars mooching off the system. All liberals are sexual deviants. All conservatives are racists. Moderates are sheep, and they're gonna get what's coming to them. Immigrants are just terrorists waiting for their orders. Caring is for commies. Death to degenerates! Death to anyone who disagrees!'" The cowboy laughed bitterly. "You can even be infected with multiple, conflicting, self-destructive ideals. The more of these thoughts you have, the more likely you are to congregate in large groups, thus spreading and receiving cross-infection."

"And you, my dear," said Rabbit Ears, "you seem to be carrying every strain at once! How economical!"

"But...why?" Mary asked. "Why the hell would you make me do this?"

Rabbit Ears handed a copy of the *Washington Post* to the cowboy, who gave it to Mary. On one side of the headlining picture was an orange-faced bombastic man, facing a sprawling audience. He posed, frowning mightily with his chin up, glaring down his potato-shaped nose at his worshippers. The motley crowd was blurry with low-lit action. Some had thrust forward their right hand toward the speaker. The rest had turned inward with fists flying, and bloody boots stomping someone on the floor.

"Why waste our own precious resources destroying the West," said the cowboy, dropping the Texan drawl, "when we can get *you* to make it destroy *itself*?"

"And I can't argue with the profit margin," said Rabbit Ears.

"Seatbelts, everyone," the attendant said. "Y'all might as well settle in and get cozy. Washington's a long way off."

YELLOW BOY

James Wood

"Would you walk a little faster?" said a voice behind Snail.

Snail glanced back to see a miner's sallow face, his eyes gleaming white against the burnt umber of his stained skin. There was no malice in the man, just a weary impatience borne from long hours underground.

"Sorry," Snail said, ducking his head and matching the stride of the rest of the procession. He allowed himself to get lost in the rhythm of their iron-shod boots as they trudged along. Apologetic and invisible, that was the trick. He had no intention of making a scene. No one knew his face and he meant to keep it that way.

The men passed through the favela in a long trail of mottled red and brown, like a snake prowling the jungle floor. Snail didn't know any of the miners by name, but a few of their faces looked vaguely familiar. Most of them were old, though it was difficult to tell under the grime and silent despair. Any amount of time in the mines eroded a man's youth like summer rains. Even the boys, some younger than Snail, were cut from mountain stone. Snail made a point of scrunching his face to accentuate whatever faint lines his eighteen years above ground had given him and walked on, just another broken soul in the crowd.

It was a long trudge through Lagoa to the hill gate and all the while, high atop Corcovado, the golden spires of the great palace loomed. That was the destination of the metal these men had pried from the earth. It came from the bowels of hell and would soon pass through the gates of heaven.

Above the palace, the statue of Cristo Redentor watched impassively as the procession made its way toward the hill. The men moved silently among the husks of bone-white apartments, spun with clothesline like cobwebs. Snail had once seen a book with pictures of Lagoa long before the ocean had swallowed the rest of Rio. The pages were full of smiling *mauricinhos* and *patricinhas*, Rio's rich, most of them gringos. Now, anyone with money lived up on Corcovado, as far from the sea and as close to Cristo Redentor as they could get. There they held great dances while the rest of Rio's population, those who had fled the flooding of the favelas, starved in crumbling Lagoa, below.

The miners followed the curve of the lagoon from which Lagoa got its name, though Snail knew from the pictures that the water hadn't always looked like piss. The miners called the runoff that poisoned the lagoon "yellow boy," said it had something to do with the acidity in the mine. Whatever it was, it had turned the whole thing a soupy yellow. When Snail was little, his mother and the rest of the women of Lagoa would wash clothes at the lagoon's shore. Now, they had to go to the retaining wall that held back the sea, and risk their lives by the swells.

Snail glanced furtively at the water as he passed and caught his own stained face. The yellow boy affected skin differently, especially the dark skin of the miners. Instead of bright yellow, it dyed the men rust red and it had taken Snail several days to get the tint just right. He worried whether it would hold up when he sweat but he hadn't had time to test it thoroughly. There was a dance at the palace tonight and that meant there would be trading at the gate.

A crowd had already formed when the miners arrived. Old women with blankets, young girls and boys with colourful crafts, men too old to work the mine holding carvings, all of them were hoping to make a sale. Snail had stood with them once, but he'd quickly learned that the gringos only wanted one thing: gold. A single ounce could get you enough rice to last a week, strike a rich vein and your whole family was set for months. The gringos loved gold, though Snail could hardly understand why. It was pretty enough after it had been buffed and polished, but there were other pretty things in the world and none of them filled a hungry belly. Snail absently patted the satchel at his side and lined up with the rest of the men.

The hill gate, a massive iron latticework of spikes and barbs, stretched across the road leading up the mountain. It was the only entrance to Corcovado, so that meant thick-necked soldiers with eyes dark as the polished metal of their submachine guns patrolled it day and night. They kept watch, vigilant for anyone looking to sneak through. Every once and awhile in the dead of night, the maraca rattle of an MP5 sounded as some fool tried his luck on the mountain, then the inevitable barking of dogs, then the heavy stillness of nothing.

The guards were also responsible for the safety of the gringos who came to trade at the hill gate. Goods could be exchanged through the gate's portholes. When the miners arrived, the guards parted the crowds and led them to the bars.

There were enough men in line that Snail couldn't see the gringos at the gate, even as the line forked to the various portholes. Snail ran through his lie while he waited his turn but soon found himself eavesdropping on the conversation behind him.

"Is it true that they sometimes bring lobsters up to the palace?" a thin voice asked.

"Don't use that word," came the stern reply. "That's what *they* call us."

"Sorry."

Snail glanced back to see a craggy-faced miner and what could only be his son. The boy didn't have his father's creases, and the yellow boy had only just started to redden his skin, but they shared a nose.

The old man put a hand on his son's shoulder. "It is true. But don't get your hopes up. I've worked the mine for thirty years and I've never been asked."

"Why do they only ask the lob...us?" the boy said.

The old man shrugged. "I suppose to reward us for bringing them gold. They bring us to serve the nobles."

The boy nodded and opened his mouth to say something else but Snail would never know what it was.

"You," a guard barked, waving his submachine gun at Snail, "come." He nodded toward one of the portholes and kept his gun trained on Snail, his finger on the trigger.

Snail hurried forward, his eyes downcast, playing the part of the broken miner. That was ninety percent of it after all, being broken. Yes, these men came down from the hill for gold but capitulation made the gringos' eyes dance more than any metal. He only glanced up once when he reached the porthole, to get a look at the man he was dealing with.

Snail had studied the gate for weeks before attempting his miner act. In that time, he'd learned that the gringos came in two types. The nobles flaunted their wealth like a child who has discovered a bird's nest. They bought gold in great swathes, their only concern the number on the scales and that it was higher than that of their neighbours. Then there were the merchants, pinch-faced men with spectacles who cared more for quality than quantity. They came with more than scales, bringing loupes and acids to test the product. Snail had traded most of his meager possessions for a small pinch of genuine gold dust just in case he came before a merchant. If that happened he would simply trade the dust for a small portion of food and keep his painted iron for another day.

When he glanced through the porthole he found neither a merchant nor a noble. Snail didn't know what this gringo was. The buyers, whether noble or merchant, stood at the gate to inspect the gold. Instead, this one lounged a few yards back on a worn-out wicker chair. His bizarre clothes, while ragged, possessed an unmistakable despotic pomp. A leather coat bleached white from the sun hung like a cloak from his narrow shoulders, the hide cured so dry that a million tiny cracks webbed its surface like polished chain mail. A threadbare topper teetered on his smudged brow and he'd tucked a playing card into the band which, as far as Snail knew, was a fashion that had long gone out of favour with the gringos. He didn't look wealthy but he had the air of an old, bored emperor. Sunlight basked his face, and his limbs draped across the back of the chair as if he hadn't a care in the world. He was a spindly man despite his belly, and his posture made him look like a spider, apathetic in its confidence that the flies would find their way to its web.

When Snail approached he leaned forward, a gleam in his cold, blue eyes.

"My name is Whiting and I have a proposition for you," he said before Snail could open his mouth. His voice was like stale wine, sickly sweet, but it left a sour note hanging in the air.

"What?" Snail said, looking up in confusion, any pretense of meekness gone. "But you don't even know what I have to sell. I've brought gold."

"I have no interest in gold," Whiting said, leaning back.

Snail's cheeks grew hot and he opened his mouth to speak but couldn't find the words. No interest in gold? Why else would a gringo come to the gate? He'd spent months preparing. He'd given up nearly all he had for the dust, the paints and the iron. He had to trade today or he would starve.

"If you don't want gold, why are you here?" Snail said hotly.

"I deal in lobsters," he said. "That's why I've come."

Snail hesitated. "Then you mean to make me a servant?" he said slowly.

"I said I deal in lobsters and you're no lobster."

"Yes, I am," Snail said defensively.

"If you're a miner then I'm the king of Corcovado." Whiting sighed. "Let me see some of your gold."

Snail didn't like the way Whiting said gold, so when he reached into his satchel he pulled out the tiny bag of gold dust. Whiting didn't get up, so after an awkward moment Snail tossed the bag through the porthole. Whiting caught it with a surprisingly quick hand and peeked inside.

"I'm glad to see you're not a complete fool. How about another."

Snail stared at Whiting warily.

"Well?" Whiting said. "Let's have it."

Snail pulled a small chunk of iron from his satchel and did his best not to check it before tossing it through the gate. Whiting rolled it around in his palm and said something to himself. After a moment, he looked back up at Snail. "You know, this isn't half bad. You did a better job here than with your skin."

Snail couldn't help but look at his painted hands.

"What's your name?" Whiting said.

Snail looked over his shoulder but the guard still had his gun trained on him.

"Relax, boy, I'm not going to give you up. Tell me your name?"

Snail thought about lying, but that hadn't worked so far. "Snail."

"There's a good boy," Whiting said with a wolfish grin. "Now, Snail, as I said before, I have a proposition for you. Here's how I see it. You have two choices. You can leave now and I won't tell the guards about your little scheme. I'll even let you keep your iron and you can try again next time. Or, you can take this." Whiting tossed something through the gate.

Snail caught it and when he opened his hand a golden ring glinted in his palm.

"A ring?"

"Look closely," Whiting said.

Snail brought the ring close to his nose and saw that there was a strange beast carved into the band, like nothing Snail had ever seen before. It had the shell of a turtle but the head of a hare.

"What is it?"

"Meet me tonight at sunset on the wall and I will tell you."

Before Snail could ask another question, Whiting motioned to the guard who pressed his gun against Snail's back and drove him away from the gate.

◉ ◉ ◉

The retaining wall always teemed with activity. Women did their washing, men fished from its ramparts and young lovers walked under the stars. This was the first time Snail had ever seen it so empty. There wasn't a soul around save the top-hatted silhouette of Whiting, sitting at the edge, his spindly legs dangling while he stared out to sea. He didn't turn when Snail approached.

"There he is," he said, his voice oozing down the wall and into the sea.

"Where is everyone?" Snail asked.

Whiting only shrugged. "Did you bring the ring?"

Snail fished it out from his pocket and let it sparkle under the moonlight.

Whiting's eyes glistened with a wistful sheen. "You know, it took me eight years to get my hands on that. And another six to find you. But it was worth the wait; you're perfect," he said appreciatively.

Snail closed his hand on the ring and eyed Whiting. Snail was wary of gringos; they were dangerous, but this one had come into the favela with no escort, and sat as if he hadn't a care in the world. That made him deadly. "What do you want from me?"

"You can really have no notion, how delightful it will be," he said, looking far off into the sea. He turned to Snail, the moonlight shining silver in his eyes. "I can make you rich, you know."

Snail took cautious a step back. "How?"

"By bringing you to Corcovado, to the palace up on the hill."

"Are you insane?" Snail said with a look askance.

Whiting barked a coarse, dry laugh. "Maybe," he said. "But so are you, coming to the gate with painted rocks."

"Safer than going up the mountain. Look at me." Snail held his hands out to the moonlight. He'd washed the paint off since their first meeting but his skin was still caramel, even without the fake yellow boy.

Whiting only smiled. "Like I said, you're perfect. You look just like him."

"Who?" Snail asked.

"A boy who was lost long ago. Out there." Whiting pointed to sea.

"Who was he?"

"He was the crown prince. A bastard to the king. The old letch could never keep his hands to himself. Of course, that was before the pox rotted his mind and before he and the late queen conceived an heir. What else could the king do but send the boy away? He was on a ship slated to cross the sea but there was a storm and it was lost. He was assumed dead, that is, until now. It seems I've found him."

"Me?" Snail said. He opened his hand and looked at the ring again. "That's what this is. You want me to replace him?"

"That's right," Whiting said. "I've spent years buying lobsters to serve at the dances, but I've kept my eye out, looking for someone who might wear that ring. Now I've found you, and not only do you possess the look, but you're clever. I may have been able to see through your little scam, but us rogues can smell our own. You'll have those fools in Corcovado wrapped around your finger."

Snail considered this. "What do you get out of this?"

Whiting snorted. "I get to be the good friend of the heir to the throne. The king isn't long for this world, Snail."

"What about his son? He is known even in Lagoa."

Whiting shrugged. "What about him? Bastard or not, you'd be the eldest; you inherit. It's not as if he gets nothing. He has no interest in ruling. As long as he gets to have his little dances he'll be happy. Just placate him and you'll get on."

"The dances are his?"

Whiting nodded. "So, what do you say? Will you or won't you?"

Snail stared across the water, weighing his options when the soft note of a violin drifted from Corcovado. He turned and looked up at the palace. Its massive windows glowed with golden light, while dark shapes slipped back and forth like apparitions.

Whiting put a bony hand on Snail's shoulder and a chill ran through him. "Come now, Snail, won't you join the dance?"

◎ ◎ ◎

The little carriage rumbled up to the hill gate and the guards barked orders at the crowds who'd gathered to listen to the music. Their voices sounded harsh against the gentle strings that fluttered from the palace windows and the people shuffled aside, their necks still craned up at Corcovado. High above, Cristo Redentor looked down on them, his arms outstretched.

Snail watched from inside the carriage, unable to take his eyes off the iron gate as it swung open. How many had dreamed of this moment? How many had longed to pass through that gate. By some divine stroke, luck had chosen him.

"Relax, boy," Whiting said, tapping his walking stick on Snail's bouncing knee. "It's an easy job. I've already done most of the leg work. They know you're coming. They're quite excited actually."

"But I know nothing about their world," Snail said.

Whiting leaned in conspiratorially. "I've already told you, that's the beauty of it. No one expects you to. The prince was hardly two when he was lost at sea. It shouldn't be a wonder that he knows nothing about his past. You just stick to the story. You were found washed up on a distant shore, taken in by a fisherman and his wife. You lived your early years knowing nothing of who you were. All you had from your past life was that ring, which you kept on a string about your neck. Then one day, not too long ago, one of my agents happened upon you at the docks. You looked a bit familiar and on a whim he asked to see the ring around your neck. Low and behold, the heir to the kingdom was found and brought to me and I, in turn, bring you to the palace to be presented to your father much to the jubilation of the entire court."

"Won't they care about...this?" Snail held up his dark hands.

Whiting raised an eyebrow and then smiled. "They will care about what you tell them to care about when you are king."

The carriage came to a sudden halt and when the driver opened the door music poured in. Snail paused at the sound. Like the rest of Lagoa's poor, he too had once listened from the gate but he'd never heard it so clearly, so pure.

"Beautiful, isn't it?" Whiting said. He gave Snail a reassuring pat. "Welcome to the dance."

Men and women dressed all in red attended them as they dismounted and even with their visors Snail immediately marked them as former miners. They were all lobsters. They'd clearly been bathed and scrubbed, but there was no mistaking the yellow boy stains on their skin.

They were led across a courtyard of high white walls and sprawling topiary. Snail did his best not to stare. Whiting had told him it didn't matter. He could gape all he wanted. As far as the people knew he was just a kid from a poor fishing village.

However, Snail had decided early on to keep some illusion of sophistication. Foundling or not, appearing an uncultured rube would not win these people over.

Yet, it was impossible to keep up appearances when he entered the grand ballroom. Clearly, all the gold exchanged at the hill gate ended up here. Everything was gilded, and sparkled under the light spilling from golden candelabras and braziers. The cutlery, bowls, cups, all of it was gold. The guests wore gold too. Dresses sparkled and jewelry glinted. Even the floor was inlaid with golden filigree. At the far end of the room, watching men and women spin and twirl, stood a young man in a golden mask atop a dais. When he saw Snail and Whiting he clapped twice and the music stopped.

For a long, silent moment he simply stared at Snail, then he raised both arms. "My lost brother has returned."

The ballroom erupted with applause, except an old man who slouched in a chair upon the dais.

"That would be the king?" Snail asked.

Whiting nodded. "Come, let us present you."

They crossed the dance floor, flanked by partygoers who continued to applaud. Snail had never seen so many white faces in his life.

When they reached the dais, the prince clapped his hands once again. A bow pulled across a string and as the other instruments joined in, so too did the dancers until once again the room swayed with a tide of movement.

"Come, let Father have a look at you," the prince said. He placed his hands on Snail's shoulders and guided him to the king. Even with the wrinkles, there was no denying that Snail had elements of this man's face. There were differences, of course, a bit less here a bit more there, but if Snail didn't know the truth of it, he might even believe the lie himself.

"Your son has returned, Father," the prince said.

The king said nothing, and didn't even look up.

"Thank you," the prince said to Whiting. "I will be able to sleep much easier knowing he is accounted for. You have done this court a great service and you will have your reward."

So, there was a reward. Of course, Snail should have thought of that. He wondered just how much Whiting stood to gain from this. Looking at the decadence of the room he decided not to bother asking. Money no longer mattered. Let Whiting have his reward.

"Thank you, my lord," Whiting said with a bow.

The prince turned back to Snail. "It is good to have you home, brother. You must be tired from your journey. Come, sit with me."

Snail was ushered to a seat between the prince and the king. They watched the dancers for some time, while lobsters in their red outfits scurried about the room pouring drinks into golden chalices. Snail nursed his, careful not to let any of it get to his head. He did not want his mind hazy should he have to answer any questions. Much to his surprise he was asked none. They sat in silence, watching the spectacle, though every once in a while the prince looked over and studied Snail's face. Snail politely ignored him.

Finally, after what seemed like hours of silence, the prince spoke.

"So, brother, shall we begin the dance?"

Snail put down his chalice. "I thought this was the dance."

The prince's mouth twisted into a predatory grin that chilled Snail.

"This? Oh my, no." He stood up and clapped his hands once. The music stopped. The dancers stopped, then they parted to make a large square in the middle of the room. Against the walls the lobsters pulled vials from their uniforms and quaffed a sparkling golden liquid. In the long silence no one moved, except the lobsters who began swaying unsteadily where they stood. A wandering toot of an oboe rose from the band and, in a shambling dance, the lobsters moved to the center of the ballroom. Some were close enough that Snail could see the clouded eyes behind their visors.

"What is happening?" Snail asked.

"The dance," the prince said with savage hunger.

Every instinct in Snail's body told him it was time to leave, yet he couldn't for the life of him get up.

The oboe continued to pipe away and the lobsters came together in the center of the room. Then the strings joined in and more servants poured into the ballroom. These were not lobsters but men and women in black suits with black masks. Snail's stomach twisted when he saw the long knives and shining hatchets they carried.

The drums rumbled as they drove the song toward a crescendo. The servants in black advanced on the lobsters and with a crash of the cymbals they swung their cruel implements. The lobsters did not run, they didn't even defend themselves. Whatever those vials had contained hollowed them out. They simply danced while they were hacked down. By the time the song ended the ballroom floor was slick with gore. Then the strings plucked up and began a jaunty tune. The servants in black held up grizzly trophies and the assembled patrons clapped.

Snail watched in horror as the servants brought the ghastly red morsels to the guests, who took them in their bare, bloody hands and sank their teeth into the flesh.

A servant with a golden tray approached the dais. Snail tried not to look. The prince took a severed hand and held it out to Snail.

"Won't you join the dance, brother?"

Snail recoiled and the prince laughed. "You were a fool to return," he said, though his voice was distant, as if hidden behind clouds. He threw the hand into the crowd and the guests scrambled for it. Then another servant in black handed him a knife and hatchet. He turned back to Snail and smiled, his teeth gleaming golden. "Turn not pale, beloved brother. Lobster is an acquired taste. Perhaps you'll have more of a stomach for the main course."

"What's the main course?" Snail heard himself say. His head was suddenly very foggy and when he tried to rise to his feet he found he didn't have the strength. He rolled his eyes toward his cup and saw the golden flecks floating in his wine. From somewhere outside the fog he heard drums and the crash of a cymbal. Then a voice like stale wine whispered in his ear.

"Escargot."

JAUNE

CATHERINE MACLEOD

The way station entrance was below street level, and the rain splashed down the stone stairs behind him. A small neon sign reading *Jaune* buzzed quietly above the door.

It opened as he approached, and a tall, burly man said, "Hurry, come in before you wash away."

Henry Knight said, "Thank you. Are you the owner?"

"No, I just saw your taxi pulling up." The man took his coat and hung it on a rack. "I'm Andrew Barrett, fellow seeker. Isn't this the worst weather you've ever seen?"

Henry said, "Not even close."

There'd been the flash flood in Lima that had carried off a good chunk of the city, including his hotel. The tornado in Arkansas that had sucked his driver's dog out of the back of the truck. The Nebraska blizzard that had taken two of his toes and his status as a card-carrying atheist. He'd travelled through worse than this to get a story.

Tonight's was already writing itself in his head. Not that he'd be filing it, but as Emma, his long-time editor and some-time lover, used to say, old habits died hard. She'd also said old reporters died harder.

Most stories about La Maison Jaune *have the flavour of urban legend. Surprisingly few of them mention ghosts and unsuspected intruders. The house may well have ghosts, though – those invited to its annual tour seem to know a great deal about being haunted.*

No one will admit to knowing how the guests are chosen or by whom, but it's said they all have one thing in common – they all long for a second chance. Every September twenty invitations, each painted with a picture of a yellow door, are sent with letters explaining that this is a one-time offer. You're under no obligation to accept your second chance; but if you refuse it, or turn back at any point in the journey to Jaune, you'll never get another.

Most stories about second chances say they can be had for a price. But it's also said that those invited to La Maison Jaune have already paid.

Not bad for a first draft, Henry thought. Writing articles in his head was a habit he'd picked up as a stringer. He started writing them on the way to the nearest word processor, and by the time he got there they were half-polished. In fifty years he'd never missed a deadline, and only once failed to finish a story.

(*Mama?*)

He closed his eyes wearily. It had been a long trip. But he'd travelled further than this for a story, too, back in the day.

◎ ◎ ◎

Andrew said, "I'm trying to get a poker game going. Do you play?"

He did, but, "No, thanks."

"No problem."

Looking around the bar, Henry felt…off, somehow. There was something not quite right about the place. He had the feeling that if he walked back out that door he wouldn't recognize his surroundings.

The bartender was a dark, handsome woman with a pretty smile. Her name tag read *Nadia*. He said, "May I ask you a question?"

"Sure."

"Where are we?"

She said, "If you've come this far, does it really matter?"

He decided her question was better than his, and watched her get the drink he hadn't ordered. He considered himself in the mirror as he slid onto a stool. When he was a boy everyone had said he looked like his mother; that he had her big mild eyes and gentle expression. He didn't think his eyes looked so mild anymore. He turned away, swivelling in half-circles, watching the other customers. No one had brought luggage, but he imagined they all had baggage to spare.

Once, he would have tried to guess their stories. Tonight, he didn't much care. He noticed most of them were wearing yellow, though.

Jaune. He'd read somewhere that yellow was the colour of optimism, and somewhere else that it was associated with betrayal.

(*Mama?*)

He shook his head. The past was close tonight. Yellow had been Emma's favourite colour, but he'd always favoured blue. Emma's eyes were the bluest he'd ever seen, like the sky at dusk.

Alice's eyes had been more like the sky at dawn, waiting to fill with light.

Gran's had the blue of approaching thunder.

His mother's had been the colour of soft, comfortable denim.

Three of them gone, none of them forgotten.

Nadia brought a glass of red wine, so dark it was almost black. "Is there anything else you'd like?"

"No, thank you, I'm fine."

He wasn't, but he doubted he was alone in that. The bar resembled a scene from an old movie: strangers gathered from around the world for some mysterious purpose. They kept their voices down. A few nursed drinks and watched the basketball game playing on a TV mounted on the back wall, its volume turned low. A red-haired woman sitting near the door read a paperback volume of Robert Frost. Andrew had found a fourth for his poker game.

Henry counted nineteen customers, including himself. One more and they could leave. He realized he didn't know what would come next. He thought he didn't much care about that, either.

He sipped his wine slowly. It was very cold, and smelled of raspberries and distant lightning; of spruce and the cold wind off the lake by Gran's house. It smelled of the fog rolling in the morning he'd joined a search party to look for a missing girl in the town of Traverston. He'd been there for a rare long weekend, wanting to be out of the city for a while. But the waitress at the coffee shop had served his breakfast with a side order of gossip that ended his vacation. There was a story there, and with any luck he would get it first.

He had. But he hadn't felt lucky.

He'd been the one to find Alice, stumbling into a clearing and seeing her curled up on the grass with her head in her dead sister's lap. Her sister's head had rolled away into a pile of leaves.

He'd forgotten about calling for help, about not touching anything. He'd forgotten everything but the too pale, wide-eyed little girl who kept whispering, "Snicker-snack, snicker-snack."

He'd lifted her away from the body, and carried her back the way he'd come, toward the river. Neither of them looked back. When the search party found them, they were both in shock and weeping.

He'd known it was going to be bad for her. She'd been eight when she told her parents she'd gone away to Wonderland, the same age he'd been when Gran told him his mother had gone away.

"She left, Henry. She just didn't want to be your mother anymore, okay?"

Of course, it wasn't okay. And she was *lying*. But he knew better than to call her on it. (Yellow: the colour of old bruises.) She'd stomped back to the kitchen to make something she knew he wouldn't like for supper, and he'd slipped into his mother's bedroom.

Her suitcases and all her clothes were gone. She hadn't had much else. He'd known she was planning to leave – which Gran *hadn't* known – and that she was taking him with her. "Even if I have to stuff you in my backpack," she'd said, making him laugh. Softly, though; Gran didn't like laughter.

He peeked down the hall, making sure Gran wasn't coming, then slid under the bed. The brown envelope was still there, wedged between the springs. He pulled it out and hid it in his own room, behind the bureau mirror.

He'd have to keep changing hiding places, though, because Gran would go through his room and take anything good. Anything pretty or fun. Anything she wanted. The envelope contained a half-dozen photos of him and his mother taken in the photo booth at the mall, and a smaller white envelope containing his birth certificate and eight hundred dollars in cash. And, most telling, two bus tickets to Larson, a town three states away.

Mama hadn't planned to go without him.

"Supper's ready!" Gran hollered, and Henry knew better than to keep her waiting. But halfway down the hall there was a little alcove with a rough plank door in the ceiling, a hatch that could be pulled down by a wooden rod with a blunt hook on the end, and he stopped to look inside. There was some-thing…off about it. The floor was usually dusty in there; no one went in the attic much, except to get the Christmas orna-ments.

The dust was scuffed, as if something had been dragged in there. The little gold key that locked Mama's suitcase glinted in the corner. He picked it up.

He remembered the rain the night before, voices raised and the shush of hard wind across the lake. He thought it had been a good night for doing bad things.

◎ ◎ ◎

Nadia said, "Sir, are you all right?"

He started back to the present and smiled tiredly. "Yes, just wool-gathering."

She might have been thirty. Or fifty. She was one of those women who could be called timeless. Like Emma. Or Alice. His mother. Hell, even Gran, except that she'd only been beautiful if you didn't know her.

"What do you know about La Maison Jaune?" he asked.

"Not much. I've never seen it. But I once heard about someone who changed his mind about going there, and got the shuttle driver to stop so he could walk back."

"What happened when he got here?"

"He never did."

"Have you ever seen any of your customers again?"

"No."

He said, "One of them just forgot his cell phone on the bar."

She didn't look around. "He didn't forget. He just doesn't want it anymore. Look around – lots of people checking their messages, right? But I've never seen anyone make a call. By the time they get here they've probably said everything they need to."

That definitely would have gone in his story.

She says they leave photos, letters, money. Jewellery, some-times. A lot of wedding rings. "I put it all in a lost-and-found box. No one's ever come back for anything, but it seems right to wait. After a year I claim it."

Emma would have enjoyed publishing this. She loved drama and intrigue. Although knowing that the illness which had taken her from him was going to reunite them might have been too much even for her.

Nadia took a teapot and a box of teabags from under the bar. Henry went back to people-watching. He wasn't impa-tient to leave. Even the bad memories weren't bothering him much tonight. He didn't mind that back in the day wasn't that far back.

Then the door opened and the last customer walked in.

◎ ◎ ◎

She closed the door and shook the wet from her coat. She'd buzzed her blonde hair short, and apparently sworn off make-up, but she still wore that tiny gold key on a chain around her neck, and made no effort to cover the scar that curved across her right cheek like a disembodied grin. She carried a narrow wooden box under her arm.

He took her coat and hung it beside his own. She slid her arms around his waist and said, "Hello, Henry."

He hugged her back gently. "Hello, Alice."

The website hosted by the world's governing chess body, the Federation Internationale des Echecs (FIDE,) rates Alice Liddell as Europe's best active female player.

There are perhaps 1,000 chess grandmasters living today – grandmaster being a title bestowed by the FIDE upon players who have attained 2,600 points in tournament play, and won at least twenty-seven sanctioned FIDE tournaments.

Odds were good that Alice would join their ranks this year. Instead, she all but retired from public life.

A chess star with a shadowed past and training in several martial arts, Alice has always been a fiercely independent woman, determined to do things for herself.

The story of finding her in the woods had been one of his best. The interview he'd done with her fifteen years later in Oslo had been better. It was the only interview she ever gave. Between matches, she'd talked candidly about how her sister's death had torn her family apart. How she sometimes still had trouble recognizing herself in the mirror. About getting help to deal with her PTSD. How both chess and martial arts made her feel as if she had a measure of control in her life.

She talked about Wonderland. When asked what she thought of the movies based on her life, she said, "Not much."

She'd emailed him when the article came out, saying it had been nice to see him, and thanking him for being a good listener. Henry, who knew about the stories children told themselves to survive, printed the note and saved it.

They didn't saw each other again, and Henry wasn't sure following each other on Twitter constituted a relationship. But he was glad she was here now.

Nadia came to their corner table with another glass of wine and a pot of tea. As Alice poured, Henry said, "It's funny what we remember, isn't it?"

She said, "Sometimes."

"You know the first thing I always remember about that day?" She didn't ask which one. "Just before you got in your father's car, you turned and waved to me."

"I remember that. I had the strange idea it might encourage you."

And, strangely, it had. She'd come out of the woods with all kinds of wounds, including gaps in her memory; the victim of things she was simply too young to understand. But even splattered with blood and obviously in distress, somehow she'd still thought to turn and wave goodbye. He'd wondered if kindness was so much a part of her nature that she hadn't had to think about it.

She opened the wooden box and set the small carved figures on the table, the queens and kings, bishops and knights, rooks and pawns, then turned the box over and opened the hinges wide. The box itself converted to a chessboard. She set the pieces on their squares, and began moving them immediately. "Do you often do that?" he asked.

"Do what?"

"Play against yourself? Pretend to be two people?"

"I always did, even as a child."

He wondered if it was the only way she could find a decent opponent. Her gold key glinted in the low light. She'd had it in her hand when he found her that day, and, walking back to the river, she'd said, "Will you keep this for me?

They'll take it away from me if you don't. They take everything good."

He knew better. He knew he should give the key to the police, her father, someone. There'd be hell to pay if anyone found out, and it was *wrong*. But he couldn't refuse her. She was being so brave, and her words cut deep into his memory, making it bleed. She dropped the key in his shirt pocket, and he didn't think of it again until that night when he undressed for bed.

He went to see her the next morning, carefully cleaned up and on his best behaviour. The police had checked out all the members of the search party as a precaution, and Alice showed no fear of him, but still – he thought her parents would be wary of a stranger at the door. He'd brought Alice an arrangement of yellow carnations and daisies in a small blue mug, and said he just wanted to say goodbye to her, and he was glad to see she was okay. Which was stupid, of *course* she wasn't okay; but she offered her hand politely, and he slipped her the key as they shook. Her smile was small and pleased. She waved goodbye as he left.

She finished the game, and said, "Play with me?" It sounded like an invitation to slaughter. She held out two pawns. "Offensive or defensive?"

"I've been called both." He chose white. "Are you still in therapy?"

"No. After a while it was just a waste of time and money."

"It didn't help me, either." His wine smelled of wild mint and Gran's lavender hand lotion; of slippery stones, and things dropped in the water late at night.

"Do you still think of Wonderland?" he asked.

"Every day. That garden was so beautiful. A little peace and quiet would be nice, don't you think?"

He did. "Why did you keep the key? Didn't your parents ever ask where you got it?"

"Once. I said I'd taken it from my sister's jewellery box because I wanted something to remember her by."

As if you'd ever forget, Henry thought.

"As if I'd ever forget," she said.

"Did you ever remember where you got it?"

She said, "I remembered everything, eventually. Starting with my sister's string of boyfriends, and how she played them off each other, making them vie for her attention. They didn't like it. One of them followed us into the woods that day. When he attacked her I just went haring off into the woods. I tripped over the roots of an old stump. The key was on the ground there."

"Did you ever see him again?"

"About a year ago, in New York. That's when it all came back to me."

"What did the police do?"

"Nothing. I didn't tell anyone."

"Why not?"

"Oh, you know me, Henry. I prefer to take care of things myself."

She snapped the head off one of his pawns and whispered, "Snicker-snack."

◉ ◉ ◉

Alice poured herself another cup of tea. "My therapist used to say I became so independent because I was trying to distance myself from my parents. But I think it was the other way around – I was just making it easier for them. We didn't talk much after the murder, true. But we hadn't talked much before, either. My sister was their favourite. I knew it. *She* knew it. They just didn't seem to know what to say to me. I think they were relieved when I started playing chess. They didn't have to spend so much time trying to deal with me."

"My mother used to talk to me all the time," Henry said.

"Not now?"

"She's dead." It was the first time he'd ever said it aloud, and it opened the door for all the other words he'd kept to himself.

He told Alice about the night his mother had disappeared. About Gran and Mama yelling at each other, sounding angrier than usual. Something about his father, he thought. Gran's voice high and cold and shrieking like the night wind. He remembered both falling silent at the same time.

He had pulled his blanket up around his ears and closed his eyes tight, telling himself it was okay, it was okay. Mama had said it was the last night they'd ever have to spend in Gran's house.

"When I was a little boy I thought that at least *she'd* got out of the house."

"And now?"

"I think she never left."

He thought Gran had kept him only because she knew it was the one thing Mama wouldn't want. She *was* that spiteful. Growing up in her house was hard. He didn't have many friends, and none would ever visit him because they were scared of her. He understood, but it was still lonely.

She wouldn't talk about his parents. The only time she'd ever mentioned his father had been to say Henry would grow up to be dirt like his daddy. And there'd been anger in her look, but also something young Henry had never seen before. Looking back, he thought it had been a kind of hunger. He thought Gran and Alice's sister must have shared the same appetite for attention. People said Gran had been lovely back in her day. But when they didn't know Henry was nearby they also said her parents hadn't done her any favours by spoiling her. That she was too used to getting what she wanted when she wanted it.

Henry suspected she'd wanted his daddy for herself.

(Yellow: the colour of madness.)

She'd never liked competition. She'd never liked the word *no*.

He'd spent his evenings studying hard, hoping good grades would help him get out. They did. Local· college, local part-time jobs, and finally full-time work at the local newspaper. He wrote well and worked to get better, knowing his success would infuriate Gran. He got noticed and moved up.

And moved out, never to see Gran again.

"Did you ever look for your father?" Alice asked.

"I did. His name was on the birth certificate. Mama's bus tickets would have taken us to a place called Layton. I put two and two together – and found nothing. I don't know why she wanted to go there. I tracked every lead I could think of. I hired a private detective. I never found him."

"Do you think your grandmother knew where he was?"

"I'm afraid she might have."

He thought of things hidden and voices gone silent. He thought of things dropped in the lake, and ripples that spread forever.

He thought of all the places he might have lost the key to his mother's suitcase.

He thought of memories so jumbled that neither he nor Alice might ever sort them out.

She moved her queen, finally putting him out of his misery. "You know the first thing I always remember about that day?" she said, and he didn't ask which one. "I knew right away you were going to be my best friend."

"Excuse me?"

"You hid my key. You kept my secrets." She folded the chessboard back into a box and began stashing the pieces. "I always had the feeling that I mattered to you. Was I wrong?"

"No."

"And I was always sure I could call you if I needed help."

"Yes."

"And you could've called me."

She hadn't been born when he'd really needed help, but he appreciated the sentiment. He looked into his empty glass, thinking that at one time he'd hated himself for not doing anything to protect his mother. (Yellow: the colour of cowardice.) But he'd been a child, and it was all he could do to save himself. Though he didn't know that he'd done such a good job of it.

He thought, *I wish none of it had ever happened.*

Alice said, "I wish none of it had ever happened."

◎ ◎ ◎

Nadia rang the bell for last call at 10:45. The shuttle to La Maison Jaune was scheduled to leave at eleven. No one asked for another drink. Alice left the chessboard and her cell phone on their table. Henry checked his one last time. No messages, no surprise.

Andrew tossed a heart flush beside the pile of money on the table. The red-haired woman left her book on the end of the bar. A quiet rustle went through the room as people collected their coats.

The shuttle bus was small and sleek. Henry and Alice sat together. "I was nervous about accepting the invitation at first," she said. "All I'd ever heard about La Maison Jaune was rumour. You know why I finally accepted?"

"Because the card looked like a door?"

Her smile was small and pleased. She leaned against him to look out the window. The rain had stopped. The clouds were parting. She said, "Do the trees look different to you? Does…everything look different?"

It did. *Where are we?*

The trip seemed short. He'd lost track of time. Or maybe, he thought, time was different here. The article had stopped writing itself in his head, not finished but as done as it was going to get.

La Maison Jaune was huge, and a truly disturbing shade of yellow. It was all wrong angles and unmeasured walls. The door opened as they approached. Alice took Henry's hand as they walked in.

◉ ◎ ◉

"Welcome to La Maison Jaune."

Their guide was a shadow clothed in shadows, Henry thought. Male, female, human, all, none, he couldn't tell. Maybe it was an unmentioned ghost. But…if they'd come this far did it really matter?

There were no introductory speeches, no explanations. No stories about the history of the house or their unknown benefactor. There were no answers.

He supposed they'd find their own soon enough.

Their guide gestured to a registration book on a table near the door. It was old and yellowed, and looked thousands of pages thick. "Please sign in."

Henry recognized some of the signatures on the page. He wondered who needed to keep track of who passed through. He signed and didn't ask.

"Now we begin," the guide said. "La Maison Jaune has many doors. You may open one. *Only* one." Henry glanced at Alice, who was glowing quietly. "When you find the door you wish to open you separate from the group and go in alone."

The tour began. "It's like a maze," Alice murmured. Some of the hallways were long, some short; some panelled in golden maple, some made of mortared stone. There were no windows, but in the first ten minutes Henry thought they must have passed a thousand doors.

The redhead went first, pausing before a faintly shining, milky glass panel in a brick wall. She reached out tentatively, and tapped a forefinger against it. The glass shattered musically, falling in slow-motion shards, revealing a quiet winter woodland. A cold breeze freshened the hallway, ruffling her hair. She stepped into the Christmas-card scene, her footsteps trailing her into the woods, and vanished among the trees.

They moved on. There were doors and doors and doors. Some pushed in, some pulled out, others slid. Some revolved.

They passed a great dirty gap in the wall, a pile of dusty bricks in front of it. Henry wondered if a hole in the wall could actually be considered a door. A hole in *anything*, like a cave entrance or a rabbit hole. He guessed that if it led you somewhere else, then yes, it probably could.

Andrew evidently agreed. He stepped through and was gone.

Alice tugged at his sleeve. He turned back to her. "Everyone's gone ahead," she said. They were alone in the hallway.

She said, "Is it my imagination, or are the doors getting bigger?"

There was a small wooden door in the wall behind her. A short glass table stood beside it. Henry hadn't thought to look down before.

Alice was looking up.

He recognized the plank door in the ceiling immediately. The rod to open the stairs leaned against the wall beneath it. He pulled them down. There was darkness at the top of them. He said, "You realize, of course, this is all impossible."

If Alice's laughter was the last memory he had of this world, he thought, it would be just fine. She said, "It's been a long time since I've believed anything else."

She knelt and used her gold key to unlock the door. He caught a glimpse of yellow carnations and daisies beyond. She set the key on the glass table and waved to him. He waved back. She crawled through.

The door closed behind her. It did look bigger.

Mama?

A hard wind blew down. He heard the shush of black water. He put Alice's key in his pocket, hoping, and started to climb the stairs as they folded up behind him.

WONDERBAND

Alexandra Renwick

Me and Eagle are bumming smokes down by the liquor store when Deuce and the rest of the Hearts show up looking for trouble. I've managed to avoid those a-holes for months, curled up in my sister's basement, sweating through my sheets each night, turning my skin yellow from nicotine, ridding myself of some habits worse than chain-smoking and forgetting to sleep.

"Look, boys," coos Deuce to his crew, "it's our crusty old pals, Duckie and Eaglet, playing at being regular upstanding members of society by digging ciggie butts from the gutter and panhandling change."

Eagle's shoulders tense. "It's Eagle now, crumplebait."

The Hearts all laugh, Deuce and his brother Ace louder than the rest. They're a bunch of skinny fuckers, rich but mean, and bullies too. Hardly worth the paper they're printed on.

"Deuce." I nod his direction, playing it cool, wishing I'd preened a bit more this morning before leaving home. "Ace. Fellas. Accidentally caught the tail end of your show a couple weeks back, after they opened the doors for free 'cause nobody would pay the toonie cover. Hope your mom's planning on redecorating the club; you guys' new sound reeked hard enough to peel paint off the walls."

Beside me, Eagle busts out in a raucous caw. "You guys sucked!" he squawks.

Ace makes ready to knock Eagle a good one square on the beak, but Deuce waves him back. "Ignore these losers, bro. At least we *have* a sound, which is more than anyone can say for these dizzy feathered fucktits. And after this weekend, everyone will know who rocks hardest in this town. Hells, they'll know it all up the coast. And once our album drops, they'll know it all over the world."

Deuce has a forgivable faraway-sorta look in his eye, dreaming the dream we've all been dreaming in this town since we were big enough to strap on guitars and step up to a mike. This is a music town, man. Everybody's got dreams. Got no problem with that. I've only got a problem with the Hearts.

So does Eagle. "Nobody never will sign you flap-hards," he says, looking puffy. His feathers get easily ruffled. Gets him into trouble sometimes. More trouble than he needs.

I eye Ace warily but he seems to have lost interest in bopping Eagle, or maybe he's forgotten who we are. He's a real bruiser but not the sharpest card in the deck. "Underland will sign us," he grunts. "Once we take the Wonderband title this weekend at Queenie's."

The Wonderband Battle of the Bands, sponsored by the hottest indie label this side of the rabbit hole, first prize a sweet cash advance and contract for a debut album plus limited tour. Every rocker in town would give a left foot to sign with Underland Records. This is the second Wonderband Battle ever held. Last year the win would've gone to us, if I hadn't pulled one of my more royal mess-capades and monumentally screwed the best band in town out of making the gig. As it was, Underland declined to name a winner and nobody got signed. But here they are again, a year later, back for round two.

Thought of a second chance sends a zip of electricity up my tail.

I preen a bit now, smoothing along the side of my head, still trying to play it cooler than I feel. I never liked Deuce. He and I go way back. Got a history. None of it good. "Yeah," I say, knowing I shouldn't, hating the smug look on Deuce's flat pasty face. "We were thinking about signing up to play. We thought competition might be kinda stiff, but if you guys are setting the bar…"

I'm expecting Eagle to laugh. He's a good wingman in all sorts of social situations, and plays hella decent second guitar. But he's goggling at me wide-eyed and wary. Our band isn't exactly together anymore, and by *together* I mean on speaking terms. Even before last summer we'd been struggling, fighting, missing gigs and burning bridges, pissing off all the wrong people. Artistic disagreements, we told everybody. That's what everybody tells everybody when their band falls apart. My shitwaddity under the myriad influence didn't help. One thing about losing your job, losing your band, and alienating almost all your friends: it sure does free up time for what you might call honest self-reassessment.

So Eagle doesn't laugh. But the Hearts do. They're slouching off smirking and snickering, though a year ago they'd have been lucky to be slotted our warmup band even though their mom, Queenie, owns Queenie's Place, the best live club in town. It hurts like a sucker punch to the ribs to have those peckweeds so sure we're not a threat, musicwise. Makes me want to get the lead out, crank up my apologies and mend some fences like I've been intending to all summer but somehow never got around to. Makes me want to scrape the gang together, show those cover-hack wannabees what a real band looks like, show everybody what a real band can do. Suddenly makes me want it really, really bad.

"Come on, Eags," I say. "We've got social calls to make."

◉ ◉ ◉

Eagle and I are both currently in what you might call the wheelless state, so it takes us an hour to slog the whole way to Dodo's westside 'hood. Nice houses, trimmed lawns. No peeling paint I can see, and not a single car up on blocks choked with parched weeds and drowned plastic bags. Of us all, Dodo's the only one with what my sister would call a real job. Works for the city, takes home some sweet pay. Not stuck up about it though, and like all good bassists, he's got the perfect garage for band practice.

He's in there now with the door rolled up, wearing frayed cut-offs. His threadbare flannel is ripped at the shoulders to give him room to play, make the most of those stumpy little arms of his. And he's *playing*, man. He's *playing*. He's riffing up, riffing down, not tight-kneed like inferior bass players but loose, man. Loose and leaning into that lowdown sound of his, crouching low like the thump reeling outta his spiffy amp, crouching so low his knees practically bend backward and his wumbles wiggle.

He looks up at last, sees me and Eagle shading the perimeter of his driveway, peering in like we're mimes at an invisible wall.

Dodo's so cool, man. The absolute coolest. He studies me without surprise. Nothing in his expression to make you think we haven't stood in the same room or breathed the same air for a year after all those years living practically in each other's laps, touring and playing and gigging, the whole band eating and sleeping together in a big pile like a litter of gigantic puppies. Gigantic boozing, hard-rocking, occasionally stoned-to-the-tails puppies.

"Whassup?" he says, no emotion in it, the way he does.

Man, did I miss this guy.

◎ ◎ ◎

So me and Dodo and Eags are cruising down the freeway. Dodo's ride is wicked sweet, a vintage finned motherflipper with an ass-end like a rocketship and tail lights like full moons. I'd barely even had time to finish my pitch before Dodo was nodding, putting away his equipment, grabbing his keys. Eagle backs me up the whole time, squawks with fresh outrage when I relate our morning run-in with the Hearts, puffs up his chest, beady eyes full of that rage he gets.

The car may be vintage, but the sound system isn't. Dodo loads in an old demo we made back when the gang was together and still in love with each other, in love with our sound. Makes me nostalgic as all get-out, makes me tear up a little. Eagle smirks at me and I gotta tell him some ash flew into my eye, blowback from the ciggies Dodo's laying on us like candy while the freeway's yellow ribbons flutter by below.

We draw up to the curb in front of the place I know so well I can practically taste the air in its kitchen, though I haven't stepped inside for a year. The flowerbeds are new. Pansies and marigolds spill over edges of little pebble walls someone's stacked to mark borders. But the house is the same, ivy licking its front, screen door propped open to sunshine. Screen door is decorated with a scrolling iron flamingo silhouette, painted an in-your-face, lick-me-please, creamed-strawberries colour few hard rockers I know would even think about thinking about.

The guys hang back, leaving me to stumble up the winding pebble path on my lonesome. I step onto the shaded porch, pretending my brain doesn't swim with a hundred memories, a hundred moments, a hundred kisses. Cool air drifts out of the dark living room, blinds drawn against the day's heat. I smell cookies. Cookies and generosity and more chances wasted than I ever deserved.

I knock on the wooden doorjamb and she calls from the back: "Coming!"

And there she is, rounding the corner from her kitchen. So beautiful, so vivid. My little lorikeet. My little Lory. Except not mine, anymore.

"Hey, Lory," I say. "It's good to see you. Really good. Really, really good."

Her smile is better than sunshine and warm cookies and a dozen record deals all rolled into one. A hundred record deals. A thousand.

"Hi, Duckie. It's good to see you too."

◎ ◎ ◎

Now we've really got the music cranked. Our music. The best music. I'm in the back seat with Eagle, thinking exactly this as he shouts to me over the whomping fugue of Dodo's runaway bass, "Hells-yeah! I forgot how bleeding good we were!"

Lory twists back to smile at us from the passenger seat, all-over ruffled by wind whipping in the open window as Dodo's vintage beast eats up the highway. Her voice isn't super loud but I hear it anyway, each syllable a silky cord winding around my heart as she says, "We're still that good."

The song hiccups, a perfect intentional pause, the sort of thing that makes every difference there is between a nothing bunch of posers like the Hearts and a bona fide rock-n-roll band like us. Pause like that swallows your heartbeat for a moment, one-two-three, then serves it right back to you for an appetizer, bon appetite. It's as if no time at all has passed between the day we mixed this and now. In the car, our four heads bob the beats *one-two-three-four*…and Lory's drum solo crashes down, an aural tsunami.

Girl drummers are rare even in a music town like this one. And Lory's the best I ever heard. The best there ever was. The best. I'm so happy right now I could explode in a puff of eiderdown. It's a monument to my general pre-dried-out depths that I let things go so long before looking up my old bandmates. Eagle's like me: kind of an odd duck, slow to make friends, quick to alienate people when he feels threatened or insecure. But Dodo and Lory have tons of friends, lots of fans no matter where they go, even without the rest of us.

I scrub at the corners of my eyes again, trying to get rid of the wetness before Eagle notices. Can't blame ashes this time; Lory doesn't like it when we smoke around her, so we never do. She hates smoking almost as much as the Gryphon does.

The Gryphon.

My testes tighten, everything shrinking along with my happiness bubble. Good as I'm feeling, good as things are going here, getting the old crew back together, getting everybody to agree to thrash it out this weekend at Queenie's for the Wonderband title, I've been avoiding thinking much ahead. Dodo, Lory, Eagle and I are birds of a feather, but the Gryphon's not like the rest of us. It's possible he won't let me past his front door, seeing as how I'm the main reason our band fell apart. Not the *only* reason – I'm not diva enough to claim that – but being the *main* reason for the end of our collective musical hopes and dreams is bad enough, isn't it?

The Gryphon has moved since I saw him last. It's a stellar pad, rundown in all the right ways, cool in all the right ways, a prime street in a prime part of town, hip-wise. Makes sense. There's nobody hipper than the Gryphon.

We all trundle out this time. I resist the urge to nudge Lory to go first up the flagstone walk between crumbled curb and impressive front door with big iron knocker. She'd do it, I know. And our chances at getting in the front door might be better if I let her. But everybody's waiting for me, pretending they're not. It's me who's got to grovel if we're going to get the Gryphon to agree to put the band back together, even for a single gig. His vocals were always our glue, our saving grace. Our secret weapon.

Without remembering having taken any steps between the curb and here I find myself on the porch. Lory's behind my right shoulder. I can smell her, like jungle flowers kissing dark chocolate. Behind my left shoulder stand Dodo and Eagle. In front of me at eyeball level sits the massive iron ring of the knocker, nestling smug in the hammered groove of its plate. I should just reach for it. I'm going to reach for it. Everybody's waiting for me to reach for it. I take a deep breath and reach for it and the door swings inward.

Off balance, I trip onto the threshold, flail a bit. The Gryphon's shirtless chest is a wide wall of muscle and sinew, feathery as the rest of us but a million times more solid. That's the only word I have for the Gryphon right now: solid. Other than fighting the sudden urge to pee, I'm blank beyond that.

"Been expecting you guys," he says, his voice that deep unforgettable lather of woodsmoke and coffee beans and melting ice cream. "Come in."

He turns and disappears back into his house, leaving me to shoot a what-the-fuck googly-eyebrows look over my shoulder at Dodo and Eagle. Far as I know, none of us have spoken to the Gryphon since last summer, not even Eagle who is some kinda way-distant cousin. Dodo murmurs, "I didn't call him," at the same time Lory gives a *don't-ask-me* sorta shrug. A soft involuntary squawk escapes Eagle, who looks as in need of a urinal as I do. The Gryphon has that effect on people.

Inside, his décor is same as it ever was: mid-century guru meets high-style loft. White painted brick and rough wooden beams, and fancy imported carpets scattered everywhere that may have cost a mint or been salvaged off the curb, one or the other. The Gryphon settles cross-legged on the highest mound of carpets, yogi-style, and watches the rest of us straggle into the room to perch awkwardly or, in Lory's case, prettily, on various tufted poufs and pillows. And he's just looking at me, man, with those inscrutable half-lidded liony eagle eyes. And he's just waiting, man, waiting for me to start.

I begin with an apology – a whole tangled string-ball of apologies – for all the gigs I flubbed, the calls I blew off, the money I stole from the band's kitty to get my next hit. But I'm barely into round one when he waves one of those massive front talons at me, all benediction of forgiveness and shit, and smooth-rumbles in a voice pure cinnamon and whipped honey, "Tell me about this morning."

There's the Gryphon all over: knows everything before you tell it, practically before you know it yourself.

Without too much tongue fumbling I tell about me and Eagle, minding our own business, set on by those flatwad Hearts. How they bragged about winning the Wonderband title this weekend. Tell him how it sent a thousand diamond and spade points piercing my guts to think a dead-end crap-tastic outfit like those flatties could sign the Underland deal my a-holery caused us to miss out on last year. Work myself into a lather, telling it like I'm telling it, sweating it like I'm sweating it, till I finally get to the end of everything I have to say other than the ten billion more apologies that could never make up anyway for letting down my band. I owed these guys everything. Still do. Owe them everything that counts for anything.

And now I'm here. The clincher, the crux of the matter, the seal of the deal unsealed. "So I really hope," I tell the Gryphon, pausing for the first breath in what seems like a year, injecting it into a silence so intense I know the rest of the crew is holding their collective breath too, "we all hope you'll let us put Gryphon and the Birds on the sign-up sheet. With you, we could rock this town like it's never been rocked, blow the feathers off that Underland rep and finally record that album we were made for. But without the Gryphon, that is to say, without you…"

Lory brushes my shoulder. She and Eagle and Dodo have come to stand near me during my monologue, a tight flock of four, same as in the good old days.

"…without you, we're only birds."

◎ ◎ ◎

Practice that week is brutal. Brutal in everything but the music.

It's me and Eagle, Dodo and Lory, and at first it's awkward as all get-out. But Dodo's working his second-favourite bass like it's thinking of breaking up with him and he can't stand the thought – wooing that chunk of lacquered wood with every stroke and lick and slap he can wring out to get it to make beautiful music with him. Eagle's okay; he and I have been riffing in secret for a couple months now in my sister's basement, me on my broke-down thrift store rig and him on his dad's latest guilt gift. Lory pounds those drums like she's pounding biscuits for rising, and there, here, in Dodo's garage, things start to come back together. We, *we* start to come back together.

I know I can't get Dodo's favourite bass back from the shop where I pawned it, even if it was still there, even if I did have the cash. But every day that week I take the bus an hour each way, coming early to practice and staying late, digging through Dodo's dusty milk crates of old equipment, bundles and tangles of stuff he's given up on, moved on from. Mikes and amps and pedals and cords his full-time job doesn't leave room for repairing, for rewiring and re-soldering and cleaning and coiling. By the end of day one I've dug up an old effects pedal whose reappearance he treats like a return of the prodigal. Day two and we've got enough mikes for full practice. Day three earns me Dodo's first genuine smile and I feel things knitting inside, bones and other body parts I didn't notice were broke.

Making good with Lory's way easier and much, much harder. No amends to be had for the tears she shed over me – enough tears to wash us all off on a river of sorrow. So no; there's no way to atone for the tears and the years, and no promises I can make to make up for the promises I broke. But that's the easy part, figuring all that out, knowing it in my heart, accepting it for truth. The hard part is that she totally forgives me.

I bring Lory flours each day, a tiny apology for the injuries I caused – massive in scope if not scale, whatever relationship we had dead by a thousand papercuts long before it got incin-erated by the missed Wonderband gig. But I bring her those flours, buckwheat and millet and sorghum and rye. I smile and watch her from the corner of my beady eye, knowing she's got things good now, glad for her. It's accepting this that's the hard part: Lory has nothing in her heart for me but love, but she'll never love me again.

It's the Gryphon I can't get back to. Dead lines and dead silence and no answer no matter how often I call from my sis-ter's place. No matter how often I hike to his 'hood, stare at that big iron knocker taunting me from its grooved iron bed. I lift and drop it, CLAAHNK CLAAHNK CLAAHNK, but it never summons the only lead singer the best band in town would ever want.

He doesn't answer Dodo's or Eagle's calls either. Doesn't even answer Lory's, and it's all because of me. But we keep practicing and it gets less brutal, and I keep telling everybody the Gryphon won't let us down. I remind them I'm a bit of an expert in the letting down department, and the Gryphon's not me. I do that all week, and all week we practice like there's no question we're playing. No question we're rocking it, thrashing it out. No question we'll win, and make Gryphon and the Birds the next Underland Wonderband.

◉ ◉ ◉

Queenie's Place is jumping. It's the go-to joint for local rock most weekends, but I've never seen it like this. Never seen it stuffed so far past the point of fire-regulation-safety no return.

We get there in the middle of the Tweedles' set. As a duo they're okay, but Dee's voice doesn't hold a candle to Lory's, not that she sings much. She should. Note to self: if I survive the plunge-gut cotton-mouth jiggle-brain sensations turning my whole body to suet, I'll write her more songs for the band to play. Maybe duets with the Gryphon, her spun sugar bouncing off his deep mahogany spice…if he ever sings with us again.

Because here's the thing: the Gryphon never did agree to sing with us here tonight.

But here's the other thing: he didn't *not* agree, either.

The rest of us are ready to rock as we've ever been. Without ever actually agreeing, we've all agreed to push the pause button on every single thing in our brains that isn't rock and roll. Even Lory, who has people in her life. Even Dodo, with his good job. All week we slept rock. We ate rock. We dreamed and breathed and shit rock. We're all sweating rock and roll right now from every pore of our brain-busted no-sleep bodies. But who needs brains to play when you've replaced all your molecules with music? So the Birds are ready. The Birds are good, but with the Gryphon, man…with the Gryphon, we're *golden*.

Eagle and I are unloading the van in the alley when Deuce and his brother shuffle up. If the Gryphon were with us those Hearts would've made themselves scarcer than roosters at a rotisserie.

"Lookie, lookie," says Deuce. "Somebody left the latch off the pigeon coop, let all the birdies out."

Eagle drops Lory's drum case and flies at him, screeching, "I look like a motherplucking pigeon to you, deckshit?"

I pull him off, calm him down, tell those Hearts to go stack themselves. Eagle's on edge because he's afraid the Gryphon won't show tonight. They're all afraid. But I keep telling them not to worry. Telling them he'll be here. I've got to believe that. Got to believe it in the deep place where you believe something so hard, you make it come true. After this week, after getting the band back, getting my friends back, I've got to believe this more than anything else I ever believed.

We stash our equipment and join the others inside. For laughs, we stick around for the Hearts set. We laugh. We also keep craning our necks to watch the door, hoping to see the Gryphon's big rounded shoulders gliding through.

Dodo sucks back his beer like it's water in the desert and says, "We're up next."

Eagle looks like he might lose his lunch. "He's not coming."

Lory pats Eagle's shoulder, worry in her eyes.

I try to beam belief at them, infect them with my universal yesness. "He'll be here," I tell them. "He'll be here. You'll see."

No chance for a real sound check in Battle of the Wonderbands. A few seconds and a *check check check* and a couple plugs plugged and that's all you get. Eagle's growing restless and Lory's shoulders are drooping and Dodo's fiddling with his gear, stalling the moment when we all fail because I couldn't convince the Gryphon to give us a second chance. Give me a second chance. Give the band one last chance to strike it big like we always deserved.

Time's up. The Underland MC comes over the system, face washed blue by the little screen he reads from: "*Up next: Gryphon and the Birds! Put your beers down and your hands together. Let's hear it for Gryphon and the Birds.*"

Smatter of clapping, but mostly a murmur-mumble of locals wondering what the fuck, because nobody's seen or heard Gryphon and the Birds in over a year. I feel it though, the anticipation. Up on stage you figure out quick how to read a crowd, how to feed it. Every performer worth salt and cuttle knows it's not about you up on that stage; it's about them. Every single one of them. Because without you, they're still waiting, but without them, you're just a flock of colourful plumage, birds of a feather strumming together on strings tied to sticks in a suburban garage.

The sound and tech guys decide our warm-up is over. Light blossoms bright, brighter, brightest, a row of white-hot suns rupturing my retinas from above the stage. Hush settles across the crowd the way it does, a Schrödinger's blanket of anticipation ripe with possibility, ready to cut this way or that, ready to reveal one reality or another. Is the Gryphon out on the floor, waiting in darkness to see whether I'll make good on my promise this time? Waiting to judge whether we're worthy? Whether we're ready? To decide whether this moment is everything, or whether it's nothing at all?

I refuse to acknowledge the sense of defeat blistering my back, the eyeballs of my band burning into the flesh of their lead guitarist, who's led them nowhere but down. I step up to the mike and suck a deep breath, like I always do. I close my eyes, like I never do. Squeeze them tight shut. Grip the neck of my guitar and lift the other arm high, arc it up over my head ready to plunge into that first chord, the chord that sets the set, man. The chord that makes the whole gig cut one way or the other. The chord that, if everything goes right, heralds the entrance of the Gryphon.

My arm drops. The chord vibrates up past my shoulder, down my ribs, echoes through my hollow bones and shoots out the scruffy ends of my wingtips. The room's hush swells, swallows me in what-ifs and what-could-bes, everything crowding close the same instant. Everything possible, even – especially – the impossible. I let the note draw on, not wanting to play the next. Not opening my eyes. Not knowing whether the Gryphon has taken his place on stage. Not really wanting to know which way the razor's slicing, because until it falls one way or the other, everything's possible, everything exists.

Under the fading twang I hear Lory's breath catch. But then she counts it, clicking her sticks against each other for the beat: one, two, three. Dodo jumps in the way he does, and he is *on*, man. We've been practicing so hard this week, we're all blistered and bloody in every place it counts. Eagle kicks in with a little plucking sequence, something he only does when he's really happy, when all his stars are aligned and his ships have come in. But still I don't open my eyes. Not until—

Music swells in the air. Our music, my music. Fills up all my bones, spills out my chest and into my guitar. And it's time, man. I feel it. It's really time. This time is the time, is it. Is now.

I open my eyes, and we're golden.

ABOUT THE AUTHORS

Colleen Anderson of Vancouver is a writer of fiction and poetry who has been twice nominated for the Aurora Award in poetry, and longlisted for the Stoker Award. As a freelance editor she co-edited *Tesseracts Seventeen*, and *Playground of Lost Toys* (Exile Editions) which was nominated for a 2016 Aurora Award, while *Alice Unbound: Beyond Wonderland* is her first solo anthology. Some of her recent works have appeared in *Grievous Angel, Futuristica, Starship Sofa, Transition* and *Magazine*. She is currently working on an alternate history dark fiction novel and a poetry collection. Black Shuck Books, U.K., will publish a collection of her dark fiction in 2018, and she has a poetry chapbook, *Ancient Tales, Grand Deaths and Past Lives*.

www.colleenanderson.wordpress.com

Patrick Bollivar is an air traffic controller living in Vancouver. He has previously published in *Pulp Literature Magazine* and *Tesseracts Nineteen*, and will soon be published in the WCSFA fundraising anthology *Power: In the Hands of One, In the Hands of Many*.

Mark Charke of Surrey, British Columbia, is an aspiring novelist with over forty-five roleplaying game publications, among them *Chronomancer: Time Travel for Everyone, The Complete Guide to Vampires* and *DragonMech: Steam Warriors*. In 2018, he will release his first novel, *Blue Water Hero*, on Amazon.   @markcharke

Christine Daigle has had short fiction appear in *Apex Magazine, Grievous Angel*, the *Playground of Lost Toys* anthology (Exile Editions), and the *Street Magick* anthology. Her first novel, *The Emerald Key*, co-authored with Stewart Sternberg, was released in 2015.

Robert Dawson teaches mathematics at a Nova Scotia university. He has read just about everything that Lewis Carroll (or Charles Dodgson) ever wrote, and once published a paper in the *Journal of Recreational Mathematics* about one of Dodgson's probability problems. Robert's fiction has appeared in *Nature Futures, AE, Compostela,*

Tesseracts Twenty, and many other periodicals and anthologies. Apart from mathematics and SF writing, he enjoys fencing, cycling, and hiking, and volunteers with a Scout troop.

David Day of Toronto is the author of *Alice's Adventures in Wonderland Decoded: The Full Text of Lewis Carroll's Novel With It's Many Hidden Meanings Revealed.** He has written and published fifty books of poetry, history, fantasy, ecology, natural history, mythology and fiction. Day's books – for both adults and children – have sold over three million copies worldwide and have been translated into twenty languages.   * YouTube: David Day Books – Decoding Alice
www.daviddaybooks.com

Linda DeMeulemeester of Burnaby, British Columbia, has had her short fiction appear in anthologies with Exile Editions and Tesseracts, and in the magazines and zines *Neo-opsis, Twilight Tales* and *Chizine.* Her first children's book, *The Secret of Grim Hill,* won the Silver Birch Award and was named one of Canadian Toy Testing Council's best books. Her spooky middle grade series has been translated into French, Spanish and Korean. Her forthcoming autumn 2018 novel is a tween adventure, *The Mystery of Croaker's Island.* www.grimhill.com

Pat Flewwelling of Oshawa, Ontario, is a part-time writer, part-time editor, part-time publisher, part-time travelling bookseller, and full-time data problem solver at a major telecommunications company. Aside from her seven full-length works, her short works have been included in the anthologies *Sirens* and *Equus* and *Purgatorium*, and in the magazine *Pulp Literature.* Find out where her Myth Hawker Travelling Bookstore, will appear next at www.mythhawker.ca

Geoff Gander of South Mountain, Ontario, was heavily involved in the role-playing community prior to writing fiction, and penned many game products. He has been published by ChiZine Publications, Metahuman Press, AE SciFi, Exile Editions, McGraw-Hill and Expeditious Retreat Press. He primarily writes horror, but is willing to give anything a whirl.   geoffgander.wordpress.com   @GeoffGander

Cait Gordon is originally from Verdun, Quebec, and has been living in the suburbs of Ottawa since 1998. She is the author of *Life in the 'Cosm*, a story about a little green guy who's crushing on the female half of his two-headed colleague. She is currently working on its prequel called *The Stealth Lovers*, a rom-com military space opera. She worked for over two decades as a technical writer, publishing user guides about everything from software applications to airplane simulators. When she's not writing, Cait edits manuscripts for indie authors and runs *The Spoonie Authors Network*, a blog whose contributors are writers with disabilities and/or chronic conditions.

caitgordon.com   @CaitGAuthor

Costi Gurgu of Toronto has had fiction published in Canada, the United States and Europe. Collectively, his three book and more than fifty stories have won twenty-four awards. His works include the anthologies *Ages of Wonder, Tesseracts Seventeen, The Mammoth Book of Dieselpunk, Dark Horiz-ons, Street Magick* and *Water*. His novel *RecipeArium* was recently released.   www.costigurgu.com

Kate Heartfield of North Gower (Ottawa), Ontario, is a former newspaper editor and columnist. Her first novel, a historical fantasy called *Armed in Her Fashion*, will be published in 2018, as well as an interactive novel for Choice of Game, inspired by *The Canterbury Tales*. Her short fiction has appeared in several magazines and anthologies, including *Strange Horizons, Escape Pod* and *Lackington's*. Kate's story "The Seven O'Clock Man," published in the Exile anthology *Clockwork Canada*, was longlisted for the Sunburst Award. Her novella "The Course of True Love" was published in 2016, as part of the collection *Monstrous Little Voices: New Tales from Shakespeare's Fantasy World*.   www.heartfieldfiction.com   @kateheartfield

Elizabeth Hosang of Kanata, Ontario, is a computer engineer who has branched into writing fiction. She has been published in a number of mystery and science fiction anthologies, and was short-listed for the 2017 Arthur Ellis Award for Crime Writing in the Short Story category. A fan of a well-told story in any genre, she especially enjoys mystery, urban fantasy and science fiction.   facebook.com/eahosang

Nicole Iversen of Sechelt, British Columbia, sees her first publication in these pages – something Exile Editions is recognized for in their decades-long support of emerging writers. She is currently writing a young adult High Fantasy series, and a short story will appear in the 2018 WCSFA fundraising anthology *Power: In the Hands of One, In the Hands of Many.*   www.nicoleiversen.wixsite.com/nicolewriter

J.Y.T. Kennedy lives in Ardossan, Alberta, and writes eclectically, with an emphasis on speculative fiction and poetry. She has been fond of Lewis Carroll, and has been easily reciting several of his poems since childhood.   sites.google.com/site/jytkennedy

Danica Lorer of Saskatoon, Saskatchewan, finds adventure and inspiration in fields, forests, riverbanks, cities, and small towns (her name comes from the Slavic word "morning star" for explorers). She is a professional storyteller, freelance writer, face and body painter, poet, and the host of Shaw TV Saskatoon's literary arts program *Lit Happens.*   @DanicaLorer

Catherine MacLeod of Tatamagouche, Nova Scotia, has published short fiction in *Nightmare, Black Static, On Spec, Tor.com,* and anthologies including *Fearful Symmetries, Playground of Lost Toys* (Exile Editions), and *Licence Expired: The Unauthorized James Bond.* Her short story "Hide and Seek" (from *Playground of Lost Toys*) won the 2016 inaugural Sunburst Award for Short Story.

Bruce Meyer of Barrie, Ontario, is the author of some 50-plus books in all genres. He was winner of the Gwendolyn MacEwen Prize for Poetry Award in 2015 and 2016, and received the IP Medal for *The Seasons* for Best Book of Poems in North America in 2014. He is the editor of Exile Editions' *Cli-Fi: Canadian Tales of Climate Change* and *That Dammed Beaver: Canadian Humor, Laffs, and Gaffes* (both 2017). He was the inaugural Poet Laureate of the City of Barrie, and teaches at Georgian College in Barrie and at Victoria College in the University of Toronto.   facebook.com/BruceMeyer

Dominik Parisien of Toronto is the co-editor, with Navah Wolfe, of *Robots vs Fairies*, and *The Starlit Wood: New Fairy Tales*, which won the Shirley Jackson Award and was a finalist for the World Fantasy Award, the British Fantasy Award, and the Locus Award. He is also the editor of *Clockwork Canada: Steampunk Fiction* and the co-editor, with Elsa Sjunneson-Henry, of *Disabled People Destroy Science Fiction*. His fiction, poetry, and essays have appeared or are forthcoming in *The Fiddlehead*, *Uncanny Magazine*, *EXILE/ELQ* magazine, *Augur Magazine*, *Those Who Make Us: Canadian Creature, Myth, and Monster Stories* (anthology, Exile Editions) as well as other publications. www.dominikparisien.wordpress.com @domparisien

Fiona Plunkett of South Mountain, Ontario (and partner of the co-authored story with Geoff Gander) is an editor, photographer, researcher, and high financier. Born in England and transplanted to Canada's capital region by her Canadian parents, she has a university degree in History, and a college diploma in Interactive Media Management. In her spare time she drives a hearse, plays the bagpipes, tenor drum, and bass drum, and terrorizes local children on Halloween as The Witch of South Mountain.   @FionaTheCarver www.beyondtherealm.ca   facebook.com/fiona.beyond.the.realm

Alexandra Renwick grew up Canadian in Los Angeles, Philadelphia, Austin, Yorkshire, Copenhagen, and Toronto, but currently spends most of her time in a crumbling historic manor in downtown Ottawa. Her genre-elastic fiction has been translated into nine languages and adapted to the stage. Find her most recent stories in *Asimov's, Interzone, Alfred Hitchcock's Mystery Magazine,* and in audio at *Cabinet of Curiosities*.   www.alexandrarenwick.com

Andrew Robertson is an award-winning queer writer and journalist from Toronto. He has published articles in *Xtra!, fab magazine, ICON, Gasoline, Samaritan Magazine, neksis,* and *Shameless*. His fiction has appeared in literary magazines and quarterlies that include *Stitched Smile Publications Magazine* Vol 1, *Deadman's Tome, Sirens Call, Undertow, katalogue, Feeling Better Yet?,* and in anthologies *Gone with* *the Dead, Group Hex Vol. 1 and Vol. 2, A Tribute Anthology to Deadworld, Cuarenta y Nueve, First Hand Accounts,* and *Abandon.* A lifelong fan of horror, he is the founder and co-host of *The Great Lakes Horror Company* podcast, official podcast to *Library of the Damned,* and a member of the Horror Writers' Association.

Lisa Smedman of Richmond, British Columbia, is the author of more than twenty books, ranging from science fiction and fantasy novels to non-fiction histories of Vancouver. In 2004, one of her novels made the *New York Times* best sellers list. She is also the author of dozens of adventures for the *Dungeons & Dragons* role-playing games, and other tabletop RPGs. She worked as a journalist for twenty-five years, and now makes her living teaching video game design and interactive fiction writing at a local college. She has also written three one-act plays, all produced by an amateur Vancouver theater group, and is the author of numerous short stories.

www.lisasmedman.wix.com/author

Sara C. Walker of Kawartha Lakes, Ontario, is a writer, editor, and library clerk. She received her first copy of *Alice in Wonderland* when she was eight years old, a gift from her father, a Yorkshireman. Urban fantasy is her favourite playground, and her novels and shorter works can be found online. www.sarawalker.ca

James Wood of Oakville, Ontario, is a high school English teacher with a passion for getting young men to turn off their video games and pick up a book. He has been published in *Burning Water* magazine and the anthology *Circuits and Slippers.* @James_N_Wood

Cover and interior art is by **Maeba Scutti** (aka Ellerslie) from Rimini, Italy. She is an illustrator, painter, dreamer and poet who has published three books of poetry and had her art appear on the covers of a variety of publications and books. www.shutterstock.com/g/ellerslie

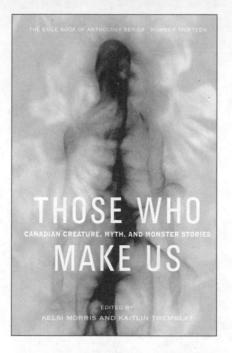

THOSE WHO MAKE US: CANADIAN CREATURE, MYTH, AND MONSTER STORIES

EDITED BY KELSI MORRIS AND KAITLIN TREMBLAY

What resides beneath the blankets of snow, under the ripples of water, within the whispers of the wind, and between the husks of trees all across Canada? Creatures, myths and monsters are everywhere…even if we don't always see them.

Canadians from all backgrounds and cultures look to identify with their surroundings through stories. Herein, speculative and literary fiction provides unique takes on what being Canadian is about.

"Kelsi Morris and Kaitlin Tremblay did not set out to create a traditional anthology of monster stories… This unconventional anthology lives up to the challenge, the stories show tremendous openness and compassion in the face of the world's darkness, unfairness, and indifference." —*Quill & Quire*

Featuring stories by Helen Marshall, Renée Sarojini Saklikar, Nathan Adler, Kate Story, Braydon Beaulieu, Chadwick Ginther, Dominik Parisien, Stephen Michell, Andrew Wilmot, Rati Mehrotra, Rebecca Schaeffer, Delani Valin, Corey Redekop, Angeline Woon, Michal Wojcik, Andrea Bradley, Andrew F. Sullivan and Alexandra Camille Renwick.

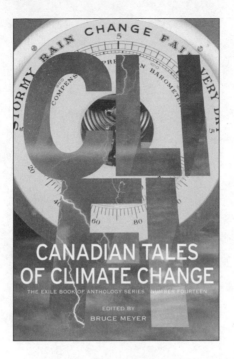

CLI FI:
CANADIAN TALES OF CLIMATE CHANGE

EDITED BY BRUCE MEYER

In his introduction to this all-original set of (at times barely) futuristic tales, Meyer warns readers, "[The] imaginings of today could well become the cold, hard facts of tomorrow." Meyer (Testing the Elements) has gathered an eclectic variety of eco-fictions from some of Canada's top genre writers, each of which, he writes, reminds readers that "the world is speaking to us and that it is our duty, if not a covenant, to listen to what it has to say." In these pages, scientists work desperately against human ignorance, pockets of civilization fight to balance morality and survival, and corporations cruelly control access to basic needs such as water....The anthology may be inescapably dark, but it is a necessary read, a clarion call to take action rather than, as a character in Seán Virgo's "My Atlantis" describes it, "waiting unknowingly for the plague, the hive collapse, the entropic thunderbolt." Luckily, it's also vastly entertaining. It appears there's nothing like catastrophe to bring the best out in authors in describing the worst of humankind. —*Publishers Weekly*

George McWhirter, Richard Van Camp, Holly Schofield, Linda Rogers, Sean Virgo, Rati Mehrotra, Geoffrey W. Cole, Phil Dwyer, Kate Story, Leslie Goodreid, Nina Munteanu, Halli Villegas, John Oughton, Frank Westcott, Wendy Bone, Peter Timmerman, Lynn Hutchinson Lee, with an afterword by internationally acclaimed writer and filmmaker, Dan Bloom.

playground
of
LOST
toys

Edited by Colleen Anderson and Ursula Pflug

PLAYGROUND OF LOST TOYS

EDITED BY COLLEEN ANDERSON AND URSULA PFLUG

A dynamic collection of stories that explore the mystery, awe and dread that we may have felt as children when encountering a special toy. But it goes further, to the edges of space, where games are for keeps and where the mind plays its own games. We enter a world where the magic may not have been lost, where a toy or computers or gods vie for the upper hand. Wooden games of skill, ancient artifacts misinterpreted, dolls, stuffed animals, wand items that seek a life or even revenge – these lost toys and games bring tales of companionship, loss, revenge, hope, murder, cunning, and love, to be unearthed in the sandbox.

Featuring stories by Chris Kuriata, Joe Davies, Catherine MacLeod, Kate Story, Meagan Whan, Candas Jane Dorsey, Rati Mehrotra, Nathan Adler, Rhonda Eikamp, Robert Runté, Linda DeMeulemeester, Kevin Cockle, Claude Lalumière, Dominik Parisien, dvsduncan, Christine Daigle, Melissa Yuan-Innes, Shane Simmons, Lisa Carreiro, Karen Abrahamson, Geoffrey W. Cole and Alexandra Camille Renwick. Afterword by Derek Newman-Stille.

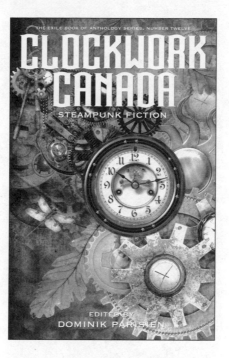

CLOCKWORK CANADA:
STEAMPUNK FICTION

EDITED BY DOMINIK PARISIEN

Welcome to an alternate Canada, where steam technology and the wonders and horrors of the mechanical age have reshaped the past into something both wholly familiar yet compellingly different.

"These stories of clockworks, airships, mechanical limbs, automata, and steam are, overall, an unfettered delight to read." —*Quill & Quire*

"[*Clockwork Canada*] is a true delight that hits on my favorite things in fiction – curious worldbuilding, magic, and tough women taking charge. It's a carefully curated adventure in short fiction that stays true to a particular vision while seeking and achieving nuance."
—*Tor.com*

"…inventive and transgressive…these stories rethink even the fundamentals of what we usually mean by steampunk." —*The Toronto Star*

Featuring stories by Colleen Anderson, Karin Lowachee, Brent Nichols, Charlotte Ashley, Chantal Boudreau, Rhea Rose, Kate Story, Terri Favro, Kate Heartfield, Claire Humphrey, Rati Mehrotra, Tony Pi, Holly Schofield, Harold R. Thompson and Michal Wojcik.

FRACTURED:
TALES OF THE CANADIAN POST-APOCALYPSE

EDITED BY SILVIA MORENO-GARCIA

"The 23 stories in *Fractured* cover incredible breadth, from the last man alive in Haida Gwaii to a dying Matthew waiting for his Anne in PEI. All the usual apocalyptic suspects are here – climate change, disease, alien invasion – alongside less familiar scenarios such as a ghost apocalypse and an invasion of shadows. Stories range from the immediate aftermath of society's collapse to distant futures in which humanity has been significantly reduced, but the same sense of struggle and survival against the odds permeates most of the pieces in the collection… What *Fractured* really drives home is how perfect Canada is as a setting for the post-apocalypse. Vast tracts of wilderness, intense weather, and the potentially sinister consequences of environmental devastation provide ample inspiration for imagining both humanity's destruction and its rugged survival." – *Quill & Quire*

Featuring stories by T.S. Bazelli, GMB Chomichuk, A.M. Dellamonica, dvsduncan, Geoff Gander, Orrin Grey, David Huebert, John Jantunen, H.N. Janzen, Arun Jiwa, Claude Lalumière, Jamie Mason, Michael Matheson, Christine Ottoni, Miriam Oudin, Michael S. Pack, Morgan M. Page, Steve Stanton, Amanda M. Taylor, E. Catherine Tobler, Jean-Louis Trudel, Frank Westcott and A.C. Wise.

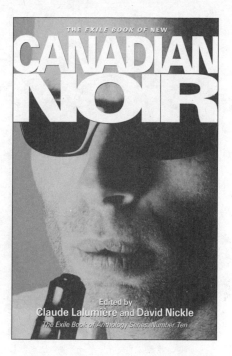

NEW CANADIAN NOIR

EDITED BY CLAUDE LALUMIÈRE AND DAVID NICKLE

"Everything is in the title. These are all new stories – no novel extracts – selected by Claude Lalumière and David Nickle from an open call. They're Canadian-authored, but this is not an invitation for national introspection. Some Canadian locales get the noir treatment, which is fun, since, as Nickle notes in his afterword, noir, with its regard for the underbelly, seems like an un-Canadian thing to write. But the main question *New Canadian Noir* asks isn't "Where is here?" it's "What can noir be?" These stories push past the formulaic to explore noir's far reaches as a mood and aesthetic. In Nickle's words, "Noir is a state of mind – an exploration of corruptibility, ultimately an expression of humanity in all its terrible frailty." The resulting literary alchemy – from horror to fantasy, science fiction to literary realism, romance to, yes, crime – spanning the darkly funny to the stomach-queasy horrific, provides consistently entertaining rewards." —*Globe and Mail*

Featuring stories by Corey Redekop, Joel Thomas Hynes, Silvia Moreno-Garcia, Chadwick Ginther, Michael Mirolla, Simon Strantzas, Steve Vernon, Kevin Cockle, Colleen Anderson, Shane Simmons, Laird Long, Dale L. Sproule, Alex C. Renwick, Ada Hoffmann, Kieth Cadieux, Michael S. Chong, Rich Larson, Kelly Robson, Edward McDermott, Hermine Robinson, David Menear and Patrick Fleming.

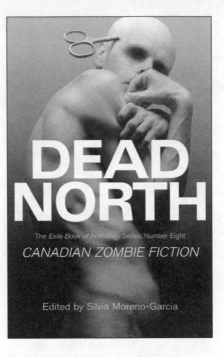

The *Exile Book* of Anthology Series, Number Eight

CANADIAN ZOMBIE FICTION

Edited by Silvia Moreno-Garcia

DEAD NORTH:
CANADIAN ZOMBIE FICTION

EDITED BY SILVIA MORENO-GARCIA

"*Dead North* suggests zombies may be thought of as native to this country, their presence going back to Aboriginal myths and legends…we see deadheads, shamblers, jiang shi, and Shark Throats invading such home and native settings as the Bay of Fundy's Hopewell Rocks, Alberta's tar sands, Toronto's Mount Pleasant Cemetery, and a Vancouver Island grow-op. Throw in the last poutine truck on Earth driving across Saskatchewan and some "mutant demon zombie cows devouring Montreal" (honest!) and what you've got is a fun and eclectic mix of zombie fiction…" —*Toronto Star*

"Every time I listen to the yearly edition of *Canada Reads* on CBC, so much attention seems to be drawn to the fact that the author is Canadian, that being Canadian becomes a gimmick. *Dead North*, a collection of zombie short stories by exclusively Canadian authors, is the first of its kind that I've seen to buck this trend, using the diverse cultural mythology of the Great White North to put a number of unique spins on an otherwise over-saturated genre."—*Bookshelf Reviews*

Featuring stories by Chantal Boudreau, Tessa J. Brown, Richard Van Camp, Kevin Cockle, Jacques L. Condor, Carrie-Lea Côté, Linda DeMeulemeester, Brian Dolton, Gemma Files, Ada Hoffmann, Tyler Keevil, Claude Lalumière, Jamie Mason, Michael Matheson, Ursula Pflug, Rhea Rose, Simon Strantzas, E. Catherine Tobler, Beth Wodzinski and Melissa Yuan-Ines.

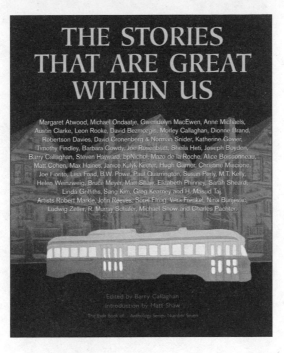

THE STORIES THAT ARE GREAT WITHIN US

EDITED BY BARRY CALLAGHAN

"[This is a] large book, one to be sat on the lap and not held up, one to be savoured piece by piece and heard as much as read as the great sidewalk rolls out…This is the infrastructure of Toronto, its deep language and various truths." —*Pacific Rim Review of Books*

Among the 50-plus contributors are Margaret Atwood, Michael Ondaatje, Gwendolyn MacEwen, Anne Michaels, Austin Clarke, Leon Rooke, David Bezmozgis, Morley Callaghan, Dionne Brand, Robertson Davies, Katherine Govier, Timothy Findley, Barbara Gowdy, Joseph Boyden, bpNichol, Hugh Garner, Joe Fiorito and Paul Quarrington, Janice Kulyk Keefer, along with artists Sorel Etrog, Vera Frenkel, Nina Bunjevac, Michael Snow, and Charles Pachter.

"Bringing together an ensemble of Canada's best-known, mid-career, and emerging writers…this anthology stands as the perfect gateway to discovering the city of Toronto. With a diverse range of content, the book focuses on the stories that have taken the city, in just six decades, from a narrow wryly praised as a city of churches to a brassy, gauche, imposing metropolis that is the fourth largest in North America. With an introduction from award-winning author Matt Shaw, this blends a cacophony of voices to encapsulate the vibrant city of Toronto." —*Toronto Star*

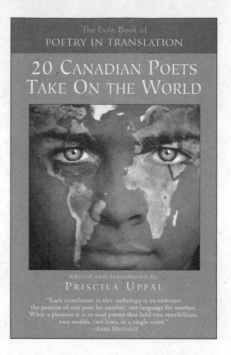

20 CANADIAN POETS TAKE ON THE WORLD

EDITED BY PRISCILA UPPAL

A groundbreaking multilingual collection promoting a global poetic consciousness, thisvolume presents the works of 20 international poets, all in their original languages, alongside English translations by some of Canada's most esteemed poets. Spanning several time periods and more than a dozen nations, this compendium paints a truly unique portrait of cultures, nationalities, and eras."

Canadian poets featured are Oana Avasilichioaei, Ken Babstock, Christian Bök, Dionne Brand, Nicole Brossard, Barry Callaghan, George Elliott Clarke, Geoffrey Cook, Rishma Dunlop, Steven Heighton, Christopher Doda, Andréa Jarmai, Evan Jones, Sonnet L'Abbé, A.F. Moritz, Erín Moure, Goran Simic, Priscila Uppal, Paul Vermeersch, and Darren Wershler, translating the works of Nobel laureates, classic favourites, and more, including Jan-Willem Anker, Her-man de Coninck, María Elena Cruz Varela, Kiki Dimoula, George Faludy, Horace, Juan Ramón Jiménez, Pablo Neruda, Chus Pato, Ezra Pound, Alexander Pushkin, Rainer Maria Rilke, Arthur Rimbaud, Elisa Sampedrín, Leopold Staff, Nichita St˘anescu, Stevan Tonti´c, Ko Un, and Andrei Voznesensky. Each translating poet provides an introduction to their work.

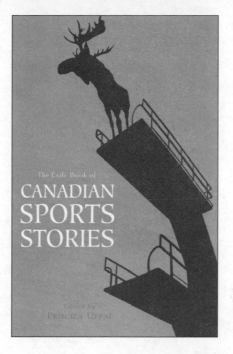

CANADIAN SPORTS STORIES

EDITED BY PRISCILA UPPAL

"This anthology collects a wide range of Canada's literary imaginations, telling great stories about the wild and fascinating world of sport… Written by both men and women, the generations of insights provided in this collection expose some of the most intimate details of sports and sporting life – the hard-earned victories, and the sometimes inevitable tragedies. You will get to know those who play the game, as well as those who watch it, coach it, write about it, dream about it, live and die by it."

"Most of the stories weren't so much about sports per se than they were a study of personalities and how they react to or deal with extreme situations…all were worth reading"
—goodreads.com

Clarke Blaise, George Bowering, Dionne Brand, Barry Callaghan, Morley Callaghan, Roch Carrier, Matt Cohen, Craig Davidson, Brian Fawcett, Katherine Govier, Steven Heighton, Mark Jarman, W.P. Kinsella, Stephen Leacock, L.M. Montgomery, Susanna Moodie, Margaret Pigeon, Mordecai Richler, Priscila Uppal, Guy Vanderhaeghe, and more.

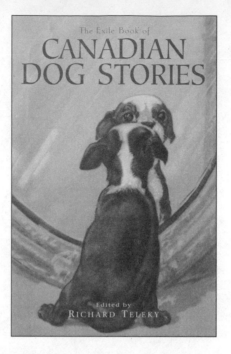

CANADIAN DOG STORIES

EDITED BY RICHARD TELEKY

Spanning from the 1800s to 2005, and featuring exceptional short stories from 28 of Canada's most prominent fiction writers, this unique anthology explores the nature of the human-dog bond through writing from both the nation's earliest storytellerssuch as Ernest Thompson Seton, L. M. Montgomery, and Stephen Leacockand a younger generation that includes Lynn Coady and Matt Shaw. Not simply sentimental tales about noble dogs doing heroic deeds, these stories represent the rich, complex, and mysterious bond between dogs and humans. Adventure and drama, heartfelt encounters and nostalgia, sharp-edged satire, and even fantasy make up the genres in this memorable collection.

"Twenty-eight exceptional dog tales by some of Canada's most notable fiction writers... The stories run the breadth of adventure, drama, satire, and even fantasy, and will appeal to dog lovers on both sides of the [Canada/U.S.] border." —*Modern Dog Magazine*

Marie-Claire Blais, Barry Callaghan, Morley Callaghan, Lynn Coady, Mazo de la Roche, Jacques Ferron, Mavis Gallant, Douglas Glover, Katherine Govier, Kenneth J. Harvey, E. Pauline Johnson, Janice Kulyk Keefer, Alistair Macleod, L.M. Montgomery, P.K. Page, Charles G.D. Roberts, Leon Rooke, Jane Rule, Duncan Campbell Scott, Timothy Taylor, Sheila Watson, Ethel Wilson, and more.

NATIVE CANADIAN FICTION AND DRAMA

EDITED BY DANIEL DAVID MOSES

The work of men and women of many tribal affiliations, this collection is a wide-ranging anthology of contemporary Native Canadian literature. Deep emotions and life-shaking crises converge and display the Aboriginal concerns regarding various topics, including identity, family, community, caste, gender, nature, betrayal, and war. A fascinating compilation of stories and plays, this account fosters cross-cultural understanding and presents the Native Canadian writers reinvention of traditional material and their invention of a modern life that is authentic. It is perfect for courses on short fiction or general symposium teaching material.

Tomson Highway, Lauren B. Davis, Niigonwedom James Sinclair, Joseph Boyden, Joseph A. Dandurand, Alootook Ipellie, Thomas King, Yvette Nolan, Richard Van Camp, Floyd Favel, Robert Arthur Alexie, Daniel David Moses, Katharina Vermette.

"A strong addition to the ever shifting Canadian literary canon, effectively presenting the depth and artistry of the work by Aboriginal writers in Canada today."

—*Canadian Journal of Native Studies*

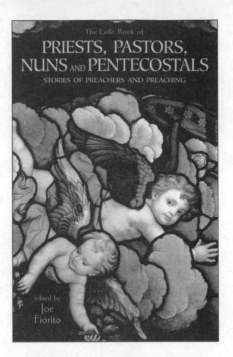

PRIESTS, PASTORS, NUNS AND PENTECOSTALS

EDITED BY JOE FIORITO

A literary approach to the Word of the Lord, this collection of short fiction deals within one way or anotherthe overarching concept of redemption. This anthology demonstrates how God appears again and again in the lives of priest, pastors, nuns, and Pentecostals. However He appears, He appears again and again in the lives of priests, nuns, and Pentecostals in these great stories of a kind never collected before

Mary Frances Coady, Barry Callaghan, Leon Rooke, Roch Carrier, Jacques Ferron, Seán Virgo, Marie-Claire Blais, Hugh Hood, Morley Callaghan, Hugh Garner, Diane Keating, Alexandre Amprimoz, Gloria Sawai, Eric McCormack, Yves Thériault, Margaret Laurence, Alice Munro.

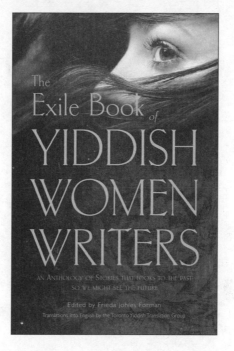

YIDDISH WOMEN WRITERS

EDITED BY FRIEDA JOHLES FOREMAN

Presenting a comprehensive collection of influential Yiddish women writers with new translations, this anthology explores the major transformations and upheavals of the 20th century. Short stories, excerpts, and personal essays are included from 13 writers, and focus on such subjects as family life; sexual awakening; longings for independence, education, and creative expression; the life in Europe surrounding the Holocaust and its aftermath; immigration; and the conflicted entry of Jewish women into the modern world with the restrictions of traditional life and roles. These powerful accounts provide a vital link to understanding the Jewish experience at a time of conflict and tumultuous change.

"This continuity…of Yiddish, of women, and of Canadian writers does not simply add a missing piece to an existing puzzle; instead it invites us to rethink the narrative of Yiddish literary history at large… Even for Yiddish readers, the anthology is a site of discovery, offering harder-to-find works that the translators collected from the Canadian Yiddish press and published books from Israel, France, Canada, and the U.S."
—*Studies in American Jewish Literature*, Volume 33, Number 2, 2014

"Yiddish Women Writers did what a small percentage of events at a good literary festival [Blue Metropolis] should: it exposed the curious to a corner of history, both literary and social, that they might never have otherwise considered." —*Montreal Gazette*

Exile's $15,000 Carter V. Cooper Short Fiction Competition

FOR CANADIAN WRITERS ONLY

$10,000 for the Best Story by an Emerging Writer
$5,000 for the Best Story by a Writer at Any Career Point

The shortlisted are published in the annual *CVC Short Fiction Anthology* series and many in *ELQ/Exile: The Literary Quarterly*

Exile's $3,000 Gwendolyn MacEwen Poetry Competition

FOR CANADIAN WRITERS ONLY

$1,500 for the Best Suite of Poetry
$1,000 for the Best Suite by an Emerging Writer
$500 for the Best Poem

Winners are published in *ELQ/Exile: The Literary Quarterly*

These annual competitions open in November and close in May.
Details at:
www.ExileEditions.com
www.ExileQuarterly.com